☢ THE NINEVEH PROJECT

By

CRAIG ALEXANDER

Cover design by Jeremy Robinson

BREAKNECK BOOKS
PUBLISHING COMPANY

Published by Breakneck Books (USA)
www.breakneckbooks.com

First printing, June 2007

Visit Craig Alexander on the World Wide Web at:
www.craigalexander.com

ISBN: 0-9786551-7-6

ATTENTION: SCHOOLS AND BUSINESSES
Breakneck Books' titles are available at bulk order discount rates for educational, business or sales promotional use. They are also available for fundraiser programs. Please e-mail: info@breakneckbooks.com or write us at: Breakneck Books - PO Box 122 - Barrington, NH 03867 for details.

For Stephanie and Darby

ACKNOWLEDGEMENTS

Thank you to the leadership of Pinelake Church both past and present, especially, Tommy Politz, Larry Herndon, Bob Buckner, Dr. Chip Henderson, Tim Smith, Robert Green, and Rick Psonak. You have all had a profound influence on me and have been instrumental in my spiritual growth.

Thank you to the guys in my Bible study group, especially, Greg Buie, Byron Galloway, Hal Sherman, Jim Stefkovich, and Derek Wells. Your support for this book and your friendship through the years means more to me than you'll ever know. You guys are great.

Thanks to Dr. Tommy Cabell and Tim Wickersham for putting up with me droning on-and-on about this story as I wrote it, for your input on earlier drafts, your help with some of the fight scenes and technical details about weapons. Also, thanks to my friend Special Agent Joe Hess of the Secret Service for your help with some of the lingo in the book.

Thank you to Breakneck Books for taking a chance on an unknown writer, and to editor Charity Heller-Hogue for helping me put the final touches on the manuscript.

I have a special debt of gratitude to writer and editor Donna Fleisher. With patience and kindness you took the time to not only help me polish the roughest of manuscripts, but to teach me what I needed to know (which was a lot) about the craft of novel writing. Without you this book would never have been published. I am eternally grateful.

Thank you to my entire family for their continuing love and support, especially my wife Stephanie, and my daughter Darby.

Last but certainly not least, thank the Lord God Almighty.

The word of the LORD came to Jonah son of Amittai: "Go to the great city of Nineveh and preach against it, because its wickedness has come up before me." **Jonah 1:1-2**

PROLOGUE

DEATH marches. The wrath of God is upon them. While his family waits, Simeon stands alone at the edge of a precipice gazing into the valley below. An arid wind tousles his hair and whips his clothing. Eyes crinkled against the rising sun's glare, he absorbs the view, drinking it in, pressing it into his memory. The scene below him is one of beauty and tranquility: a vast metropolis carved in the midst of this oasis in the desert. The great river Tigris winds lazily past the city's walls, bringing with it life and abundance.

Why couldn't his countrymen recognize the danger?

In the distance, past the walls of the city, the rising sun glints off of a multitude of swords, spears, and shields. The banners of the Babylonians, Medes, and Scythians are harbingers of doom. His family is one of the few leaving. The rest foolishly believe what they were told: no army could penetrate their defenses, breach their walls, or withstand their army. The king, in his arrogance, even planned a banquet in the hours before the city's invasion.

The dust from the feet of the soldiers, horse's hooves, and chariot's wheels creates a cloud that seem to reach to the heavens. The morning sunlight shines through the dust, giving it a blood-red caste, an omen of death.

They had been warned. Jonah's call to repentance had briefly persuaded them to turn from their sinfulness, but once the threat of destruction was forgotten, the wickedness returned.

Simeon looks for the last time at the city he calls home. When the king's herald's raised the alarm, warning of the army's approach, Simeon gathered his family and belongings and fled.

As the prophet foretold, this great city is about to be destroyed, razed to the ground for its wickedness.

He tears his eyes away and turns to join his waiting family.

Northeastern Iraq: January 2003

HUSSAAM Uzeen Zaafir stood among a copse of trees at the edge of the desert. The night was tranquil and quiet, the sky clear. The sands surrounding the trees seemed to glow from the light of the stars. Nearby mountains were black silhouettes on the horizon. A cooling breeze rustled the leaves overhead.

Although his two bodyguards were loyal and well trained, fully capable of keeping watch and identifying danger, Hussaam trusted no one. There was no margin for error, and he could not risk anyone noticing them enter the hidden entrance in the rock face. He had taken a great risk coming here himself, but this was too important to leave to someone else.

The day of his vengeance was at hand.

The concealed door they were about to enter, far from the visible remains of the Sennacherib palace site, led into a vast underground labyrinth beneath the ruins of what had once been the greatest city in the world. The city had stretched for miles along the Tigris River in the area commonly known as the Fertile Crescent, a literal island of green in a sea of sand. All that was left on the surface were ruins, long-ago scavenged for the valuables they once contained.

With a final scan of their surroundings, Hussaam swept aside the brush covering a hidden locking mechanism and punched a code into an electronic keypad. With a quiet hiss and a rush of cool air, a door opened. Behind the door would seem, to the casual observer, to be the entrance to ancient catacombs. A more thorough inspection would reveal hi-tech surveillance and detection technology.

Hussaam and his two companions followed the dark passageway, the sand softly crunching beneath their feet. After a slight bend, out of sight of the exterior entrance, they encountered a large metal door. He keyed in another code and it opened.

Two guards snapped to attention. "Mr. Zaafir, the prisoner is being held in his office," said one.

With a nod, Hussaam continued into the corridor. Even in his disgruntled state, he looked around him and admired the facility. After the 1991 invasion by U.S.-led forces, the vast catacombs, and tunnel systems of this once great city had been turned into a state-of-the-art research and manufacturing facility. Its purpose: the production of chemical and biological weapons, out of sight of the U.N. inspectors and the prying eyes of rest of the world.

His people encountered little resistance convincing Saddam Hussein to allow this facility to be built. The dictator's insatiable desire for power and revenge made him easily swayed. Saddam had, of course, been convinced that the lion's share of the weapons would be at his disposal.

Everything possible had been done to convince the dictator to at least show the pretense of acquiescing to the U.N. sanctions, but Sadam's ego made him openly defiant of their demands, potentially jeopardizing Hussaam's plans.

He regretted having to cease operations prematurely, but there was no alternative. An attack by the U.S. was inevitable. Over the last few weeks, the laboratory equipment and weapons created with them had been removed.

After traversing several corridors, they entered the director's office. Hussaam's bodyguards surveyed the room as they took up positions on either side of it.

Two members of the facility's security team stood on either side of a seated man. His name was Abdul. His eyes were large and pupils dilated. Beads of sweat lined his brow. Hussaam had known the man since college and had personally put him in charge of this operation. He had been caught leaving in the night with materials that would have compromised the entire operation.

Hussaam wouldn't allow that to happen; he had spent his entire adult life bringing his plans to fruition. "Why did you do it, Abdul?" He kept his voice steady, without a hint of anger or frustration.

"Do what? Please, I did nothing."

"Have you told anyone of our plans?"

"No, of course not. I have always been loyal to you."

"Then why were you sneaking out in the night with plans to this facility and papers that could compromise me? Haven't I always been good to you and paid you well?"

Before the man could answer, Hussaam held up a hand for silence. He moved to the intercom on the desk. Pressing a button, he called the chief of security. "Has this traitor gotten any information to anyone on the outside?"

"No, sir. I can't find any evidence that he has. Before we caught him, he had not left the compound in weeks."

"Keep looking. We must be absolutely sure. If you have the slightest doubt, inform me immediately." With a wave of his hand, Hussaam motioned the security officers away from the captive. "Stand up, Abdul." It was a command, not a request. "I will make you a deal. If you can get past me, you can leave."

Abdul stood, obviously digesting what he had just been told. His facial expressions ran the gambit from fear to a brief flicker of hope.

The moment Hussaam registered hope in the man's eyes, he lashed out with a claw-hand strike. The blow smashed the traitor's throat with a crunching, tearing sound. The man dropped to the floor, his feet no longer able to support him. Air passage crushed, unable to draw breath, he writhed in wide-eyed agony on the floor. With a final convulsion, his movements ceased.

Turning from the corpse, Hussaam uttered a quiet command. "Get him out of my sight." He punched the intercom button again. "Make sure there is nothing left here that could expose us if this facility is found, and make sure the entrances are sealed and security measures are in place after we leave."

"Yes, Mr. Zaafir. It will be done."

Hussaam would be a god, and the nations would tremble. No one would be allowed to stand in his way, not even a man he considered a friend, of which he had few.

He glanced around the office ensuring everything of importance had been removed. Satisfied, he walked to the far wall and placed his palm against a concealed biometric scanner. A section of the wall slid to the side, revealing a hidden cabinet. He eyed the two black metal cases within and a smile touched his lips. He caressed the tops of the cases and a tingle coursed through his fingers. The power contained within intoxicated and thrilled him: two briefcase thermonuclear bombs, each with more destructive capability than the bombs dropped on Hiroshima.

His fingers moved to the case on the right and tapped a code into the locking mechanism. He lifted the top and inserted a key. The bomb's electronic readouts flashed to life, bathing his face in green and amber light.

Although the invisible and silent killers created in the labs down the hall were capable of much greater damage, these devices had a much more dramatic effect.

PART I

An attacker advances against you, Nineveh. Guard the fortress, watch the road, brace yourselves, marshal all your strength! **Nahum 2:1**

CHAPTER 1

Present day: Flowood, Mississippi

THE answer is in Nahum.

This strange and unusual phrase had passed through Aaron Henderson's mind all day. No, that didn't quite describe it. The phrase bounced, banged, careened, and jolted through his mind. The arcane passage had been spoken to him in a dream the previous night, and he couldn't clear it from his thoughts. Disturbing images plagued his sleep of late, each night growing in intensity, ripping him from slumber with cold sweats and shakes, leaving him tired and eyesore by day.

The foot zooming toward his face snapped his attention to his present situation. No time to block. He dropped his head beneath the kick, stepped to the side, and the foot grazed the back of his skull as it passed.

A flurry of punches and kicks flew at his face and body. He blocked and parried, using his palms to sweep away the blows. The attacker seemed to sense an opening and moved in for the finish, pressing the assault, one strike flowing into the next. Aaron backpedaled as he deflected the onslaught. A kick slipped beneath his guard and caught him in the ribs, forcing a whoosh of air from his mouth.

Focus.

His opponent stood much shorter than Aaron's own six-foot-three-inch frame, but the man was fast, aggressive, and skilled. A heel slashed toward him—a side-kick unleashed in the direction of his forehead. He deflected the strike with the inside of his forearm, unbalancing his attacker. His opponent's eyes squinted, telling Aaron the block had inflicted some pain. Good.

He pressed the attack with a flurry of his own, a series of alternating punches and kicks. A low kick followed by a high punch. Low punch, high kick. The last kick was blocked but left an opening. He slid in and delivered a short right to the sternum. The technique brought them close together. Sweat poured from Aaron and his breathing was labored. The fight needed to end. He followed the punch in and grabbed a shoulder, preparing to lever his opponent onto his hip and toss him to the ground.

The answer is in Nahum.

The world turned upside down. The ceiling, flag-decked walls, and a flash of white uniform with black trim flickered past as he was thrown to the floor, his own attack stymied and reversed. Aaron smacked into the mat with a loud whap. He absorbed the impact on an outstretched arm, leg, and the lateral muscles of his back.

He glanced at the black belt tied around his white uniform, its ends splayed on the floor, three gold stripes adorning the left side. Those stripes were more than decoration. They were supposed to mean something. He slapped the mat with his palm. He should never allow himself be distracted that way. On the street it could be fatal.

His opponent leaned over, face split by a white-toothed grin beneath close-cropped brown hair. The smiling face belonged to Joseph Harris, agent in the Secret Service, training partner, and friend. "You okay, old man?" Joseph extended a hand.

At thirty-six, the nickname was more the result of Aaron's demeanor and conservative attitude than his age. Ignoring the barb, Aaron grasped the offered hand and jumped to his feet. "I'm fine. Wipe that grin off your face." He tugged his uniform into place before bowing formally to his opponent.

* * * * * *

Dressed in street clothes, a blue tee-shirt and jeans, Aaron dropped his gear bag and leaned against the hood of his car, waiting while Joseph locked the school. A long standing tradition, their informal Friday night training sessions were as much about hanging out together as improving skills.

Joseph rounded the hood and plopped against the car, crossing his arms. "What's up?"

Hands stuffed in his pockets Aaron stared at the headlights of passing cars. The glare burned his tired eyes.

"I said what's up? Where are you tonight?"

"Oh, sorry. I'm just a little distracted. A little tired."

His friend glared, apparently waiting for Aaron to elaborate. "Well?" Joseph asked. "What's going on?"

"Dreams. Weird, strange, disturbing dreams. I haven't gotten a good night's sleep in weeks." Aaron waited, expecting a sarcastic comeback.

"What are they about?"

Aaron narrowed his eyes, surprised by the lack of a smart reply. "You must be losing your edge. That was a great opening for a zinger."

Joseph shrugged his shoulders. "I'm a man of many layers. You just fail to see my depth."

"Uh, uh. Layers."

"Are to going tell me about the dreams or not?"

"They're about death. Destruction. Strange disjointed images of carnage in an ancient city. And last night a voice spoke to me." He nodded his head. "Yep. Now I'm hearing voices in my sleep."

"Come on. I'll buy you dinner. Sarah and Abby will be asleep when you get home anyway." Joseph slapped Aaron on the back. "You can tell me all about it. I won't even make fun of you. At least 'til the salad comes."

"You're a real prince, Joseph."

* * * * * *

Amman Jordan: 7:03 a.m.-Eastern European Time

From the office of his international headquarters, Hussaam Udeen Zaafir stared through the windows at the city, his hands clasped behind him. In the parking lot below, a large sign displayed his company's logo: a white outline of a hawk on a field of blue and printed beneath in white letters was the company's name, Hawk Pharmaceuticals. The sight of it never failed to please him. The nickname "Hawk" had been bestowed upon him as a youth due to his dark brown, almost black, eyes, and penetrating gaze.

He turned and glanced toward a framed photo on his desk. It pictured him on his wedding day with his bride, Fatima, and her uncle, the former monarch of Jordan, King Hussein. Hussaam had been granted the privilege of marrying into the royal family as a reward for his service to the former king. Upon the monarch's death from cancer, his son, Abdullah II, Fatima's first cousin, was crowned. Like his father before him, Abdullah betrayed his people by signing a peace agreement with

Hussaam's enemies. He bit back the bitter taste of anger and allowed the trace of a smile to play across his lips. Soon, the price of that betrayal would be paid in full. Soon, his goals would be achieved and his people would be liberated.

Hussaam eased into his chair and removed a leather wallet from his coat pocket. He laid the wallet on the desk and extracted three photos from a recessed pouch. The pictures were yellowed with age and though he did not understand why he kept them, he was unable to part with them. He traced a finger over the images of his mother and father before picking up the photo of a young boy. A boy he had not seen in years. A boy whose features closely resembled Hussaam's. *It will not be much longer, my brother.* Hussaam gently tucked the photos into place and returned the wallet to his pocket.

On a wall opposite him, one of the many mounted TV monitors showed an American twenty-four-hour news channel. Hussaam still could not believe his fortune. Mere days before the Americans invaded Iraq, he completed the transport of his chemical and biological weapons out of the hidden base. In the end, all it cost him was time. But now, all the pieces were in place.

A large cache of weapons and a new base were hastily set up in the mountains of Northeastern Syria. At first he feared America was doing more than saber rattling toward Syria. They had proof that Syrians were crossing the border into Iraq to lead terror attacks on their troops, and the Syrian government continued to allow terror training camps to remain in operation. It looked as if the Americans would not be dissuaded from taking action. It could have been disastrous, further delaying, possibly even ruining, his plans.

He chuckled to himself. It was one the few times he was glad to be wrong: the Americans had done nothing. The American's own political games made them doubt themselves and weakened their resolve. Confidence in their intelligence was so eroded that even if they somehow got wind of his plans, they would probably be too hesitant to act. There was only one remaining person from Saddam's regime who could identify Hussaam and his role in the base in Iraq: Izzat Ibrahim al-Douri had been found, and any threat he might pose would soon be removed. Al-Douri had been smarter than the rest of Saddam's henchmen. He left Iraq before the Americans struck, taking millions in cash with him. But he would not escape his fate. In the end, it would be the same as his dead compatriots.

The fact that no "weapons of mass destruction" had been found in Iraq caused great rifts within the American populace. Even now it seemed as if every other news report asked, "Where are the WMDs?" WMDs, WMDs, this term was ingrained in the American lexicon. Now, the American government concluded there never were any weapons.

Another small smile formed on his lips. He had no idea his subterfuge would have such an unintended, yet so welcome, consequence.

* * * * * *

Colombia: 1:10 a.m.-Eastern Standard Time

Captain Derek Galloway peered through the dense foliage at his objective: a large ranch-style mansion in the midst of a jungle on the lower slopes of the Baudo mountains, near the pacific coast. He absorbed every detail of the terrain and the heavily guarded grounds. The stars above shone so bright and close it seemed as if he could reach out and touch them. It was moist and hot; the air pressed upon him with a palpable force. Sweat dripped from his pores, causing his black fatigues to cling to his skin. He resisted the urge to wipe his damp forehead, instead blotting it with a sleeve so as not to risk smearing his black face-paint.

He glanced at the men behind him—a group of the most elite fighting men in the world. All of them experienced and battle-hardened, and each hand picked to be part of this team.

He reached down and clutched the silver cross in the side pocket of his black fatigues. He shouldn't have it on him, but he didn't believe it would give away his identity if found. Members of units involved in black ops were forbidden to have anything on their person to identify them in case they were captured or killed.

He mouthed a silent prayer, steeling himself for combat. Many had questioned his seemingly at-odds career and faith. How could a man of God be a soldier? The answer was that he believed he was doing right, protecting his country and the world from evil. Although America had her problems, he believed in her inherent goodness. Derek believed she was a bastion of freedom and light in a largely dark and oppressive world. His beliefs also affected his decision to pursue a career in special operations. There was less gray area. He had clearly defined targets and objectives. Sometimes indiscriminate killing was a necessary evil in conventional battles.

After all, as he was fond of telling his men, where better to have God on your side than in battle? His favorite scripture said, "With God on my side, who can stand against me?" Although his men gave him a hard time about his devotion to his faith, they would follow him into hell, and often had.

Tonight they were after a big fish, someone who might be able to tell them what actually went down in Iraq before it was invaded. They had come to capture Izzat Ibrahim al-Douri, the former Vice Chairman of the Baath Party's Revolutionary Command Council and a longtime confidant of Saddam Hussein. He was also the highest-ranking member of Saddam's regime left at large.

Derek and his team needed to make it quick, in and out, no hitches. They were operating in a foreign country without its government's permission. Despite repeated requests from Colombia's elected government for aid in squelching the rebel forces attempting to overthrow them, it was the strict policy of the United States to remain "hands off" in Colombia. The Baudo mountains were controlled by a rebel group known as the FARC, *Fuerzas Armadas Revolucionarias de Colombia–Ejército del Pueblo*, the Revolutionary Armed Forces of Colombia–Peoples Army. Utterly ruthless, the "people's" army was funded by extortion, kidnapping, and the illegal drug trade. The mountains were crawling with them. Obviously al-Douri had their blessing, or he wouldn't be there.

His capture wouldn't be a cakewalk. The house was well lit and well guarded.

He raised his hand and signaled the men to fan out and take their positions. He clutched the mike at his throat and whispered, "Anvil, this is Hammer. We're in position. Do we have a green light on mission?"

The reply came quickly: "Hammer, this is Anvil. You have a green light."

* * * * * *

From his office and ops center deep in the bowels of the CIA's old headquarters building in Langley, Virginia, Harold "Hal" Bouie studied a bank of monitor screens. The screens showed infrared- and night-enhanced aerial views of the compound that Captain Derek Galloway's team was about to infiltrate.

"Hammer, there are no rebel forces near you. I have infrared of the guards. It doesn't look like they know you're there. Most are smoking and talking to each other. I count two stationary in front, two stationary in the rear, and four patrolling the perimeter. Do you have their positions?"

"Anvil, we have their positions marked."

"Hammer, there will be more of them inside. I don't know exactly how many. Hit them hard and fast, and be careful."

"Affirmative, Anvil. We'll return soon with a house guest for you. Hammer out."

A tip from a friend, the U.S. Deputy Director of National Intelligence, had alerted Hal to al-Douri's location. His capture could be a coup on a grand scale. The information al-Douri might possess could alter the world's opinion of the United States and its actions. Not to mention their own populace.

Hal plopped into a chair. There was nothing to do but wait and let Captain Galloway do his job.

By special order of the president after September 11th, a unique twelve-man terrorist strike force had been created. For the first time, Delta and Seal operatives had been put together in a single unit, in the utmost secrecy, for one reason: to hunt down terrorists wherever they might be. The mixture of Delta and Seal team members would enable them to operate anywhere on land or sea. They worked outside of the normal chain of command which enabled them to act quickly and avoid red tape.

He watched the bank of monitor screens. Galloway was moving in— it was crunch time, the most difficult period of an operation for Hal. All he could do was watch. His fingers strummed the arm of the chair as his foot tapped. Nervous energy finally overcame him. He pushed himself out of the chair and began to pace.

When the president created the special terrorist strike force, he had requested Hal by name to be its eyes and ears. Hal ordered and organized their missions and answered only to the president. He helped direct the movement of Captain Derek Galloway's team, using his own resources as well as those of the NSA, FBI, and CIA. After a long career as a field operative, he had become a CIA analyst in the '90s. His was one of the loudest voices urging the government to pay attention to the growing threat of terrorism and to step up their anti-terror efforts. The

failure to stop September 11th and the seeming debacle over Iraq's missing weapons was something he had taken very personally.

Now, he had been given the resources to hunt down America's enemies, no matter what hole in which they were hidden.

He glanced at his watch. The action was about to start. He extracted
a cigarette from his pocket and stuck it between his lips. He dug out a
lighter and flicked it to life with his thumb before placing the flame to
the cigarette's tip. He puffed a deep, satisfying drag, blowing a cloud of
swirling smoke toward the ceiling.

Godspeed, Derek.

* * * * * *

"All right, we have a green light," Derek whispered into his throat mike.
"Move in. Hands signals only from here." His fingers slid across his
weapons, ensuring they were in place and secure. Four groups of three
would take out each set of guards. Derek and two of his corporals,
Chavez and Johnson, would take out the guards at the front and go in
after al-Douri.

His group's targeted guards paced back and forth before the front
entrance of the mansion. The moment they turned away, Derek led his
men silently forward, like black wraiths melting into the shadows. When
the guards completed their patrol and turned back, Derek held up his
hand. His men went still, barely breathing. When the guards turned away
again, he lifted his sleeve to look at the glowing dial of his watch. He
pulled his night-vision goggles over his eyes just as the power to the
compound was cut, blanketing the men in total darkness.

Derek signaled again, and his group sprinted toward the two guards.
As they drew near, one of the guards sensed their approach and turned,
brandishing his weapon. In the green light of Derek's goggles, the barrel
of the man's .44 Magnum looked as large and dark as a cave. Fortu-
nately, the man appeared more worried about survival than duty, in de-
fending himself rather than raising an alarm. With an open-handed slap,
Derek knocked the pistol away. He grabbed the guard by the shoulders
and with a quick push-pull motion, twisted the man around so a rear
choke hold could be applied. Once Derek had him secured, Johnson
stabbed a tranquilizer into his neck.

The third member of Derek's group, Chavez, approached the remaining guard. Chavez stayed low, moving in a crouch. Once in position, he seized the man from the rear, applying a submission hold.

Johnson moved quickly to the second guard and repeated the tranquilizing process.

Chavez and Johnson dragged the two unconscious guards into a clump of bushes. Derek peered at the waiting house, which glowed green through his goggles. He reached up and flipped a switch, making his vision infrared. The view changed from green to black, spotted with red. The red indicated heat signatures which he used to seek out any hidden guards. Satisfied, he switched back to night-vision. He cocked his ears, listening to sounds of the night: the trilling of bugs, the skittering of small animals, the wind rustling leaves. Nothing seemed wrong; it remained quiet. After scanning the front of the house a moment longer, they moved into the covered entry porch where the darker shadows swallowed them.

A beam of light pierced the glass beside the front door, momentarily blinding him until he pushed his goggles up on his forehead. Derek and his men flattened against the wall, melting into the heavier gloom. The front door swung open and a huge form stepped into view, one hand holding a flashlight. A pistol was tucked underneath an arm, placed there to free up a hand which had twisted open the lock. The man was huge, his bulk filled the entrance. He yelled, "You guys okay out there?"

Derek launched from his position. The man's eyes moved toward the motion before going wide, and he reached for his gun. He opened his mouth and sucked in air to shout an alarm. As the sound welled up in the guard's throat, Derek delivered a vicious kick to the man's sternum. A small groan escaped his lips as he doubled over. Johnson stepped forward and jabbed the man in the neck with a tranquilizer.

He still had some fight in him and tried to raise his gun, but Johnson intervened with a solid right hand to the head. The large man staggered and fell to his knees, succumbing to the punishment and chemicals.

Chavez muscled his way past the guard, gun at the ready, to cover the interior of the mansion. Derek followed and crouched on the opposite side of the doorway, sliding his night-vision goggles into place as he moved. He surveyed the interior. They stood in a large foyer with checkered marble floor tiles, and fluted columns rising to the high ceiling. Paintings adorned the walls and statuary filled darkened niches. Two large staircases, bordered by intricately carved balustrades, curved up either side of the room. The steps intersected at a landing on the second level and two shorter sets of stairs split away, connecting with hallways on left and right. The hallway on the left led to the master suite.

Satisfied there was so immediate threat, Derek waved his men ahead. Chavez took the left staircase, Johnson the right. They bounded up the stairs to take positions on the landing.

On their signal, Derek moved to join them. As he crossed the foyer, a shadow moved to his left. He spun toward the motion, raising his gun. His finger caressed the trigger.

A woman whom he assumed to be household staff crept forward, one hand on the wall, feeling her way through the dark.

Derek released the pressure on the trigger and continued. The woman was oblivious to his presence.

He climbed the stairs two at a time. At the upper landing, he placed his finger to his lips and pointed to the woman below, alerting his companions to her presence. He didn't want an innocent bystander shot.

Chavez and Johnson proceeded to the hallway on the left, while Derek crouched on the landing. As he moved to join them, his goggles filled with unbearably bright blinding light. His eyes squeezed shut against the flash just as a shot boomed out and plaster erupted from the wall behind him. The woman downstairs screamed. A second shot exploded and Derek dove away, peeling off his goggles. He rolled on to his stomach and aimed his gun toward the shots.

At the bottom of the stairs, a guard held a revolver in one hand and a large electric lantern in the other. The shaft of light from the device filled the upper landing, throwing shadows on the wall behind Derek. The guard lined up for another shot, but Derek returned fire. His silenced rifle bucked slightly in his hands one time. The guard slumped to the tiles with a bullet through his heart. The light's beam fell with him, pooling on the floor around him, returning Derek's position to relative darkness. The woman below stood still, horror filling her eyes, mouth slightly opened. She glanced at the fallen man, then at Derek, and ran away, another scream exploding from her lungs.

Derek's eyes moved from the retreating woman to the dead man on the floor. His death was unfortunate, but there hadn't been another option.

Drawn by the sounds of the firefight, Johnson crouched in the entry. Derek signaled all was clear and vaulted the remaining steps to join him.

The three men re-grouped and discovered the entrance of the master suite where their quarry was presumed to be residing.

They found themselves in a long passage with plush carpeting, more paintings, and lined with doors one either side, some of them open. At the end was the set of double doors—their destination.

Johnson moved ahead with Chavez following. As they came to an open door, they pressed their backs against the wall. Johnson readied his weapon in front of him and swung away from the wall, aiming the barrel through the dark portal to cover its interior. Satisfied, they continued thus, each man alternately repeating the process until they reached the end of the hall.

Derek brought up the rear and joined them in front of the large double doors. He nodded, and Chavez tried the lock, but it didn't turn. Silence no longer necessary, Derek smashed the door with his foot. The wood around the lock shattered, and the three men stormed into the room, brandishing their weapons.

Along the left wall of the huge room was an equally large bed. In its middle, with the sheets pulled up around his neck, sat their wide-eyed objective.

Chavez ripped the sheets back and pulled al-Douri to his feet. To his credit, he didn't resist, beg, or bargain. He seemed resigned to his fate, as if he had known it was only a matter of time until he was found. Chavez bound the man's hands and a tied a gag over his mouth.

* * * * * *

After incapacitating their assigned guards, the rest of Derek's men were able to escape the mansion without resistance. At their rendezvous point in a clearing in front of the compound, the twelve-man team gathered around Derek. He issued terse commands: "Johnson, take the rear. Pearson, you take point. Let's hoof it to the LZ and get this package home!" He hesitated a moment. Something didn't seem right. He could almost sense eyes upon him. Alarm bells clanged in his head. His nerves were raw; the mission was not yet complete.

The wind picked up, not cooling, just stirring the tepid air. The clouds parted to reveal a moon so large and brilliant it lit the clearing like day compared to the thick darkness. The moon's light bathed the entire valley. Derek peered at the thickly vegetated hills surrounding the compound. He felt exposed, naked. The sense of being watched made his skin tingle. He had relied on his instincts to live this long, and he would not ignore them now. "Move it to the trees now! Double-time." He and his men dashed toward the tree line, half dragging, half carrying their prisoner with them.

"Ahh!"

Derek turned as al-Douri cried out. His men reacted quickly, making an outward-facing circle, guns at the ready. Corporal Chavez sprinted to al-Douri's side and applied pressure to the entrance wound in the man's back and the exit wound at the front. His efforts did little to staunch the flow of blood. He met Derek's gaze and shook his head.

Derek knelt at al-Douri's side. The man's breathing become shallow, his skin pale. He was not going to make it out alive. "Who did this to you, and why?" Derek didn't expect an answer.

Al-Douri stared at him, lucidity returning to his liquid brown eyes. With fading strength, he grabbed Derek by his lapel and pulled him down. He whispered, "The Hawk. Look for the Hawk. He did this to me. He has the weapons. He is going to . . ." The man's voice trailed off as his body failed.

Derek said to his men, "Did anyone see where the shot came from?"

"It came from up the slope in the trees, that way." Two of his men pointed in the same general direction.

Derek weighed his options and decided against taking his team to pursue the shooter. They had to get out. He pulled a blanket from his pack and draped it over the corpse. He said a silent prayer for the man's soul. Nothing else could be done. "Wagner. Chavez. Grab him." He stood and scanned the horizon while his men formed a makeshift stretcher out of the blanket. "All right, let's move out. Keep your eyes open."

* * * * * *

Amman Jordan: 10:15 a.m.- Eastern European Time

Hussaam toweled the sweat from his forehead and switched off the treadmill. He sipped from a bottle of water and admired the scenery. The training room's window afforded him a view of the pool and the mountainous countryside surrounding his estate. The brilliant morning sunshine glistened off ripples on the pool's surface, and small puffs of cumulous lazily floated in the azure sky.

He exercised twice a day: a light work-out in the morning and an intense one in the evening. His bodyguards, Basil and Rashad, were required to join him. One of Hussaam's phones rang. Under normal circumstances, it would have been a source of agitation for him. His morning exercise period was not to be disturbed. But he hoped this was the one call he anxiously awaited. Basil brought the ringing phone to him. The satellite phone, good. This could only be one man. A deadly and useful man whose services Hussaam had utilized many times. He placed the phone to his ear.

"The target has been neutralized."

"Did they have a chance to question him?"

"No."

"Are you sure?"

"Positive. I witnessed the whole operation."

"Well done."

Without further comment, the call was disconnected from the other end.

Hussaam tossed the phone back to Basil. Al-Douri was dead. It was going to be a good day. He rubbed his hands together. Now, what had the cook prepared for brunch?

CHAPTER II

THE ancient city lies in ruin, not the victim of time and decay but ravaged by fire and violence. The buildings, what little of them remain, are crafted of large hand-hewn stone-and-clay bricks and stout bracing timbers. The devastation, whatever the cause, is complete. Overturned stones litter the ground, and the bracing timbers are nothing but charred remains. The city still burns. Bright red-orange flames radiate heat that even from a distance feel as if they are baking his face, drying him out, and making his skin feel taut as old leather. The fire's light casts the entire scene in a red hue. Bodies are everywhere, lying over each other, in doorways, on the streets. Their clothing is in tatters, their skin smolders. It is a scene of doom, of chaos, of death.

In the midst of the devastation a man kneels, his body wracked by sobs of grief. A large book is open before him. He is out of place in this ancient, gruesome, scene. His clothes are modern and well kept. His hair is short, his shoulders broad. He turns his head, revealing an intense gaze. "Save us." The words are spoken in a whisper yet seem to reverberate and echo.

He lifts the book, and its pages become visible. It is a Bible, old and worn, its edges slightly frayed. He points to words on the left side of the page. Without perceptible movement, he is suddenly close. A few feet separate them. His intent green eyes appear troubled and haunted, enhanced by the glimmering firelight. He speaks again. "The answer is in Nahum . . ."

Aaron's eyes popped open and he bolted upright, the swift motion shaking the bed. Sweat poured down his forehead, down his back. His skin was cold and clammy. His heart raced. Blood throbbed against his temples, and he couldn't seem to catch his breath. For a moment he didn't know where he was, disoriented by sleep-clouded eyes, until details of the room coalesced. The shadow of a pine dresser and armoire, the humming of a ceiling fan, the scent of laundered sheets. His bedroom.

A groan beside him told him he had woken his wife.

Sarah rolled over and propped on an elbow. "What's wrong? Are you okay?"

"It was a dream. *The* dream. Again." His voice was quiet, words spoken in a whisper, as if speaking louder would provoke the demons haunting his sleep.

Sarah stroked his arm. The touch was tender and it still made his heart leap. She studied his face. "Try to relax. It was just a dream." There was worry in her eyes. "You fell asleep with the news on again."

It was true: news of tensions in the Middle East, terrorist bombings, terror threats, nuclear threats, continuing unrest in Iraq, and natural disasters dominated the headlines.

The problem was that deep down, in the depth of his being, Aaron sensed his were more than mere dreams, more than nightmares, and even worse than any of the terrifying images he could remember conjuring in sleep as a child. There was something in him, in a place he couldn't bear to explore, screaming to him that these were more than just nightmares, more than his subconscious identifying an unresolved issue in the waking world.

Sarah still stroked his arm, and Aaron covered the back of her hand with his palm. "I'm fine. Go back to sleep." He squeezed her hand for assurance.

Though she appeared unconvinced, she rolled over and settled into the sheets.

Save us.

Save who?

The answer is in Nahum.

Who, what, where was Nahum?

He wiped the perspiration from his brow and lay back on the pillow. Though he closed his eyes and forced his tense muscles to relax, sleep was a long time coming.

* * * * *

Aaron, normally an early riser, could tell by the glow through the curtains that it was much later than he preferred to get up. Even on Saturdays he usually woke long before his wife, affording him precious quiet time with his daughter. At nine months old, Abigail was his pride and joy.

"Time to get up," he told himself, but his body just didn't agree. With a groan, he forced himself upright and stepped out of bed. He heard the sounds of cooking, and as he drew closer to the kitchen he smelled his favorite breakfast: bacon and eggs. "Wow, sweetheart, it smells great. What's the occasion?"

"What; there has to be an occasion for me to cook now?" She blinked her blue eyes and smiled.

Aaron gave her a quick kiss, poured a cup of coffee, and sipped it for a moment. He set the cup down and crossed his arms, his thoughts returning to the dream. Even by the light of day, he couldn't shake its effects. It seemed so real; he had been there, experienced every detail. It was also very unusual. He dreamed every night but rarely remembered the details. As soon as he woke up, the memory usually disappeared like vapor.

His neck and shoulders tightened, and his back became stiff. He massaged them to ease the tension. Then he heard two precious words that could cheer any heart: "Da, da!" Abby screamed with delight when she saw him.

With teetering toddler steps, she ran to him with her arms outstretched. Aaron picked her up and her tiny arms squeezed his neck. His arms encircled her and clutched her tightly, inhaling her fresh baby scent, feeling her tiny heart beat against his chest. Holding her like this was when he felt the most like a man. Most of the time he saw himself as a little boy, trying to fill a man's shoes. His arms were so strong and hard against her tiny soft body. This precious life was his to mold and protect. Careful not to scrape her face with his unshaved stubble, he planted a kiss on her cheek. His spirits lifted, he gave her a tickle to hear her giggle.

"I've had a tough time keeping her out of the bedroom. She just didn't understand why you weren't up," Sarah said. "Now wash up. Breakfast is ready."

The meal was delicious and just the way Aaron liked it: lots of eggs, lots of bacon. As usual, Abby spent more time looking at the birds out the window and dropping food on the floor than eating.

Aaron's sense of dread returned, draping him like a blanket, weighing him down. Unbidden, a question formed on his lips. "Do we still have the Bible Sis gave us?"

"Yes, I think so. Look in the study bookshelf." Sarah's eyebrows lowered in a quizzical manner, an indication of how strange she must have thought the question.

He walked into the study, steps heavy, pulse quickening. He located the Bible on a shelf. It was a gift from his sister, one of her many not-so-subtle hints to get him involved in religion. He held the book in his hands, gauging its weight. It was a large and heavy volume with scripture and study notes. It was the first time he had picked up a Bible in a very long time.

He started to open it but hesitated without knowing why.

A blast from a car horn nearly caused him to jump out of his skin. "Easy, calm down," he mumbled to himself. It was just someone picking up one of the neighborhood kids. *Get a grip. You're a grown man. It was just a dream.*

He scanned the cover of the Bible: the New International Version. It was supposed to be easier to read. Slowly, he opened the cover, its binding stiff from lack of use. After flipping a few pages he found a list of the books of the Bible. Using his finger as a guide, he scanned the page.

The skin at the back of his neck rippled with goose flesh. There, toward the end of the Old Testament list of books, was the word he hoped wasn't there but somehow knew would be. *Nahum.*

He stood absolutely still, staring at the word. Or was the word staring at him? The five letters leapt from the page, separating from the words around it. His fingers seemed weak and the book impossibly heavy. *How?* As far as he knew, he had never seen or heard of the book of Nahum. He had passing knowledge of the Bible from his youth but had not read it since. He wasn't even sure he believed it anymore.

He placed the open book on his desk and sank into his chair. What, if anything, could this mean?

CHAPTER III

STILL dressed in his robe and slippers, Aaron returned to the study. Sarah was in the shower, and Abby was down for her morning nap.

He sat at his computer, logged onto the Internet, and typed one word into his search engine: Nahum. As the computer finished its search, he let out a deep breath. Several web sites appeared. They all seemed to be religious or archeological in nature. He picked one at random.

As he read, the skin at the back of his neck tingled again. Apparently Nahum was one of the Bible's minor prophets. His book foretold the destruction of Nineveh, the capital of the Assyrian Empire. The ruins of the once-thriving city of Nineveh were located in modern day Northern Iraq, near Mosul.

Toward the end of Saddam Hussein's regime, there had been a great effort to preserve the integrity of the ruins and completely excavate them. According to the article, Saddam's goal had been to preserve Iraq's rich cultural heritage. There seemed to have been a great deal of plundering during the years of U.N. sanctions.

Aaron realized as he read that his face was tight, eyes squinted and brow furrowed. He looked away from the screen and massaged his forehead. This was all very interesting, but how could he have possibly dreamt of this obscure book of the Bible which he could not recall having ever read?

He hadn't attended church since he was a teenager. He didn't miss it, either, especially the guilt. He could never measure up, so why even try? And so many of the people who went to church were phonies. Sunday morning they sang, nodded their heads in agreement with the preacher, said amen. Smiled and put a large offering envelope in the plate for all to see. On Monday they were cutthroat businessman. They would lie or cheat to make a profit, fire without compunction, and avoid their families in the name of the dollar. Further souring Aaron were the televangelists with their coifed-up hair and shiny suits. They said things like "Geeezus," and "Gawwd," or, "Place your hand on the Tee Vee and be heeeled." Healing, of course, had to be accompanied by check, money order, credit-card number, or deed to one's house.

Gathering his courage, he picked up the Bible again. There had to be a simple explanation. He opened it, turned to the book of Nahum, and began to read.

The book was definitely not feel-good reading. It was about a terrible siege, the deaths of men, women, and children. According to the prophet, it was a result of their own wickedness. This was hard for Aaron to understand. Wasn't God supposed to be kind and loving?

He decided to call his sister. The phone rang only once before she answered. "Rachel, it's me," Aaron said.

"Well, hey, sport. I was going to call you today. I haven't talked to you in over a week." In sister code that meant: I am a single girl all alone, and you haven't even bothered to make sure I'm all right.

Aaron couldn't help smiling. His sister was eternally optimistic and could find the positive side of any situation, yet make him feel guilty in an instant. "I'm *very* sorry," he said.

"Well, there's no reason for you to feel guilty, I'm fine. Really."

Shaking his head, Aaron ignored the gibe. "Sis, I'll tell you all about it later, but do you think your minister might be willing to talk with me?"

She didn't say anything. After a second, when Aaron was about to repeat the question, she finally responded, "I'm sure he would. Do you mean you would like to start attending church?"

Aaron had shocked her. Good. "Slow down. I just need to get some advice."

He deftly avoided her questions about what was going on and eventually was given her minister's phone number.

* * * * * *

Aaron decided to put off making the call until later. He stood and stretched, a groan escaping him. He rotated his neck and worked his shoulders. He was tight all over. Some exercise might be the remedy.

He changed into workout clothes and went into the garage, where he kept an exercise area. He would warm up by doing some Hyung, or forms, predetermined patterns of kicks and punches. His fascination with the martial-arts began at an early age with movies and television. He begged for lessons as a child and though he'd never been able to sway his parents into agreement, his interest didn't wane. He began lessons in college and never quit. An unexpected bonus had been the contacts and relationships he wouldn't otherwise have, including his friendship with Joseph.

After stretching for several minutes, Aaron executed a few impromptu kicks and punches to loosen up. He eased into position and began a black belt form called Koryo.

Block, kick, kick, strike, block, punch. He stopped, holding the last move, unable to recall the next one. With a shake of his head he started over, with the same result. He continued to lose his concentration after a few moves. He couldn't keep his focus. He glanced at the mixture of swords, sticks, and staffs mounted on the wall. The way his mind was wandering, there was no way he would even attempt to work with one of them. That would be a sure recipe for bruises and lacerations.

Instead of continuing, he turned to his heavy bag. He slipped on training gloves and began hitting the bag at random, alternating between hands and feet. After about fifteen minutes of mindless drumming, he stopped. His heart raced, his chest heaved, and perspiration dripped off him. Taking air in through his nose and blowing out through his mouth, he gained control of his breathing. He flexed tired muscles, now loose and relaxed. His anxiety was gone, almost as if the sweat had purged him of his sense of dread. Not the best workout, but it seemed to have done the trick.

* * * * * *

After a quick shower, Aaron decided to call Pastor Jenkins. He doubted the wisdom of doing it, but it was worth a try. Rachel sang the man's praises, saying he was both young and wise, and acted like a regular guy. Aaron needed someone versed in scripture.

"This is Aaron Henderson," he said into the phone. "I'm Rachel's brother."

"Yes, Aaron, how are you?"

"I'm fine, Pastor." His grip tightened on the phone. "I just wondered if, well, um, I . . . this is going to sound crazy, but I'm having strange dreams. I really don't know why I called you but, I'm a bit confused and . . ."

"Wait, Aaron, why don't you just slow down and start from the beginning?"

"All right. This is going to sound crazy, but here goes." Aaron explained the recurring dream and its culmination last night with the man holding a Bible and the reference to the book of Nahum.

"You mean you've never read the book of Nahum?" Pastor Jenkins asked.

"No. Not that I can remember, anyway."

"Well, that wouldn't be too surprising. It is a somewhat obscure book, and I myself have rarely studied it."

"Pastor, do you have any thoughts on what, if anything, it could mean? I hate to waste your time. It's probably nothing. It's just that the dreams are so real and vivid."

"Is there anything going on that may be causing you stress? Work, financial strains . . . anything like that?"

"No, nothing I can think of."

"Aaron, I'm no expert on dreams, but it seems to me there are two possibilities here. Either these are just nightmares caused by physiological or psychological events, or you're actually having visions."

Visions. Right. Next he would be building an ark or telling fortunes at the carnival. "What do you mean by 'visions'?"

"Aaron, do you believe in God?"

"Yes. I think so. Maybe. Sometimes, to be honest, I'm not too sure. That's one of the reasons I haven't been to church in a long time." *Here comes the sermon.* He almost hoped for it. That would make it easier to dismiss whatever else the man had to say.

"Well, in the Bible, God commonly sent dreams to reveal the future or give insight."

Aaron took a moment to respond, surprised by the lack of rebuke. If there was anything he knew about clergy, it was that no opportunity to pile on the guilt would be wasted. "Pastor, I doubt that I am the type of person God would be sending messages to."

"I wouldn't be too sure. The Bible is full of unlikely and unwilling people who were used to accomplish great things. One of the most well known stories in the Bible is about Jonah and the Great Fish. The reason Jonah was in the fish in the first place was that he ran from God's instruction. You're not running from God, are you, Aaron?"

He began to doubt the wisdom of making this call. Maybe he needed to talk to someone trained in dream analysis.

"Hey, why don't you come to church services in the morning? We can get together face-to-face afterward. I'll think about this and maybe we can come up with an answer together. At the least it will make your sister happy to see you in church, and maybe you can get her off your back about it, for a few weeks anyway." The pastor laughed.

"Well, that might not be such a bad idea. My wife would probably enjoy it."

"Great, I'll look forward to seeing you tomorrow morning. Church starts at ten-thirty. I'll do my best to keep you awake."

Aaron hung up the phone. He hadn't received any answers, but his burden seemed lighter just discussing the dreams with someone else. It was almost as if a weight had been lifted from him. Maybe the man could help him. It wouldn't hurt to find out.

CHAPTER IV

AFTER fighting the nightly battle to get Abigail to sleep, Aaron strolled into his bedroom and plopped heavily on the bed. With a sigh, he sunk into his pillows.

Over the course of the day, he read the book of Nahum twice. He still couldn't fathom any meaning from it or figure out how it related to him in any way. It was the prophecy of the destruction of the city of Nineveh, destroyed in 612 BC. It didn't seem to relate to him in the slightest.

He grabbed a novel from his nightstand, longing to be captivated by its story, to be swept into its fictitious world, transported to another time and place. He thumbed through the pages and found his bookmark. He held the book in his lap and began to read. Turning the page, he realized he had no idea what he just read. His eyes had taken in the words, the words just hadn't registered. He tried a couple more times before giving up. He turned off his bedside lamp and grabbed the remote.

Sarah leaned over and kissed him on the cheek before rolling onto her side and curling up in the covers. Within moments, her breathing was even and deep.

Aaron stared at the television. His thumb kept pressing the channel change button on the remote control; images flashed on and off. The bedroom flickered in its light as one channel came on and lit the room then went dark as it switched to the next. Without realizing it, his finger pressed the button faster and faster.

Out of the corner of his eye, Aaron noticed Sarah staring at him. "I'm sorry. Did I wake you?" The question was rhetorical; he most assuredly had woken her.

The look of annoyance on her face softened. "It's all right. What's the matter?"

"I can't get this dream out of mind. What do you think? Am I losing it?"

She stared into his eyes for just a moment before answering, almost as if she needed a minute to think about it. Her eyes sparkled, just the way they usually did before she smiled. The smile in her eyes reached her lips, and she extended her fingers to stroke his hand. "I don't think so. You are, without a doubt, the most centered and stable man I know."

"Hmm, if I didn't know better I would say you were calling me boring." He laughed.

"Well, I have certainly learned to pay attention to your dreams."

Aaron considered that for a moment. Although it was rare for him to remember dreams, every so often he did. Usually they were powerful ones about the people he cared for the most. Two came to his mind immediately. He had dreamed of his grandmother's death, and an accident his sister had been in, before they happened. "Yes, I see what you mean," he said. As vivid as those dreams had been, as true as they had turned out to be, this was different somehow. He could feel it.

Sarah patted his hand and turned to settle back into the covers. "Whatever it is, I have no doubt you'll figure it out. In the meantime, why don't you try to get some rest? Oh, did you let Rachel know we were coming to church tomorrow?"

"No, I thought we would surprise her. So, you really don't think I'm nuts?"

"No more than I always have. Now, go to sleep."

Aaron found an old movie to watch. He was very tired and his eyes were getting heavy. He blinked and rubbed his eyes, doing his best to stave off sleep. An ancient city, fire, death, and destruction plagued his thoughts. He had no desire to revisit this nightmare. No longer able to fight it, he finally succumbed to fatigue and fell asleep.

* * * * * *

In a conference room deep in the bowels of the White House, Hal sat next to Derek. Across a large polished wood table from them sat the president of the United States, the National Security Advisor, the director of National Intelligence, and the deputy director of National Intelligence. The room was secure, shielded from electronic surveillance.

"That was all he said, Captain Galloway?" the president asked. The question referred to the failed attempt to capture Izzat Ibrahim al-Douri and his final words.

"Yes, sir. That's all he said." Derek cast his eyes down. His jaw worked and his fists were clinched on his lap. "I'm sorry I didn't bring him in, sir."

Robert Russell, the director of National Intelligence, or DNI, slammed a palm on the table. "Pardon me, Mr. President, but this is unacceptable."

Hal glared at the man. "Excuse me." The man was a career politician with bottle black coifed hair and a tailored suit. A pompous ass with no intelligence experience, completely undeserving of his position. It still rankled that the president appointed him.

"You risked an international incident for this crap. 'The Hawk.' Come on. That could be anyone or anything. You failed, Mr. Bouie. That's why from now until this matter is settled you will be reporting to me."

"What?" Hal turned to the president. "Sir, I thought the whole idea was to keep us free from red-tape and bureaucracy."

The president cleared his throat and adjusted his tie. "It's just temporary, Hal. With Robert's resources, he can help you. I'm asking you to be a team player. For now." He shot a glance toward the DNI and turned to Derek. "I know you did your best, son. That's why you were chosen you to lead your team." He returned his gaze to Hal. "Do you have any idea who 'the Hawk' is?"

"No, sir. I have my staff poring through every bit of data and transmissions we can get our hands on, but no luck yet."

The president looked down at his hands for a moment and seemed to be in deep thought. "I know I don't have to tell either of you what the implications of al-Douri's murder may be. It could be revenge, or it could mean someone wanted him silenced. If he did have information on Iraq's weapons and he was killed for it, then it is likely whoever killed him knows where they are." He paused, taking a deep breath before continuing. "I don't care about the politics of this thing. If Saddam Hussein or any of his lackeys had chemical and biological weapons, we have to know where they went and who has them now."

Both Derek and Hal nodded in agreement. No other response was necessary.

Fixing both of them with her intent brown eyes, the NSA turned and spoke. "Mr. President, I think we should release the news that al-Douri has been *captured*. I can handle what details will be released."

"You're right. Some good press couldn't hurt." The president rose to leave, saying, "Hal, you find this man, and be prepared to send Captain Galloway's team wherever necessary. I'll give you both any help you need."

Hal remained in his chair. "I'll find him, sir. Don't worry."

Derek stood and snapped a salute.

The president and the NSA retreated from the room, but the DNI remained. He stood and loomed over the table, pointing a finger. "Bouie, you will keep me in the loop. I want to know what you know as soon as you know it." He inclined his head to the deputy director, Tim Greene. "Tim will be your liaison and you'll report to directly to him. I know how you feel, but I don't care. Maybe your relationship with Tim will make it easier for you to swallow. Maybe not. I really don't give a damn." He grabbed his briefcase and moved to the door. "Tim, I expect a briefing by this afternoon."

When the man disappeared Hal turned to Tim Greene. "*You* weren't any help."

The man lounged in his chair and examined his nails. "Sorry." He glanced in Hal's direction and stared a moment before a gleaming white smile erupted on his face.

"Sorry?" Hal moved around the table and hovered over the seated man. "That won't cut it. You better keep him off my back." He reached out a hand. Tim clasped it and Hal used it to pull him from his chair. Hal returned the smile while they shook hands. The two men had met right out of college early in their careers at the CIA, while still training at Langley. During field operations in the early eighties where both men distinguished themselves, they had saved each other's lives countless times. But that was where the similarities ended. Tim was tanned and toned. Though well under six feet, he seemed taller. He wore a navy Italian suit, impeccable as usual, and his wavy dark hair was combed to perfection. Hal glanced at his rumpled shirt and tie stretched across his growing paunch and mentally shrugged his shoulders. What could he say? Where was the joy in life without good food, bourbon, and cigarettes?

"Captain Galloway." Tim reached a hand to Derek. "Good to see you. I'm sorry about that. We all know you did your best. That you *are* the best."

"Thanks."

"Tim, I'm not joking. You keep that blowhard away from me." Hal waved his finger between himself and Derek. "We've got a job to do."

"Take it easy, Hal. The guy has a tough job himself. You can't imagine the pressure he's under. He's actually an okay guy who means well."

"Yeah, he's stressed all right," Hal said. "Because he doesn't have a clue what he's doing. He's nothing but an empty suit. An ass-kissing, sycophantic, glad-handing, opportunistic, career politician. I still can't believe the president appointed him."

"Come on. You know better than anyone how the game is played," Tim said. "These guys come and go. To help this country you have to put up with it." He turned to Derek and spread his hands. "Can you talk some sense into him?"

"No. I've given up. Tim's right, though." Derek fixed his gaze on Hal. "Our commander-in-chief put the man in charge. I think you should show him the proper respect."

"Aw, shi . . ." Hal stopped when Derek's glare hardened. "Sorry." Hal pointed a thumb toward Derek. "Sister Theresa here is trying to reform me. Who ever heard of a soldier who doesn't like swearing?"

"Good luck with *that*," Tim said. He tapped a finger on Hal's gut. "I've been trying to reform him for years."

Hal swatted the finger away. "Will you be able to make dinner tomorrow night? Anne and the kids are expecting you."

"Of course." Tim lowered his voice. "I'll pick you up at the house early and we'll go to the club for a game of racquetball. We can talk more." He grabbed his briefcase. "Maybe we can sweat off some that spare tire." With a wave over his shoulder he walked out of the room. "Call me later so I can update Greene."

CHAPTER V

HE is floating. Below him is the perfect sphere of the earth. He has seen it in many photographs, but they've never done it justice. The white swirls of cloud move lazily, the vivid blues of the oceans are dazzling, and the green hues marking the land are truly beautiful to behold.

Without warning he drops. His stomach and his breath are lost behind him, much like the feeling when a roller coaster crests its first slope and plummets over, or when a speeding car plunges over the top of a hill. He moves fast, the wind whips his hair, and the skin on his face is pulled tight. The panoramic views disappear as he finds himself passing through the mists of the clouds, water vapor collecting on his face. Below the clouds, his riotous descent ends and he hovers.

Beneath him he sees the desert, and in its midst a large city with a river running past it. He knows this place all too well.

As he watches, the familiar flames of devastation seem to take on a life of their own. From his vantage point, high enough that details of the terrain below are barely recognizable, the fire spreads in thin lines like the strands of a spider's web. Accelerating rapidly, they reach to points east, all ending in small points of flame. His eyes are drawn back to the city below as two more lines of fire erupt from the blaze. They are larger and burn more intensely than the others. One ends in a large flaming mass in the mountains to the northeast; amidst the flames he sees a small building surrounded by rocks, hidden from casual observation. The other mass of flame moves to the edge of his vision, crossing the Atlantic Ocean and, for the first time, he tastes real fear. He strains to see its terminus, but before its destination is reached, he again drops so quickly it steals his breath.

He is now at ground level, and again he sees the devastation and death in this ancient city. Flames and bodies are everywhere, it is a horrible scene. Movement catches his eye and he turns to see the tall, broad-shouldered man. The man walks closer, fixing him with intense green eyes.

As the man moves, the landscape transforms around him, and the ancient city turns to vapor. From the haze morphs a new landscape, and he is in the midst of a stark region, void of man-made structures. The few trees are scattered, excluding a large thicket a short distance away. It is bright and clear; sand lies all around his feet, glimmering as if filled with diamonds reflecting the starlight. The breeze blows across his face, bringing with it a hint of moisture. Water is nearby. In the distance, mountains are dark silhouettes against the sparkling sky.

The man speaks. "Aaron, the answer is in Nahum."

Surprised to hear himself reply, Aaron says, "Wait, I don't know what that means. Please help me understand."

The man stops and, rubbing his square jaw, seems to consider whether or not to answer. "The Hawk plots evil. He knows not the extent of the devastation he will wreak on us. There is a message in chapter one, verse eleven, and chapter three, verses one through three." The man motions to the copse of trees over his left shoulder. "You will find answers in there." As he turns to walk away, he glances over his shoulder. "You have been chosen."

"Wait . . ."

Aaron's eyes flew open. He was winded as if from great exertion. He concentrated to control his breathing and wiped the cold sweat from his forehead with the back of his hand. The glowing numbers on the clock indicated it was a little after four in the morning. He took a moment to gather his thoughts and rose from bed, using care not to disturb Sarah. Treading lightly, he made his way toward the study. With every step his dread mounted.

He picked up the Bible and, having already marked the book of Nahum, flipped to it. Taking in a great gulp of air, he found the eleventh verse of the first chapter. He started to read, and the words seemed to leap from the page: "From you, O Nineveh, has one come forth who plots evil against the LORD and counsels wickedness."

After reading the verse a second time, he turned to the first three verses in chapter three. "Woe to the city of blood, full of lies, full of plunder, never without victims! The crack of whips, the clatter of wheels, galloping horses and jolting chariots! Charging cavalry, flashing swords and glittering spears! Many casualties, piles of dead, bodies without number, people stumbling over the corpses."

Aaron placed the book in his lap. He stared at the wall, allowing the words and their implications to sink in. This was beyond comprehension.

He grabbed a pen and paper and began scribbling notes. He may not know what it meant, or why, but he didn't intend to forget it.

* * * * * *

Aaron sat motionless at his desk, leaning back, staring out the window but not actually seeing the gray light of dawn breaking. Around him sat stacks of paper, the result of two hours of furious Internet research.

Many of the printouts were topographical maps, road maps, and aerial photographs. On some of the maps and photos he had drawn red circles. To the best of his ability, he placed marks where each point of fire in his dream had been located. On one map of Syria, he drew a large X mark. He looked back down at the map and tapped the X with his pen.

He was so wrapped up in his thoughts that his mind barely registered what his ears were hearing.

"Da, Daaa!"

He jumped out the chair and made his way to Abby's bedroom. "There's daddy's little angel. How are you this morning?"

Abby grinned as he picked her up and squeezed her. He carried her into the living room and turned on the TV, making sure it was on her favorite channel. He tickled her tummy and changed her diaper. Then, holding her with one arm, he walked into the kitchen to start a pot of coffee.

His thoughts returned to the dream. Maybe he had a grip on what the dreams could mean. He muttered to himself, "The real question is, am I losing it or is it really happening?"

Small fingers grabbed his cheek as Abby, not to be ignored, pulled at his face. Her little eyebrows furrowed as if to say, "Are talking to me?"

Her puzzled looked caused Aaron's lips to part in a grin. He leaned in and put his forehead to hers. "So, what do you think, Abby? Is Daddy losing it?"

His only answer was a giggle and a big wet kiss.

* * * * * *

Hal Bouie stared across the table at Derek. They had been at it all night. Surrounded by paper, Hal's team was in the process of sifting through every data base they could access and all the intelligence reports they could get their hands on. They worked feverishly, trying to find a lead on the identity of the Hawk. So far they had come up empty.

The NSA called a press conference to release the news about the "capture" of al-Douri so that by the next morning the news shows could give it their full attention. Hal couldn't guess how she would spin it.

Derek's eyes were dark and sunken from fatigue. He had rested very little since returning from Columbia. Even though data sorting was not his area of expertise, he asked to help. Hal knew him well enough that there was no doubt in his mind Derek had taken the mission's failure personally, and he needed something to keep him occupied. "Why don't you go home and catch a few hours of sleep? There isn't much you can do here," he said to Derek. "You need to be fresh. I sent out an all-agency query, maybe someone else has a lead on this Hawk character. As soon as we find him, you may have to go back into the fray. I'll let you know the second we find anything."

Derek released a huff of breath. "I don't know."

The two men had bonded in a relatively short time, their camaraderie grown from implicit trust. Hal considered Captain Derek Galloway a friend, though still somewhat of an enigma. Derek was a kind and gentle man, but a born soldier and leader of men. Anyone with eyes could tell by Derek's bearing and physical presence that he was a warrior. Yet he could disarm a person just as quickly with a smile and a kind word as with his hands.

"I need a smoke. We wouldn't want to damage your finely-tuned lungs. So, get out of here already." Hal glanced at his watch. "I'm about to pack it in, anyway. I've got to brief Tim, then I need to get home."

Derek fixed him for a moment with his intense green eyes, considering, and nodded his head. "You're probably right. I need to check on my men anyway. I'm sure they need my help to sweat off hangovers." He stood and leaned over the desk, riveting Hal with another stare.

"I'll call," Hal said, "I promise."

CHAPTER VI

EYES squinted against the sun, Aaron pulled onto Old Fannin Road and drove northeast toward the church. The once small, winding, and unevenly paved road was now a smooth, three-lane boulevard. It had been improved to accommodate the population explosion in the area. Over the past twenty years, the crime rate had gone up in the state capital of Jackson, Mississippi and its population scattered to several suburbs as residents fled the urban decay. In Aaron's high school years, the only thing on this road had been trees; now there were neighborhoods and businesses its entire length.

It was a beautiful day, and the worries of the pre-dawn gloom were far away. In the bright morning light, his trepidation over last night's dream seemed ridiculous. Sarah's attitude was also contagious; she had been positively bubbly all morning. As they dressed for church, she went on and on about how glad she was that they were going. It was no secret she wanted them to begin attending services, but Aaron had been reluctant. Sarah didn't like going without him and was considerate enough not to badger him.

As they pulled onto campus at the Shady Pines Church, Aaron was surprised by the number of cars in the parking lot. He saw several friends and acquaintances going in ahead of him.

They approached the building and were greeted by smiling people wearing name badges who all made a point of shaking their hands. As a matter of fact, everyone seemed to be in a good mood; people were laughing and talking to each other, and they appeared genuinely glad to be there.

While Sarah checked Abby into one of the children's Sunday school classes, Aaron searched for Rachel. With the help of an usher, he found the sanctuary, a large, bright, airy room. Windows lined both walls, and vaulted ceilings adorned with wood beams arched overhead. There were three sections of pews: a larger one in the middle and two smaller ones on the sides. At the front stood a stage with a small podium in the center and a choir loft behind it. Beyond the choir section, blue water glistened in the baptistery pool. High in the rear wall, the morning sun beamed through a large stained-glass window, dazzling the eye.

Aaron spotted his sister halfway down in the middle section of the sanctuary. He took the aisle on the right and made his way toward her. "Rachel, hey."

She turned around and Aaron waved to her. The surprised look on her face was priceless. She ran over and hugged him as if she hadn't seen him in a year. "Oh, I can't believe you're here!"

"Me either. Well, Sis, so far you are right: this is nothing like I expected."

Sarah joined them and the service began. The songs were joyful and accompanied by a full band. For the religiously impaired, such as Aaron, the words to the songs were projected onto a screen behind the pulpit.

Pastor Jenkins spoke about ways to experience joy in their turbulent world. It was an upbeat message mingled with humor. Aaron enjoyed it, despite some long-dormant feelings it aroused, and even began to look forward to meeting with the pastor.

In the process of singing the closing song, Aaron, not much of a singer, mouthed the words that appeared on the screen. Music filled the hall, and he even found himself tapping his feet to the rhythm.

"Do not run from me, Aaron."

Aaron's mouth and feet stopped. His head swiveled in an attempt to identify the speaker. Had he actually heard something?

"The answer is in Nahum."

Aaron's head snapped around. A little girl behind him caught his eye and smiled. A man nodded his head in greeting. A lady gave him a nod and a smile also. Aaron turned back to the front. *Who said that?*

"Heed my words. Do not be like Jonah. Jonah chapter one, verses three and four."

He nudged Sarah to get her attention. "Did you hear that?" he whispered in her ear.

"Hear what?"

"I thought I heard someone talking."

Sarah shook her head. "No, I didn't hear anything but the music."

She looked as if she was about to say more, but Aaron turned to Rachel. He repeated the questioning with the same response. Neither had heard anything.

The song ended and the pastor said a closing prayer. The crowd began to exit, and the sanctuary filled with the buzz of conversation. People discussed lunch plans, the sermon, the weather.

As they waited for the crowd to clear, Aaron grabbed a Bible from behind a pew, found the book of Jonah in the index, and flipped to chapter one. Goosebumps sprouted all over him, like thousands of icy needles lightly pricking his skin. "But Jonah ran away from the LORD and headed for Tarshish. He went down to Joppa, where he found a ship bound for that port. After paying the fare, he went aboard and sailed for Tarshish to flee from the LORD. Then the LORD sent a great wind on the sea, and such a violent storm arose that the ship threatened to break up."

"Oh boy," Aaron muttered under his breath. His buoyancy turned to dismay. The sounds of the throng around him faded. All he could hear was the pulse pounding in his ears. His tingling skin was cold. *"Don't run from me."* He stood holding the Bible, his surroundings forgotten.

Rachel gripped his elbow to get his attention. Aaron hadn't noticed Sarah moving toward the aisle, or the line of people waiting patiently for him to move out of their way.

"Are you all right?" Rachel asked.

Aaron returned the Bible to its resting place. "Oh, sorry. I'm fine. Can you introduce us to Pastor Jenkins, please?"

They made their way to the aisle, and Rachel led Aaron and Sarah to the front. The pastor stood near the stage, a small horde of worshipers surrounding him. He smiled and shook hands with some, leaned in close and prayed with others. Each person who approached was given a warm greeting.

They neared the pastor, and Aaron was struck by the man's youthfulness. Dark hair framed a friendly face. He was casually dressed, wearing slacks and a crisp white button-down shirt open at the collar. He noticed the three of them waiting and moved to greet them. "Rachel, let me guess: this is your brother Aaron." The pastor reached out and shook Aaron's hand with a firm grip. "It's nice to finally meet you."

"It's nice to meet you too, Pastor Jenkins."

"Please, call me Paul." The pastor turned to greet Sarah. "I am very glad to have you both here. Aaron, if you'll give me a few minutes, we can go back to my office and talk. If you still want to, that is."

"Please. I know you're busy, but I would really appreciate it."

"Okay, I'll be right back." The pastor turned to speak with some others who were waiting.

Aaron faced his sister. Her mouth was opening to speak, and Aaron knew he was about to be flooded with questions. "Hey, why don't you take Sarah and Abby to lunch? I'll meet you guys back at our house afterward."

Rachel gave him an appraising look. "I don't guess you want to clue me in on what's going on, do you? You looked pretty shaken up at the end of the service."

"I'll tell you all about it later. I promise."

With a fake groan she turned and stalked away.

A few minutes later, Aaron sat in Pastor Jenkins office. It would take some time to get used to calling him Paul. The office was large, and the shelf-lined walls were crammed with books. In the corner was a large, slightly cluttered desk. In the center of the room, two leather chairs faced each other, which the two men now occupied.

Aaron leaned back in the chair. His foot tapped and his hands gripped the chair's arms like a vice, hard enough to make indentions in the leather.

The pastor leaned forward. "Well, Aaron, did I keep my promise? Did I keep you awake?"

"Oh, yeah. Well, Rachel kept elbowing me, so I didn't have a chance to nap. I'm kidding, of course. Actually, I have to tell you I have been pleasantly surprised since I arrived here. This isn't the way I remember church. In the church I grew up in, the only time anyone smiled was on their way out the door."

Paul chuckled. "Yes, Rachel has told me some of it. I don't want to stick my nose where it doesn't belong, but is that why you quit going to church?"

"Well yes, that's part of it, but there's more to it than that. I always felt that I couldn't measure up to the teachings, that I would never be the person I was supposed to be, so why even try? I also watched my grandmother spend her life's savings on TV hucksters calling themselves preachers. It just all gave me a sour taste."

"I'm sorry you feel that way, but that's not the way it is supposed to be. I hope you saw something different today. As for televangelists, it's my opinion that they are to religion what professional wrestlers are to sports. All show no substance. All foam and no beer." Paul settled into his chair and clasped his hands together. "Well, most of them, anyway."

Aaron's hands relinquished their stranglehold on the chair. He shifted his weight to find a more comfortable position. The analogy brought an unexpected smile to his face. "Well, there's a little more to it than that." He stared into the pastor's eyes. "I look around and see violence, pain, evil, sickness, disaster, and suffering. It seems as if God has forgotten us. Rachel has told me she now believes that God is kind and loving. How can He allow it?"

"Oh, I thought you were going to ask me some tough questions." Paul chuckled. "I can tell that you must view God as a scowling father looking down on us pitiful mortals and shaking His head in dismay, doing nothing to help us. The fact is, He created us, and even though we may not always do exactly as He would like, He still loves us. Just like when Abby or Sarah do something that makes you mad, you still love them the same. Our fellowship with God may change, but He is still our father, and nothing we can do will change that. The best way to handle what life throws at us, whether it is adversity or fortune, is to develop a relationship with Him." Paul took a deep breath and seemed to collect his thoughts.

Aaron leaned forward, placing his elbows on his knees. He was surprised at his own interest in what the man had to say.

"Aaron, as to suffering, the truth is that man has been trying to answer that question since Adam and Eve left the Garden of Eden. Without getting to *preachy*"—Paul held up his fingers to make the quotations sign—"I'll answer that the best I can. Somewhere, somehow, people have gotten the idea that we are not supposed to suffer any hardships. The fact is, that's completely contrary to what the Bible teaches. Throughout the stories found in the Bible there are wars, plagues, pestilences, you name it. The Bible does not promise us peace on this earth . . . but it does promise us peace. God promises us that if we completely give ourselves to Him, and completely trust Him, He will give us peace in spite of our circumstances. I believe God has a plan, that He is in control, and that in spite of the fact that His plan doesn't always fit into our way of thinking . . . it is still the case."

Aaron found himself leaning farther forward, trying to absorb the man's words, as if proximity could help him better understand. A question tumbled through his mind but he held it. Words spilled out of the pastor's mouth, and Aaron didn't want to interrupt. The man was obviously passionate and exuberant about the subject.

Paul reached down and picked up his Bible, brandishing it before Aaron. "I believe this book. So, I believe that when it tells me something, even when I don't understand it, it is the truth. I have seen much pain, suffering, and loss right here in this very congregation, much less in the wide world around us. But I haven't lost faith or hope. One of my favorite scriptures, Jeremiah, chapter twenty-nine, verse eleven, says, 'For I know the plans I have for you,' declares the Lord, 'plans to prosper you and not to harm you, plans to give you hope and a future.'" He placed the Bible in his lap. "Look, I don't want to give you a sermon, but remember, you asked." His smile and raised eyebrows seemed to say, *You asked for it and now you're getting it.*

Aaron returned the pastor's smile. Something about the man's enthusiasm was infectious.

"I can only speak about what I know from my own experiences. I have witnessed terrible tragedy strike people who I know and love. But it is my experience that God never wastes a hurt. What I mean is that usually something positive comes from a bad experience. Some sort of growth occurs." Paul looked out the window and sighed softly. "You may not know this, but I lost my wife to cancer a couple of years ago and I won't lie to you, it has been difficult. While visiting her in the hospital, her two brothers, who had not spoken to each other for years over some forgotten feud, embraced each other and, with tears flowing, held onto each other. They have been inseparable since. That is just one of many examples I could cite you."

"Paul, I'm sorry, I didn't know." Aaron could tell the man's wounds were still fresh. That the loss still weighed on him.

Paul shook his head, as if shaking off the grief. He held up his hand. "Please don't mention it. I didn't tell you that to minimize what you are going through, or to get sympathy. I just want you to know that I believe what I'm telling you."

During the pause, Aaron took a chance to ask a question. "You said something earlier about developing a relationship with God. I've heard that, or something like it, my entire life and I've never understood what it's supposed to mean. How does a person develop a relationship with a God he cannot see or hear?"

This brought yet another smile from Paul. He leaned forward, elbows on his knees in the same manner as Aaron. "That's the crux of the matter, isn't it? See, I believe we can see and hear Him."

Aaron leaned back in his chair, crossed his arms, waiting for elaboration.

"How is a relationship developed?"

"By getting to know someone, spending time with them, talking to them," Aaron said.

Paul clapped his palms together then spread them in front of him. Using his hands for emphasis, he said, "Exactly!" as if Aaron had just revealed the secret to one of life's greatest mysteries.

Aaron felt the skin of his face tightening as his eyebrows knitted and his lips pursed. *Huh?*

Paul left him in contemplation for only a moment. "Yes, spending time together is how a relationship is developed. Prayer and Bible study are the best way to begin and develop a relationship with God."

Aaron forced his face to relax. Some questions answered, so many more remained.

"Why don't you just give that some thought. I've given you quite a bit to chew on," Paul said. "Now, why don't we talk about your dreams? I've been thinking about what you told me, and I'm fascinated."

"Well, now there's more." Aaron told him about the previous night's dream.

Paul stroked his chin. "Interesting."

"You mentioned Jonah yesterday when I spoke to you. Can you tell me some more about his story? I mean, I know about him being swallowed by the whale, but what else?"

Paul looked a little surprised by the change of topics but answered quickly. "The Lord told Jonah to go to the city of Nineveh to get them to repent, and he didn't want to go. He fled on a ship. While at sea, a great storm came on them and threatened to capsize their ship. Jonah admitted to the sailors that he was fleeing from God. So to save their ship, the sailors threw him overboard. That was when he was swallowed by the great fish. After three days, the fish spat Jonah onto dry land, and he then went to Nineveh."

Aaron pulled air through nostrils and released it with a sigh. "So Jonah was running from God."

"What makes you ask about Jonah? Is it because his book is also related to the city of Nineveh, as Nahum is?"

"No. I didn't know the story of Jonah well enough to even know that." Aaron hesitated, gauging whether or not to tell the rest. After a moment's consideration he told the pastor about the words he heard during the service. To add emphasis, he repeated the scripture from Jonah he'd read after the service, verbatim.

The pastor's eyes widened and he took a long deep breath. He silently mouthed the word "Wow."

"Paul, you've never met me before today, and I realize how this all must sound. It sounds crazy to me, and I'm the one saying it."

"You don't strike me as delusional, Aaron, so I don't think we should dismiss it out of hand. Do you have any clue what any of this could mean?"

He gathered his thoughts and his courage. He had developed a theory, but a theory based on what? He decided to press on. "I think something terrible, something evil, is going on in the ruins of Nineveh, and this Hawk is at the root of it. Before I came here today, I still thought these dreams were more than likely the product of an over-active imagination. But after what I just told you, I don't think I can believe that anymore. I don't feel like I'm crazy . . . but what crazy person does?"

"I tell you what. If you don't mind, I will e-mail a few of my friends in the ministry. Maybe we can put our heads together and help you out. It will probably be a day or two before I can get back to you. I would like a chance to give this some thought, too."

"Please do. I can't tell you how much I appreciate it. If you get any ideas, please call or e-mail me." Aaron handed the man a business card.

Glancing at the card, Paul read the company name embossed across the top. "'Graphic Solutions.' What do you do for a living?"

"I own a small graphic design company."

Paul tucked the card into a drawer.

As Aaron turned to leave, Paul said, "Rachel tells me you are into the martial arts, and pretty good at it, too."

Aaron froze. Here it was. The condemnation. He turned to face the pastor. "Well, I … yes. I know you may not think that—"

Paul held up his hands up, waved them back and forth, then gave the time-out signal. "No, no, Aaron, I don't think it's a bad thing. I was actually going to ask you if you would be willing to give me a few lessons." He held his fists in front of him in a boxer's pose. "I boxed for exercise while at seminary and really enjoyed it. Besides, you just never know when I may have to protect the offering plate." He laughed.

Ashamed at how quickly he had become defensive, Aaron shook his head and laughed as well. He held up his hands in mock surrender then reached out and gave the pastor a firm handshake. "Paul, you've got a deal."

As Aaron walked out the office, Paul said, "All joking aside, it will be all right. We'll figure it out."

"Thanks. I sure hope you're right."

* * * * * *

Sarah and Rachel were already home when Aaron arrived. Rachel was putting Abby down for her afternoon nap. He and Sarah sat together on the couch in their living room where they waited for her. Sarah kept her questions at bay so Aaron wouldn't have to repeat everything. They both knew his sister would not be denied hearing the story.

She walked in, plopped down on a chair, and said, "Okay, sport, spill it. What's going on?"

Aaron took a deep breath and began to talk. He told the women about the dreams and filled them both in about *the voice* at church. He ended his story with the conclusions he had shared with Paul.

"Well, what are you going to do?" Rachel asked.

"Do? I don't know. There's nothing to do. I am going to wait and see what happens. If, I mean *if*, these dreams have some meaning, I'm still not absolutely sure what it is. Even if there was no doubt in my mind, who would I tell? What would I say? I don't have any tangible evidence."

Sarah picked up the remote; the TV had been muted on the Fox News channel. "The National Security Advisor is giving a press conference," she said. "Let's see what it's about." She turned up the volume so they could watch and listen.

"Yesterday, in a joint operation with the Iraqi security forces, an attempt was made to capture Izzat Ibrahim al-Douri. He was found near the northern town of Zakho, near the border of Turkey, where he had apparently been hiding since he fled Baghdad at the onset of Operation Desert Shield. We believe he had been responsible for leading insurrectionists against coalition and Iraqi forces. He was being guarded by Saddam loyalists, and there was an intense fire fight in which al-Douri was unfortunately killed."

The NSA continued speaking, but Aaron no longer heard her voice. The mention of Iraq and the death of this al-Douri character struck a chord. Something about the story nagged at him, but he couldn't quite put his finger on it.

The NSA fielded questions from the reporters packed into the room. Aaron's attention wasn't on her; it was on the Secret Service agents that unobtrusively surrounded her. They all stood still, stoic and calm amidst the throng of reporters. But their eyes took in every detail, assessing any threat. Lions poised to spring.

Secret Service agents. Joseph.

Aaron bolted from the couch and ran to the study. He closed the door and grabbed his cell phone. He scrolled to Joseph's number and dialed. "Come on. Pick up." Just when he thought he was going to be directed to voice mail, Joseph answered.

"Hey, old man."

"I see. You recognized my number and let it ring five times before you answered."

"Well, I wasn't sure you were worth interrupting my nap."

"Sorry. Joseph, you know the dreams I told you about. Well, I had another one. I'll explain it all when I see you. But, I wanted to see if you could do me a favor? If it's too much trouble just tell me. It will sound crazy."

"And what's unusual about that? Come on, it's me. Spit it out."

"Well, I was watching the NSA's press conference about this al-Douri guy. Something about it … I don't know. I just wanted to see if you would check something for me. Could you see if you have anything in your database about anything going on at the ruins of Nineveh, or anything about someone named Hawk?" Aaron blurted the questions out, realizing how odd they must sound.

"I'll do it in the morning. It's not a problem." Joseph paused a moment, as if considering what to say next. "Aaron, if there is any information, and I'm not saying there will be, and it happens to be classified, I won't be able to give you details."

"I wouldn't expect you to. I just want to know if anything pops up. That's all."

CHAPTER VII

HAL glanced in the mirror and patted the paunch beneath his shirt. He grimaced at his reflection, uncomfortable in the workout clothes. The white tee-shirt, shorts, and tennis shoes weren't flattering.

The doorbell rang and Hal grabbed his gear bag from the bed. His shoes squeaked on the pine floors as he navigated the steep stairs of his colonial row house. He loved this place: a two story home nestled on a quiet tree-lined street, no front yard and just enough grass in the back to allow room for the kids to play. Nope, he didn't miss the life of a field operative. His hours were far from regular, but at least he wasn't jaunting across the world. Anne had been ecstatic when he'd become an office analyst, allowing them to have a somewhat normal existence. They had moved to the "burbs" and even had children.

As his feet left the stairs and touched the living room floor, two sandy-haired forms streaked past in a blur. His boys. Nine-year-old Benjamin and seven-year-old William were masses of hyperkinetic energy.

They raced to the front door and flung it open, chiming in unison, "Uncle Tim!"

"Hey guys!" Appearing as if he just stepped from a Ralph Lauren catalogue shoot, Tim wore a white polo shirt, matching shorts, and a sweater draped over his shoulder. He placed his bag by his feet and crouched down to hug the boys, then pushed them to arm's length. "Man, you guys have grown a foot." He stood and rubbed the tops of their heads.

Benjamin and William stared at him with their big brown eyes, waiting, hoping, but polite enough not to ask.

A smile beamed from Tim's face. "What's wrong, fellas?"

They shifted their feet and looked at the floor.

"Okay, okay. Take a look in my bag."

The boys' faces lit up and they pushed past Tim to unzip his bag. Benjamin reached in and pulled out a box. "Cool!" They turned the box toward Hal. "Look, Dad. A model plane. A fighter!"

"What do you say?" Hal said.

They both hugged Tim again. "Thanks."

"You're welcome."

Anne walked from the kitchen rubbing her hands on a towel and kissed Tim on the cheek. "You boys don't be late. Dinner is at six."

Hal grabbed his bag. "We won't. This shouldn't last long."

* * * * * *

The squeak of rubber soles on the floor rang in Hal's ears, echoing off the walls of the racquetball court.

Tim slammed the ball into the front wall, low at an angle. It bounced to the right wall and shot to the floor. Hal sprinted forward, racquet in front of him. The ball hit the floor and bounced low. He lunged, stretched, and swung the racquet. He missed the ball and his forward momentum sent him flying into the front wall, smashing into it with his shoulder.

Dropping his racquet, he slumped to the floor, peeled off his goggles, and used the edge of his un-tucked shirt to mop the sweat pouring from his face. He waved his hands in front of him. "No more. Uncle. I'm done," he gasped between ragged breaths.

Tim sat down next to him. "Are you okay?"

"Don't act like you care. You enjoy seeing me suffer." Hal leaned against the wall and closed his eyes until he caught his breath. "Now. What did you want to talk about?"

Leaning in close, Tim spoke in a hushed tone. "The DNI doesn't think this lead is going anywhere. He wants to pull you off of it. He didn't give me any details, but some intel crossed his desk about a possible two-fronted terror attack." He bent close to Hal's ear and whispered, "On the British parliament and the Saudi royal family."

"By who?"

"I don't know. Like I said, he didn't tell me much. I do know that if he verifies it, he plans to send your team after the perpetrators."

Hal sat up straight. "What? That bastard has no say in our missions."

"He's got the president's ear right now. You know how much pressure the man is under. The DNI is trying to convince him that you're a loose cannon. That you're actions need more oversight."

Teeth clenched to keep from yelling, Hal pointed a finger. "We'll see about this. This is total crap."

Tim held up his hands. "Hey, don't get mad at me. I'm just giving you a head's up." He lowered his voice again. "You may want to just drop this 'Hawk' business."

Hal took long slow breaths through his nose to calm down. The way his heart beat and the blood pounded in his ears, he feared he might suffer a stroke. He blew a breath out of puffed cheeks. "Thanks for the info." He patted Tim on the shoulder. "Let's grab a beer and get home for dinner."

*   *   *   *   *   *

Hussaam's leaned on the edge of his desk, arms crossed, eyes scanning the faces of the men filling his office, searching for any signs of weakness or duplicity. On the books, they were executives in his research and development division, but their areas of expertise and their loyalties were a bit more exotic than that. They were trusted members of his private army and would be critical in the completion of his plans. "I know that you will not fail me," he told them. "I am loathe to leave you, but my attendance at the Conference on Inter-Faith Relations is vital to our mission." Hussaam also knew if any of them failed, or if he made the slightest miscalculation, Israel would retaliate first and ask questions later. In the event that happened, he intended to be far from harm's way. "Remember, there can be no traces that would lead back to us, or to Jordan."

Nods and promises not to fail him passed through the room. There was no screaming, no ranting, no shouting to kill the infidels. No. These men were stoic and professional. There were uses for zealots, many good uses, but there was no room for them in his organization. He dismissed them with promises of glory and wealth.

With his bodyguards, Basil and Rashad, in tow, Hussaam stalked down a flight of stairs. He reached his destination: a room which would not show on any plans or architectural drawings. The walls were lined with state-of-the-art computers, their sole purpose to monitor all unsecured communications. Any e-mail, radio, or phone transmissions that were intercepted were scanned for key words. If any of the computers detected anything, he would be alerted immediately. Before leaving, he wanted to check one last time to ensure there was no "chatter" that might indicate any leaks concerning his plans.

A young man named Ahmed, whom Hussaam recruited out of college and an expert in all things technical, sat scrutinizing several computer screens while his fingers flew over a keyboard.

Hussaam cleared his throat, and the youth jumped to his feet, startled at the interruption. "Anything?"

"No, sir."

Hussaam fixed the youth with a hard stare. "Keep at it. I have to be sure al-Douri did not talk. If you get *anything*, alert me at once."

The young man's eyes widened and he bobbed his head feverishly. He fumbled out. "Yes, sir, Mr. Zaafir. Yes, sir."

Hussaam unlocked his gaze and spun away, leaving the room as quickly as he arrived.

* * * * * *

Hussaam glanced up from his laptop, its glowing screen bright in the dim interior of the plane. The jet soared high over the Mediterranean Sea en route to Madrid, the first leg of his journey.

The sky was dark and clouds obscured most of the celestial light. With no points of reference, the slight vibration of the plane's engines gave the only hint of its velocity as the sleek aircraft pierced the night sky. His bodyguards sat on opposites sides of the two rows of seats, one asleep, one awake, ever vigilant. Hussaam glanced at the slumbering forms of his wife and son. He searched his heart for the love he should feel, but found little. Fatima was a tool, a beautiful one, but only the means to an end. And although fond of his son, Hussaam knew he, too, was an instrument. At eight years old, Haytham was still pliable enough to be swayed by his father, and once Hussaam's plans succeeded, the obedient boy would remain useful. The two of them had not wanted to accompany him on this trip and miss the annual royal celebration. He had been forced to insist, but to soften the blow he promised them a few days of entertainment and shopping in New York.

The king of Jordan had been none too pleased that they were leaving, either, but he realized Hussaam could not turn down the invitation to speak at such a prestigious event as the Interfaith Convention. An event Hussaam had worked hard to insure took place in the city and time of his choosing. He seethed at having to explain his actions. Soon, very soon, the obstacle the king presented would be gone.

His thoughts were interrupted by the vibrating cell phone in his pocket. He retrieved the phone and flipped it open. "Yes."

"Your man screwed up."

"What?"

"Your man didn't make a clean kill. Al-Douri lived long enough to talk. Before he died, he named you. Not specifically, but he gave your nickname."

"Have they connected me to it?"

"No. I'm doing damage control. I have to go. I'll keep you informed."

Hussaam folded the phone and pressed it between his palms, resisting the urge to crush it. Given the chance, he would strangle the assassin with his bare hands. The phone vibrated against Hussaam's hands and he flicked it open with a thumb.

"Sir, it's me, Ahmed. We got a hit. We intercepted an e-mail and a phone call. They both mention the city of Nineveh and the name Hawk." The young man paused, taking in a long breath before spitting out his next words. "Sir, the phone call mentions Nineveh, Hawk, *and* al-Douri."

"What agency?"

"Well, that's the thing. The call and the e-mail came from two different addresses. Both of them are private residences."

"Where?"

"Both came from addresses in the United States. From a town named Flowood, in the state of Mississippi. That's as far as I've gotten."

"I want the transcripts from the call and the e-mail. Find out everything you can about these people and call me back immediately. Once you are finished, pack and leave for the base."

"Yes, sir. It may just be a coincidence."

Hawk disconnected the call. He had not progressed this far by believing in coincidences.

He returned his attention his laptop. Using his mapping program, he located Flowood, Mississippi. According to the map, it was only about two hundred miles south of Memphis, Tennessee. That was too close.

The headquarters of his U.S. operations were located in Memphis. It was also this trip's final destination.

He dialed Thomas Cable, the head of security in his Memphis office. After two rings the call was answered. Hussaam issued a command. "We have a possible security breach. Send two teams toward Flowood, Mississippi. I will get you more specific information as soon as possible." He flicked the phone closed. His eyes narrowed. Clenched teeth caused his jaw muscles to bunch. One word slipped into his thoughts: *How?*

He scanned the cabin, seeking someone on whom to vent his anger. Basil glanced toward him then quickly averted his eyes.

Hussaam's phone vibrated in his hand. It was Ahmed. "Speak."

"Sir, I have names and addresses."

"Give them to me." He wrote down the information. "Who are they? Who do they work for?"

"Neither is involved in law enforcement. One is a graphic designer and the other is a minister."

"Keep digging." Hussaam thumbed the end key. *What?* His grip on the phone hardened. His other hand tapped a pen on the writing pad, staring at the two names. Clutching his pen like a knife, he raised it from the page. His hand hovered just a moment before stabbing the pen's tip into the paper. Its point stabbed the beginning letter of the first of the two names written there. Aaron Henderson. For some inexplicable reason, the name raised bile in the back of his throat. He pulled his gaze to the second name. Paul Jenkins.

Whatever these men knew, however they found it out, Hussaam would soon know as well. If by some means they knew anything of his plans, they'd better pray to whatever god they placed their faith in. Because hell would be brought to their doorstep.

CHAPTER VIII

JOSEPH Harris arrived at his office at five-thirty Monday morning. He was a little skeptical about Aaron's request but, to placate him, he planned to keep his promise and research the names. There were few agents in the room at that hour, and Joseph knew he wouldn't be bothered. While his computer booted up, he inhaled the aroma of the steaming coffee in his hand before taking the first sip. He leaned back in his chair and swallowed a second larger mouthful of the hot brew. He set the cup down and rubbed his hands together, about to begin the search.

"Special Agent Harris." The voice cutting through the silence belonged to Robert Carlisle, his supervisor.

A little annoyed at the interruption, Joseph turned toward his boss. "Yes, sir."

"Can I see you for minute?"

"Sure." He followed the man into his office.

"Joseph, I'm sorry to interrupt you," Robert glanced around the empty room outside the office, "but you're the only one here." He passed Joseph a manila file folder. "This came on the wire yesterday afternoon. It's an all-agency query from the CIA. The MCI has been checked. But all offices have been asked to individually check their files. I hate to dump this on you, but I have to leave."

Joseph knew if the Master Criminal Index database hadn't turned anything up, this was probably the morning's second wild-goose chase. But in the post 9/11 era, they couldn't afford not to respond to the CIA request. Although he agreed with the philosophy, he still chafed at being the one with the dubious honor of spending hours of research for nothing.

His lack of enthusiasm must have shown. His boss reached over and patted his shoulder. "Don't put too much time into it."

With a nod, Joseph left the room and returned to his desk. He flipped open the folder and scanned the page inside. "What the ...?"

The CIA query requested any information that would lead to the identity off a person know only as "Hawk."

Joseph spun his chair toward his supervisor's office. What to do. He scanned the room, debating his next course of action. Share with his boss or ...

He grabbed the phone out of his pocket and dialed. *Aaron, what's going on?*

* * * * * *

Aaron's night had been free of nightmares. He woke up early, rested and refreshed. Discussing the dreams with others must have been therapeutic. Comfortable in his leather recliner while sipping his second cup of coffee, he enjoyed his favorite morning cable news show. The morning ritual was soothing and familiar.

The chirping of his cell phone interrupted his peace. Doing his best not to spill the contents of his mug, he raced to grab the infernal device. The caller ID indicated it was Joseph. "Hello." The words were barely out of Aaron's mouth before his friend began speaking.

"How quickly can you get to my office?"

The question sounded more like a command than a request. "What's going on?"

"That matter you asked me to look in to. The CIA is looking in to it as well."

"You sound like you're serious."

"I've never been more serious."

Aaron attempted to absorb the information. He wasn't scared, confused, or surprised. The words left him numb.

"Aaron, get to my office. I want to talk to you alone before I go to my supervisor." Joseph hesitated a moment. "You know I won't let anything happen to you. Whatever is going on, I'm with you. You know that."

"I know." Aaron's fingers stroked his forehead. "All right. I have to grab a shower and then I'll be right there."

Ending the call, he stared out of the window. The CIA? It could just be a coincidence. No, it had to be a coincidence. Anything else ... well, he didn't even want to think about it.

* * * * * *

Aaron backed out of his driveway, shower-dampened hair the only evidence of his haste. He wore his usual work attire: a dark suit and white shirt, opened at the neck. The sun was still only a hint on the horizon as the dawn broke. Aaron had neglected to tell his wife about Joseph's call. No need to worry her without need. He would explain once he knew more.

He fiddled with the knob on the car radio, fingers searching for a song to fit his mood. The perfect *I'm having weird dreams and they are real or I'm losing my mind and now I may somehow be involved in a CIA investigation* song. He finally settled on an eighties tune, but as soon as his hand left the controls the song was forgotten, lost in the tumult of his thoughts.

As he drove, manicured neighborhoods turned to gleaming new strip malls, which in turn gave way to aging business establishments. He glanced in the rearview mirror. Two nearly identical black vans followed at a distance. How long had they been there? They were only noticeable due to the lack of traffic. Were they following him? He shook his head and laughed off his paranoia.

Before long he was downtown where the relatively few high-rises were located. The Secret Service office was in a large government building on the corner of Farish and Capitol streets. Rather than navigate the road construction on Capitol Street, he picked a spot two blocks east on Mill Street, near the Amtrak station.

He stepped out of the car and slid a coin into the meter. It was a beautiful day, one of the very rare days in Mississippi when it wasn't hot and sticky or cold and wet. The temperature was in the eighties, the sky clear and blue. A gentle breeze swirled dust and bits of paper scattered on the sidewalk.

He stretched his tight muscles while he scanned the area, taking stock of his surroundings. It wasn't exactly the safest part of town. Across the street stood the once-magnificent Prince Edward hotel, now in a state of ruin and a terrible eyesore. The high-rise hotel had no glass in any of the windows and was a rotting haven for vagrants and drug addicts. The city was finally planning to refurbish it. Construction materials lay stacked around it inside of a six-foot cyclone fence. Aaron still planned to walk on the opposite side of the street.

He passed an alley between two buildings and stared into it: a mugger's paradise. After quick-stepping to get past it, he strolled toward the corner of Capitol and Farish, where he would turn left and head east toward the Secret Service office. He glanced down and saw a homeless person, surprised because he hadn't noticed him before.

The man sat with his back against the gray concrete of a building in an upright fetal position: head bowed and arms wrapped around bent knees. His clothes were disheveled and dirty, blond hair long and unkempt. He raised his head and looked Aaron squarely in the eye before averting the stare.

Aaron was struck by the intense blue and clarity of the man's eyes. He had expected to see the hollow red-rimmed gaze of someone in a drunken stupor. He was hesitant to give money to street people, afraid they would use it to get high. They were only a couple of blocks from the Gateway Rescue Mission where anyone in need was offered a meal and a bed.

Without knowing why, Aaron said, "Excuse me, sir, but when was the last time you had something to eat?"

The man looked up, his expression seemed almost mirthful with just the hint of a smile at the edges of his lips. "I can honestly say it has been a very long time."

Aaron pulled a twenty out of his wallet and handed it over. "I know it's not much, but it will at least get you a hot meal."

The man reached up with both hands to accept the money. He nodded in thanks and tucked the money to his chest. "God bless you, sir."

Aaron nodded in return and continued down the sidewalk. As he was about to turn left at the corner, the man called to him, "Aaron, wait."

Startled, he turned around. "How did you know …?" The question hung in the air when he looked into the vagabond's eyes. The blue orbs were riveted on him, unwavering, and their depths seemed to hold the key to the secrets of the universe. Instinctively, Aaron slid his feet into a defensive posture.

"You don't need to fear me. I'm sorry, but your life is about to change."

"I don't understand. Who are you? How do you know my name?"

"Hush, be still, listen." The man pointed. "They're coming. Don't let them take you."

Aaron turned in the direction of the pointing finger. A black van with tinted windows raced toward him, was almost on top of him. He turned back, another question forming on his lips, but the vagrant was gone. Aaron scanned the area, but he couldn't locate the mysterious stranger. The man simply vanished.

With a screech of tires the van skidded to a halt a few feet away, one tire bouncing onto the curb. The driver's side door flew open. A dark-haired man jumped out and rushed towards Aaron, arms spread, shoulders low, preparing to tackle. His left hand held a small canister.

Aaron dove to the left. He reached for the ground with his right palm, rolling away from the take-down. He rose to face his assailant, left foot forward, hands ready.

The man adjusted his course, closing the gap and pointing the canister at Aaron's face. Overcoming the instinctive reaction to flinch away, Aaron launched himself forward and grabbed the man's left wrist, pushing the canister to the side. He stepped in and turned his back to the attacker while reinforcing his grip with his opposite hand. He turned the man's palm up and pulled him in close, pushing the arm up.

When his assailant attempted to pull away, Aaron pulled the man's arm across his shoulder with all the force he could muster. He heard and felt the sharp crack of bone breaking and ligaments tearing; the elbow was hyper-extended past the breaking point. Aaron pivoted left and delivered an adrenaline-rushed elbow to the man's nose. Blood blossomed from the impact as his head snapped back. Aaron released his grip, and the man crumpled to the concrete.

Motion caught his eye, and he realized his mistake.

A second attacker.

A foot flew at his face with no time to block it. Using gravity for assistance, Aaron dropped toward the ground. A flicker of pain registered as a shoe brushed his ear. He spread his arms and legs to absorb the impact of the pavement and took the brunt of the fall on his forearms, palms, and feet.

The moment he hit, he rolled onto his left side, snaked out his left foot, and hooked the man's base leg behind the Achilles tendon. While the leg was trapped, Aaron blasted out his opposite foot and delivered a full powered side-kick to the man's knee. The joint shattered with a pop, followed by a moan of pain.

Unable to support himself, the man dropped, joining his companion on the sidewalk.

Aaron reached over and snatched the canister out of the first attacker's hand and jumped to his feet. He studied the two men rolling in agony on the ground. Both were dark skinned, with dark hair and distinctly Arabic features.

Clutching a broken arm, the assailant who had been holding the canister gazed at him fiercely, murder in his dark eyes. He started to rise, sliding his good hand into his coat as he moved.

Aaron pointed the canister at the man's face. "I don't know what this is, but if you don't lie down and stay still, I *will* spray you with it. Then I'm going to break your other arm." He poured all the anger and venom he could muster into his voice. He prayed the man would buy it and no more violence would be necessary.

The man paused, staring. He looked like a trapped animal, calculating the risks against his chances of escape. He let out a sigh and began to sit back down. In that instant his hand darted into his coat and whipped out a pistol.

As the gun's barrel came to bear on him, Aaron depressed the trigger on the canister. A concentrated mist shot out of the nozzle, splattering the man's face. On impact his eyes rolled back and he slumped to the concrete.

Aaron turned his gaze to the second man. He still lay on ground, unable to rise due to his useless leg. His hand was sneaking toward his own jacket pocket. "Don't. I'll spray you, too."

Blood streamed down the fallen man's face, pouring from his battered nose. His hand stopped moving, and he gazed toward his unconscious companion.

"Roll over on your stomach. Now."

With a grimace of pain the man moved.

"Spread your hands out so I can see them."

The man complied and Aaron scanned the area, seeking help. He saw nothing but an empty street. No one had witnessed the altercation. What seemed like a lifetime actually lasted only a few moments.

As Aaron reached for his phone to call for help, another man stepped from the alley. Relief turned to horror as a gun appeared from beneath the man's blazer. The barrel seemed elongated for such a small weapon. A silencer. Aaron couldn't get to his car—the man and the alley he came from were between them.

Run.

Aaron spun and raced toward the intersection of Farish and Capitol. As he reached the junction he heard a sound. A loud spit. *Sppht.* Across the street from him, something impacted the brick façade of the King Edward Hotel. Dust plumed from a small gouge in the wall. A gunshot.

Aaron ducked around the building on the corner. He was about to put on a burst of speed but slid to a stop as he noticed another van with two more men standing beside it. They spotted Aaron and walked toward him, arms sliding into their coats.

Where was everybody? Other than his attackers, not another soul was visible on the street. In thirty minutes the area would be flooded with traffic. Fighting panic, Aaron turned and sped in the opposite direction, feet scrambling for purchase in his slick-bottomed loafers. He angled away from the sidewalk and into the wide boulevard, seeking an avenue of escape. The shooter appeared at the corner along with a fourth man on the opposite corner.

Aaron was boxed in ahead, rear, and right. Only one option—left. He dashed across the street, eyes searching. His pursuers closed in, converging on him from three sides. With no other option, Aaron ran headlong toward the six-foot high chain link fence surrounding the old hotel. He stuffed his phone and the canister into his pockets and hurdled into the fence, planted his left foot about halfway up, and grabbed the top. The sharp edges bit into his palms as he used his momentum to vault over. He dropped the six feet to the pavement. Hitting hard, he bent his knees and rolled forward to diminish the force of the impact. He finished the roll and came up in a run. Scrambling into the darkened portico of the King Edward Hotel, he ducked behind stacks of construction materials piled beneath the covered entry. Aaron intended to lose his stalkers in the expanse of the rotting building. Immersed in shadow, his feet tripped through trash and sent empty bottles clanging into the walls where they shattered.

He reached the double doors that served as the entrance. The glass was boarded over and the metal handles chained. He had run headlong into the proverbial boxed canyon. His heart stuttered and his stomach churned. He searched for an exit. The windows on both sides of the entry were covered in boards.

He pushed against the boards, gauging their strength. Could he kick through? His fingers probed the edges of the wood covering the doors. At the lower left edge, the board moved. One of the bolts fastening the wood to the door was loose. He sat, grabbed the board with both hands, and placed his feet against the wall. He pulled with all his might until the wood splintered and bent. He crawled through.

Shadows blocked the sunlight to the right and left. His only hope was that the eyes of his assailants wouldn't adjust to the gloom in time. Aaron crawled into the gap and squeezed past the board as bullets ripped into it, spraying his face with splinters. Scrabbling through the hole, he ripped his pants and blazer. He jerked his legs through the opening, crawled away from the door, and leaned against the wall.

He needed a place to hide.

Aaron glanced at his surroundings. He was in a once grand lobby which now appeared to be a snapshot of hell. The interior was dim; the sun streaming through the glassless second floor windows provided the only light. Plaster and trash littered the floor. Gouges were ripped into the ceiling and walls. Decorative columns appeared to be the only thing holding up the high ceilings. Graffiti stained the walls. Straight ahead, a seemingly antique escalator rose to the second floor. It was as if he had stepped into a futuristic sci-fi movie where his present was the ancient past, and all that was left of his civilization was this relic.

A thump against the boards in the door made his thumping heart skip a beat. They were coming in after him. Aaron patted his pants pockets. His cell phone remained in the left one but the gas canister was gone; dangling cloth was the only remnant of his right pocket. He shrugged out of his coat and used it to wipe the sweat from his face.

A hand gripping a pistol appeared in the gap. Aaron surmised that the men didn't intend to kill him right away. Otherwise they would have simply pulled up in a van and shot him, rather than try to anesthetize him with the spray canister.

When a head appeared through the hole, Aaron blasted a soccer-style kick into the hand holding the gun. The weapon clattered across the floor. Using the impetus of the kick, he spun and struck his pursuer in the forehead with his heal. The man's head snapped back and he cried in pain, the first sound any of the four had made. Aaron followed the kick with a punch to the jaw. The man slumped, blocking the entrance. *Sppht. Sppht.* Holes erupted in the boards over Aaron's head.

He dove out of the way. On hands and knees, he searched for the pistol but couldn't locate it on the littered floor. The fallen man's torso disappeared as his companions pulled him out of the way. No time.

Aaron sprinted toward the escalator and bounded up it two and three steps at a time, attempting to ignore the groaning of its structure and the stairs crumbling beneath his shoes. He thought he must be running fast enough to defy gravity as he reached the top and dove behind a half wall overlooking the floor below.

He plucked the cell phone out of his pocket and prayed for a signal. Using his thumb, he scrolled until the correct number appeared. He mashed the send key. "Please, pick up. Pickup-pickup-pickup."

* * * * * *

Joseph paced the floor and studied his watch for the fifth time in the last minute. He plopped into his chair and leaned back. The room around him bustled with activity as other agents filtered in to start their day. Phones rang, fingers tapped keyboards, voices filled the air. Many of his colleagues stole glances at him, curious as to the source of his agitation.

Where is Aaron? He should be here by now.

The cell phone clipped to his belt rang. Aaron. "What's taking—?"

"Joseph, I'm on the second floor of the King Edward Hotel. Men are chasing me. With guns. They're shooting at me. There's three of them outside and three more are following me. Please, I need your help"

"I'll be there in two minutes." Joseph sprang from the chair and grabbed the agent at the next desk by the shoulder. "Come with me." As they sprinted toward the elevator Joseph patted the holster under his coat. *Hang on, buddy. I'm coming.*

* * * * * *

How long would it take Joseph to reach him?

A squeak of footsteps on the treads of the escalator told him his pursuers were approaching. Aaron was in a large open area, the mezzanine floor. Double wooden doors in varying states of decay led to darkened chambers, more than likely ballrooms once used for meetings and receptions. Probably all dead-ends. A gaping elevator shaft led nowhere and to either side of it, two exits led to crumbling staircases. He scanned for a place to hide or the best way out.

He crawled to the edge of the half wall until he was out of view of the escalator. As he stood, his feet bumped into a form on the floor. "Whaa ..."

Aaron barely stifled a scream as a vagrant rolled onto his back and fixed him with a vacant stare. Aaron raised his fingers to his lips. "Shh."

He pointed toward the escalator. He whispered, "You may want to get out of here." The man didn't move.

Damn!

Afraid his pursuers would simply kill the man, Aaron pulled him to his feet by his armpits. Gagging from the stench, he guided the man toward the nearest set of doors.

"What are you . . .?"

The fetid alcoholic reek from the man's mouth made Aaron choke. "Please. Be quiet. There are men chasing me. They have guns. Stay here and take your chances, or come with me."

The man didn't answer and allowed himself to be led along. They walked through a set of sagging wooden doors into a large chamber. Intricate flowered wallpaper hung in strips between holes in the walls, and green carpeting lay in tatters on the floor. It appeared to be a ballroom. Another set of doors to the left was the only exit.

Aaron guided his charge past the doorway. Hiding in the shadows, he peeked back toward the escalator. Two men mounted the top step and began searching the mezzanine. Aaron grabbed the homeless man tighter and dragged him toward the second set of doors. The doors were intact but lay askew. He squeezed between them into what appeared to have once been a kitchen or service area. A dead end.

He set the drunken man on the floor beneath a bank of glassless windows. A glance through them told Aaron they would provide no escape. Below was a two-story drop to a concrete courtyard and nothing to use to climb down.

He raced back to the doors and tugged them in place; any who followed would have to open them to get in. He searched for a weapon with no luck. Aaron picked through a pile of litter in the corner and found an aged and empty quart beer bottle. Not much, but better than nothing.

He crouched to the right of the doors and waited. How long ago had he called Joseph? A glance at his watch told him it had only been a couple of minutes. Could he risk calling again? Sweating profusely, Aaron attempted to get his fear and his breathing under control. He wouldn't make it if he panicked. *Think.*

Footsteps approached slowly and cautiously, then grew faint. They were searching the shadowy ballroom and it wouldn't take long. There was nowhere to hide. The footsteps approached the door. Fear seized

Aaron like a stranglehold, constricting his throat, tightening his muscles. The doors rattled as someone pushed against them.

Aaron slid up the wall and stood with his back to it. He clutched the quart bottle in his right hand near its tapered mouth. Something banged the door—probably a foot—pushing it open far enough to squeeze through. A foot followed by a man's torso pushed through the gap. An arm extended, its hand holding a gun pointed at the homeless man across the room. His eyes widened and he seemed to finally emerge from his haze. He raised his hands and yelled, "Please, no!" His eyes strayed toward Aaron's hiding place.

Aaron sprang from the wall and lashed out with his left foot, striking his pursuer on the back of the elbow. The gun wielding arm was knocked to the side. Bullets spit from the silenced barrel of his gun, ripping into the plaster.

Swinging the bottle like a hammer, Aaron struck the man near the crown of his skull. Glass erupted in a glittering shower and the attacker stumbled through the door. He took one step into the room, groaned, and sank to the floor.

Aaron ducked behind the door and snuck a quick look into the ballroom. Empty. They must have split up.

He grabbed the gun from the fallen man's outstretched hand. The vagrant lay in a ball with his arms over his head. "Stay here," Aaron said.

He pulled the pistol's slide open far enough to glimpse a bullet in the chamber. He crept into the ballroom clutching the gun. He strained his ears and heard nothing. Careful not to disturb any of the litter on the floor, he moved toward the double doors, praying his light footsteps wouldn't find a groaning floor joist. Aaron crouched in the shadow of the fallen doors and studied the mezzanine. No one was visible.

Holding the pistol in a two-handed grip, he moved into the room, eyes darting.

A shout from downstairs broke the quiet: "Freeze!"

Joseph. Halleluiah. A few moments of silence were followed by another shout and gunfire. On the other side of the escalator, a form appeared in the doorway opposite Aaron. He froze.

He had been spotted. The man ran forward with gun raised. Aaron raced toward the exit to the right of the elevator. Probably a dead-end, but at least it might provide shelter.

Sppht. Sppht. Bullets split the air around him.

Shooting blindly, Aaron fired his gun in the general direction of his attacker as he sprinted. As Aaron reached the exit, a hole in the floor appeared. With nowhere else to go, he planted his left foot and hurdled the space. His right foot just bridged the gap and he landed in a hall. He slid into a wall and found himself in a passage behind the elevator. The stairs to the next floor were crumbling and useless. Light streamed through the remains of a glass door halfway down the hall.

As he ran toward the door, a shadow darkened the floor on the opposite end of the passage. He reached the door and stooped beneath the glassless lower panel. A glance back told him his pursuer was on his heels. Aaron straightened and ran.

He was on a large second story terrace at least a hundred feet long and had nowhere to hide. There had to be a way down. He ran, heels clicking and arms pumping as his feet flew across the brick flooring. Aaron risked a peek over his shoulder. His pursuer was chasing him, gun aimed at his back.

Aaron's footsteps thumped and echoed beneath him now, rather than clicked. He was running across some sort of rectangular cover in the middle of the terrace. As he placed his next step, his foot pierced the cover's shell. He stumbled forward and fell. His weight hit the cover and he crashed through it. He released the pistol and spread his arms and legs to absorb the impact as the ground rushed at him. He landed on an unyielding surface. The bottom of a pool. He seemed to have landed in the shallow end.

He scrabbled with his right hand until he located the pistol and flipped onto his back, pointing the gun toward the opening. His hands shook from the adrenaline pumping through his system. He attempted to slow his breathing and still his arms. A shadow loomed over the opening. Aaron steadied the gun and eased the slack on the trigger.

"Hold it! One more step and I'll fire," Joseph shouted.

The shadow filled the hole over Aaron and his pursuer stared down at him, gun pointed. As Aaron was squeezing the trigger, a shot boomed and Joseph yelled again, "That was a warning! Drop it."

The man glared at Aaron for a moment and raised his arms over his head, pistol dangling by the trigger guard from his fingers.

"Set it down and back toward me." Joseph's voice sounded closer. Still staring at Aaron, the man sat the pistol by his feet and backed away. The shadow receded, sun filtered in, and Aaron lay still, gun still trained on the empty hole above him. He heard the metallic click of handcuffs being snapped. He lay back with a sharp exhalation of breath. Tension drained from his body, and his muscles felt weak and watery. A head peeped over the side of the hole and Aaron's heart leapt.

"You all right, old man?" Joseph reached through the hole and stretched out his hand.

* * * * * *

Two ambulances pulled away. Aaron's injured attackers were in the rear, accompanied by Secret Service. The others had been taken into federal custody until the assault and the reasons behind it could be discerned.

Surrounded by police cruisers and unmarked Secret Service sedans, Aaron leaned against the hood of a black Grand Marquis while a paramedic swabbed the blood from his ear.

"Do you have any other wounds?"

"No. I'm fine. Thank you."

The medic packed her medical kit and walked toward an ambulance.

Joseph sat next to him, arms crossed in apparent amazement. "You sure did a number on those guys." His head tilted toward the retreating ambulance.

"I was lucky."

Joseph cast his eyes down, seeming to consider what to say. "You know this has to be more than coincidence, Aaron. The request from the CIA, your knowledge of the information they are looking for, this attack. What have you gotten yourself into?"

Something began nagging at Aaron. A new train of thought eased through the corridors of his mind, abruptly gathering momentum before crashing into the station. His head snapped around as a cold wave of fear washed over him. He wasn't the only one who knew. Others had been told. Paul. His family. They could be in jeopardy. "How could they have found out about me, Joseph?"

"More than likely your phone calls or e-mails. It's not difficult with sophisticated software and equipment. The Secret Service has a keyword program that searches the body of e-mails, scanning for threats to the president."

Aaron's heart thumped in his chest and he felt the light-headed.

"Are you okay? You just went pale."

"My family. Paul." Aaron grabbed Joseph's shoulders. "I need you to go to my house. Protect my family. I'm not asking you as a Secret Service agent. I'm asking you as my friend."

"Aaron, we're in the middle of—"

Squeezing Joseph's shoulders harder, Aaron stared, his eyes making a silent plea.

Joseph considered only a moment and nodded. "All right. Let's go."

"No. Not we. You. I have to get to the pastor." Aaron ran toward his car.

"Wait."

Aaron called over his shoulder. "I'll call you. Make sure you answer your phone. Please go now!" He reached his car and glanced back. Joseph's car door slammed closed and a moment later it sped away, tires scratching on the pavement.

CHAPTER IX

AARON sped down the six lanes of Lakeland Drive, the stores and restaurants a blur as he passed, his emergency flashers engaged in a feeble effort to avoid being pulled over.

The decision to send Joseph to his house was desperate and strictly selfish. There was no doubt he would get there before Aaron could. Joseph would drive at a frenetic pace without police interference and, more important, protection was his business. Aaron chose Sarah and Abigail over Paul. If Paul was in danger, it was up to Aaron to find out.

He reached into his pocket and pulled out his cell phone while weaving in and out of traffic. When he raised his eyes back to the road, he saw the bumper of the car ahead of him brake as it stopped for a light. He wouldn't be able to stop even if he tried. Without slowing for the now-red traffic light, he swerved left, narrowly avoiding the rear of the vehicle. Horns blared as he careened through the intersection, dodging cross traffic.

He dialed information, requested the number of Paul Jenkins, and had the call automatically connected. After five rings an answering machine picked up. "Paul, this is Aaron Henderson. If you're there, please answer. If not, I need you to call me as soon as you get this message." He left his cell number on the machine and disconnected the call.

He pressed and held a number on the phone's keypad, automatically dialing his sister's number.

Rachel answered on the second ring. "Hello."

"Rachel, it's me. Do you know were Pastor Jenkins would be this morning?"

"Well, the church office doesn't open until noon on Mondays, and I know he usually goes in early because he likes the peace and quiet. Why? What's going on? You sound stressed."

"Sis, no questions. Pack an overnight bag and go to my house. When you're on the way, call ahead and let them know you're coming. I know this seems strange, but you have to trust me. Get going. Do you understand?"

"Aaron, you're scaring me." He expected her to press the matter further, but after a moment she said, "All right. I'll be out of here in five minutes."

He hung up and dialed information again. He was now on Old Fannin Road, its curves and neighborhood entrances making cell phone use even more dangerous. As he looked down, the scrape of gravel jerked his attention back to the road. The road curved away and a ditch loomed in front of him. He yanked the wheel to the left, and the car fishtailed in the loose detritus before finding purchase on the pavement. Over his heart's wild thumping, he heard a voice through the phone. "Hello, information." He risked a glimpse down—the phone had dropped on the seat between his legs.

Keeping his eyes locked on the road, he scrabbled for the phone and asked to be connected to Shady Pines Church. After five rings, a recorded message started to play. Aaron hung up. He would arrive at the church long before anyone heard the message.

He turned right onto Spillway Road, the pine trees on either side flashing by. The road ahead narrowed from four lanes to two, and the right lane he occupied ended at the light ahead of him. He raced past a line of traffic in the opposite lane and veered left at the last second, his tires throwing up gravel. He glanced in the rearview mirror to see the driver behind him shaking a fist.

The first of the two entrances to Shady Pines Church was just ahead. He pounced on the brakes, slowing enough to make the turn. As he pulled onto the campus, the pine trees of the aptly named church immersed his car in shadow. He slowed further, allowing his eyes to adjust while he drove up the narrow entrance. The rear parking lot came into view and his heart began to thud.

Only two vehicles were parked in the large lot: a small burgundy truck and a black van.

Aaron pulled into the pooled shadow of a particularly large tree and shut off his engine. Veiled in shadow, he stared at the entrance to the church offices and clutched his steering wheel. *What to do?* He whipped out his phone with the intent of calling 911, but he hesitated. What if it was someone who was supposed to be there? Black vans were not uncommon. He envisioned the police storming in with guns drawn, only to find Paul counseling a little gray-haired lady.

By the time the police arrived, it might be too late anyway.

* * * * * *

Derek intently watched his men. A nap on the flight back to Fort Bragg and a couple of hours in his bed had been all the inactivity he could stomach. After lunch, he mustered the team together for a drill session. His gut told him they would soon be deployed. One of the most difficult things about their job was staying ready between missions. They sometimes went weeks or months without a combat assignment, and it was imperative that they remained sharp.

Derek wiped the sweat from his eyes. He had been leading the men through evasion maneuvers. He just successfully finished his third trip through the obstacle course, an area fifty yards wide and one hundred yards long. Objects of various sizes were scattered about, some large, some small, some large enough to take shelter behind, others not. On the opposite end of the course perched a sharpshooter, using a modified rifle containing rubber cartridges. Not deadly, but painful. The goal was to traverse the course without getting hit.

The pager at his belt vibrated. Reaching down, he shut it off. There was no need to check the number; only one person had it.

He walked over to his gear bag and rummaged for his cell phone. He pressed and held the one key, automatically dialing Hal's number.

Hal answered on the first ring. "Derek, do you feel like taking a trip?"

"Where?"

"I just received a call from a Secret Service agent in Mississippi. He has some information on the Hawk. I'll pick you up and explain en route."

"I'll be waiting at the hangar." Derek ended the call. This was an intriguing turn. He shouted to his second in command, "Lane, front and center."

"Yes, sir!" The man ran toward him.

"I'm leaving and I don't know how long I'll be gone. You have command. Keep these guys sharp, and try to keep them out of the bars. I have a feeling we may be on the move soon."

"Will do, Captain."

After returning Lane's quick salute, Derek sprinted to the showers.

* * * * * *

Hal reached for his desk and used it to push out of his chair. Every muscle in his body screamed in protest. *Okay, that's it: you're going on a diet.* Opening a desk drawer, he grabbed a bottle of aspirin and popped two pills into his mouth. He washed them down with a glass of lukewarm water retrieved from his cluttered desk.

Reaching for his briefcase, he glanced around the untidy office. The small room was tucked away in a corner of original CIA headquarters building. A desk, a phone, a computer, little else. No personal photos on the walls. No family connections here. He realized it was a little paranoid, but once a field operative, the habits were hard to break.

He punched the intercom and called his secretary. "Is the plane ready?"

"Yes, sir. Fueled and ready for take-off."

"Thanks." Hal grabbed his blazer and headed for the door. The lead probably wouldn't pan out, but he wasn't ready to give up yet. Until the president told him to back off, he would keep on it, DNI be damned. Al-Douri said what he said for a reason. Even a craven miscreant wouldn't utter useless information as his dying words. No. Hal *would* hunt down the Hawk.

CHAPTER X

AARON slipped out of his car and eased the door shut. The shadow of a large pine engulfed him, the gloom beneath its branches in stark contrast with the brilliant morning sky. He hunched over and crept through the shadows, angling toward the rear of the church. Pine needles lay like a carpet beneath his feet, their scent clean and fresh. He had no idea where, or even if, anyone threatened Paul inside the building. If there were, Aaron's only advantage would be surprise. He longed for a weapon of some sort.

He paused and leaned against the trunk of a tree. From his vantage point, he could view Paul's office but the angle of the sun didn't allow him to see through the window. He realized anyone inside would be able to see out.

Skulking about in the shadows, he felt a bit ridiculous. He scanned the grounds, hoping no one else was around. Weighing his possible embarrassment against the very real possibility of danger, he continued.

Remaining low and in shadow, he snuck to the rear of the building, out of view of the office window. He slunk to a set of double doors at the rear entrance to the building which connected the sanctuary to the school. He pushed the doors and entered a small foyer. The walls on either side extended a few feet then opened into a hallway. Straight ahead was another set of doors leading outside. The hall to his left led to the school, and the one to the right led to the rear entrance of the sanctuary and the staff offices. Paul's office was the last one on the right.

Aaron slipped off his loafers and socks to enable stealthy movement. He hoped this was a false alarm, but embarrassment was preferable to the alternative.

His back to the wall, he leaned his head out and scanned the hallway in both directions. Seeing no one, he tiptoed toward Paul's office, the plush carpet masking his movements. As he moved, his uneasiness grew. Unbidden, the theme to *Mission Impossible* began to play in his head and the hilarity of the situation momentarily replaced his fear. There he was, sneaking through a church hallway in bare feet, fulfilling his boyhood fascination with cloak-and-dagger scenarios. He craned his neck to ensure no one else was watching.

He closed on Paul's office and peeked into the reception area in front of it. Empty. Ears pricked, Aaron continued. Approaching the doorway, his mirth turned to alarm.

"–just leave. I don't know anything else. How dare you defile a house of worship?" Paul spoke softly, but he sounded angry.

The soft guttural pronunciations of a man speaking in English with a heavy Middle Eastern accent responded. "I grow tired of this game. Tell us, now. How do you know of the Hawk? If you refuse to cooperate, it will not be pleasant for you."

"How many times do I have to repeat myself? It was heard in a dream. I was intrigued and e-mailed some colleagues to get their thoughts on the dream. There's nothing else I can tell you."

Aaron was unsure how to proceed. It appeared they had been speaking for a while. The man asking the questions sounded professional but perturbed, as if he was losing patience. If nothing could be gained from direct questioning, they might just kill Paul, or take him elsewhere to torture the information out of him then kill him.

Heart pounding, mouth dry, and palms sweaty, Aaron made up his mind. He swallowed hard to combat the lump in his throat. He stole a glance around the door frame exposing only his right eye and jerked his head back. Two men. Although neither held a gun, both wore coats which undoubtedly concealed them. The man speaking gripped a familiar spray canister.

Aaron leaped from the wall, spinning left through the office door. The adrenaline rush jangling his nerves gave him the urge to yell, but he suppressed it to keep his presence unknown until the last possible second. He knew he wouldn't be lucky twice. He was going to get hurt; it was just a matter of how severely.

The closest man faced Paul and stood with his back to Aaron. As Aaron cleared the doorway, he turned sideways, planting his front foot and stepping behind it with the other. Unleashing his coiled legs, he blasted a kick into the man's back. The contact was solid, and the man pitched forward, falling across Paul's desk.

The second man, looking not at all nonplussed, calmly reached into his coat as Aaron turned toward him. Before the gun could clear its holster, Aaron slammed into him with his left shoulder, forcing him into the rear wall. He continued forward and kicked the man's abdomen. As the man doubled over, Aaron rammed the palm of his hand into the man's chin.

The first man roared in anger and as Aaron turned, two hands clutched his throat, cutting off his air supply. As he moved to break the hold, the other man rose to join the fray.

Paul leaned over his desk and swung a vicious left hook followed by a right cross. The blows rocked the man's head, and he collapsed to the floor.

Aaron focused on the matter at hand: the two hands strangling him and forcing him into the wall. He reached over and grabbed the crook of the man's arm while stepping to the side and pulled sharply down. The man's grip tore free and his head pitched forward. As his momentum carried him past, Aaron slammed the man's head into the wall. The impact gouged a hole in the paneling.

As the attacker fell, Aaron turned to Paul. "Quick. Dial 911."

Paul punched the numbers into the phone and held the receiver to his ear. He glanced up from the keypad and shouted, "Look out!"

Aaron turned, sensing the blow before it landed. He raised his hands to cover his face and tucked his chin. The man pushed off the wall and spun, using the turn to increase the force of the vicious backhand strike. It connected on the top of Aaron's skull, and the thicker bone there absorbed the blow. But it still hurt and made his eyes swim.

He swept an arm up, forcing the man's arm out of the way, and blasted his right fist into his opponent's sternum. Propelled by fear, pain, and adrenaline, Aaron continued to rain rights and lefts until the man dropped.

Chest heaving, he said,, "Help me, Paul!" Using their belts and Paul's tie, they bound the men well enough to hold them until the police arrived. They dragged them into a closet and closed the door. Aaron grabbed a chair and jammed it under the door knob, blocking it shut. He scrawled a note informing the police where to find the prisoners, along with Joseph's number and instructions to call him. "Paul, I have to get to my house, and you're coming with me."

"What's going on?"

"We'll talk in the car." He grabbed Paul's arm and led him away at a run.

"Don't we need to wait on the police?"

The sounds of sirens could be heard in the distance, but Aaron did not want to get held up—they would ask questions he didn't want to take the time to answer. "I have to get to my family, and I don't want to leave you here. Let's go."

Retracing his, steps the men made their way to Aaron's car and climbed in. As they pulled away, he tossed his phone to Paul. "Find the preset number that says 'Joseph cell' and call it for me, will you? When he answers, put the phone to my ear."

Doing as he asked, Paul found the number and dialed, then held the phone to Aaron's ear. Joseph answered on the first ring. "Aaron where are—?"

"Joseph, are you with my family?"

"Yes, everything's fine. I have three agents here. Where are you? Sarah is worried sick."

"I'll be there in five minutes. How fast can you get someone to the Shady Pines Church on Spillway Road?" Aaron explained what happened and the location of the assailants.

"I'll contact the local police, make sure they're found, and have them transferred to our custody. Someone in the CIA wants to talk to those guys badly, and to you, too. I'll sure be glad when you can tell me what the heck is going on."

"When I find out, I'll let you know. I'm on the way."

Aaron glanced over at Paul, whose face was ashen. As the adrenaline faded, Aaron began to feel the affects of the punishment he had taken. The accelerator beneath his foot was cool and a little gritty. He wiggled his toes and realized he was still barefooted. "Paul, I'm really sorry about all this. I don't know how or why, but I've gotten us both into a mess." He explained his encounter downtown and the warning from the stranger.

Paul took a deep breath and seemed to collect himself. "Well, I guess it's safe to assume that these dreams you're having are more than just dreams." He glanced over at Aaron. "I can also assume I need to be much more careful about whom I invite to church in the future."

Aaron's head swiveled toward his passenger, momentarily diverting his attention from the road. The stinging words were a bolt from the blue until he noticed the sardonic smile on Paul's face. The grin and the return of color seemed to indicate the pastor had regained his composure. "Paul, why me? Why us? Why would God allow you to be in danger this way? You serve Him!" Aaron clamped harder on the steering wheel. He hesitated for a brief instant as the day's events flashed through his mind. "And I don't mind telling you, either . . . I'm scared to death."

"I don't understand this any more than you do. But I do trust God. I know you have doubts and fears right now. But it's amazing how perspectives can be so different. When those men were questioning me, I had never been so scared in my life. I prayed fervently for God to help me, to save me. Then you came rushing through my office door, and I knew He had heard me. You see? You doubt, while I'm grateful to Him for sending you to save me."

An interesting perspective, Aaron thought. He didn't know what to say.

CHAPTER XI

THIS side trip was not on Hussaam's public itinerary. Upon landing in Madrid, his entourage had pulled into a private Hawk Pharmaceuticals hanger. After making excuses to Fatima and explaining his intent to meet her and Haytham in New York the next day, he and Rashad climbed into a second plane. Basil remained with Hussaam's family. The flight to Syria took a little over three hours in the custom Citation X, a plane capable of nearly sonic speed. Another covert landing and a short jaunt via helicopter brought them to a base in the hill country of north-eastern Syria. The covert travel was as necessary as the speed. Hussaam believed his presence at the impending meeting was crucial. The two men about to arrive were vital to Hussaam's plans. They just didn't know it.

Hussaam would watch, wait, and listen. The soon-to-be-arriving guests were arrogant and powerful men, leaders of two of the world's most infamous terror groups. Of course, they achieved their status, and retained it, at Hussaam's whim. His financial support and intelligence allowed both men's organizations to prosper. Let them swagger for now, Hussaam thought. Soon they would be brought to heel by their master. A master they did not yet know existed.

Hussaam stood shoulder-to-shoulder with Rashad. From their place behind a small rock outcropping at the rear of the base, they surveyed the surrounding hills. Nothing seemed out of place.

Faint orange light hinted at the coming dawn, the horizon broken by dark silhouettes of the mountains surrounding the small canyon. The western expanse of the sky burst with stars reluctant to yield their dominion to the rising sun.

Hussaam raised his binoculars and turned his attention to the caravan approaching the base. A line of SUVs traversed the only navigable pass into the canyon. As instructed, a green flag waved from the antenna of the lead vehicle.

Jalal, Hussaam's second in command of off-the-books operations, served as the reception committee. Jalal stood alone in front of the larger of two buildings in the canyon, hands clasped in front, entirely unthreatening, patient. He man was one of the few Hussaam trusted.

The serpentine line of vehicles surged into the canyon accompanied by a cloud of dust. *Come to the snare, my little rabbits.* Hussaam touched his companion on the shoulder and they melted into the shadows of the rock wall which allowed them to see without being seen. Their position also placed them out the line of fire.

As the lead truck braked to a halt in front of Jalal, several armed men sprang forth and fanned out to surround the caravan. Guns at the ready, they scanned the base. Apparently satisfied, one opened the door of the middle vehicle. The tall, gaunt figure of Abdul-Qadir Rayhan stepped out: self-proclaimed cleric and leader of the Fist of Allah.

The action was repeated at the next vehicle, and the pockmarked face of Sheikh Malik Farraj emerged. Though not as widely recognized, the leader of the Hammer of the Crescent was equally, if not more, dangerous. Both men were pursued by law enforcement agencies across the globe.

Jalal escorted the two men inside and Hussaam strode into the center of the compound with Rashad in his wake. The visitors' guards turned at their approach. When they recognized Hussaam, their expressions became a mix of bewilderment and awe. None attempted to impede him as he marched in the front door.

Making his way to the meeting room, Hussaam heard raised voices. Through the small rectangular window in the door, he saw Jalal staring across the table at the terrorists. His voice sounded strained and frustrated. "Please explain to me again why you won't do this. Both of you are sworn to defeat our enemies by any means. I do not understand."

The men appeared aghast at Jalal's tone. They exchanged a glance and Sheikh Malik Farraj bounded to his feet. He jabbed a finger at Jalal and his shout echoed off the wall. "I told you I would not do it! It is just the excuse the Israelis need to destroy us in open warfare, without the world intervening. I am leaving. Now!"

Hussaam threw the door open and stepped into the room, silencing Farraj's rant. He shoved the sheikh on the forehead, forcing him back into the chair. Jalal reached under the table and whipped out a concealed small-caliber pistol.

"I told you they were yellow dogs," Hussaam said to Jalal. "Revered and respected by their followers. Feared by their foes. Ha!"

Abdul-Qadir opened his mouth to reply, but Jalal centered the barrel of the gun on his brow.

Hussaam gestured toward the seated men. "You see? These two are perfectly willing to send others to their deaths for their causes but won't risk anything of themselves. Without a cave wall or a young boy to hide behind, their bravado vanishes." He nodded to Jalal.

Jalal grabbed a small two-way radio, depressed the call button, and spoke one word: "Now."

From outside, the rat-a-tat of automatic gunfire erupted as Hussaam's men sprung the ambush from their concealed positions in the rocks above the ravine. The barrage ceased in seconds.

A voice squawked through Jalal's walkie-talkie. "It's done."

"Your men are all dead," Hussaam said. He grabbed the gun from Jalal's hand and took aim at each terrorist in turn. He waved the barrel back and forth, alternately targeting each of them, moving the pistol in slow lazy circles. He lowered the gun and some of the alarm in the men's faces disappeared. In a flash, Hussaam whisked the gun up again, settling the barrel on Abdul-Qadir's forehead. "Last chance. Help us or die. Your people are dead. You're all alone."

Before either man could reply, he aimed the gun's barrel toward Sheikh Farraj. He pulled the trigger; the noise was thunderous in the small room. Smoke and the acrid smell of gunpowder filled the air. The man's head snapped back and his sightless eyes stared at the ceiling, then he slumped forward onto the table.

Two of Hussaam's men rushed in and unceremoniously dragged the body from the room.

Hussaam turned his attention and the gun's barrel to Abdul-Qadir. "You *will* make the recording. You will claim responsibility for the attacks. If you cooperate, you may stay here as my guest. If not"—he placed the cold steel of the pistol barrel on man's nose—"you may join your friend."

Apparently at a loss for words, the leader of the Fist of Allah frantically bobbed his head up and down.

Hussaam tossed the pistol back to Jalal and spoke to him in English, which the cleric couldn't speak. "I'll call you when I reach New York."

Hussaam glanced at the terrorist. "If he will not cooperate, there are more where he came from."

CHAPTER XII

AARON rolled into his driveway, reassured by the presence of Rachel's car as well as the two black sedans along the curb. A Secret Service agent sat behind the steering wheel of one of the cars.

Aaron climbed out of the car and groaned. He was already stiffening up. Paul in tow, they moved toward the house. The words of his instructor Mr. Haversham popped into Aaron's head: *"You fight like you train. If you are lazy and sloppy in the dojang, you will be lazy and sloppy on the street, and you will get hurt. Do it again."* These remarks came after a night of *nok-sul*, or break-fall training. Everyone had been tired after slamming into the mat time and again, and their landings became sloppy. He reminded them if they could not fall well on mats, they would be in serious trouble if someone threw them onto the hard ground. Aaron realized that a little muscle soreness was a small price to pay. It could have been much worse. A lot of training and luck had more than likely saved two lives today.

They approached the back door just as it flew open. Sarah rushed out and hugged Aaron fiercely, burying her head in his chest. She gave another squeeze for emphasis and released her hold. She brought her gaze to his face and a frown crossed her own. Her eyes roved, scrutinizing his features. She reached up and gently caressed a sore spot on his face with her fingertips. "Aaron, are you all right? Will you *please* tell me what's happened?"

Aaron covered her hand in his own and nuzzled it. "I'm fine." He brought her hand down, entwining his fingers in hers, and tugged her after him. "Come on. Let's get inside and I'll tell you all about it."

* * * * *

Aaron lounged against the kitchen counter and outlined the morning's events for Rachel and Sarah. Though they both seemed concerned for Aaron, the two women absolutely fawned over Paul, forcing him to offer repeated assurances of his health and well-being. Aaron caught the pastor's eye. Paul shrugged his shoulders in supplication, his eyes pleading for help.

Aaron returned the look with a brief side-to-side shake of his head. There was no way he was getting in the middle of that. *You're on your own, brother.* Discretion was the better part of valor. Soon enough the women would remember to blame Aaron for placing Paul in danger. The amusing part was they had no inkling of how tough the soft-spoken cleric really was. The situation seemed to have left him unfazed, whereas Aaron was developing a case of the shakes.

Joseph pulled Aaron into the living room. "There are two CIA guys flying in to talk to you. They'll be here in a couple of hours."

"Great. This just keeps getting better."

Joseph's gaze fell away and he shuffled his feet in obvious discomfort.

"Spit it out. What's wrong?"

"After the CIA guys get here, I've been ordered to report in, and to leave you in their hands."

Aaron's gaze turned to his wife and sister, who still fussed over Paul, then to the door of his baby's room. What had he brought on them? He returned his focus to Joseph. "Please. Don't leave. I'll beg if I have to."

"I thought you knew me better than that. When they get here I'll see what can be done. I won't leave you without protection, even if I have to take vacation and operate off duty."

"Thanks."

Joseph reached out and gave Aaron's arm a squeeze. "Don't be such a wimp, old man."

Aaron appreciated the insult, the familiar jibe lifting the dark cloud settling over him. "What do you think I should tell the CIA people?"

Joseph answered without hesitation: "The truth."

* * * * * *

Explanations to his family made and all information shared, Aaron sought a moment of solitude. He shut the bedroom door behind him and strode into the bathroom. He peeled off his shirt and assessed his bruised and mottled skin. Probing with his fingers, he examined the welts, which were sore but not serious.

Someone had just attempted to kidnap and probably kill him over something seen in his dreams. A cold sweat popped from his forehead, and his hands shook. He wiped at the perspiration on his brow, the skin beneath his hand cool and clammy. Bile rose in the back of his throat, and he dashed to the toilet as a heaving wretch twisted his guts. Barely making it, he vomited until the contents of his stomach were purged.

* * * * * *

Aaron lounged on his bed after a long, scalding shower; the hot water had rinsed away some of his stiffness. His eyes drooped and he sunk into the pillows, body heavy and relaxed. As drowsiness settled over him and slumber beckoned, the doorbell rang. His eyes popped open and he heard Joseph instructing everyone to get away from the door.

Aaron pulled a shirt over his head and stepped out of the room. Joseph holstered his weapon as he opened the front door and allowed two men to step inside. The first was an unremarkable man dressed in a suit with a jacket draped over his arm. The sight of the second man was startling. The familiar face belonged to a stranger, yet was as familiar to Aaron as the mirror's reflection.

It was *him*.

Introductions were made as everyone shook hands. Stunned and awed to silence, Aaron clasped hands with an apparition made flesh.

"I'm Derek Galloway. Good to meet you." The words were spoken in a conversational tone, but the timbre of the man's voice was deep and resonant, as if the quiet tone held a tempest at bay, a powerful storm to be unleashed on the unwary.

The reality of meeting a man who stepped from his nightmares caught Aaron off guard. He stood transfixed, grasping the man's hand, staring at him dumbfounded. Galloway's grip was firm, hinting at the strength in his hands, his green eyes just as intense as in the dreams. His hair was dark with a hint of gray at the temples and shaved close to his head.

"Are you all right, sir?" Galloway asked.

Aaron snapped out of his reverie. "I . . . I'm sorry. It's just . . . well, seeing you here rattled me. When you hear my story, you may understand why."

The group assembled at Aaron's dining room table. Joseph and Paul sat beside him, Hal Bouie and Derek Galloway opposite them. Rachel and Abby played in the living room, while Sarah brewed a pot of coffee for their guests. As Aaron unabashedly recounted his story, he scanned the newcomer's faces, gauging their reactions, searching for any indication of their thoughts. Galloway's expression remained impassive, but Bouie appeared skeptical. Aaron studied his hands as he talked and squirmed in his chair. Trying not to allow the CIA man's attitude to shake him, Aaron told all: the content of the dreams, Derek Galloway's appearance in them, the words he had spoken, and finally, the morning's attacks.

"So, Mr. Henderson, what do you think this all means?" Hal asked. The tone of his voice and the way he squinted his eyes indicated the question was asked out of sheer curiosity, as if Aaron's response didn't matter to him in the least.

Aaron swallowed. The man didn't believe him. "Please, just call me Aaron. Assuming my dreams have some meaning, which is becoming easier by the hour . . ." He glanced at Galloway before dropping his eyes to the table. "My theory is there were weapons of some kind being produced in the ruins of Nineveh. Now they've been moved to other locations." He raised his head to meet Hal Bouie's gaze. "I'm afraid the weapons are going to be used for a terrible purpose." He didn't know what type of response his statements would garner. He didn't really blame them for not believing him. What would he think if he were on their side of the table?

He was surprised when Hal simply asked, "What makes you think that?"

"I'll show you." Aaron stood up. "I'll be right back." He dashed to his study and hastily collected a small pile of printouts of maps and scriptures, and his Bible. He returned to the table and spread it all out. "Bear with me a second." He shuffled the papers until they were in the proper order. "Okay, here goes. The dream told me the answer is in 'Nahum.' Nahum is a book about Nineveh, the ruins of which are in Iraq. I was led to this scripture." He flipped to the correct page of his Bible and read aloud. "'From you, O Nineveh, has one come forth, who plots evil against the LORD and counsels wickedness.'" Aaron read the frightening passage in its entirety. When he finished, he hesitated, allowing the gravity of the scripture to sink in. He raised his gaze to his audience. "I believe the Hawk I dreamed about is the one who plots evil, and he is going to use what he made at Nineveh to wreak devastation on the world."

No one moved.

Aaron considered what to say. He raked his eyes over each of the seated men, finally resting his stare on Hal Bouie. "Look. I wish I had the luxury of accepting your disbelief. That I could just forget about this. But my family and I are now in danger. I have no doubt that the men who tried to kidnap Paul and I would have killed us."

Paul spoke up for the first time. "I can vouch for that."

Hal exchanged a glance with Derek. "Um, Aaron. Can you give us a few minutes to discuss this?"

Aaron nodded.

"Derek, Agent Harris, may I have a word with you outside?" Hal said.

As the three men left the table, Joseph turned to give Aaron a pat on the shoulder. "Don't worry," he said.

"I'll try."

* * * * * *

Derek scanned the neighborhood, inventorying his surroundings out of habit. For an early Monday afternoon, there was quite a bit of activity. People walked, jogged, and pulled weeds out of their flowerbeds; many looked retired. There wasn't much traffic, and the neighborhood had only one entrance. It seemed like a pleasant place to live. Even so, he studied all the activity at a glance. Were he asked, he would have been able to describe in detail all he observed: The color of the band on the knee-high socks on the elderly gentleman tending his yard. The color and style of the jogging suits worn by the grey-haired ladies sauntering down the street. Even the hair and eye color of a passing motorist. Each detail of his environment was carefully assessed and catalogued as he searched for threats, instinctively seeking avenues of escape and defensible positions.

The men took up positions in the yard, and Hal faced Joseph Harris. "Agent Harris, how well do you know Mr. Henderson?"

"Very well," the man replied.

"Is he in to drugs? Does he owe the wrong people money?"

"What are you implying?"

"Nothing," Hal said. "I'm just asking." He turned to Derek. "What do you think?"

"I think those two men have stepped in it. I also believe they are in serious jeopardy." Derek blew a puff of breath over his lips. "Whew. I have to tell you guys, Mr. Henderson's story gave me a bit of a chill."

Hal rolled his eyes. "Oh, come on guys. You can't tell me you're buying this religious mumbo-jumbo." He raised his hand and wiggled his fingers. "Whooo, *whooo*, voices from beyond."

Agent Harris glared at Hal.

"Take it easy, Hal," Derek said. "I think there's more to it. What about the attacks on those men?"

"The people that attacked them could be anybody," Hal said. "We have no idea what they were after or who they are. You can't really expect me to take this back to the DNI. For all we know Mr. Henderson just ate some bad pizza. He could have gotten the wrong people mad. I don't know."

"We've got their attackers in custody," Derek said. "We may get some answers when they're questioned." He glanced toward the house. "I have a feeling there's more to this. Don't ask me why, I just do. The least we can do is see if Mr. Henderson is willing to come with us. We can question him some more, see if he really is on to something." He turned back to Hal. "Right now this is the *only* lead on the Hawk we have."

Hal stared back and considered for a moment. "Okay. We'll bring him in. I'll get on the phone. I'll see if I can get temporary protection for these people. At least until we get to the bottom of this. Maybe the local FBI office will lend us a couple of agents."

"No way," Harris said. "I want these people properly protected. I'm not knocking the FBI, but protection is the Secret Service's business." He inclined his head toward the house. "Those people are like family."

"I know, but you guys aren't authorized to protect civilians," Hal said.

"I know someone who can change that."

"Who?"

"POTUS," Harris said, using the acronym for president of the United States. "Special order of the president will allow me to keep a team here to protect these people. Aaron's first priority will be to keep his family safe, and he will be little help to you if he doesn't have confidence that they are. I won't be able to assure him that they will be, unless we protect them." He raised his eyebrows and looked Hal in the eye. "So, I suggest you make it happen."

"I don't kn—"

"Do it, Hal," Derek said.

"Okay, okay. I'll make some calls. I'm not making any promises." Hal turned away, indicating he wanted privacy, and dialed his phone.

Agent Harris stared after Hal.

"He'll do what he can," Derek said. "Let's wait inside."

CHAPTER XIII

THE Citation X soared over the Mediterranean Sea. The day's events could not have gone better and Hussaam had no doubt Abdul-Qadir would cooperate.

The chirping of the satellite phone interrupted Hussaam's musing. He clutched the device to his ear. "Report." Trusting no one, as always, he implemented a back-up plan. The man on the line was the same sent to silence al-Douri, extorting double his usual fee for the rush required by this new assignment, refusing to even acknowledge his earlier blunder.

"I've located your quarry. Somehow, they eluded capture before we were able to get information from them. Both men survived."

It seemed Hussaam's caution had paid dividends. "Can you get to them?"

"I reconned the residence. After a drive by, I listened with a directional mike. I didn't get much, but there is some law enforcement activity at the house. I should act now. I've identified the principle target, and there's a way to blend in to get close."

Hussaam wanted more information but kept his curiosity in check. The line was secure, but one never knew who could be listening. "Do it. No more mistakes."

* * * * * *

Seated on the couch, Aaron surveyed his home and family. This house was his safe haven, his fortress of solitude, invaded by his nightmares. He scanned the faces of his beloved wife, his sister, his beautiful baby.

Abby slept cradled in his arms, snoring softly, the movement of her tiny chest barely perceptible.

Fear. Its icy fingers clutched, grabbed, squeezed, engulfing him in its frigid grip. Why had this been brought to his doorstep? Their lives were being turned upside down. He feared for himself, but much more for his family. Paul had also been sucked into this whirlwind of events but seemed to be handling it better than any of them.

Hal Bouie strode into the room, flipping his phone closed with a click. "From this moment forward, there will be no unsecured communications regarding this matter. For now, we're considering this a matter of national security. Mr. Henderson, your family is now officially under the protection of the Secret Service." Hal addressed Joseph. "Agent Harris, I expressed your concerns. I've been assured that you'll be given operational control." Hal turned away from Joseph, and focused his eyes on Aaron. "For as long as Mr. Henderson is helping us."

Aaron returned the stare. *Point taken, message received, roger that.*

"Just in case, I think it's a good idea if your sister and Pastor Jenkins stay with your wife. At least until we figure this thing out."

Sarah spoke up. "Aaron, you may have to go with them, but *I am* going with you."

Hal was about to speak, but Aaron held up his hand. "That's not a good idea, Sarah. I want you and Abby to stay here with Rachel and Paul. I won't be able to do what I need to do if I don't know that you're safe. And if you're here with Joseph, you will be."

Joseph moved to sit by Sarah and patted the back of her hand. "I'll take care of you. Aaron will be much better off if he doesn't have to worry about you. He'll have enough to worry about."

Sarah acquiesced with a slight nod of her head.

"I'm sorry, but we need to leave," Hal said. "Soon. Unfortunately, I can't tell you where we're going."

Sarah's head snapped in his direction, eyes blazing.

Derek shot a scathing glare at his associate before turning to Sarah. "Mrs. Henderson, I'm sorry. This cloak and dagger routine is for your family and your husband's safety." He knelt before the couch, placing himself at her eye level. "You don't know me and you have no reason to trust me, I realize that. But I will do everything in my power to take care of your husband. And as soon as possible, I will see that he's able to call you."

It has been said that the eyes were the windows to the soul. If that was indeed true, then Sarah became fully acquainted with the soul of Derek Galloway. Her eyes bore into his, unwavering, as if her stare was capable of measuring his words and his worth. Apparently satisfied, Sarah gave another nod, and Galloway rose to his feet.

A tear pooled in the corner of her eye. "Give us a few minutes, please," Aaron said. "I need to throw some things in a bag." He wrapped his free arm around Sarah's shoulders. "And say my good-byes."

Derek tugged Hal's elbow, nudging him toward the door.

* * * * * *

Abby in one arm, Aaron set down his hastily packed bag. "You be a good girl for momma. Daddy loves you." His kiss was met with a smile, and he passed her to Rachel. He wrapped his arms around Sarah for a long moment and then pulled his sister into the hug with them. After kissing their foreheads, he disentangled himself. With a caress of his thumb, he gently swiped the tears from Sarah's cheek. "I'll be fine, don't worry. I'll call you as soon as my feet hit the ground. Oh, and call my office in the morning for me will you? Tell them they'll have to handle things for a couple of days without me."

She nodded, stood on her tiptoes and brushed her lips across his. Rachel gently pulled her away.

He stuck his hand out to Paul. "I can't tell you how sorry I am about this. You shouldn't have to stay here too long." They clasped hands. "But since you're here, please take care of them while I'm away."

"I will, you have my word. Try to have faith. It will all work out. I know you have your doubts, but I feel God is using you for a grand purpose. He'll watch over you." Paul smiled. "Besides, I've been in much worse places than this."

Aaron responded with a feeble smile of his own. He turned to Joseph. "I don't even know what to say. I won't ever be able to thank you enough for—"

Joseph cut him off. "Oh, come on. You know you don't have to thank me. But you do owe me a steak, and I expect to get it soon." He grasped Aaron's shoulders. "Don't worry about your family. I promise I'll keep them safe. You just take care of yourself." He pulled Aaron close, giving him a strong embrace and a pat on the back. "Don't underestimate yourself, you are good. But this is a different game, and you can't be afraid you'll hurt someone. If you have to defend yourself, hit hard and fast, and do what's necessary to survive. I want you home in one piece." He pushed Aaron away and held up his thumb and forefinger two inches apart. "I want a steak like this. No little gristly one, but a big, thick, juicy one."

Aaron stole a last look at his family, absorbing every detail, carving their images into his mind. As confident as he had sounded to them, he had no idea what was about to happen or how long he would be away. Without further delaying the inevitable, he blew them a kiss and turned away.

Paul said, "Wait. You may need this." He pulled a small book out of his back pocket and tossed it over.

Aaron grabbed it from the air with his free hand and inspected the cover. It was a pocket-sized copy of a Bible. "Thanks." He slipped the book into his pocket and gave the pastor a small smile.

* * * * * *

From the front sidewalk, Agent Derek Galloway surveyed the area, drawing the pine-scented air through his nostrils. This neighborhood represented what he fought for. Home and family. Things he found himself longing for of late. A bell rang in the distance, and the laughter and joyous screams of children was carried on the wind from the school beyond the trees. How could he burden a wife and a child with his lifestyle? Gone all the time, at tremendous risk of dying in action. And they would never be told what really happened. No.

Hal stepped in front of Derek and glared, speaking to him through clenched teeth. "I don't like this. I can't believe I let you talk me into this. I'm already on the hot seat with the DNI."

"Blame me," Derek said. "I don't see that we have any other choice. If I'm right. If this man is really on to something, it may be a matter of national—no, international security. Let's just get him to Langley and assess the situation from there." He stared back at Hal. "My instincts are buzzing. Something tells me Mr. Henderson can help us."

Before Hal could respond Aaron approached them. "I guess I'm ready."

As they traversed the sidewalk toward the car, alarm bells clanged in Derek's head. Scanning the area, he identified the source of his unease.

Although there were several people walking and jogging, something about an approaching jogger seemed peculiar. He had been down the street doing warm-up stretches, seemingly unhurried. But as soon Aaron came out of the house, the man rushed toward them. Coincidence? Maybe. Without looking directly at him, Derek studied him. The clothes seemed somehow wrong and the face . . . this man had driven by earlier. Not necessarily incriminating.

He snuck a hand beneath his blazer and flipped the snap on his shoulder holster.

* * * * * *

As they moved to the waiting car, Aaron examined his yard and his neighborhood, attempting to draw comfort from the familiar scene. Leaving his home and family like this, he never felt so alone. Derek Galloway dropped back to walk next to him.

They neared the end of the sidewalk, and Aaron saw a blur of motion out of the corner of his eye. A man dressed in jogging gear stopped abruptly across the street from them and whipped a gun out of his belt pack.

Aaron was shoved to the side. As he fell, he glanced over to see Derek retracting his arm while in the opposite hand a large black handgun materialized from beneath his blazer.

The jogger leveled his gun. As Aaron hit the ground, three booming shots deafened him. He flinched, waiting for the pain.

Instead, the jogger's chest erupted in a shower of blood as three successive bullets ripped into him. The first shot nearly knocked him off his feet and he fell into the side of a parked vehicle. Unable to fall further, the second two bullets struck him, pinning him to the side of the car. He jerked like a marionette, his strings pulled by a macabre puppeteer in a spasmic death dance. No longer able to support his own weight, he pitched forward, falling face first in the street.

Aaron scrambled to his feet and saw a shudder course through the body of the jogger as a crimson pool spread from beneath it. Silence filled his ears, the yells of his neighbors ceased, the birds no longer chirped. It seemed as if even the wind stilled.

Derek moved to check the body, but there seemed little doubt of the outcome. Aaron's relief was only equaled by his horror. That man came to kill him. *Him.* He was the intended victim. His blood might very well have been fertilizing the lawn beneath his feet. Another shudder wracked him.

Breathe. In through the nose, out through the mouth.

Hal shoved Aaron into backseat of the waiting car. Gun in one hand, Derek slid in next to him and slammed the door shut with the other.

Joseph raced through the front door, gun drawn, just as his partner rounded the corner of the house wielding his own weapon.

Hal flung open the driver's side door. "We're getting out of here. We weren't here. You guys handle this." He dropped into the driver's seat, slammed the door shut, and jerked the gear shift into drive. With a screech of tires, they sped away. Hal glanced at Aaron in the rearview mirror. "Well, I'll say this. You sure ticked *somebody* off."

Aaron peered out of the rear window to watch all he loved disappear from view. Turning back to the front, he looked at Derek and simply said, "Thanks."

PART II

Keep me, O LORD, from the hands of the wicked; protect me from men of violence who plan to trip my feet. **Psalm 140:4**

CHAPTER XIV

THE whir of lowering flaps and the whine of the jet's engines roused Aaron. His eyes fluttered open as the plane bumped to the runway. Sunlight streamed through the windows, forcing him to squint. Tires screeched, and he pitched forward as the plane decelerated. He assumed they had arrived at their destination, Bolling Air Force Base in Washington D.C. His eyes adjusted and he scanned the opulent interior of the private plane. Hal remained on the phone as he had been since take-off. Derek appeared to be sleeping in a seat across the aisle.

As they came to a stop, Derek jumped to his feet and moved to the exit at the rear of the plane. He twisted the locking mechanism and lowered the door. Steps on its back provided a passage to the Tarmac. He motioned for Aaron to come with him and exited the plane.

Aaron grabbed his bag and followed. Stepping through the portal, wind and sound blasted his senses. The jet was parked outside a large metal hanger. The whump-whump of chopper blades assailed his ears as a sleek blue and white helicopter came to rest a few yards away from them. The gust of air from its rotors stirred dust and grit as its skids came to rest. Face stinging from tiny flying particles, Aaron held a hand in front of his eyes to shield them.

Hal emerged from the plane and touched Aaron on the shoulder, then pointed toward the helicopter. "That's our ride."

Derek opened the chopper's door and motioned them ahead.

Aaron ducked beneath the whirling blades as he approached the craft. "Where are we going?" he shouted over the din.

"Langley," Derek said. "CIA headquarters."

"Wonderful," Aaron said. They climbed aboard, and Hal tapped the pilot on the shoulder. Just as Aaron touched the seat they lifted off.

What a day. It seemed as if he hadn't slept in days and the short nap on the flight did little to assuage his fatigue.

He clutched the armrest of his seat as the craft was buffeted. He glanced around the cabin but no one else appeared in the least bit alarmed. Seated next to the pilot, Hal talked animatedly into a headset.

Derek tapped Aaron on the shoulder and pointed to headsets hanging near their seats. They placed them over their ears, and Derek's voice, sounding tinny, broadcast through the speakers. "First time in a helicopter?"

"Yes. What's all the shaking and bumping?"

"It's just cross-drafts, nothing to worry about."

"If you say so." The helicopter lurched again and Aaron swore his stomach was no longer in his body.

Derek pointed below. "It's the river. Once we're over it, the flight will be smoother. That's the Potomac, by the way."

They flew low over the body of water. Aaron guessed, by the position of the setting sun, their flight was generally northwest. The receding sunlight danced on ripples in the languid current to their left, and the helicopter's shadow stretched away to their right. Beneath them the water was churned by the spinning rotors. The vessel lifted abruptly as they approached a bridge and angled toward the tree line at the edge of the waterway.

As they rose above the trees, Derek pointed out landmarks. "That's the Arlington Memorial Bridge there. Just across it is the Lincoln memorial." He pointed to their left. "And over there is Arlington National Cemetery." Even in the dusk, row upon row of white headstones were visible, testaments to the high price of freedom. "That road is George Washington Memorial Parkway."

The sun sank beneath the horizon, leaving a pink-hued skyline in its wake. Streetlamps, headlights, and neon signs lit the area beneath them. The craft banked left and they passed over a heavily congested area. In a few minutes, the lights of the city faded as they flew above a forested area. They reached an open area in the dense forest. In its midst was a large complex, the surrounding trees separating it from the eyes of the world. It looked like a college campus. A nice one.

They descended to a clearly marked helipad behind a large glass and concrete building dominated by a large arched entrance. Hal turned. "Welcome to CIA headquarters." He pointed to the building. "That's the new headquarters building." He pointed to another obviously older, more traditionally constructed building. "That is the original headquarters building."

A large courtyard filled with trees and shrubbery, manicured grass, water features, and picnic areas separated the two structures.

"Okay, that's it for the tour," Hal said. "We've done a thorough background check on you, and the director has authorized me to take you into classified areas. But you have to sign this." He reached into his briefcase, extricated a document, and passed it over.

Aaron grabbed it and flipped through the pages. It was a confidentiality agreement.

"The gist is," Hal said, "if you breathe a word of what you see or hear during your stay, the United States government will jail you without impunity, with no trial." He held out a pen. "Just sign the last page."

Aaron accepted the pen as the helicopter settled to the ground with a little thud as the skids met the pavement. He turned to Derek. "Should I trust him?"

Derek looked at his associate for a moment. "No. But the document is pretty standard."

Aaron flipped through pages. Placing the pen on the signature line, a sense of foreboding welled within him. His name was hardly scrawled in the blank before Hal snatched the paper away, stuffing it into his briefcase.

"Let's go," Hal said.

The group stepped onto the helipad beneath the whirring rotors. Shoulder to shoulder with his new companions, Aaron was ushered into the original headquarters building of the Central Intelligence Agency. As they passed through the entrance, his feet trod across the CIA emblem, a large circle framed by granite flooring. Inside the circle, an eagle hovered over a shield which bore a sixteen point star.

As he was rushed past the infamous symbol on the floor, Aaron stopped. He was surrounded by a large atrium full of statues, pictures, and other memorabilia. Turning in a slow circle he stared at the room, awestruck. Some malevolent hand had surreptitiously pulled him from the world he knew and dumped him into some nightmare spy movie.

His companions finally noticed his dawdling and returned to usher him through the entrance hall. They arrived at a set of doors framed by two armed guards. Hal nodded in greeting and slid his ID into a card reader. The doors opened with a magnetic click and a hiss of air. As they passed through the portal, Aaron gaped at the passage beyond. *Toto, I have a feeling we're not in Kansas anymore.*

* * * * * *

Hussaam's limo seemed like a cage, and the oppressive New York skyline did nothing to alleviate his apprehension. Rashad sat in the front seat next to the driver, overtly avoiding eye contact in the mirrors. Hussaam swallowed his urge to lash out, to pummel something, anything. The lack of contact from the assassin—he slammed the edge of his fist into door. He closed his eyes and smoothed the front of his suit in an attempt to regain his composure. He dialed his Memphis head of security. "What is the situation?"

"None of the teams have reported in, and we have no idea what happened. I'm not very optimistic."

Hussaam squeezed the phone. "Find out. Now. Do not fail me." He resisted the urge to fling the phone through the window. When it rang again he stared at it a second before answering. "Tell me you know something."

"Your man failed. Again. For the last time. The others failed, too. Those who aren't dead are in custody. Can they connect you? Did any of them know of our plans?"

"No," Hussaam said. "Nothing. They do not know who hired them or why." He bit back his anger. The man was not questioning him, simply being cautious. "Have we been compromised?"

"No. And I'll keep it that way."

* * * * * *

Aaron slumped in a chair. He sat alone in a hallway outside the door to the office where he had spent the last three hours being interviewed. He leaned forward, elbows on his knees, right thumb and forefinger massaging his eyes.

It was almost midnight, and this was now officially the longest day of his life.

His eyes roved past non-descript office doors lining the hallway. Bright white floor tiles matched the walls. The glowing overhead lights reflected off the stark whiteness, irritating his burning eyes. The CIA building's corridor seemed a study in twentieth century bland.

Hal and several colleagues had questioned him for over an hour. The bulk of the questions were about his personal life. Finally they produced satellite surveillance photos showing aerial images of Nineveh and the surrounding areas and asked him to point out anything that seemed familiar. Throughout the questioning, Derek Galloway sat quietly, speaking little.

Then Aaron had been asked to wait in the hall. Hal reluctantly agreed to allow him to call home with the strict stipulation that he tell them nothing about where he was or what he was doing.

Everyone was worried but all right. Joseph had gone home, but there were three agents on duty. At least Aaron could sleep with the knowledge his family was safe.

Finally, the office door opened. Derek strolled into the hall. "Let's grab a bite and find a place to sack down."

After grabbing a quick meal in the commissary, Derek led Aaron through a maze of corridors until they exited the building, then to a smaller building a short distance away. An armed security guard handed them keys and directed them to some sleeping quarters. Derek explained that the rooms were for agents working long and odd hours, who couldn't or wouldn't take the time to go home. There were also the occasional visitors like themselves in need of a place to sleep.

Aaron was led to a small unadorned room containing a single bed, a lamp, a metal night table, and a metal bureau. Very Spartan.

As he undressed, he cleared his pockets of keys, wallet, loose change, and the small Bible in his back pocket. He had almost forgotten it was there. Turning the book in his hands, he smelled the new paper scent. He caressed the leather binding with his thumb before laying it on the night table.

He stowed the rest of his things and located the public bathroom down the hall. The shower was decorated in typical locker room fashion: large and open, lacking curtains and barriers, with small off-white squares of ceramic tile covering the floor and walls. He chose one of the eight shower heads sticking out of the wall at random. For twenty minutes he allowed the hot water to cascade over him, the steaming water rinsing away the stiffness in his neck and shoulders.

After plodding on heavy feet back to his room, he plopped onto the bed and the ancient springs groaned in protest. Ready to sleep but wide awake, he reached over and grabbed the Bible. Ripped pieces of paper of various sizes were stuck between some of the pages. He chose one of the homemade bookmarks at random and flipped the book open. The marked passage was the first chapter of the book of James in the New Testament. Several sentences of the text were highlighted, and his eyes roved to the first of them, verse twelve: "Blessed is the man who perseveres under trial, because when he has stood the test, he will receive the crown of life that God has promised to those who love Him."

Did Paul highlight that passage for Aaron's benefit? He couldn't have, could he? It was so . . . applicable. He turned his attention to the beginning of chapter one and began to read, soaking in the words. To his surprise, he found they provided some comfort. By the end of the chapter his eyes began to droop.

CHAPTER XV

HE stands on a hill above the city of Nineveh, the capitol of the ancient Assyrian empire, the world's mightiest nation pre-dating the Romans. The construction of this mighty fortress city began in 9th century BC, and the city was destroyed in 612 BC. According to the books of Jonah and Nahum, the destruction was due to the ungodliness of its people and rulers.

Below him is the city in its former glory: a vast metropolis dissected by a labyrinth of streets and alleys, built of stone excavated from the surrounding mountains. The mighty Tigris, life-bringer to the desert, flows past the city's western walls.

In the distance under the red glow of the setting sun is the city's doom: an advancing army, the most powerful coalition of nations in history advancing to annihilate this metropolis and all who dwell within it.

Movement catches his eye and he turns to the north. A family is fleeing into the hills, one of the surprisingly few attempting to escape the impending siege. The man leading them turns and stares at the city below. The gentle breeze rustles his hair and clothing. He pauses for a moment, gazing with obvious remorse at the city that had been his home. With a slight wave of his hand, almost as if he is saying farewell, the man turns and ushers his family into the hills now known as the Kurdish mountains.

The dreamer's gaze returns to the city and the scene changes. The city melts into vapor, vanishing into the mists of time. From the haze emerges the modern day ruins of Nineveh, an unimpressive collection of grass and dirt covered mounds the only evidence of the once great city's existence.

He surveys his surroundings, soaking in the lay of the land, inexplicably knowing the exact distance to the river and to the distant mountains. He also recognizes two mounds: Kuyunjik, the former site of one of Nineveh's many palaces, and Nebi Yunus, which once housed the king's arsenal . To the north, exactly one mile away, he recognizes a familiar copse of trees. Within them is an entrance to subterranean passageways. How he knows this is a mystery to him. The landscape surrounding the thicket is dappled with trees and green grass, in sharp contrast to the desert beyond the river.

Abrupt movement grabs his eye as a large white bird launches itself from the branches of one of the trees in the copse. He believes it to be a large pigeon or dove, but as it draws closer he can see details: powerful wings, large claws, the head of a raptor. A body designed for hunting. The unmistakable cry of a hawk pierces the air. A white hawk? He didn't know they existed. The bird flies toward him, the beating of its powerful wings draws closer and closer. He realizes the bird is immense, one of its claws could engulf his head. It is almost on top of him, claws reaching. He wants to flee, but some unseen force holds him immovable. His heart beats to a crescendo in his chest as the bird of prey reaches for him, talons extended. He braces for the pain, waiting for the claws to rend his skin. But it doesn't come. Before his eyes, the hawk dematerializes into vapor; in its place a face appears. The face is angular and dark, the predatory eyes bear into him with malevolence, its features even more savage than that of the great bird. It vanishes as quickly as it appeared.

With a jerk, he is ripped from his hillside perch, pulled up and away so sharply his stomach feels as if it remains on the ground below.

Hovering high over Iraq, he sees the lines of destructive fire begin to spread from Nineveh. Like before, streaks of flame move to an area he believes is northeastern Syria, from there, as before, lines of destructive fire spread to Israel and Jordan, then over the Atlantic Ocean.

This time, however, it doesn't end there. To his horror, destructive flames flare from Israel and strike first Syria, then all the countries surrounding them. In the distance, an immense cord of fire blazes from across the Atlantic Ocean.

Fire erupts from the east. A conflagration rages across the globe until the world is engulfed in an inferno.

Fear courses through his veins, knotting his stomach. Man's worst nightmare. Nuclear Armageddon.

A disembodied voice speaks. "You must make him believe."

The sky, the earth below, and the flames consuming it disappear into mist. The mist parts. He stands on the roof of a ramshackle adobe dwelling looking over a one street village. No lights are visible. The only light is provided by the stars. The town is surrounded by lush green hills, dense with towering trees. The silence is broken by gunfire and yells.

On the dirt lane winding through the village, two men run past followed by shots. They near the edge of the village and soldiers pour into view, rushing after the fleeing men, automatic rifles spitting fire after them. One of the men stumbles and a wound in the leg forces him to the ground. His companion whirls at his cry and rips free a machine pistol carried on a strap over his shoulder. He kneels by his fallen companion and strafes the pursuing soldiers. Several fall and the rest duck for cover. The man releases his weapon, allowing it to hang free from his shoulder. He grabs his wounded comrade by an arm and maneuvers him onto his shoulder. With a final burst of shots he runs into the darkness the other man on his shoulder.

"Tell him you know about the scar on his leg. Tell him it happened in Nicaragua in nineteen eighty-six. He will believe."

The village vanishes and the dreamer sees himself lying on the bed, sheets twisted from his tossing and turning.

"You must save them. You must save him."

As the ethereal words float to his ears, Derek Galloway's image forms in his mind. "To save them you must save him. Go with him to the great city, Nineveh. Jonah three, three." The dreamer plunges toward the bed and raises his arms to cover his head. He opens his mouth to scream but no sound escapes.

Aaron bolted upright. Cold sweat covered him, an occurrence that was becoming all too familiar. Maybe he should go to bed with a towel. He rubbed the sleep from his eyes with the palm of his hand, flicked on the bedside lamp, and retrieved the Bible on the nightstand. Thumbing through the pages, he found the book of Jonah. He located chapter three, verse three and read the first line of the passage: "Jonah obeyed the word of the LORD and went to Nineveh." He pressed the book shut between his palms, hard enough for the pages to snap. Clutching the Bible to his chest, he stared at the wall. He was supposed to go to Nineveh? In the midst of a war? He was supposed to save Derek? Not likely. Aaron's heartbeat, just beginning to slow from the nightmare—the dream, the vision—began to thump again in his chest. His lungs heaved as if from running.

Nineveh? Me? No.

He flung the sheet off and fell to his knees. Clutching the Bible between his palms, he took a position of supplication. For the first time in his adult life, he prayed. *Lord, I don't know what to say. I don't know how this works. Please. Help me.*

* * * * * *

A tap on the door ripped him from slumber, interrupted sleep apparently being his new lot in life. Aaron groaned and raised his head from the pillow. He had been sleeping hard and was momentarily disoriented. His head was thick and it seemed as if he had just fallen asleep. The sun streaming through the windows told him it was early morning.

He swung his legs over the side of the bed and stepped toward the door. "Coming." He ran his hands through his hair, attempting to straighten it. He opened the door expecting Derek but was surprised to see Hal Bouie. He looked exhausted.

"Aaron, I'm sorry to wake you so early, but you have thirty minutes. You have just enough time to grab a shower and get to the commissary for some breakfast. I need to ask you a few more questions."

Stifling a yawn, Aaron looked Hal in the eye. "Okay."

"I'll come get you in the commissary."

"Hal." Aaron turned to grab his shaving kit from his bag. "I had another . . . dream." He turned to face the man. "I may know what Hawk looks like after all."

Hal stared back, his face impassive. "Um . . . sure. We'll talk about it later." His tone said what his face didn't. He still thought Aaron was a crackpot.

CHAPTER XVI

THE chapel was quiet and tranquil. Sun filtered through the lone window behind the podium, its rays caused floating dust particles to glow like thousands of small moons. Six pews covered in emerald green cloth were all empty. Derek was the room's lone occupant.

There were no religious symbols in evidence since the small sanctuary was for the use of all CIA employees, regardless of theology or denomination. But that didn't matter; the room provided a place of peace and tranquility. He knelt in front of the podium, clutched the small silver cross attached to the chain on his neck, and bowed his head.

Lord, grant me wisdom. Guide and direct me. Give me the courage to do what I have to do.

He opened his eyes, took a deep breath, and raised his head. The sun's rays fell warm against his face. Thoughts of Aaron Henderson occupied his mind. The dreams fascinated Derek and he hoped they would have a chance to discuss them more before he left for Fort Bragg.

Derek wondered again if maybe, just maybe, he was in the presence of a man in communication with God. Could he be witnessing a miracle? A testimony to the power of God? A miracle to rival those in the age of miracles?

He rose from the floor with a shake of his head. Using his thumb and forefinger, he pinched the crease of his dress uniform trousers, pressing the wrinkles from the knees. He tugged the bottom of his formal tunic and flattened the front with the palm of his hand. Satisfied that he was presentable, he retrieved his hat from a pew and tucked it under his arm. Turning on the heel of his gleaming black shoes, he exited the chapel.

* * * * *

Aaron followed Hal through a set of thick wooden double doors. The conference room was quite large; in the center sat a table big enough to accommodate twenty or so people. Two of the chairs were occupied.

Captain Derek Galloway wore a dress military uniform and leaned his elbows on the table, hands clasped in front him. He smiled. "Good morning."

Aaron nodded in greeting. The other occupant was a young blond man with glasses, half hidden behind a mass of computer equipment and a video camera. He didn't speak and wasn't introduced.

Hal led him to a chair across the table from Derek, and pulled it out. "Have a seat." He walked around the table and plopped into the chair next to Derek. "Okay. I want you to go through your story again."

"Is this really necessary?" Derek said.

Hal didn't respond. He just nodded to the young man who stood and moved toward Aaron. "He's going to attach some electrodes to your skin," Hal said. "It won't hurt. Among other things, this equipment serves as a sophisticated lie detector."

Derek leaned back and crossed his arms. He appeared disgusted.

As Hal spoke, the young man hooked Aaron to electrodes on the arms, chest, neck, and head, then plugged the wires into the equipment on the table. Aaron settled back into the chair and tried to relax. Was it hot in here? He was starting to sweat.

* * * * * *

Hussaam stared at the New York skyline from the balcony of the Four Seasons penthouse. He clenched the railing like a vice for a moment and relaxed. Squeezed and relaxed. He realized what he was doing and released the rail.

In the room behind him, his bodyguards dragged the furniture to the edge of the walls. Hussaam was leaving for Memphis soon and his nerves were raw. He was close, very close. Now there was an unknown element, a loose thread, a fly in the ointment. A threat? As yet unknown. That was the problem; he didn't like unknowns. He pounded the railing with a fist. The sounds of moving furniture ceased, and he stepped through the sliding glass doors. He needed to take the edge off to allow clear thinking and focus. To remain sharp.

His protectors stood with their arms crossed, waiting a command. Hussaam motioned Basil to the center of the room, and Rashad moved against the wall. Easing into defensive postures, Hussaam and Basil circled each other. Each feinted attacks, searching for an opening.

The bigger man lunged at Hussaam, attempting to grab and use his bulk to advantage. Hussaam stepped to the left at a forty-five degree angle, pushed the hands away, and blasted a roundhouse kick into the man's stomach. The kick wasn't pulled, he delivered it with full power. The top of his foot made a satisfying smack as it impacted, doubling Basil over.

A hiss of escaping air was the only sign any pain was inflicted. By Basil's standards, it was almost a scream of anguish.

Expecting the counterattack, Hussaam saw the kick coming and easily deflected it as he stepped away. As Basil retracted his right foot, his right hand followed with a vicious overhand punch. Hussaam stepped in, deflecting and grabbing the arm with his left hand. He bent slightly and heaved the man onto his right hip, throwing him to the floor.

Hussaam shifted into a defensive position, and his thoughts wandered back to the X factor that had been introduced. Nine men had been sent to Mississippi. One was dead, eight were in custody.

This loose thread would soon be tied. As much faith as he had in his comrade, some things were better done himself. Once Basil gained his feet and moved out of the way, Hussaam motioned Rashad to the center of the room

CHAPTER XVII

WHILE Aaron re-told his story, Hal alternately stared from him to the monitor screen. Thermal imaging showed the man's silhouette in hues of red, yellow, green, and blue. The device was state-of-the-art, utilizing a combination of voice stress analysis, functional magnetic resonance imaging, and electroencephalography. When Aaron finished, adding a new bit of delusion from last night, Hal turned to the tech. "Well?"

"He's telling the truth." The tech moved around the table to remove the electrodes from Aaron.

Hal stood, loosened his tie, and clasped his hands behind his back. He strolled around the table. Okay, just because Aaron believed what he said didn't make it true. Would it hurt to check it out? This was too crazy. Hal had gotten where he was by analyzing and acting on facts. *Facts.* Sure, intel often came from unlikely sources. But this. This insane hoo-doo. He just couldn't bring himself to buy it. No. He couldn't risk his career on this. He had a family to think about now. Even with Tim in his corner, he believed director Russell wanted his head. And Hal didn't know how loyal the president remained to him. With the DNI chewing his ear, would he intercede on Hal's behalf if he fouled up? Since he couldn't be sure, he made up his mind. "Aaron, I appreciate your help. We'll take it from here. I think it's time we sent you home."

"So that' it's it?" Aaron said. "You're just going to blow me off?"

Yes. "No," Hal said. "We'll take the information you gave us and act appropriately. Don't worry."

Aaron stood and jabbed a finger toward Hal. "Don't worry. Easy for you to say. People tried to kill me." Aaron drew in a breath and sat down. "Look, I understand. If I were you, I would think I'm crazy, too. But, come on. How do you explain this?"

Hal searched for an answer but couldn't find one.

Aaron walked to the window. He bent his head and rubbed his temples with the tips of his fingers then turned and snapped his fingers. "Wait." He stared into Hal's eyes. "Your leg. You have a bullet scar. You got it in Nicaragua in 1986."

Hal stared, realizing his mouth hung open. "What? You couldn't . . ." Hal turned to the tech. "Will you excuse us?"

The young man nodded and walked out of the conference room.

Hal turned to Aaron. "How could you know about that?" Maybe five people in the world knew about it. All of them with high echelon security clearance. And two of the people aware of the incident were there.

"The same way I know everything else. The dreams."

Awed and staring at the man who just revealed something he couldn't know, Hal's thoughts swirled. Nicaragua. 1986 . . .

He and Tim had been in a small village on the mosquito near the Caribbean Sea in the *Puerto Cabezas* region. The town was a collection of ramshackle wood and adobe dwellings, home to poor and desperate people. The area was controlled by the *Frente Sandinista de Liberación Nacional*, the Sandinista National Liberation Front. Most knew them simply as the *"Sandinistas."* They fought a bitter revolution against the Nicaraguan government in the seventies, finally seizing power in 1979. In 1981, President Reagan condemned them for joining with Cuba in supporting Marxist revolutionary movements in other Latin American countries. The president authorized the CIA to begin arming and training the *contrarrevolucionarios,* the anti-communist counter revolutionaries who became known as the *"Contras."*

Hal and Tim had been arranging for a shipment of arms to reach a contingent of peasant military Contras, anxious to strike at their enemies. The air had smelled clean, purified by a recent rain shower. The streets were quiet and mud squelched beneath their feet. Not so much as a barking dog broke the silence. A rain-scented breeze caressed Hal's face. He sniffed the air and caught a faint whiff, a tinge, beneath the freshness. He angled his nose to better catch the wind. Beneath the fresh scent the unmistakable aroma of burned flesh. He reached over and tapped a finger twice against the back of Tim's hand.

Their contact and an interpreter led them into a crumbling ruin of a cantina. The need for an interpreter was a ruse; Hal and Tim spoke flawless Spanish.

They were ordered to remove their weapons and they complied, removing the straps of their small ARES FMG submachine guns and laying them on the table. Next they removed the holstered forty-fives at their belts. They weren't patted down. The man posing as their contact would live a while longer. The second Hal stepped into the candlelit remains of the bar he realized his nose hadn't misled him. It was a trap. If any of the villagers remained alive, they would be far away by now. At a center table sat a dark skinned man, upper lip covered with a black *mustacho*, dressed in an olive drab military uniform. No peasant he, but a Sandinistan officer. Lounging around the room, soldiers with similar, if more shabby, uniforms, stared at them through black eyes glistening in the candlelight. All carried rifles.

The officer smiled, his jagged teeth gleaming against his dark skin. Hal crossed his arms and slid his hand beneath his unbuttoned shirt.

In broken English the officer informed them of their fate. "I will enjoy this. Watching you dogs scream what you know. Begging me for mercy."

When he tilted his head back to laugh, Hal whipped a Glock 18 from the holster under his arm and put a bullet in his forehead. Hal thumbed the selector switch and put the pistol on full automatic. He sprayed the room with bullets, and Tim's gun joined the barrage.

They fled from the room, gunfire bursting around them. As they passed the table, they grabbed their other weapons and ran into the street. Both men sprinted toward the outskirts of the village where there Jeep waited, hidden in the edge of the jungle. Yells and shots pursued them as Sandinista troops poured in to the streets. As he stepped to round the corner of a building and melt into the night, fire erupted in Hal's leg and he went down. Tim turned to lay down cover fire, momentarily driving back their pursuers. He scooped Hal up, fired again, and carried him to safety. Tim dressed Hal's wounds in the sheltered roots of a giant tree. Sandinista troops guarded their Jeep, so they had been forced to crawl through the jungle, avoiding patrols and snakes the entire night, until they reached their rendezvous point and called the chopper. Tim had dragged and carried Hal the entire way.

* * * * * *

"Well?" Aaron said. "Is it true? Did you get injured in Nicaragua?"

Hal's face had gone pale and he stared blankly. Aaron knew his words had hit home.

"Hal?" Derek said.

Rubbing a hand across his forehead Hal exhaled, seeming to deflate. "Geez. This just isn't possible. This can't be happening."

"Look," Aaron said, "something is or was going on in Nineveh. At least attempt to verify my story. Send someone to take a look. If you find anything, you'll know whether this is as insane as it sounds."

"Why don't you give us a minute, Aaron?" Derek said.

"Okay." Aaron moved to the door and grabbed the handle.

"I can't believe I'm even asking this," Hal said, "but do you think you can give a description of the guy you think is the Hawk to a sketch artist?"

"I think so."

"I'll have one sent down."

* * * * * *

After fifteen minutes of pacing in the hall, Derek invited Aaron to back into the conference room. He took a seat and leaned his forearms on the table.

"We're sending a team to check out Nineveh," Hal said. "Do you think you can pinpoint the location of the entrance on a map?"

"Maybe." Aaron glanced at the table then brought his eyes up to meet Hal's. "Are you sending Derek to Nineveh?"

The two men exchanged a quick look. "Why do you ask?" Derek said.

Turning to meet his eyes, Aaron said, "It's important. Please."

"Yes," Hal said. "I'm sending his team."

Aaron swallowed. His pulse quickened and a knot formed in his stomach. He couldn't believe what he was about to say. "I have to go with him."

"I really don't think that's a good idea," Hal said. "In a long list of bad ideas, that's got to be at the top."

"Wait a minute, Hal," Derek said. "Aaron, why do you think you have to go?"

Aaron debated whether or not to reveal everything said to him in the dream, but something held him back. "If I don't go, the mission will fail. Don't ask me how or why. I don't really know. I just know I'm supposed to go."

"You realize you're asking to go to a country in the middle of a war," Hal said.

Aaron nodded.

"No. I'm going to have enough trouble explaining why I'm sending a team. If a civilian goes too . . . If something goes wrong . . ."

"At this point, he's all we've got," Derek said. He rubbed a hand over his jaw. "I don't like it, either. But maybe we should let him go. I don't see how we can risk not following through. We won't be traveling near any population centers. The area should be relatively secure." He looked at Aaron's face. "If he says the mission will fail without him, at this point I have to believe him."

Hal smacked his palms on the table and pushed out his chair. "You guys are going to give me an ulcer." He leaned over the table and stared at Aaron. "Are you sure about this?"

Uh-uh. No way. Absolutely not. "I'm sure," Aaron said. "To be honest, I don't think it's a good idea, either. I don't want to go. I want to go home, kiss my wife, hug my baby, and resume my life. Unfortunately, I don't have that luxury. If I don't go, the mission *will* fail."

"Okay," Hal said. He glanced at his watch. "You two get to Bragg. I want you prepped and in the air ASAP." He moved to the intercom. "Send the sketch artist down, please." He released the call button. "After you work with the artist, I want you guys out of here. I need you in the air and on the way before I brief the deputy director. That will give me a little time to figure out what to say."

Aaron worked with the sketch artist for about an hour. Using his description, the artist reproduced an image of the Hawk as clearly as he had appeared in the dream. The black and white image staring from the page caused Aaron to shudder. Neither Hal nor Derek recognized the man.

CHAPTER XVIII

AARON perched on the edge of a wooden packing crate, sweat dripping from his nose. He swiped the drops away with the back of his arm. After the meeting, they had flown to Fort Bragg, where Derek's unit was based. They ended up in a large metal building, almost identical to a typical Quonset hut barracks, but on an immense scale. The ribbed metal walls curved upward, meeting some fifty feet overhead. Equipment and training areas littered the floor of the cavernous interior.

Once the decision was made to send Derek's team, plus one, to Iraq, Aaron was caught in a whirlwind. Shortly after arriving, he was introduced to the eleven other men comprising Derek's unit. All were imposing physical specimens and each eyed Aaron warily during the mission briefing.

Aaron just completed a crash course in desert and combat survival. He was shown how to look for cover, evasion techniques, how to react when fired upon, and desert survival. He was forced to familiarize himself with every weapon and gadget the team would be carrying. The deluge of information overloaded his mind. He didn't think he could absorb anymore.

During weapons instruction, Corporal Chavez questioned him. "Have you ever fired a gun?"

"I'm from Mississippi: home of the four-wheel drive and the gun rack," Aaron said. "Are you kidding?"

The stoic look on the corporal's face indicated Aaron's humor was lost on him.

Aaron wiped the smile from his face. "Yes. I've fired a gun. Recently."

Over the course of the day, he worked with every man on the team. All had been curt yet polite. Aaron realized his presence was tolerated, not appreciated.

The sweat now pouring from him was a result of the last exercise. Derek put him through the paces of hand-to-hand combat techniques to gauge Aaron's skill.

"You move pretty well," Derek said. "How long have you trained?"

"Since college. About sixteen years."

Derek sat on the crate opposite Aaron and reached into a gear bag near their feet. When he leaned over, Aaron noticed a silver cross fall out of the collar of his black tee-shirt. He extracted a folded blade and a hand gun. "I don't expect any trouble. The area we are going into is relatively secure. It's sparsely populated and open. The fighting in Iraq is mainly going on in population centers where the insurgents can hide among the civilians." He paused and looked at Aaron. "But you have to be ready just in case. I want you to carry these when we get there." He passed the knife over. "This is an Emerson CQ-7 combat knife, arguably the best all-around survival and close-quarters combat knife made, and you never know when it may come in handy. The blade is sturdy enough to cut through metal."

Aaron accepted the knife. Balancing the folded blade in his palm, the weight surprised him; it was much heavier than it appeared. The dull black handle, even folded, was nearly six inches long. With his right thumb he flicked the blade open, locking it in place with a click. This brought the knife's length to nearly a foot. It looked deadly, like a shark's tooth or serpent's fang. The blade was thick on the top with serrated edges like a saw and tapered down do a razor sharp edge. The point looked as if it could pierce anything. He depressed the lock on the handle and folded the blade into the hilt.

Derek passed over a gun. "This is a forty-five automatic. It has incredible stopping power. I want you to carry these weapons when we get there. I want you to be able to defend yourself."

Aaron turned the weapon in his hand. Its dark finish seemed to absorb the light. The grip fit perfectly into his hand. He ejected the clip and pulled the slide back to make sure a round wasn't chambered.

Derek nodded in approval.

Aaron raised the gun and sighted down the barrel. The sites were almost like a rifle's. Two prongs were mounted at the rear and at the business end of the barrel, mounted between the prongs, was a single metal protrusion with a green dot on it. Aaron snapped the clip back into the butt of the pistol and handed it back.

"The green dot is tritium. It glows in the dark," Derek said. "It allows for sighting at night without giving your own position away. Before we leave, I want you to fire a few rounds with it. All this is a precaution only." He bent over and returned the weapons to the bag. He straightened and then leaned forward, placing his arms on his knees, the movement bringing his face inches from Aaron's. "Let me be very clear. You are only going to guide us. You *will not* participate if we come under fire. The weapons are only for last resort self defense." The captain's eyes bore into Aaron. "You will keep your head down, and stick close to me. I expect you to do exactly what I say, when I say it. For the duration of this mission, you belong to me. If you follow orders, everything will be fine." He paused giving his words a chance to sink in. "Do you have any questions?"

Aaron considered a moment. There were many questions. "Can I ask you a personal one?"

"You can ask. I won't promise an answer."

"If you don't want to answer, I understand." Aaron paused, attempting to choose the right words. "My beliefs, or the lack of them, have really been challenged. In my dreams you were holding a Bible, and I noticed the cross around your neck. Are you a believer? In God, I mean?"

"Yes. Does that surprise you?"

"Well you seem to have chosen an unusual career for a man of faith."

The Bible Paul had given Aaron sat with the rest of his things next to him on the crate. Derek nodded toward it. "Have you read much of that?"

Aaron shook his head.

"Well, you'll find it is filled with stories of all sorts of people using their talents for the good of mankind and living lives devoted to God, including soldiers. After all, what are men like Samson and David famous for? The world is unfortunately filled with those who would do evil and harm the innocent. So, as long as evil exists, someone must protect the innocent." He scanned the area around them, making sure no one could eavesdrop. "I don't know what these dreams you're having mean." He reached over and clasped Aaron's shoulder. "But I will do everything in my power to get you through this." Derek glanced toward the ceiling. "With His help, of course."

Aaron stared into Derek's intense green eyes, and the man's conviction provided him a measure of confidence.

"Enough questions. Get some rest. We're leaving in a couple of hours. I have to finish briefing the team."

* * * * * *

Derek watched Aaron until he entered the locker room. When he was sure the man was out of earshot, he shouted, "Front and center, guys!"

A chorus of "Yes, sirs," was shouted in reply. The eleven men gathered from various points around the building where they had been making preparations for the mission. They formed up in front of him, stood ramrod straight, arms clasped behind their backs, eyes front.

"I know you don't like the idea of taking a civilian on a mission." Derek paced in front of them, heels clicking on the floor as he scrutinized each face. "But you'll have to deal with it." He tilted his head in the direction of the locker room door. "He may be able lead us to what we believe could be a hidden weapons lab in Iraq." He stopped pacing and stood facing them. "I expect you to do your jobs as usual. I also expect you to protect Mr. Henderson like he is one of our own."

The faces stared back impassive. The men were the best, and they would do their duty. "Any questions? Comments?"

When no one spoke up, he dismissed them and reached into his fatigues for his cell phone. Already in operational mode, no names were used when Hal answered. "Anvil, this is Hammer," Derek said. "Have you gotten any information from the men in custody?"

"Not yet, but they are en route to me now. We got print matches on two of them. They are, or were, Al-Qaeda operatives. My gut tells me they're freelance now. But we don't know who was directing them. When I have them here, I'll try to get some more answers." He paused. "You know this doesn't necessarily mean anything. It doesn't prove anything."

"Affirmative. Have you contacted SOC?" Special Operations Command directed the efforts of all other special operations units in the world, and Derek didn't want to get tangled in any other operator's mission.

"Yes. The area you're moving into is supposed to be clear."

"Thanks." He ending the call and returned to directing mission prep.

* * * * * *

Hussaam strolled into his office in Memphis, Tennessee, the home of Hawk Pharmaceuticals' U.S. headquarters. As his operations grew, more of his time was spent there, so the office was appointed to his liking. It contained elegant furnishings: a large desk, fine art, and weapons. His office in Jordan was designed to impress, being the location of meetings and interviews. This space was more of a reflection of his tastes. Hanging on one wall were weapons from a variety of countries and eras: katanas, broadswords, rapiers, scimitars, staffs, and spears.

The office was located in a large three-story brick building on the corner of an industrial complex, situated on a bluff overlooking the Mississippi River. Here they produced and distributed pharmaceuticals to the entire western hemisphere. Memphis was a choice location for a number of factors: the ease of shipping freight on the river, the primary mode of waterborne transportation in the U.S., and the airport housed one of the largest Federal Express fleets in the country. The city had also been most generous in their tax incentives.

He moved to the window and took in the view of the nearly mile wide expanse of the Mississippi River. The brown waters flowed with deceptive calm, rippling with small waves and whirlpools.

His thoughts turned to what lay before him. Soon the throne of Jordan would be his. Israel would be severely weakened by the "terrorist attacks" which would soon occur, and it would take little convincing for Syria to finish them in their weakened state. Egypt would never interfere. When the smoke cleared, Hussaam would be the most powerful force in the Middle East. And then the world.

Everything would soon be in place.

He flipped open his cell phone and called Jalal. "I am here. Is everything prepared on your end?"

"Yes. Everything has been loaded, and the transport planes will be landing shortly. The videotape is finished."

"Did the palace receive our package?"

"Yes."

The king ruled Jordan, but the administrator ruled the palace. Hussaam had spent years befriending the doddering old fool. A gift from Hussaam Zaafir would not be scrutinized. Even so, measures were taken to conceal the gift's true nature. A case of wine was given to be opened for a toast after the king's speech. Each bottle contained a deadly combination of liquid and gaseous toxins. The poisonous vapor would spread to every corner of the ballroom, killing everyone in it and anyone else unfortunate enough to be in the general vicinity. Even if the bottles were not opened all at once, they would still kill. Each top held a tiny detonator timed to go off within fifteen minutes of the beginning of the king's speech the night of the celebration. There would be no survivors. The royal line of Jordan would be eradicated. The only exceptions would be Hussaam's wife and son.

Hussaam turned from the window. "Jalal, my faithful friend, it will be over in a few days." Ending the call, he pressed a button on the intercom, buzzing the receptionist. "Please send in Mr. Cable."

The head of Hussaam's American security team, Thomas Cable, stepped into the room, his pace slow and measured. Hussaam could tell he was anxious and doing his best not to reveal it.

"Are the loose ends being tied?" He accompanied his question with a glare, leaving no mistake what he expected the answer to be.

Thomas shifted his weight. "Yes, sir. The problem should be taken care of tonight."

"I am counting on you. I do not expect to be disappointed."

"I'll handle it."

The man's tone was a bit too brusque. Hussaam glared at him a moment longer then dismissed him with a wave.

* * * * * *

Jalal stepped to the rear of the C-5 Galaxy and pressed the ramp control. With a hydraulic whir and a small bang, the hatch thudded to the runway of Ben Gurion International Airport. The cavernous interior of the plane held eight parked vans, all painted identical to the plane: light blue with a large white hawk on both sides. A customs official spoke to the pilot while he leafed through a copy of the cargo manifest. The list told him the vans parked in the cargo hold contained relief supplies to be delivered to the Palestinian territory. Due to the shortages of food, clothing, and medicine in the Gaza strip, the Hawk Pharmaceuticals Humanitarian Aid Division had easily obtained travel permits from the Israeli government. How could they refuse?

The Zionist functionary shook hands with the pilot. Jalal signaled and eight van engines roared to life.

* * * * * *

Jalal pointed to an arched entrance, indicating that the van's driver should pull through. Forced to pass through multiple military checkpoints, the caravan had slowly snaked its way toward their destination in Gaza. The trip from Tel Aviv took over two hours as each van was repeatedly searched. Jalal glanced in the side mirror to make sure the vans behind were following. A few feet after pulling into the archway, they encountered a closed gate guarded by two men. When the van reached the gate, the men pulled it open, allowing the convoy access to a large enclosed courtyard. Once all eight vans were parked, and the gates closed behind them. Men rushed out of doors to greet them and unload the vans. Once their deadly cargo was off-loaded, it would be distributed to their points of deployment. The local Palestinians used for the operation had no ties to Hawk's organization. Nor did they care who provided the weapons. They only wanted to kill Israelis. There would be no culpability for Jalal or his boss. If anything went wrong, it would seem business as usual for these men.

A black metal suitcase was already hidden in Israel, tucked safely away until it was time for it to be placed and armed.

CHAPTER XIX

JOSEPH blinked his eyes to stave off sleep. Uneasiness gnawed at him. He planned to move Aaron's family and Paul to a safe house in the morning. He didn't like the feeling of having the wagons circled, just sitting and waiting for an attack. Joseph's apprehension made him regret the decision to wait.

He pushed himself out of the recliner where he had been dozing. The living room was dark; the only light was from the moon through the windows and a night-light in the kitchen. A gusty wind stirred the trees outside the windows. The shadows of their waving branches danced on the walls, skeletal silhouettes evoking memories of childhood fears. The hissing of the wind whipped leaves made a noise like ghostly feet creeping toward the house.

David, the other agent stationed in the house, walked quietly into the room. Joseph whispered, "All clear?"

"Yeah. It's quiet."

A cloud passed in front of the moon, immersing the house in shadow, deepening the darkness.

Joseph activated his radio and contacted the agents stationed outside of the house. "How does it look out there?"

"Clear in front."

"Clear in back."

A fifth agent stationed in a parked car in the driveway relayed the same message.

Joseph peeped into the guest bedroom and heard Paul's deep, even breathing. He did the same in the baby's room where Rachel slept and again in the master bedroom where Sarah and Abby were sleeping. Everything seemed fine, but Joseph remained anxious.

He peeked through every window and studied the street, the neighbor's houses, the backyard, looking for something, anything, out of the ordinary.

He disengaged the deadbolt on the front door and pulled it open. Through a full-length glass door, he scanned the neighborhood. The agent stationed at the front paced the street bordering the front yard, a Hechler and Kock MP5 submachine gun carried discreetly beneath his blazer so as not to alarm the neighbors. More than they already were, anyway. Another good reason to move the family. Across the street, the houses bordering the woods were all quiet as well. He shook his head and mumbled, "I must be tired."

The clouds parted and shafts of moonlight bathed the front yard in white light. As he turned away, he sensed movement in his periphery and snapped his eyes toward it. Two men dressed in black emerged from the trees across the street and sprinted toward the house.

Joseph lifted his sleeve mike to his mouth as the men stopped and raised their weapons. The agent in the front yard stumbled backward, arms waving, finally crumpling to the street. There was little noise—the assailant's weapons were sound suppressed. "We're under attack!" Joseph shouted into his mike. "Agent down!" He whipped his SIG Sauer P229 out of its shoulder holster and called to the other agent stationed in the house. "David, secure the master bedroom. I've got the guest rooms."

He heard return fire from MP5s and knew the agents outside were engaging their attackers.

As he rushed toward the master bedroom, the sliding glass doors leading to the rear patio imploded with a crash. The eruption of glass was followed by a black-clad figure. Joseph whisked his gun up and snapped off three quick shots, the blasts reverberating of the walls. Each shot scored a hit.

The attacker fell, but another figure burst through the broken door, firing an automatic weapon from his hip. Bullets showered the living room, ripping huge gouges out of the sheetrock and furniture. Feathers from the couch cushions exploded into the air. As the deadly spray tracked his direction, Joseph dove out of the way and rolled into a crouched firing position, leveling his gun on the man's torso.

He expelled his breath and squeezed the trigger as a bullet grazed his left shoulder. His shot ripped into the assailant's chest, and the machine gun fell silent.

Joseph stood, ejected the clip from his pistol, and snapped a fully loaded one in its place. Neither of the men he shot moved. Then he heard Paul's voice. "Look out behind you!"

Joseph spun around. Another black-clad figure loomed in the foyer, gun trained on Joseph's chest. The gun roared as Paul crashed into Joseph, knocking him out of the path of the shot. Paul groaned in pain. Using the impetus of the push, Joseph again rolled to the side. Finishing the roll in a firing position, he squeezed off a salvo of bullets. The man jerked with the impact of the barrage before dropping in a lifeless heap.

Joseph placed a finger on the neck of the fallen attacker. No pulse. He moved to Paul who pressed a hand against a bloody wound in his right side. "Are you all right?" Joseph asked.

"I think so. It hurts pretty bad."

"Hang on, we'll get some help." Joseph jumped to his feet. "I'll be right back." He dashed to Sarah's room, where Abby's sobbing was loud in the quiet after the attack. As he moved, he contacted the rest of his team. They reported all clear. Joseph stuck his head into the bedroom. No one hurt.

He swept all the rooms in the house and, once satisfied, ran outside to the downed agent who was still alive, thanks to his Kevlar vest. In the distance, wailing sirens split the night air.

Joseph stood, scanning the neighborhood. Eyes tentatively peeked from behind the neighbors' blinds. Porch lights popped on up and down the street. He returned his pistol to its holster, took a deep breath, and attempted to slow his racing heart. The wound in his shoulder throbbed.

His thoughts turned to his friend. *Aaron, watch yourself.*

* * * * * *

The once quiet, dark house was brightly lit and bustled with activity. The home was surrounded by Secret Service sedans, local police cruisers, and ambulances with lights flashing.

Joseph yawned as the aftereffects of the adrenaline dump added to his fatigue. His shoulder was a little numb, a result of the shot of Novocain administered by the paramedic before it was stitched and bandaged.

There had been five attackers. All were dead. The downed agent was in serious but stable condition. Paul suffered a bloody but relatively minor wound to his right side, which a paramedic was working on currently. Rachel sat beside Paul, holding his left hand, her eyes puffy and red from crying.

Joseph spoke to the paramedic. "Is he all right?"

"Yes, he's going to be fine. He was lucky. The bullet took a deep gouge out of his side, but it missed the pelvic bone and passed through. No bones were broken or vital organs hit."

As the wound was bandaged, Paul winced.

"Can he go without a hospital stay?" Joseph asked.

"He doesn't have to go to a hospital, but a doctor should take a look at it. The bandage will need to be changed frequently, and it will be very sore."

The medic stood to leave. Paul disentangled his fingers from Rachel's and reached out with his left hand. He shook the paramedic's hand. "Thank you."

"No problem, sir."

As the man left, Joseph asked Paul, "Can you make it without going to the hospital for now?"

"Yes. I'll be okay."

"When we get to the safe house, I'll have a doctor brought to you." Joseph nodded and turned toward the master bedroom. He stopped and glanced over his shoulder at Paul. "Thank you." Without waiting for a response, he hurried into the bedroom. Sarah sat in a chair rocking Abby, an agent close by. "We have to go, Sarah. I know you would rather stay, but it isn't secure. Until this is resolved I'm taking you to a safe house. I have to wrap up some loose ends here, answer some questions, and then we're all leaving. Pack enough to last a few days."

"What if Aaron calls looking for me?"

"I'll make sure he knows you're leaving. He can reach me on my cell anytime if he wants to talk to you. Besides, when he called, he said he would be out of touch for a few days. This is for the best. Aaron wouldn't want you to stay here."

She glanced down at Abby sleeping peacefully in her arms, and nodded her ascent. Joseph knew she must be terrified. He didn't blame her. Her husband was God only knew where, doing only he knew what, and now this attack on her home.

Joseph knelt down before his friend's wife. "Aaron will be fine, and so will you. Trust me."

CHAPTER XX

"ARE you ready to order?" the pretty young waitress asked.

"I'll have the rib eye. Medium," Tim said.

"And for you, sir?"

Hal folded his menu. "The house Caesar."

The waitress took their menus and scurried to the kitchen to place their order.

"A salad?" Tim said. He took a long sip of his wine, staring over the glass at Hal.

Hal patted his stomach. "That beating you gave me yesterday made me realize just how out of shape I am. Give me a month and I'll blast you off the court."

"I look forward to it." Tim set his glass down and leaned over, placing his elbows on the white tablecloth. "Do you ever miss the old days?"

"Sometimes." Hal's ears picked up the tinkling of glasses, hushed conversation, and he realized that without conscious thought, while the hostess led them to the table, he had marked every person in the room. Seeking out threats, searching to see if anyone paid to much attention, or too little. He nodded. "Yeah. I do miss it. The adrenaline rush. The adventure. But I don't miss the injuries. Hiding in god-forsaken wilderness. Sleeping on the ground."

"Yeah, me, too." Tim glanced around making sure no one was close. "The director was pretty miffed that you sent the team before clearing it with him."

"I report to him. Not answer to him." Hal pointed a finger. "Until I'm told different, I still run the ops. He can kiss my —"

"Okay, okay." Tim waved his hand in front of him. "Can you just give me something? Anything to pass along to placate him."

"All right. Not here, though. After dinner." Hal spread butter over a cracker. "For you. Not him."

* * * * * *

Fire. Flames hungrily devour all in their path. Blazing lines inter-twine, weaving a tapestry of destruction. Eruptions spew. The confla-gration is all-consuming.

Aaron choked on a breath stuck in his throat. He opened his eyes and rolled onto his side, the springs of the cot squeaking beneath him. He rubbed his hand across his face. The hum of the plane's engines vi-brated his body, filling his ears with a monotonous roar. He traveled in an immense C-17 Globemaster, an aircraft designed for troop and equipment transport. The steel walls were lined with benches bolted be-tween the curved reinforcement beams. In the middle of the compart-ment, boxes of the team's gear lay stacked. Some of the other men slept on cots near him, while others spoke in hushed tones.

Fear knotted Aaron's stomach, and he felt as if he had swallowed a frozen basketball. A jolt of turbulence brought a wave of nausea.

"Can't sleep?" Derek asked from the next cot.

"No. I had another dream."

"Is there anything new you need to tell me?"

"No." Aaron flung his blanket off and swung his legs to the floor. "What do you think would happen if Israel and the U.S. were attacked by a nuclear bomb and they believed a foreign government was respon-sible?"

Derek scowled, causing deep lines to crease his forehead. "We would respond in kind. So would Israel. The outcome would more than likely be global thermonuclear war." He leaned forward. "Why do you ask?"

"My dreams. They've changed. Now, every one includes images of a fiery holocaust. I can't be sure, but I'm afraid that's what will happen if we fail. But fail at what? I don't even know what I . . . we're supposed to do."

"We'll know more when we reach Nineveh. We'll figure it out. And we won't fail."

Aaron studied the warrior's face. "You know. I believe you. There's still the chance I'm leading you on a fool's errand."

"Maybe." He shook his head. "But my instincts tell me you're on to something. I feel it." He lay back on his cot and closed his eyes. "Try to get some sleep. We still have a long flight ahead."

* * * * * *

Hussaam hung up the phone. At first a jolt of what could only be fear coursed through him at the news, and he quickly shook it off. An opportunity had presented itself. The best way to mislead was by presenting something very close to the truth. The travertine bath tiles cool against his bare feet, he strode to the door and opened it a crack. Fatima still slept.

Pulling on a robe and slipping into house shoes, Hussaam extinguished the light and moved through the bedroom. He made his way to a guest room down the hall and closed the door behind him. He flipped open his phone and called Jalal. "Send some people to Nineveh. There is a chance the base may be found. You know what to do."

* * * * * *

Sweat trickled down Aaron's spine. He used his sleeve to wipe the dampness from his forehead. The unfamiliar clothing and gear he wore amplified the heat and his discomfort. It was ironic that the heat causing his discomfort did nothing to melt the icy knot in his stomach. He was in Iraq, in the midst of a war. In what was quickly becoming a habit, he closed his eyes in silent prayer. He gave the pocket on the leg of his black fatigues a pat, the small Bible snapped securely within it.

After landing in Baghdad, they drove for over an hour in a military transport truck. They were brought to a U.S. military base and staging area on the outskirts of Tikrit.

They sat near a wire fence sequestered away from curious passersby, and Derek was speaking with the base commander. Before leaving, they had been instructed not to speak to anyone about their mission. Aaron realized the admonition was strictly for his benefit.

He scanned the faces of the men in Captain Derek Galloway's team. The heat didn't seem to affect them as they sat, appearing completely relaxed. With their black gear, black fatigues, and faces painted the same flat black, they looked deadly, like coiled vipers, ready to deliver a lethal strike in an instant.

A resounding boom shook the ground. Aaron's head snapped toward the explosion. It was some distance beyond the perimeter of the base, but close enough for the ground to quake beneath him. Gunfire erupted as smoke from the blast settled. Rat-tat-tat. Boom, boom, boom. Fire. Return fire. He wanted to dive for cover, duck his head, drop and roll, flee for his life, run screaming into the desert. Something. Anything. But none of his companions even flinched. Out of courtesy, Aaron thought, they could at least appear mildly concerned.

Corporal Chavez glanced in his direction and, seeming to sense Aaron's discomfort, gave a wink and a smile. His teeth were stark white against the black paint. The warrior gave a thumbs up and returned to prepping his gear.

The sounds of battle subsided, replaced by the drone of regular base activity. Aaron took stock of his surroundings. To the northeast lay the faint outline of the Kurdish mountains, the general direction they would be traveling. To the west, the setting sun lazily drifted beneath the horizon. The orb shimmered at the edges, the atmosphere blurring its radiance. In its wake was a master's canvas, brimming with color. Vivid hues of pink, orange, purple, and red painted the sky. Wispy tendrils of cloud drifted languidly, their bellies incandescent, brushed with the heaven's radiance. The sand below blazed a golden brown as the air danced over its surface, rising heat waves giving it a liquid and mercurial quality. Such warmth and beauty in the face of cold reality.

Lost in the scenery, Aaron didn't notice the crunch of sand beneath booted feet. A hand grasped his shoulder, startling him. At the rate his heart thudded, a massive coronary was imminent.

Derek removed his hand and spoke just loud enough for the group to hear. "We leave thirty minutes after full dark." He glanced in the direction of the setting sun. "That'll be in about an hour. Check your gear. Then check it again."

* * * * * *

Aaron stood last in line waiting to board the Blackhawk helicopter. The craft was large, sleek, and dark as pitch. One of the copter's helmeted flight crew stood to one side of the rear hatch, Captain Galloway on the other. As each member of the team climbed aboard, Derek methodically checked their gear, scanning their equipment and tugging on straps.

Once he was satisfied, he patted their back and motioned them in with a wave.

As Derek checked Aaron's pack and gear he said, "Again, this is precautionary, but we have to be ready for the worst."

Aaron wore the .45 in a leather holster on his belt, where a fastened strap held it securely in place. He was dressed identically to the other men: black leather boots, black fatigue pants and shirt, face painted black. A pack on his back held compact camping gear, ammunition, water, food, and a medical kit. He was also equipped with a radio, which consisted of an earpiece and a microphone attached to his throat.

"Where's the knife?" Derek asked.

Aaron pointed to his right boot. The CQ-7's sheath had a metal clip which he had used to attach it to the inside of his high-topped boots.

Derek nodded. "If we get into a firefight, I want you to get down and stay down. No heroics. Stick close to me. I'm your momma and your daddy. You don't so much as scratch your nose without my permission. Understood?" He looked Aaron in the eye, the glare leaving no room for doubt about the gravity of the words.

Aaron nodded. "Understood." A push nudged him into the rear of the helicopter. He found a spot in the midst of the team and settled in.

Facing the open side doors, four men, two on either side and secured with straps, held large-caliber machine guns.

Derek jumped in and the helicopter's crew chief followed. The crewman moved toward the cockpit and touched the pilot on the shoulder. The pilot and co-pilot flipped switches and checked gauges. The interior lights were extinguished, throwing the cabin into darkness. The only illumination came from the control panel in the cockpit.

The Blackhawk's engines roared to life. The rotors spun sluggishly at first, but steadily increased velocity. Wind pounded the ground until enough upward thrust was achieved to lift them into the night sky. The nose dipped and they were away. Their flight path was to the northeast. The pilot would fly them to the visible ruins of Nineveh's Sennecharib palace. From there, Aaron would attempt to guide them to the copse of trees seen in his dreams.

The bright moon made it easy to see, but it also made it easy for them to be seen, diminishing the advantage provided by their night-vision goggles.

Derek clutched the mike activator at his throat. "Anvil, this is Hammer. The bird is in the air."

Aaron was startled to heard Hal Bouie's voice in his ear. "Roger, Hammer. You have a green light. Contact me when you reach the objective. Anvil, out."

Aaron gripped a handhold as they soared into the night. Each turn of the rotors thrust him toward destiny.

* * * * * *

Half a world away, Joseph lounged in a comfortable chair, a newspaper resting in his lap. The move without incident to the secluded safe house and a few hours sleep provided him a measure of solace.

He glanced up from the morning headlines. Through a door leading to a small study he glimpsed Paul, also sitting in a chair. His back was framed by morning sun streaming through the window. An open Bible lay in his lap, but it had been quite some time since a page turned. The pastor raised his eyes to stare at the wall, wringing his hands together as if he were washing them.

Joseph was just about to check on him when Rachel emerged from the rear of the house. She nodded a good morning to Joseph and grabbed a cup of coffee from the kitchen. She stuck her head through the door of the study. "Am I disturbing you?"

Paul turned, and his eyes lit when he saw her. "No, please come in." His face beamed as if the sight of her refreshed him. Rachel's reactions were much the same.

The pastor glanced in Joseph's direction and Joseph quickly averted his eyes to his paper. Ah, love. He didn't think either one realized how the other felt. Paul seemed like a fine man. Good for Rachel.

"Are Sarah and Abby all right?" Paul asked.

"They're as fine as can be expected. I just looked in their room and they're still asleep. How 'bout you? Are you okay?"

Paul stood and a wince flashed across his face, the wound in his side obviously tender. "I'm fine. Just a little sore." He took Rachel's hand. "I don't want to worry you, but, well . . . I'm anxious for Aaron. I can't explain it, but I had a sudden urge to pray for him. Will you pray with me?"

"Of course," she said.

Hand in hand they knelt to the floor and bowed their heads. Joseph closed his eyes as well.

CHAPTER XXI

THE helicopter flew along the east bank of the Tigris River, low enough for Aaron to make out the moon-dappled ripples on its surface. As they traveled north, the desert became less arid, and the once unbroken waves of sand became increasingly scattered with trees and greenery. To the east, the faint outline of the mountains bordering Iran were visible.

In an attempt to take in the view on both sides of the chopper, Aaron's head swiveled as if he were watching a tennis match. Details of the landscape were vivid, the gibbous moon and star-flecked sky a celestial lamp that bathed the terrain in a soft white glow.

Derek tapped him on the shoulder to let him know they were getting close. A few minutes later they hovered over the Sennacherib Palace site at Nineveh. The only evidence of its existence was an unassuming metal roof covering the excavated palace ruins. Aaron scrambled forward and stood between the front seats. His eyes roved the landscape in an effort to gain his bearings, attempting to convert the terrain from his dreamscape to the real scene below. He motioned for the pilot to take them higher for a better view.

It took Aaron only a second to decide. He pointed to their right, in the direction of the Kurdish Mountains. The pilot glanced at Derek, who nodded his approval.

Aaron grasped the front seat headrests for balance as the Blackhawk banked and surged ahead. After flying what he estimated to be about two miles, there it was. The thicket of trees. He patted the pilot on the shoulder and jabbed his finger toward it. He gave Aaron a thumbs-up and instructed him to return to his spot in the rear compartment.

Derek replaced him between the pilot's seats and motioned with palms down, requesting the pilot to stay put. Their forward motion stalled and they hovered in place.

Surrounding the copse was a gently rolling plain interspersed with other smaller groups of trees and a mixture of sand and grass. Aaron stared at the grove, a place he had only seen in his dreams. Now it was real, right there in front of him, its existence verified. The surprising thing was he wasn't surprised. How quickly the bizarre became mundane. The leafy canopy swayed in the breeze, and he wouldn't have been shocked if a giant bird of prey burst forth to defend its lair.

A slight crackle in his earpiece warned him someone was about to speak.

"Anvil, we're in place," Derek said. "How long until we have eyes? Over."

After a moment's pause, Hal's voice crackled. "About thirty minutes, Hammer." They wouldn't have a surveillance satellite in position for half an hour.

"Copy that." Derek glanced at his watch. "Anvil, we're not waiting. We're going in now. Hammer out." Making sure all eyes were on him, Derek formed a V shape with his first two fingers, placed them in front of his eyes, and then pointed toward the tree line. The action was repeated toward the field and the thicket. The men nodded and turned to scan the area below them. Derek made a circular motion with his right forefinger, indicating the pilot should circle.

The copter skirted the edge of the meadow, keeping the copse to their right. A half mile on the opposite side near a smaller group of trees, a campsite came into view. There were several tents made of blankets and skins propped up with wooden poles. A fire pit, surrounded by stones, contained a campfire tended by a lone man waving a pan over the flames. A pen nearby held a few goats. Lifting a hand to shield his eyes from the rotor-created gale, the cook stared at the approaching helicopter.

As the craft passed, the soldiers stationed at the port-side doors trained their guns on the campsite. One of them shot a questioning glance at Derek who shook his head no. The chopper continued until the circuit around the field was completed.

"Drop us here," Derek instructed the pilot. "Then land out of earshot." The Blackhawk dropped until its skids were only a couple of feet off the ground. Derek placed a hand on Aaron's arm indicating he should stay put. The rest of the team poured out of the helicopter. They surrounded the craft, facing out, guns ready.

Derek scanned their surroundings like a big cat on the scent of game, ready to fight or flee, whichever was necessary. Apparently satisfied, he motioned for Aaron to join him. They stepped clear of the spinning blades and Derek motioned the helicopter away. Wind and dust washed over them as the craft lifted off.

Clutching the activator at his throat, he spoke to the team. "Stay sharp. I can't put my finger on it, but something's not right." He spoke again. "Anvil, we're on the ground and we're going in."

He pulled Aaron close to him. "I want you right behind me. Stay at least three steps back at all times, no more, no less. I need to know exactly where you are without having to look for you."

Aaron nodded.

Derek held a closed fist over his head, indicating he expected complete silence. He motioned again, and the team formed a wedge-shaped line with Derek at the point. Aaron's position put him in the middle of the triangle. Derek gestured again, and one of the men, whose name Aaron thought was Johnson, stepped out of formation. He sprinted away from the group, running low and so quiet the grass hardly stirred from his passing.

At another hand signal from Derek, the team crouched to the grass as one. Aaron scrambled to follow suit. Their black-painted skin and dark clothing blended with the landscape. From a distance they would be difficult to see.

In stark contrast to the day's heat, the night wind was cool. Aaron's skin became sticky as his sweat dried. Nerves jangled, and he gulped air in an attempt to calm down. With the absence of the helicopter's roaring engines, the night around them came alive. Insects buzzed and chirped, frogs croaked, wind rustled foliage, small creatures slid and skittered through the grass. Aaron's heart leapt at every sound, and his head whipped to-and-fro searching for a threat. At his companions' lack of alarm, he forced himself to relax.

About five hundred feet away, clearly lit by the bright moon and precisely the same as in his dreams, stood the cluster of trees. Beneath the upper canopy where the moonlight couldn't penetrate, where the boles met the ground, it was inky black. The gloom seemed malignant. Each sway of branch and swish of leaf, the raspy breath of a slumbering leviathan. The rustling of the boughs, its sinister voice. It waited. It beckoned. *Come to me.*

Aaron's heart raced as adrenaline was pumped into his bloodstream. A cold lump filled his stomach. He tore his eyes away and gave his head a shake to clear the image. *Get a grip.*

He searched for Johnson, who seemed to have disappeared. Half the distance to the trees, a spectral form separated itself from a minute patch of shadow. Johnson. He sprinted a few yards and melted into the gloom again, a shadow among shadows. An arm appeared from the patch of darkness and motioned them forward.

The team moved ahead at a slow jog. Aaron concentrated on keeping pace and focused on Derek's back. They proceeded half the distance to the trees and stopped. As soon as the team was in position, Johnson crept closer to the copse. He stopped a hundred feet away from its edge. He placed goggles over his eyes and scanned their objective, his head moving slowly back and forth. He pushed the goggles down around his neck and sprinted back, resuming his position in the spear-like formation.

His voice whispered faintly in Aaron's earpiece. "I got several faint heat signatures in the trees. There's at least six of 'em."

Derek raised both hands and pointed to the two men on the opposite ends of the wedge. He motioned forward, and the two men dashed toward the tree line with their automatic machine guns held in front of them. One veered left, the other right, and they disappeared into the shadows of the trees. Derek turned to Aaron and held his palm down. Stay put.

The rest of the team stood still and silent as statues.

Aaron exhaled a quiet deep breath in an attempt to cleanse his body of the paralyzing fear welling up within him. As he pulled a slow breath in through his nose, the silence was ripped apart. The slow inhale turned into a gasp.

Gunfire erupted in the trees. Muzzle flashes flared in the gloom. The small pulses of light were accompanied by the deep boom of large caliber rifles.

A staccato burst of shots interrupted the barrage as the two men from their team returned fire, the rat-tat-tat of their automatic weapons easy to distinguish from the rifle fire. Unlike the muzzle flashes from the first volley of shots, the automatics sprayed streaming fire into the dark.

The flaring muzzles spit, disappeared, then flashed in a different location.

The men around Aaron remained motionless, unperturbed by the sudden action. Derek waved his hand, and the rest of the team exploded from their positions and raced toward the trees.

As the group dashed toward the fray, Derek turned and whispered, "Get down. On your stomach."

Aaron dropped to the ground as instructed. He lay prone and watched as the men devoured the distance with silent ground-eating strides until they melted into the shadows of the trees.

Derek remained crouched in front of him, weapon ready, standing guard.

"Save him!"

Aaron glanced around. Who said that? Derek's lips hadn't moved, and no one spoke through his earpiece.

"SAVE HIM!" This time the voice was insistent, pleading, and loud. It came from behind him.

He rolled onto his back and raised his head off the ground. Looking between his outstretched feet he scanned the field. Nothing. He was about to turn around when the ground near him shifted. A section of grass separated itself from the field, and a figure seemed to emerge from the ground. A man rose and flung a camouflaged blanket off his back. The blanket was fashioned with a thick layer of grass and dirt, indiscernible from the field around it in the darkness.

The sounds of the gun battle behind Aaron disappeared, replaced by the pounding of blood in his ears. He reached for the holster at his belt and unsnapped it.

The barrel of the concealed man's rifle whipped up and centered on Derek's back while five more figures rose silently from identical hiding places.

A warning stuck in his mouth, Aaron snatched the gun out of its holster and pointed it in a two-handed grip. He centered the pistol's barrel on the first of the rising figures, using the green dot to aim. The gun bucked in his hands, the report deafening.

The first shot caught the man in the shoulder, spoiling his aim as his rifle discharged. A spray of dirt exploded near Aaron's left foot. He brought the gun back on line and continued pulling the trigger until the man stumbled backward. The darkness hid the destructive affects of the bullets on his flesh.

As the dying man's five companions brought their rifles to bear on Aaron, gunfire thundered behind him. He switched targets and continued frantically pulling the trigger until the slide of his gun locked open. All his bullets were spent.

Out of the corner of his eye, he saw Derek strafing the group with bullets. His gun moved from left to right, death in its wake, only hesitating long enough to spit two bullets into each target before moving to the next one in line.

The survivors scrambled and returned fire.

"Don't move. Stay down."

Aaron obeyed the order by huddling into a ball and covering his head with his arms.

Derek stepped over Aaron to shield him. Two gunmen remained standing—pap-pap—then one. Derek trained his gun on the last man but was rocked off balance as a bullet struck him in the chest. The force of the impact on his Kevlar vest forced him backward. As he fell, his aim didn't waver. His automatic spewed a final burst of bullets, and the last of the attackers fell to the ground alongside his companions.

With a slight grimace as the only sign of discomfort, Derek sprang off the ground. He scanned their surroundings while ejecting a clip from his weapon and snapping a new one home with a click. He pulled Aaron to his feet and checked him for injuries. The forty-five was plucked from Aaron's quivering fingers. Derek ejected the spent clip, replaced it with a full one, and jacked a round into the chamber. Engaging the safety with a click, Derek passed it back, butt first. Aaron just stared at the moonlit carnage. When he didn't retrieve the weapon, it was pressed into his hand.

Their earpieces hummed. "Sir, we're all clear in here."

"Did we take any casualties?"

"Negative."

"I want two of you to hoof it to that campsite. I want to question that goat farmer before he decides to bolt."

"Yes, sir."

Derek turned back to Aaron. "You all right?"

Aaron didn't answer. He had just taken another man's life. His hands trembled and he clinched his fists to stop it. From his hands the trembling spread as if he were in teeth-chattering cold. His stomach heaved and gurgled.

Derek gave him an understanding look. "The trembling will pass in a little while. You know you didn't have a choice. They would have killed us. Both of us. You just saved both of our lives."

On an intellectual level Aaron knew he was right, but that didn't change the way he felt. It was ironic; he would gladly exchange his earlier fear, which he had fought so hard to control, for the guilt he felt now.

Before he could dwell on it further, Derek grabbed his elbow and tugged him toward the waiting copse of trees.

CHAPTER XXII

AS they approached the edge of the trees, a flashlight blinked, marking the team's position. Derek released his grip on Aaron's elbow and they stepped into the shadows of the thicket. He couldn't shake the sense he was stepping into the maw of the beast. They maneuvered between tree trunks and ducked low-hanging branches. After twenty or thirty yards, they found the rest of their team in a small clearing. Several of them were bandaging each other's wounds.

A team member whose name Aaron believed was Lane, said, "There were twelve of them. All accounted for." The man nodded toward a pile of now-dead members of the ambush.

Derek glanced at Aaron and told Lane, "Get them covered up."

"Yes, sir." Lane moved to the bodies, took off his pack, and began unrolling a tarp.

Aaron tried not to look at the corpses, but morbid fascination overcame him and he glanced in their direction. As soon as he did he regretted it. Their bullet-torn and bloody bodies lay akimbo, sightless eyes staring. Rivulets of blood trickled in the dirt beneath them. Even after the tarp slid over them, the sight burned his eyes like the after-image from flash photography.

His stomach churned and he swallowed back the acid boiling up in his throat. He averted his eyes and examined the surroundings in an attempt to purge the sight from his retinas. The trees towered over them. Thick trunks rose to a dense green canopy waving in the breeze. Stars winked through the swaying leaves, allowing shafts of moonlight to stream intermittently through, dappling the ground with luminescent dots. The thick foliage, stingy with the sun's rays, allowed very little underbrush to grow beneath the leaves.

A large black outline a few yards away caught Aaron's attention, a darker shadow among the shadows at the edge of the small clearing. He moved past the team toward it, drawn. Details of the obscure silhouette became clearer with each step. His skin tingled as if from a cold wind, and goose bumps sprouted on his flesh. There it was. Moonlight flashed, revealing details, a lichen-and-vine-covered rock formation. He pointed. "That's it."

* * * * * *

Hal Bouie paced, his loafers clicking on the tile. He scanned the row of monitors for the thousandth time.

"Anvil, this is Hammer, over."

Thank goodness. "I copy, Hammer. What's your status?"

"It's exactly as Dreamtime described it," Derek said, using Aaron's codename for the mission. "We encountered some light resistance. No casualties. There's an entrance hidden in a rock formation and a concealed digital keypad. We're working now to break the code."

"Hammer, don't go inside 'til I get a hazmat team there."

"How long?"

"A couple of hours."

"Roger that. Hammer, out."

* * * * * *

Derek placed his hands in the small of his back and arched his spine, stretching. He clapped his hands and rubbed them together while his eyes roved the clearing and his men. "Let's get on that lock. When the hazmat team gets here, I want it open. Chavez, you and Mr. Henderson pick a spot and set up camp."

The rest of the group slung their packs to the ground and extracted lights and electronic equipment. Chavez tapped Aaron on the shoulder, and they collected camping gear from the packs. A laptop computer was set up near the door in the rocks and plugged into a camera-like device. A blurred image of a passage behind the door showed on its screen. A gadget that looked similar to a large calculator was hooked to the keypad and numbers cycled across its LCD screen.

Chavez collected the camping gear from the rest of the team's packs and piled it onto Aaron's outstretched arms, using him as a pack mule.

The dark-skinned soldier stacked one last bag on the heap, tucking it beneath Aaron's chin. A smile split Chavez's face, white teeth gleaming like flashlights in the dark.

The two men sent to reconnoiter the campsite they had flown over earlier returned, pulling another man along between them. He jabbered in a guttural dialect. The words spilled out his mouth so fast it was impossible to separate one syllable from the next.

Lane led the trio to Captain Galloway. "Sir, I think he's telling us he's a goat herder, but I can't make it out." He gave the man a nudge with his rifle and pointed to the ground. The man sat down, words still streaming from his mouth.

Chavez leaned in close to Aaron and whispered, "All of us have had to learn enough Arabic to get by. But there are so many dialects, it's impossible to be fluent in all of them. Captain Galloway though, he has a gift for languages."

Johnson stood on the other side of the prisoner. He pulled a large hand gun from behind his belt at the small of his back. "Sir, he had this on him. We also found a radio and some more rifles. At the campsite we counted eighteen bedrolls."

The prisoner continued to jabber. Derek knelt down in front of the man and listened with his head cocked at a slight angle. A moment later Derek raised his hand. "Shh."

The prisoner stopped talking.

Derek spoke, his words slow and stilted.

The man shook his head from side to side.

Derek grabbed him by the chin, forcing their eyes to meet and spoke again.

The man began spouting out words, waving his arms, and pointing around them. After a few moments he stopped talking and cast his eyes toward the ground. His shoulders bunched as if expecting a blow.

"Tie him up over there," Derek said. "He claims he's a freedom fighter. Here to remove the infidels from his country. He said when they heard the helicopter approaching, they set up the ambush. He's probably lying. I think there may be more to his story."

From near the door hidden in the rock formation, Wagner said, "Sir, we've got the code."

* * * * * *

The thropping of helicopter blades approached in the distance. Two large troop transport choppers soared over the tree line and landed nearby. Derek strode out to meet two uniformed officers who had each stepped from a different copter. The three exchanged words, and Derek returned to camp. Soldiers poured from the door of one the choppers and formed a cordon around the trees. From the other, boxes of gear were unloaded and brought to the camp.

Aaron paced, arms crossed, hands tucked beneath them to ward of the chill. The rest of the team lounged nearby, packs at their feet.

Chavez motioned to a spot on the ground beside him. "Have a seat. Rest while you can."

When Aaron sat down, the corporal reached into Aaron's pack and brought out a shiny thermal blanket. Aaron accepted it and wrapped it around his shoulders. "Thanks."

They watched as a large tent with open sides was erected. Floodlights attached to generators revealed all manner of gadgetry and gizmos extracted from the boxes and set up underneath the tent. In a matter of minutes, a field laboratory appeared.

The leader of the hazmat team passed out yellow bio suits to his two companions. While the scientists donned their suits, Derek grabbed a box and moved toward his team. He passed each of them a gas mask. "Keep these on 'til you're told different." He glanced at Chavez. "You keep an eye on Mr. Henderson."

Aaron pulled on the mask. Chavez adjusted the straps on the back for him so it sealed to his face. Within seconds Aaron's face was hot, the clear faceplate fogged by his breath. He reached to tug at the contraption. A hand grabbed his.

Chavez shook his head no. "You'll get used to it. If you break the seal, it won't do you any good."

The rest of the men, yellow-clad hazmat team in tow, moved toward the entrance door in the rocks.

Derek moved in front of the keypad and motioned everyone away. He leaned with his back against the wall to the right of the door. Stretching a finger, he pushed a button and ducked away, seeking shelter behind the rocks.

With a faint hiss, the door separated from the rock and swung open.

CHAPTER XXIII

AARON huddled beneath his blanket. The team had entered the cave behind the door over an hour ago. He and Chavez were kept in the loop by their radios. The team's movements were hampered by security equipment and explosive booby traps. Chavez relayed information to Hal Bouie as it was received from Captain Galloway.

Aaron was tired and impatient. The minutes passed like molasses flowing in winter, and his mask was hot and itchy.

Finally, Derek appeared at the entrance, followed by the hazmat team. "You can take your masks off. The air's clear."

Peeling his off, Aaron took a gulp of fresh air, grateful for the cool breeze on his face.

Derek radioed Hal. "Anvil, we've got some film of the interior for you. I'll upload it shortly. There's a massive complex down there. We've only scratched the surface of it. The hazmat guys said the air was clean."

"Hammer, good work. Anvil out."

"Can I see it?" The question escaped Aaron's mouth without thought.

Derek didn't answer right away. Aaron expected the answer to be a resounding no. After a moment Derek said, "Okay. Come on."

He followed Derek through the entrance in the rocks. Beyond the portal, they walked into a cave on sand-covered stone floors, past stone walls, their way lit by several portable floodlights. Around a bend in the wall, they arrived at a second door. Beyond the door the cave turned into a modern hospital-like corridor. Farther along the passage, beyond a set of double doors, other hallways bisected the corridor. The searching beams of flashlights glowed from within.

Derek placed his hand on Aaron's shoulder. "That's far enough. I thought at the least you deserved to see this much." He removed his hand and motioned toward the hall. "The complex is enormous, and it will take a while to search through, but I've seen enough to know that this was most likely a weapons lab. Maybe more. Someone took great care to sanitize it. Now we have to figure out what was made here and where it went."

"I know where it went." Aaron spoke the words in a whisper, but they seemed to reverberate off the walls.

"I know you do. You'll give us any information you can, and then you're on the first plane out."

A shout echoed from the bowels of the complex: "Captain, you should get down here."

"Okay, tour's over. Chavez, escort Mr. Henderson to the surface."

* * * * * *

Waiting only long enough to make sure Aaron left, Derek turned and trotted down the corridor toward the shout. Another bad feeling began to creep over him. They had seen enough. Time to let the eggheads take over. He arrived at a four-way junction in the corridor and stopped. He scanned the hallway to the left and the right. No sign of his guys. Rather than shout he used the radio. "Where are you guys? I'm at the first T-junction."

"Down here." A short set of steps fell away in front of him, and about fifty yards straight ahead the corridor dead-ended into a set of double doors with hallways at ninety-degree angles to the left and right. Johnson leaned through the doors. "In here, Captain."

Derek pushed through the doors into a cavernous room lit by the team's roving flashlights. It looked like a large operating room. Beds with straps were bolted into the white-tiled floor, drains beneath them. Light fixtures and large vents covered the high ceilings.

He completed a head count, nine men. One missing. "Where's Wagner?"

The group looked toward an open door at the opposite end of the room. "In there."

"Form up. We're moving to the surface." Derek walked toward the door. It was in the center of a wall of large glass windows and, as he approached, he could see through them, the interior illuminated by Wagner's flashlight. It appeared to be some sort of control room. Wagner moved around within, his flashlight passing over the banks of monitors mounted on the wall. In the center of a room stood a console with two chairs facing out toward the room Derek and the rest of the team now occupied. Wagner moved behind the console and leaned forward. A flashing red glow illuminated his face.

"Captain, it's a clock!" Wagner sprinted toward the door. "It's counting down! We've got eleven seconds." As Wagner approached the door it slammed closed. A vaporous cloud hissed into the room. "Ahh!" His scream could be heard through the glass. Wagner threw up his hands to cover his face then fell and thrashed on the floor, his skin blistering.

Donning his gas mask, Derek delivered a side kick to the glass door. It cracked but remained intact.

"Sir!"

He glanced toward the shout. A solid steel plate had begun to slide from the ceiling in front of the double doors at the entrance to the main room; at the rate it was descending, they had no more than thirty seconds to clear the room. "I'll see to Wagner, the rest of you get out, now. That's an order."

Derek turned his attention back to Wagner, who had managed to pull on his own mask. Derek reached into the side pocket of his pants and slipped on a pair of leather gloves to protect his skin. He took a couple of paces away from the door and then shot forward, slamming a step-behind side kick into the cracked glass. It shattered beneath his foot, spraying shards over Wagner.

Derek reached for his fallen companion and grabbed an arm and a fistful of lapel. With a groan from the strain, he pulled the man from the floor and hoisted him onto his shoulders in a fireman's carry. Turning from the gas-filled room, he sprinted toward the exit.

The steel plate slipped toward the floor. He wasn't going to make it. It was already halfway down.

Derek bent forward and dug in, attempting to squeeze a bit more speed from his burdened legs. As he approached, there was a scant three feet between the floor and the falling steel plate. He dumped Wagner on the floor and shoved him beneath the plate. Hands reached in and pulled the man through. Another hand jammed a tripod from one of the portable spotlights beneath the plunging metal wall. Derek dropped to his side and rolled beneath as the tripod bowed under the pressure. With a metallic groan, the tripod collapsed, and the metal plate slammed into the floor. Derek rolled through and felt steel brush his back and a gush of displaced air.

Hands helped him to his feet. "You all right, Captain?"

"Fine." Derek gained his feet as a muted rumble shook the floor and the walls. A distant explosion. Another. A sound like the thundering feet of a buffalo stampede followed. Rushing water.

He scanned their way out. Fifty feet straight ahead, two of his men struggled to hold open an exit, their backs to the wall of the corridor and their feet against another steel plate sliding sideways from the wall. In a leapfrog fashion, the men began to work their way out; as one slipped through the exit, another took his place holding the door.

Another explosion rumbled in the distance. Then another, even closer. The walls shook. Debris fell from the ceiling. The sound of rushing water drew closer.

From the corridors to the left and the right a cacophonous roar preceded two rushing walls of water, filling the passages floor to ceiling. Derek stood at the nexus of the three hallways between both roiling waves. "Go!" he shouted, sprinting toward the exit.

Two men pushed Wagner's unconscious form between their squad mates holding the steel plate open. After pushing him through, the last two men squeezed into place, holding the exit open. Derek's feet flew across the white tiled floor, the sound of his steps lost in the roar of water. The two waves met with an ear-popping crash and exploded into the passageway behind him. Halfway to the exit, Derek gulped a lungful of air as the wave crashed into him and swept him off his feet. Dark river water engulfed him and thrust him toward the door. He crossed his arms over his head and tucked into a ball as the surge rammed him into the steel plate.

The current pressed him against the door, nearly forcing the air from his lungs. For a moment he was pinned, unable to move. His men struggled to hold their purchase as the water rushed over them. Despite the effort, one was washed through the portal. The door started sliding closed. The job too much for one man.

The pressure decreased slightly as the water filled the passage behind Derek and poured past the man attempting to hold the door open. Pressed against the steel plate, Derek struggled against the current. He placed one hand on his rifle and used the other to pull the strap over his head. Lungs bursting, he jammed the rifle lengthwise into the quickly diminishing opening. As the door closed on the weapon, lodging it in place, he pushed his comrade through ahead of him. Grasping the edges of the steel door Derek pulled himself into the current. Steel scraped his skin as the water swept him past the plate into the corridor beyond.

The current forced him down until he banged into the floor. Heart pounding and lungs on fire, he gathered his legs beneath him and sprang up. As his head cleared the four-foot-high torrent, he sucked in a lungful of sweet air. The leap carried him out of the water and he dropped onto his back with a splash.

Hands grabbed him and pulled him to his feet. Coughing and sputtering met his ears as the man he had pushed through in front of him was pulled from the current. The rifle bent and buckled beneath the pressure and the steel plate rammed shut behind them. The gap left by the ruined weapon allowed water to trickle through.

Water nearly waist deep swirled around their legs. Another explosion shook the corridor, forcing Derek to place a hand against the wall to steady himself. Falling debris somewhere down the passage caused more water to spurt through the small crease between the wall and the steel plate. The place was coming down.

"Let's move," Derek said. They slogged through the water until they climbed the short set of stairs at the first T-junction. Derek stood at the top and helped each man out of the water, his footing treacherous as the ground shook from another quake.

Chunks of ceiling crashed into the floor, the walls buckled, dust clouded the hallway. Derek glanced toward the exit. It seemed to be closed.

* * * * * *

The ground trembled beneath Aaron's feet and dust flew from the artificial cave mouth. His earpiece crackled, erupting with the team's voices, and just as quickly fading out. The ground shook again.

"Stay put. I'm going in," Chavez said. He dashed into the entrance and was swallowed by dust and darkness.

Aaron paced in front of the rock outcropping, staring into the entrance. He chewed his lip and stroked his chin. Chavez gave him an order but . . . no.

Aaron sprinted into the cave. The ground quivered beneath his feet, and pebbles dislodged from the ceiling battered his head. He rounded the bend and saw Chavez fighting to hold open the large steel door. The man leaned forward with both hands on the door, one leg forward and bent, the other straight behind, as if he were stretching his calf muscles. The door swung slowly in, Chavez grunted and his boots slid across the sandy floor.

A violent quake shook the cave. An explosion? Aaron was thrown to the floor. A chunk of the cave's roof split off and crashed to the floor behind him. He covered his head with his arms and rolled out of the way. Dust swirled and filled his lungs. Stones fell and rolled to the ground. One the size of his head plopped into the dirt just inches away.

When the tremor was over, he jumped to his feet and glanced toward Chavez. Despite his efforts, the door was slipping closed. His back pressed against the doorjamb, his arms bent, only a foot or two remained before he would be pinned.

Aaron grabbed the head-sized rock from the floor and lodged it between the door and the frame. He grabbed Chavez and pulled him free as the door slammed on the stone. It remained open about six inches.

Running feet and voices approached behind the door. Chavez peeked through the opening. "Captain, we're here."

"Let's see if we can get this door open," Derek said. "We'll push, you pull."

Chavez and Aaron grasped the inner edge of the door and pulled. Nothing happened.

"Put your backs into it." Derek said.

Steel edges bit into Aaron's fingers, and the veins and tendons in his neck bulged from the strain. The door grudgingly yielded a couple of inches at a time. A gap was created big enough for the team to tumble through, two of them dragging an unconscious man. The door slammed closed and another violent tremor bowed the door frame. The ceiling and walls in the corridor beyond cracked and split and caved in on themselves, filling the passage with debris. Aaron hit the ground in a bone-jarring heap as the ground wobbled beneath his feet. A dust cloud swirled around his head, clouding his vision and gagging him. Rubble fell all around, striking his legs and back. He pushed up from the floor and attempted to gain his bearings and clear his eyes. A hand grasped his bicep and tugged him toward the exit.

He ran, guided by the strong grip. Through watering eyes he could make out the exit and his dust-clogged nostrils caught a whiff of fresh air. He was a few steps from the door when an explosion shook the ground, close enough to pop their ears. Behind them the lower half of the cave fractured and toppled in on itself. Aaron burst out of the cav-

ern followed by a cloud of smoke and dust, as if he were being spewed
in disgust from the mouth of the beast as it breathed its last.

Hands on bent knees, Aaron spit, coughed, and gagged. After swip-
ing his eyes with his sleeve, he glanced at the man beside him.

"You okay, Mr. Henderson?" Chavez said.

"Fine. Where can I sign up?"

Derek knelt beside the form of Wagner, a finger on his neck probing
for a pulse. He removed his finger and placed a hand on the fallen man's
chest. He shook his head and released a sigh. With a light touch of his
thumb and forefinger, he slid the man's eyelids closed. Leaving his hand
on Wagner's face, Derek leaned forward and shut his own eyes. "God
be with you, soldier."

The rest of the men surrounding them doffed their caps and bowed
their heads.

CHAPTER XXIV

AARON lounged in a folding canvas chair in front of his tent, sipping a mug of strong, hot coffee. He clutched the cup in both hands, allowing the warmth to spread into his palms while he inhaled the steaming vapors rising from it. The first rays of orange light peeked over the mountains to the east, a herald of the sun rising to vanquish the chill of night and bring the scorching heat of the day.

What were Sarah and Abby doing right now? It was late afternoon at home. They were safe; they had to be. His worry for them was tolerable only because of his faith in Joseph. Aaron longed to call them, hungry for the sound of their voices and a sympathetic ear. Talk about a stranger in a strange land, he was the epitome.

He drained the last precious drop from his mug, tempted to swirl his finger around the rim and suck it dry.

Derek emerged from the trees with not so much as a whisper of steps or stirring of a branch preceding his arrival. The team had been crushed by Wagner's death, and it must have been weighing on Derek. In spite of that he appeared fresh and rested, although he couldn't have slept much, if any. In contrast, Aaron's eyes were sore and his head felt thick, as if his thoughts were strained through a sieve.

"Want some breakfast?" Derek asked.

Aaron nodded and pushed himself out of the chair. He yawned as he stretched to relieve his protesting back muscles. He was not yet hungry but accepted the offer. Who knew when there would be another opportunity to eat?

They strolled toward a large tent in the center of camp, just at the edge of the trees. Inside, the smell of scrambled eggs was mingled with the low buzz of conversation as the rest of the team ate. All of them appeared rested and fresh. For a reason he couldn't explain, this irritated

Aaron. Of course, before his second cup of coffee, there wasn't much that didn't. He was greeted with nods and "Mornin's" when he entered. The men who had been so indifferent, if not hostile, to his presence yesterday seemed to accept him. The pat on the back from Chavez almost toppled him.

Derek poured a cup of juice while Aaron filled a mug to the rim with coffee. They each grabbed a generous helping of eggs and toast. The food heaped on Aaron's plate made his stomach gurgle. He was hungry after all.

They sat with the rest of the men, and Aaron shoveled food into his mouth, washing it down with gulps of coffee.

Derek took a few bites and raised his head, surveying the group. "The inspectors have found trace residue from agents used to create several chemical and biological agents," he said. "It will take awhile to sift through the wreckage, though. I assume whoever built the complex thought the explosives they left behind would take care of anyone that came to snoop around." He took a breath and another bite of food before continuing. "I'm waiting word from Anvil to find out our next move." He glanced at Aaron. "Rest while you can, we'll be on the move soon."

* * * * * *

The breeze blowing through the open tent flaps rippled the canvas and made a sound similar to a flag snapping in the wind. The sun was fully over the horizon, and it was already hot. Aaron sat across a small table from Derek. "I just got word from Hal," Derek said. "He's agreed to allow me to go to Syria." He unrolled a map and laid it on the table. "Based on what we found here, we believe it's prudent to see this all the way through. We can't afford not to. The weapons created here went somewhere. And so far, you have the only lead." He tapped the map with a finger. "I want you to show me where you think the base in Syria is."

Aaron studied the map. He was pretty sure he could use it to point the way, but something nagged at him. His eyes went to a spot on the map. Fire and flames seemed to erupt from the page. Two words leaped into his mind, seeming to scream for his attention. *"Save him."*

But he already had, hadn't he?

"I'll show you," he said, "but I'm not going home." He brought his gaze up. "Believe me, I want to. I just feel . . . well, I have to stay. What if you get there and can't find what you're looking for? You'll need me."

Derek stared back at him, unblinking. "I *am not* taking you into harm's way again. I've already lost one of my men. A good man." The steely gaze wavered for a moment then locked on Aaron like a laser sight. "We will be operating in a foreign country without its government's approval. If we're captured and they find out who we are, it will be considered an act of war. If we are caught, the United States government will disavow us—we'll get no help." He stood and leaned over the table, his hands gripping its edges. "We would be tortured and imprisoned at best, tortured and killed at worst. Well, death would be preferable to torture. I've seen the results, it's not pretty. You have no idea what you're saying. It will be doubly perilous. The people we're after will be dangerous enough, while at the same time we have to avoid the authorities." He pushed away from the table and clasped his arms behind his back. "I'm taking some additional men and I won't be able to watch you. The answer is no. I appreciate what you've done. We all do. But you're going home."

"No. I'm not."

"Excuse me?"

"I said I'm not going home. I can't. I don't know how I know, but *I know* my role in this isn't done."

"Mr. Henderson, this isn't a democracy. You do what I say. I won't risk your life or the lives of my men by taking you. This time, we know there will be opposition. It's too dangerous. No more argument."

The way he said *Mr. Henderson* was reminiscent of an angry parent calling a child by their full name. Withering beneath the man's gaze, Aaron rose to his feet, pushing the chair back with his knees. He rounded the table and stood before Derek. Although they were about the same height, the man seemed to tower over Aaron. He swallowed a lump in his throat. It was a tough sell; he hadn't even convinced himself of the wisdom in continuing, and now he was attempting to convince someone else. He wanted nothing more than to go home. He was frightened and tired. Fear, it seemed, had become his constant companion. "I can't leave. Surely after everything that's happened, you believe me?"

Derek stepped forward, close enough for Aaron to see his grinding jaw muscles.

Aaron resisted the urge to flee from the tent. The only thing keeping him still was the certainty of Derek's restraint and discipline.

"If I have to," Derek said, "I will bind and gag you and drag you to the plane myself."

A ringing satellite phone interrupted their argument. His irritation at the disturbance obvious, Derek ripped the phone from its spot on the table. He glanced at its digital readout. "It's Hal. I need to take this. Excuse me a minute." Placing the phone to his ear, he said, "I'm here, Anvil."

Aaron released a long deep breath, grateful for the reprieve.

CHAPTER XXV

FROM the front passenger seat of the desert patrol vehicle, or DPV, Aaron squinted against the glare of the afternoon sun. The vehicle's interior was open to the air, surrounded by a sturdy metal roll cage, and its large tires were treaded for traction in the sand. Behind and slightly above the two front seats, a swiveling third seat for the gunner allowed access to the assortment of weapons mounted on the roof and frame of the vehicle. The man seated there scanned the horizon while he clutched a monstrous fifty-caliber machine gun. Behind him a square net stretched across the open rear frame.

The vehicle was parked behind a sand dune in the area of Iraq known as Mesopotamia, one of the world's earliest known centers of civilization although no signs of it remained here. Heat waves swam in front of Aaron's eyes, dancing like writhing snakes. The golden sand appeared as inconstant and liquid as the Tigris and Euphrates Rivers bordering the region to the north and south. Grateful for a respite from the jouncing ride, the benefit was diminished by the sweltering heat, no longer dissipated by the wind of travel.

After flying from Nineveh in helicopters to a staging area, six DPVs had been waiting for them. They traveled in a convoy, followed by a transport truck. For the last hour they had driven across the desert at speeds between fifty and sixty miles an hour, only slowing when the terrain became too rough, as they made their way to the Syrian border. With Aaron's help, a path was chosen into the Syrian mountains through canyons and trails to the location he believed the base to be hidden.

Derek appeared to Aaron as if he walked among squirming serpents as he strode toward the crest of the sand dune. Small puffs of dust plumed beneath his boots with every step.

Sweat trickled under Aaron's collar, adding to the dark wet stain on his back, causing his shirt to stick to his skin and the seat. He wiped the moisture from his forehead and shifted in the seat. The argument on whether or not he was coming on this mission had been settled by Hal, who apparently wasn't as concerned for Aaron's safety. The man believed if Aaron was willing to go, he should; the risk to his person was outweighed by the danger posed from the missing weapons.

There was no doubt in his mind Derek would have physically dragged him to the airport. Winning an argument had never brought Aaron less satisfaction. Woo-whoo and zippity-do-da, he was going to Syria. Maybe to be shot at, captured, or killed. Who knew what fun waited?

Despite the heat, a chill caused a shiver to course through him. He was being inexorably drawn toward a confrontation with the Hawk. He prayed he would survive it. He reached down to the pocket on his leg and rested his hand on the Bible there, surprised at the amount of comfort provided by the small square beneath his palm.

* * * * * *

Derek hiked toward the crest of the dune, his progress hampered by sand sliding beneath his feet. When he reached the point where standing would skyline him, making him visible to anyone looking from the opposite side, he lay on his stomach and crawled to the top. Peering over the summit, he placed the binoculars to his eyes and scanned the horizon. He compared the images in front of him to satellite surveillance photos stored in a small handheld computer.

The mission would be assisted by satellite surveillance. A surveillance plane had already made a pass overhead to inform them of Syrian border patrol positions. Before they crossed the border into Syria, Derek wanted a look with his own eyes to be sure the area was clear. Their goal was a trail into the mountains. To get there, they had to cross an open flat area about a mile wide before they arrived at the cover of the foothills of the mountain range. They had chosen to use the DPVs for ingress since the machines were light and fast with advanced weaponry. Using helicopters, they risked being spotted on radar, even flying low.

They planned to work their way through the mountains, performing recon with their own eyes and state-of-the-art remote control intelligence-gathering devices. The strategy was to strike the base in the dark, take as many prisoners as possible, and haul out whatever they could carry. Anything else would be destroyed. Everything and everyone they found would be brought back to Iraq. They had to get in and out fast, without being discovered by the Syrians. Requesting their cooperation was briefly considered and just as quickly disregarded.

With a last glance at the horizon, Derek hurried down to the waiting convoy.

* * * * * *

From his office in Langley, Hal Bouie studied the green dots on the monitor that represented Galloway's team. It would take them about three hours to travel to the base from the Iraqi border. He glanced at satellite images of the Syrian terrain, marking the team's location against Syrian military positions. Analysts sat in front monitors and studied the data streaming in. A mission into Syria was risky, but he didn't believe there was a choice. Hal strolled around the room, looking over the analyst's shoulders, checking monitors over and again to make sure all the satellite feeds worked properly. Checking and re-checking, he was the conductor and the people and machinery in this room were his orchestra. He still couldn't believe this was happening. Dreamtime actually found a base in Nineveh's ruins. Now Derek was leading a team into Syria. Tim nearly went into a conniption when he was briefed. Sure, the base had been a find of far-reaching importance . . . but a mission into *Syria?* He had cautioned Hal that the director might go ballistic.

Hal shook it off. He had a job to do. Fears over his future could wait. He had hoped for some additional intel from the captured assassins, but none had talked. Apparently they were more afraid of whoever sent them than of the U.S. government. The real names of the assassins had been ferreted. They were all associated with known terrorist organizations. It still remained a mystery who sent them or why. To add to the frustration, the man known only as "the Hawk" had not been identified.

A man burst into the room, out of breath. Before Hal could express his annoyance at the interruption the man spoke. "Mr. Bouie, we've got him." He held out a folder.

Hal accepted the offered folder and thumbed through its contents, his eyebrows rising higher with each page. The information couldn't be right. "Did you show this to anyone else? I mean *anyone?*"

"No."

"Keep it that way," Hal said. "This stays between us for now."

* * * * * *

"Is everything in place?" Hussaam perched on the edge of his chair, elbows propped on the desk. Alone in his office, he held the phone to his ear with one hand while the fingers of the other drummed the desk. *Stop it.* He clinched his fist to cease the tapping.

"Yes," Jalal said over the line. "Everything was delivered. The planes are returning to headquarters. There were no problems."

"Where are you now?"

"On my way to the base. I will be there within the hour."

"Contact the base immediately. There is an American military unit on the way there now. You know what to do."

"Have we been compromised?"

"No. They will only know what we want them to know. This will work in our favor."

"What about the men? Should I get them out?"

"Absolutely not. Sacrifices must be made. Their loss will be unfortunate, but necessary." Hussaam leaned back and crossed his legs, forcing himself to relax. "Wait nearby. Make sure everything goes as it should."

"As you wish."

CHAPTER XXVI

Aaron lay in a pool of ink-black shadow in a small swale on the crest of a canyon wall, the stone cool against his sweat-drenched shirt. He studied the base below through binoculars, its magnified image all too familiar. The base sat in the midst of a gorge cut into a range of foothills surrounded by sheer rock walls. A few crevasses led into the canyon; one large enough for vehicles served as a road. The two lone buildings were constructed of some sort of thin metal, their tops painted the same grayish brown as the rocks, and the sides the same golden brown as the sand surrounding them.

A few small trucks and two older-model Suburbans were parked beneath camouflaged nets. Armed men patrolled the perimeter. In an open area between the two buildings, another group of men warmed their hands around a fire in a barrel. Their faces and hair were hidden beneath colorful scarves called *kaffiyeh*. The two sentries assigned to the rocks the team now occupied were already prisoners.

Aaron crouched next to one of two men placed to be sentries while the team infiltrated the base. Derek's instructions were clear and concise: Aaron was to stay put in the rocks, keep his head down, and stay out of the line of fire. The way the commands were barked, Aaron believed if he was injured, it would be nothing compared to the wounds he would receive at Derek's hands.

Aaron pulled the binoculars from his eyes for a view of the entire base. The base's sentries were cut down from silenced gunfire. With Derek in the lead black-clad figures swarmed into the clearing and surrounded the two buildings. Fingers probed the necks of the fallen sentries for pulses. Once it was certain none survived, the bodies were dragged out of the way.

Near the front door of the larger of the two buildings, Derek leaned with his back against the wall. He raised a hand, and the windows in both buildings imploded as gas canisters crashed through them. Shotgun blasts and kicks removed the two front doors, and men poured inside.

Like disco strobes, the flash of gunfire flickered through the glassless windows. Screams of pain, rage, and fear accompanied the barrage. The deep boom of a single rifle shot was followed by another volley of muzzle flashes.

A hush fell over the base; not so much as an insect chirruped. Nothing moved but the breeze, and time seemed to momentarily cease its forward march. Then, in the space of a breath, the sounds of night returned. In the space of a breath, the operation was over. In the space of a breath, men died. Aaron knew the men were terrorists with evil intent, yet in his heart he felt pangs of sorrow at their deaths. Hopes and dreams, however perverted, spilled with their blood into the sand.

* * * * * *

Derek removed his gas mask and goggles. The breeze through the open doors and broken windows quickly dissipated the gas. His earpiece buzzed. "Building one, clear." An instant later: "Building two, clear. It's here." Derek stole a glimpse at his watch. He wanted to be packed and out of the area in ten minutes. He strode to the smaller building, designated as building two, and glanced inside. Floor to ceiling, wall to wall, stacked crates and canisters filled the room. Some of the crates were open, revealing conventional weapons: rifles, pistols, shoulder-fired missiles.

There was no doubt in his mind as to what the canisters contained. "Be careful with those," Derek said. He hurried toward the larger building, issuing instructions on the way. "Move the DPVs and the truck in. Load up everything but the furniture."

"Sir, you should see this," Chavez called from building one.

Derek stepped through the door. The interior was in disarray. Bodies lay on the floor, scattered papers, open drawers and cabinets, open boxes. It appeared as if someone had been packing.

"Back here, sir."

Chavez stood in the door of an office. In the midst of a room stocked with video recording equipment, video cassette players, a television, and map-decked walls lay a body, the corpse of Abdul Qadir Rayhan, the leader of the Fist of Allah, with a Kalashnikov rifle across his chest. A bullet wound in his forehead had seeped blood into a now-congealed pool beneath him.

"Too bad we couldn't take him alive," Chavez said.

Derek knelt and placed a finger on the terrorist's neck. Cold. He stood and gazed around the room. The maps on the wall were of England and Saudi Arabia. Pictures of government buildings were pinned to the maps. A tape sat in the VCR, partially ejected. He snatched it free and turned it in his hands. He squinted his eyes. *Hmm.* Something just seemed . . . off. He passed the tape to Chavez. "Get everything on the truck. Snap some pics of Rayhan."

Derek moved outside to supervise the team's progress. Clutching the mike at his throat, he activated his radio. "Anvil, we're green light. We're loading up now. It was here. And more." He scanned the horizon, feeling exposed, nerves tingling. "I think I'm coming down with a cold."

"Are you sure? It's not flu season."

"Pretty sure. The symptoms are getting worse by the second." The coded phrase was designed to inform Hal that Derek felt something just wasn't right. Something about this setup seemed suspicious. Hal's response indicated he understood.

"Roger, Hammer. Wait a second." Derek's earpiece went silent for a few seconds, before Hal's voice burst through it again. "Get the hell out of there. We picked up a vehicle moving in your area. It was parked in a smaller canyon near you. A military unit is approaching from the south." His voice faded as if from a poor cell phone signal. "The bird is flying, so I will be out of touch for a while. Watch yourself, Anvil out." The satellite uplink went dead.

*　*　*　*　*　*

Loose pebbles skittered over the rocks behind Aaron, loud in the quiet after the raid. He turned on his side and stared into the darkness behind him. *Was someone there?* He tapped the sentry on the shoulder and whispered, "Did you hear that?"

The man nodded and placed a finger to his lips. He scanned the area with a night-vision scope and shook his head. "Probably just a small animal."

Aaron turned to watch the progress below while his companion studied the terrain. The truck and the DPVs were moved into position. Before the tires stopped spinning they were swarmed and the team began loading them. Like a teeming hive of ants, the soldiers moved in and out of the buildings apparently grabbing anything they could carry. Several men clad in yellow bio suits placed the canisters into the back of the truck.

Derek glanced toward their position and activated his throat mike. "Lookout two, get down here and help with the loading. It's going too slow. Lookout three, stay put."

As Aaron' companion rose to leave, he pointed at his eyes, then made a slow circular motion with his finger. He moved to the edge of the canyon wall slid over the side.

Aaron alternated between watching the team's progress and searching for intruders. In minutes the loading was completed. Derek waved to get his attention and motioned toward the last DPV in line. "Lookout three, get down here. We're leaving in two minutes. You ride with me."

Aaron picked his way over the top of the ledge, careful to stay clear of the side. A couple of slips on the rocky ground forced him to step carefully.

The lead vehicle in the convoy pulled away as Derek and Chavez placed explosive charges. All evidence of the base's existence and the attack on it were to be obliterated.

The transport truck pulled away from the last DPV in line. Parked with its front bumper facing the disappearing convoy, Chavez and Derek checked the cargo packed into its net.

Small muffled blasts ignited fires in the building, and flames flickered through the windows as their contents were consumed. Aaron increased his pace. After the fires, explosions were to follow and he didn't want to be around when it happened.

He reached the crest of the ridge and found a gentle slope he could climb down without too much difficulty. He lay on his stomach to swing his legs over the ledge. A single gunshot boomed in his ears then echoed off the rocky walls. He froze, moving only his eyes to locate the shooter. There was no one on the ridge with him.

"Stop! If you touch your weapon, we will shoot!" The voice in heavily accented English came from below.

Aaron pulled his feet back from the edge and twisted around to see below. He eased his head up enough for a peek. Chavez lay on the ground behind the DPV, one hand clutching his bleeding right thigh and the other hovering near the holster at his belt. Derek's hand was a hair's breadth from the automatic slung on his back. Five shadowy forms surrounded them, all pointing guns. Finally Derek said, "Stand down." The words were spoken in a near yell. Loud enough to make sure Aaron would hear.

The rear vehicle in the American convoy skidded to a stop, the front door flew open, and the driver leaned out.

The leader of the ambush pressed the barrel of his rifle against Derek's temple. "Tell them to leave. Now. If they do not, I will blow out your brains and peel the skin from your comrade."

Derek hesitated a moment before activating his radio. "Get back in the truck," Derek said. "Everything's fine back here. Stay on mission. You have your orders."

"Sir, we heard a shot. What happened?"

"I said stay on mission, soldier."

"Yes, sir." The doors closed and the truck pulled away.

Aaron lay as flat as possible and attempted to melt into the rock. He prayed his black clothes would conceal him. *What do I do? What do I do?* The .45 was strapped to his belt, the knife tucked in his boot. Could he take out five men by himself? He was responsible for this. He had not an inkling of doubt that his presence affected Derek's decision to yield.

Chavez and Derek were tied with their hands behind their backs, relieved of all their weapons and radios, and forced to march into the night at gunpoint.

After the group disappeared into the canyon, Aaron crept down the slope. He dropped to the sand and crouched in the shadows. *Think.* With one of their radios confiscated, he couldn't call for help, and the kidnappers would hear the DPV if he started it. One thing was sure, he couldn't stay here. Any minute the explosives would detonate. The base would be an inferno.

He set out on foot to pursue Derek and Chavez's captors. He just didn't know what he would do when he caught up to them.

*   *   *   *   *   *

The fires from the camp faded and the night closed around Aaron like a shroud. The stars lit his way, but their glow couldn't penetrate to the floor of the ravine. He waded through black shadow, unable to see his own feet, and he couldn't see very far ahead. The rock walls rose fifteen feet up on either side. Imaginary enemies perched on their rim, ready to pounce on him. Aaron moved with caution, stopping every few steps to listen. The scrape of the sand on his boots seemed a clarion call to any nearby ears.

The cool night air was dry and seemed to suck the moisture from his skin. His breathing became heavy and he gasped for air. The sounds of the convoy and the conversation of Derek's captors faded. The night became quiet. Aaron's pulse raced. Every sound—the whisper of the wind on dried grasses, the cry of an insect, the sound of small feet skittering among the rocks—became ominous.

A flash of light preceded an explosion that ripped through the silence. The concussion struck his back like a wave and forced him to his knees. Aaron curled into a ball and covered his head with his arms. Debris rained down, pelting his back and arms. The flare from the discharge caused sparkles to dance in his eyes. Once his vision cleared, he risked a glance back. Smoke and flames plumed into the air over the base. He crawled into the shadows near the wall, exposed by the glow from the blaze.

He hid in the shadow until he was certain no one returned to investigate. The fires dimmed until their glow no longer reached the trail. Once his eyes adjusted, he continued down the trail.

Around a bend, the trail split. A wide path lay to the right, a smaller one to the left. At the junction he knelt down and attempted to study any tracks in the sand, but couldn't make any out. He peered down both trails, searching the dark but unable to penetrate it. He strained his ears and swiveled his head. No sounds; none that belonged to humans, anyway.

He pulled out a miniature flashlight. Cupping his hands around its lens, he switched it on and scanned the ground. The path to the right was churned by the tracks of the convoy. The sand in the trail to the left had been stirred by something, possibly feet. He flicked off the light and put it back in his belt pouch.

Could he catch the convoy? Probably not. He was pretty sure his companions had been taken down the path to the left. He was also pretty sure that their lives were in his hands, their only hope of rescue. And without them, Aaron doubted he would ever make it out of here.

Lord, help me. Please.

He stepped onto the trail on the left. The walls closed in, the sky a thin ribbon overhead. The few visible stars did little to light the path. His carefully placed footsteps were loud in his ears as he inched his way along. He considered removing his boots, but slithering sounds on the sand made him think better of the idea. Move. Stop. Listen. Move. Stop. Listen.

As he approached a bend in the trail, he heard the sound of a foot scraping in the sand. He froze. His heart seemed to skip a beat then pounded like a drum.

He rushed to the left and leaned his back against the rock wall. He stood motionless except for the rise and fall of his chest, hearing nothing but the pounding of his heart.

Against the wall, he inched forward. Faint light became visible around the bend. Raised voices. Footsteps.

The rock wall curved out slightly before disappearing around the bend. He dashed on tiptoes to the beginning of the curve and flattened himself against the wall. He wiggled his shoulders in an attempt to melt into a rain-eroded groove. Against natural instinct, he looked away from the approaching footsteps. The white of his eyes would glow like a beacon against his painted face and black clothing. He focused on his peripheral vision.

The sound of feet digging into the sand grew loud. In the corner of his left eye he saw an armed man round the bend. His stomach roiled as his racing heart pumped adrenaline into his system. He held his breath and resisted the urge to watch the approaching figure.

Finally, the man passed. A few feet down the trail he paused, staring into the darkness. A rifle rested in his crossed arms.

Aaron sprang away from the wall. The armed man turned toward the approaching footsteps, but Aaron grabbed the man's neck, applying a rear chokehold. He squeezed, forearm and bicep constricting the neck, the hold reinforced with his opposite hand. No sound escaped the man's throat. The rifled dangled in his left hand and his right clawed at the arms around his neck. Aaron kicked him in the back of his knees and knelt down. The man would soon be out.

The sound of footsteps rushed toward him. A glance over his shoulder revealed a figure looming over him, a rifle raised high. With a flash of motion, the butt of the rifle slammed into Aaron's skull.

Pain. Darkness.

CHAPTER XXVII

He floats over a city in the desert where heat waves make the ground appear to move. A mighty river flows to the west, its banks separated by a mile of brown swirling water. The city is not Nineveh. The river is not the Tigris. On a plateau near the river, an immense pyramid towers toward the sky. Thousands of workers swarm the area, their clothing in tatters, dark skin blistering in the sun. Two separate groups work simultaneously, hundreds of men strain against ropes, sinew and bone near the breaking point. Using ropes and pulleys, one group raises a large triangular stone, the pyramid's capstone. Its base is larger than a small house. The final piece. Taskmasters' whips rake across the workers' backs, urging them to pull. As one man falls, another is pushed into his place.

In front of the tremendous structure, another group strains under a different burden. With the aid of pulleys and braces, they pull a statue to its feet, raising it from the ground where it had lain like a sleeping giant.

Almost simultaneously the capstone and the statue are set in their resting places. A cheer erupts from the taskmasters, their whips momentarily still.

The statue depicts a man adorned with a conical headdress, his chin and neck covered by a long goatee. He is naked to the waist, wearing only a sarong and sandals. The bare torso is muscular and strong.

Surveying the scene below, a group of men stand on a raised and shaded dais. Most wear priestly robes and hold scepters in the crooks of their arms. In front of them is a man with arms crossed, his facial features nearly identical to those of the newly erected statue. His eyes twinkle with delight.

The sands begin to swirl, the wind to blow, and the scene fades behind churning dust and mist until it disappears.

Another city appears through the mist. This one is modern and glows with artificial light. Glass and steel spires rise to sky, and congested streets and highways dissect it. Bordering it to the west is another large river, its dark waters traversed by barges. The city seems familiar to the dreamer.

He scans the area below, attempting to absorb every detail. Without warning, he drops. Air rushes past, pulling at his hair, skin, and clothes. He abruptly stops to stand in the middle of a large street. Headlights sweep over him, and engines roar as cars and trucks rush past him, oblivious to his presence. The wind from their passing buffets him. He tries to run but his feet won't move. A scream sticks in his throat as he looks up. In front of him is another pyramid very like the one in the ancient city, and a nearly identical statue stands in front of it. The pyramid dominates the skyline, at least three hundred feet tall. Instead of large hewn stones, this pyramid is constructed of steel and glass. There is an inscription in gold lettering on the statue: "Rameses the Great."

Everything goes still; there is no wind, no sound. It feels as if the air is being sucked from his lungs. He feels a blast wave and hears an explosion. Searing heat washes over him, and blinding white-orange light stings his eyes. A concussion wave hurls him into the air, like a leaf before the wind.

When his vision returns, blurred and spotted from the blinding flash, he is again above the city. The explosion radiates out from its detonation point, vaporizing everything around it. Above the devastation, a mushroom cloud plumes.

The blast radius reaches him and he is again blinded and buffeted by the wind. A voice speaks. "Save them. The answer is in Jeremiah. Jeremiah forty-six, nineteen."

Aaron's eyes fluttered. Searing white pain exploded in his skull and he squeezed his eyelids closed. He grimaced and attempted to raise a hand to stroke his aching head, but his arms were bound behind him. He ached all over. Pain radiated through his body, indicating he had received further punishment while unconscious. How long had he been out?

He forced his eyes to open. Every throb of his pulse brought a wave of pain. He lay on his left side, hands and feet bound, arms tied behind his back. Ropes bit into his skin. A shoddy eight-by-ten wood shack with a dirt floor served as his prison. Light flickered between large gaps in the plank walls. A shadow shuffled toward the door and peeked through a slit. Aaron closed his eyes and feigned sleep until his keeper's steps receded. Raised voices speaking in Arabic broke the silence, followed by the smack of hands punishing flesh and grunts of exertion.

Derek and Chavez. They were being tortured. Aaron wriggled on the ground, struggling against his bonds. He had to get free and help his friends. He pulled and strained against the ropes, but it was fruitless. The cords didn't slacken in the least and all he accomplished was to become out of breath and overtax his already aching muscles.

Relax.

Forcing the tension from his arms and legs, he gently tested his bonds, probing for any weaknesses. No luck. He scanned the interior, searching for some protrusion, possibly a nail he could use to saw through his bonds. Nothing.

The knife.

He wiggled his right foot. It was still there. The CQ-7 combat knife was tucked in his boot. He arched his back and flexed his hamstrings. His feet met his hands and he grasped his pant leg with his left hand. With his right fingers, he stretched for the knife. His hand touched it, but the ropes holding his feet were wrapped all the way past the top of the boots. From his position, he was only able to reach the bottom of his calf. He needed to reach the top of his boot to have any hope of grabbing the knife. He pulled harder against protesting back muscles, inching his hands down his leg. No good.

The yelling of their captors' intensified, then Aaron heard a voice speak in English. "I know you understand me, you American pig. My time and my patience are wearing thin. You can make this as easy or as hard as you wish."

When no response came the distinctive thwap of fists pummeling skin made Aaron shudder. How much could they take?

Aaron rolled onto his back and pushed up in an arch until only the bottom of his feet and his shoulders touched the ground. He worked his arms down his hips as far as he could and lay back down. He raised his knees to his chest and attempted to slide his hands over his rear end. He was able to get them to the widest point of his hips but no further.

Come on.

Fear for his companions renewed his vigor. Aaron ignored his protesting muscles and chafed skin to roll back and forth, wiggling, straining, pushing. His hands moved a fraction. He pushed again, straining so hard it felt as if blood vessels in his head would burst, and his arms slid over his hips.

There wasn't enough play in the ropes for him to slip his feet between his arms, but he was able to reach the top of his boots. He hooked a finger on his left hand around the rope at his feet, with the other he tugged at the fabric of the pants tucked into his right boot. One millimeter at a time, he freed his pant leg from the boot, sliding it high enough to reveal the blade. He gripped the hilt of the knife and pulled it free. Using his thumb, he worked the folded blade open. He held the knife in both hands. Now what? He could cut the ropes on his legs from this position, but he would need his hands.

Carefully, he turned the knife so the blade pointed toward his head. He brought his heels to his hands, braced the hilt between his ankles, then slid the blade between his wrists, the edge resting against the ropes. He sawed up and down, raking his bonds over the blade. Cold sharp steel bit his flesh. *Slow down.* The ropes frayed with each swipe until they finally severed. He dropped the knife and sat up.

Aaron moved his hands to the front and massaged his wrists, the left one bloody. Grabbing the knife, he sliced the bonds on his legs. He folded the blade, stuffed the knife in his pocket, and crawled to the wall of the shack. He placed his eye against a gap in the planks. In the flickering light of a fire stood four of the men who had taken them captive. One paced around the clearing, a rifle clutched in his crossed arms. The other three stood in front of Chavez and Derek. Their rifles were propped against the hood of a truck.

Derek and Chavez had both been stripped to the waist, their arms stretched and tied spread-eagle between posts.

Chavez's light brown skin looked mottled and pale, the right leg of his black pants even darker with blood. His head hung limp on his chest, eyes closed. He must have lost consciousness.

Derek stared at his captors, eyes cold, revealing nothing. Well-defined muscles bulged, gleaming in the fire's light as he strained against his bonds. His skin was bruised, and small rivulets of blood ran from his nose and mouth. Aaron was reminded of the story of Samson strapped to the posts at the temple of Dagon. Just before he ripped it down.

The man in front of Derek brandished a knife and waved it near Derek's eyes. "Tell me what I want to know, and I will spare your friends unnecessary pain. Now. What do you know of my operation?" He stabbed the knife in the general direction of the Iraq border. "What will your comrades report when they return?"

Footsteps approached, and the fifth man strode out of the shadows of the trail Aaron followed earlier. He addressed the man speaking to Derek, and Aaron thought he made out the name: Jalal.

Jalal muttered something and the other man returned to the shadows of the trail.

Jalal spoke again. "I will whittle you down, piece by piece. When I am done with you, I will start with your friends. I will leave you alive long enough to witness it, to hear their screams!" He yelled, spittle flying from his mouth, "Tell me what I want to know!"

Derek said nothing.

Aaron needed to do something soon. Relieved of his gun, the knife was his only weapon. The thought of using it to kill, burying its blade in a man's flesh, nauseated him. But if it came to it, he would do what was necessary. If he could get to the sentry with the gun, he thought he might have a chance.

He belly-crawled to the door of the shack and peered through. The armed man patrolled the ravine in lazy circles, his attention more on the captives than his surroundings.

The sentry's circuit brought him near the shack. Aaron scrambled to the spot where he had awakened and lay down, placing his hands and feet in the same position as when he had been tied.

He closed his eyes, turned his head, and put his left eye close to the ground in the deeper shadows near the floor. Squinting through his left eyelid, he was able to see the man pause outside the shack and peek in through a crack. Apparently satisfied, he returned to his patrol, his back to the shed.

Aaron sprang from the floor and tiptoed to the door. With a gentle shove he pushed it open, praying the hinges didn't squeak. He squeezed though and scrambled around the side of the shack opposite the fire, staying close to the shadow-cloaked wall. The rough wood rubbed against the cloth of his shirt, making a loud *sssst*. He flattened against the building and froze, afraid to take a breath.

Footsteps approached again. The guard ambled past the shed within a few feet of Aaron. He waited until the man's back was to him and vaulted away from the wall. The sentry turned, but Aaron drove a front kick into the man's stomach, forcing the air from his lungs and doubling him over. Aaron chopped the man's neck with the edge of his hand and he slumped to the ground.

Aaron sprinted toward the three men standing in front of Derek and Chavez. Although Derek must have seen Aaron coming, his eyes didn't waver.

The men heard his approach and turned as Aaron was almost upon them.

Jalal raised his knife. Aaron turned sideways and blasted a step-behind side-kick into the terrorist's sternum. The kick connected with bone-jarring force. Jalal sprawled backward into the sand, his head bouncing from the impact.

Aaron turned to see one of the other men running toward the rifles leaning against the truck. Aaron shot his foot out in a low sweeping arc and connected with the fleeing man's heel. The impact tangled his legs and he hit the ground in a heap.

In Aaron's periphery a fist flew toward his face. He grabbed the arm, pulled his attacker onto his hip, and hurled him to the sand. He dropped to a knee and delivered a vicious punch to the ribs.

Aaron pushed himself up and hurried to his bound companions, pulling the knife out of his pocket and flicking it open as he ran. Chavez's head was up, his eyes alert. Aaron reached Derek and slashed the ropes binding his right arm. Sensing movement behind him, he placed the knife in Derek's freed hand and spun around.

The two men he had put on the ground scrambled for their weapons. With a yell, Jalal ran at Aaron, knife raised over his head.

Aaron knew his only chance of survival lay in protecting his center of mass. He prepared himself for the pain, sure he couldn't escape getting cut. As the knife descended in an overhand stab, something streaked through the air past Aaron's face. Jalal stopped short and his eyes went wide. He reached down to clutch the knife buried in his chest.

Derek grasped the hilt of the knife and placed his foot to the dying man's chest, ripping the blade free while kicking him to the ground.

Derek sprinted to the other two men who now held rifles. The bloody blade flashed in the firelight and Derek dispatched one with the knife. The other raised his gun and Derek swept its long barrel to the side. A gunshot shredded the night air as the knife slashed in another deadly dance.

Aaron detected movement in the corner of his eye. The sentry emerged from the trail and aimed his rifle at Derek. "Look out! To your left!" Aaron shouted.

The sentry fired. Derek ripped the gun from the dead man at his feet and dove away, bullets tearing up the sand where he had stood. He ended his roll in a crouch and brought the rifle up then snapped off three shots, each striking the man in the chest, killing him before he hit the ground.

The sentry Aaron first had first grappled with after his escape from the shack stood and aimed his rifle at Derek. Another volley of shots erupted from behind Aaron and the sentry fell, joining his companions in the throes of death. Aaron glanced over his shoulder. With the frayed ends of ropes dangling from his wrists, Chavez lowered the rifle from his shoulder, a wisp of smoke curling from its barrel.

The quiet after the action was deafening. Aaron took a deep breath, attempting to still his churning stomach. More dead bodies. A crimson stain blossomed on Jalal's shirt, and his malevolent intentions departed with him. Aaron loved action movies—how many times had he dreamed of saving the day, rushing in just in the nick of time? Of using his skills to thwart black-hearted villains? Now, more than anything, he longed for his recliner and remote. He wished never to have witnessed death by violence first hand. The back of his throat burned from rising bile. *I'm not going to throw up. I'm not.*

* * * * * *

In his office at Langley, Hal Bouie studied the printouts in his hands. In fifteen minutes, a satellite would be in position to uplink with Derek's team. He took the opportunity to peruse the documents handed to him.

It must have been a mistake, or something that could be logically explained away. The man Aaron identified as the Hawk was none other than international businessman and philanthropist Hussaam Uzeen Zaafir. The white hawk on the field of blue of his pharmaceutical company and humanitarian relief force was internationally recognized.

Hal would have to proceed with caution. He called the man who brought him the documents. "I want you to dig deep. I want a complete bio of Mr. Zaafir, personal and financial, and not just what the papers printed. Remember. Keep it quiet."

"I'll get on it right away."

Hal hung up the phone and resumed his pacing. Derek's code phrase indicating he suspected an information leak had been somewhat of a shock. Hal would allow no more communications to *anyone* about their operation until he could talk to Derek in person. Director Russell could threaten and bluster all he wanted, but he would be kept out of the loop for now.

CHAPTER XXVIII

A hand on Aaron's elbow pulled him gently to his feet. "Are you hurt?" Derek asked.

Aaron swiped vomit from his mouth. "No. Just bruised." And embarrassed.

"We've got to move fast. Gather our gear while I see to Chavez."

Aaron scurried to collect their packs and weapons where they lay in a heap next to the shed, doing his best to ignore the bodies.

Derek made Chavez lie down then ripped his pant leg to reveal the bloody wound on his thigh. When the cloth ripped away the bleeding increased, a dark river streaming down Chavez's leg. Derek grabbed a first-aid kit from Aaron. He cleaned and sutured Chavez's wounds, then filled a syringe with a clear liquid and injected it near the wound. He poured some pills into his hands and passed two each to Chavez and Aaron. "Take them. It will help with the pain and give you some energy."

Aaron swallowed the bitter-tasting pills, washed down by a lukewarm drink of water from a canteen. The water tasted like honeydew to his parched mouth and throat. He was tempted to rinse his mouth and spit but thought better of it. Water was precious.

Derek inspected the kidnappers' SUV: a large older-model Suburban painted light brown. "It's too big and heavy to get us back the way we came. Our DPV may have survived the blasts. It's not far. Let's go. Now."

Aaron offered a hand to Chavez and helped him to his feet.

Derek bent over Jalal's body and grabbed his radio equipment, inspected at it, and tossed it to the ground. He rummaged through the packs of the dead men, discarded a few items, and stuffed the rest into one pack. He picked out a black tee-shirt and pulled it over his head, tossed a pair of pants to Chavez, and handed Aaron an automatic rifle and his forty-five.

Taking up positions on either side of Chavez to allow him to wrap his arms around their necks, they stood. "Give me a few minutes," Chavez said through gritted teeth. "When the meds take affect, I should be able to walk."

Carrying the man between them, they entered the dark passage they came through before. Derek turned to Aaron. "It looks like saving our bacon is becoming a habit for you. Thanks."

Chavez gave Aaron's chest a hearty pat, a grin splitting his dark features. "Yeah, nice moves, rookie. We might even make a soldier out of you."

Aaron attempted a smile. "Thanks. But, no thanks. I'll leave this to you guys." As they walked, pain and stiffness set in. He knew the other two must have felt even worse. He hoped the medication would take affect soon.

Derek stared into the distance. His lungs swelled and he released a whiff of air, the sigh audible in the quiet night. "I won't sugarcoat this. We're on our own now. The team has their orders. They won't be coming back for us."

"I had another . . . dream," Aaron said.

Derek nodded and held his forefinger to his lips to indicate the need for silence. "We'll talk it about when we get back."

* * * * * *

They approached the convergence of trails and stopped. Voices. Derek jerked them into the shadows next to the wall and eased Chavez to the ground. He put his lips next to Aaron's ear. "Stay here, I need to see what's going on." He crept away, melting without a sound into the night.

Aaron slid to the ground and leaned his head against the rock wall. His eyes drooped and he fought to keep them open.

Five minutes later, his heart leapt as Derek materialized in front of him. "There's a Syrian military patrol at the base. We can't take the DPV. I snuck past them and set a delayed charge on it. We're on foot and we have a long way to go." He glanced at his watch. "We have about seven hours 'til daybreak. Their patrol is going to be looking for whoever was responsible for that." He pointed toward the base with his thumb. He locked eyes with Aaron. "I'll get you out of here. But you have to keep your eyes on me. Move when I move, stop when I stop. Are we clear?"

"Clear."

Derek pulled both men to their feet. The three of them hiked down the trail, following the tracks of the convoy with Chavez supported in the middle. After about ten minutes they heard a muffled explosion behind them. Shortly after, Chavez removed his arms from around their necks and walked on his own.

* * * * * *

As soon as transmission was possible, Hal initiated contact. "Hammer this is Anvil, what's your status?"

To his surprise, Lane, Derek's second-in-command, responded. "Mission complete and on the way home. Anvil . . ." The man paused, and for a moment Hal believed the connection had gone dead. "We've lost contact with Hammer one. There are two others with him. Should we send someone back for them?"

The man's voice sounded hopeful, expectant, even though he realized Hal couldn't and wouldn't countermand their orders. "Continue. I repeat, continue. When you're in the green zone, leave someone to wait for them." He wished he was able to order Derek's rescue. He was afraid he already knew the answer to the next question. "Who's with him?"

"Hammer three. And Dreamtime."

"Roger that. Anvil out." Hal cursed under his breath. He scanned the images on the screens, the satellite finally in position and transmitting data. The convoy was crossing the open area between the Syrian and Iraqi borders. A Syrian military unit converged on the area. The convoy would make it, but any stragglers might not. "Come on, Derek. Get out of there."

* * * * * *

Exhausted, Aaron lost his footing and fell to his hands and knees. He didn't notice the new scrapes; he hurt all over and couldn't remember ever being so tired. The strong hands of his inexhaustible companions hoisted him to his feet. Chavez, pant leg stained with blood and face pale, had not groaned or faltered once. Derek seemed to have unlimited endurance. He served as their forward and rear scout, making multiple forays into the night to reconnoiter.

They traveled all night, hiding in shadows, behind rocks, and in small ravines. It was often necessary to find cover to avoid detection by a helicopter searching the area, passing Jeeps, and soldiers on foot.

The first hint of dawn purpled the sky to the east as they reached the edge of the mountain range. The cold dark desert spread before them and seemed endless.

Derek called a halt, and they crouched together. The trail, along with the relative safety and concealment it provided, ended at their feet and the wide-open expanse of the desert began. "We're only about a mile from the border," Derek said. "We can't wait 'til night to cross. Can you two make it?"

Chavez nodded.

Aaron was near his physical limit. Could he make it? He didn't have a choice. "I'll make it."

"All right. We travel in a straight line. I take point, Chavez in the rear, Aaron you stay between us." Derek reviewed some hand signals with Aaron. Lie down, stand up, be still, move quietly, and sprint. The three men began a ground-eating trot into the desert.

Sand churned beneath their feet, and small dunes hardly visible from a distance seemed like mountains. Every step was a challenge. Aaron's lungs burned, his legs ached, and each step became a triumph. He didn't believe he could go any further. Finally, Derek slowed their pace to a fast walk.

The sky ahead turned rapidly from purple to orange, the desert around them lightened, increasing visibility and temperature. Derek waved toward the ground, and all three of them dropped to their stomachs. Aaron hit the sand and, still cool to the touch, it was welcoming. If he stayed there too long, he might not be able to continue. A few seconds later he heard what must have caused Derek call the halt: the *throp-thropping* of an approaching helicopter.

The sound of whirring blades grew louder and the noise was soon accompanied by the roar of Jeep engines. Derek sprang from his stomach and crouched on one knee, eyes scanning, compact machine gun held in front of him. The sounds drew nearer. The sun climbed into the sky. Derek said, "They've seen us. You two move out. I'll cover the rear. Go! Move now!"

Chavez and Aaron jumped to their feet. They took no more than two steps when gunfire erupted, the sand around them exploding from the impact of bullets. Sand plumed as the slugs furrowed the ground.

Arms and legs pumping, Aaron risked a glance behind him. The helicopter was almost on top of them, the noise from its rotors and the report of the guns deafening. Aches were forgotten as fear gave Aaron's feet wings.

"Don't look back!" Chavez yelled. "Swerve from side to side."

Derek returned fire. The ground around them erupted with another volley of bullets, so close Aaron felt their wind as they passed. Searing pain ripped down his left arm and he dove to the ground, covering his head with his arms. He cold almost hear Abby's sweet giggle, smell the flowery scent of Sarah's hair, feel their skin beneath his fingertips. A tear trickled into the dirt beneath his face. He prayed for God to protect them as he cringed, waiting for the bullet that would end it. This forsaken place would be his grave.

The gunfire moved away and Aaron peered out beneath his crossed arms. Derek fired at the helicopter then moved. Fire and move. Fire and move. The helicopter ceased its advance and hovered. The pilot positioned the open side door to face them, allowing three armed soldiers a clear line of fire. When the chopper stopped, so did Derek. He hit the ground on his stomach and propped on his elbows in a shooter's tripod. The men sprayed bullets in Derek's direction. He returned fire. Two soldiers fell from his first volley, one tumbling out of the helicopter to the ground.

Chavez pulled Aaron from the sand and grabbed the automatic. The gun spit fire from its short barrel as Chavez blasted the chopper's cockpit. Glass splintered and sparks flew.

Derek dropped the third soldier, jacked a new clip into his gun, and trained his own fire on the pilot's cabin. Smoke belched from the craft and it pulled away.

Jumping to his feet, Derek shouted, "Go, go!"

Aided by a push in the back, Aaron moved, and the trio again sprinted toward the border. The sound of pursuing Jeeps grew louder. Aaron ran with all his might, forcing his arms and legs to obey. He crested a small dune.

Two hundred yards away sat a parked DPV. Two black-clad members of Derek's team, binoculars to their eyes, stood beside the vehicle, accompanied by a contingent of border guards. Hope swelled in Aaron's chest.

"That's it! Dig hard. Move!" Derek shouted. "They can't help us until we cross."

Chavez, running stride-for-stride with Aaron, lost footing and tumbled to the ground. Aaron knelt to help him, to pull him to his feet, but the injured man was dead weight.

Derek reached them and heaved Chavez across his shoulders. "Keep moving!"

They ran in lockstep, Derek keeping pace with Aaron even with burden on his shoulders. They were about a hundred yards from the waiting vehicles when gunfire exploded behind them again. The sand erupted, geysers of sand shooting into the air. The soldiers waiting at the border were yelling, "Run! You're almost here!"

When they reached a point fifty yards from the border, the gunfire stopped. Derek and Aaron sprinted to their waiting comrades, who glared with menace at their pursuers, guns raised, daring them to continue shooting. The three men tumbled across the border. Strong arms caught Aaron before he could hit the ground.

They were loaded in a truck and medics ministered to their injuries as they sped away. When they had bound the wound on his arm, Aaron lay back. He couldn't remember being this tired. The medics did all they could for Chavez until they could get him to a hospital. An IV tube pumped fluids and pain killers into his arm. He opened his eyes and caught Aaron's gaze. Chavez gave a thin smile before succumbing to the drugs.

Aaron's eyes were so heavy, he couldn't hold them open. The words from the dream streaked into his head like a flaming beacon: *Save them. Jeremiah forty-six, nineteen.* He fumbled with the buttons on the side pocket of his torn pants and extracted the Bible, its edges crinkled, the cover battered. He thumbed through pages until he found the book of Jeremiah and turned to chapter 46, verse 19: "Pack your belongings for exile, you who live in Egypt, for Memphis will be laid waste and lie in ruins without inhabitant."

He read it again.

Memphis?

He turned to Derek, held out the Bible, and pointed to the passage. "You may want to see this."

Derek scanned the paragraph. "Don't say anything. To *anyone*." He glanced around them. "I'll explain later. Trust me."

Aaron opened his mouth to ask a question, but Derek put a finger to his lips and shook his head. Puzzled, Aaron leaned against the side of the truck, attempting to find a comfortable position on the hard bench. As the truck bounced over the desert, he closed his eyes. *What now?*

PART III

"Because he loves me," says the LORD, "I will rescue him; I will protect him, for he acknowledges my name." **Psalm 91:14**

CHAPTER XXIX

THE top floor of the Memphis Marriott Hotel provided an excellent view of the city. Hussaam contemplated the scene below undistracted by the sounds of the party behind him. The cacophony of conversation, the clinking of plates and glasses, belonged to the attendees of a reception to kick off the International Conference on Inter-Faith Relations. The conference was scheduled to begin tomorrow, and Hussaam's philanthropic pursuits in diverse cultures garnered him an invitation as a keynote speaker. His speech was to be on the second day of the five-day conference. The president of the United States and the prime minister of England were scheduled to speak later the same day. Attendees included religious and political leaders from countries spanning the globe. The goal of the conference was "to promote religious harmony and tolerance in the new world order of terrorism and religious hatred."

In the distance, its reflective surfaces glinting like diamonds, stood the site of the conference: the Memphis Pyramid. The structure was a replica of the pyramid that stood in ancient Memphis, Egypt. Rather than giant stones, this one was constructed of steel and glass which gleamed in the spotlights shining on its mirrored surface.

Hussaam chuckled at the delicious irony. Andrew Jackson had named Memphis after the ancient capital of lower Egypt due to its similarity in position on a bluff overlooking a river. The ancient Egyptian city overlooked the Nile, the modern one on the convergence of the Mississippi and Wolf rivers. Hussaam knew the Jewish prophet Jeremiah had predicted the destruction of the ancient city because, according to Jeremiah, its citizens turned away from his god to worship the Egyptian god Ptah. It was all superstitious nonsense, of course. Now, in a pyramid built in homage to that ancient city, Jews, Christians, and Muslims alike would share the fate Jeremiah had supposedly predicted.

The chaos would be pandemic. Governments would demand answers, and people of the world would demand punishment for those responsible. In the wake of the devastation here and abroad, Hussaam would rise like a phoenix as the voice of reason, using the power and influence of his new throne to bring together the countries surrounding Jordan. First peace, then conquest. When Israel was no longer a threat, he would use the throne of Jordan to usurp power from neighboring countries. Hussaam would build an empire to rival Caesar's and Alexander's; his people would no longer be forced to cower on a small strip of land, surviving by the whim of others. The cache of weapons moved to his facilities in Jordan insured that his enemies would tremble. With Abdul-Qadir and Palestinian terrorists blamed for the attacks, there would be no connection to him. He planned to lead the charge in destroying the Palestinian terror groups, while relocating the law-abiding citizens who wished to go to their new home in Jordan, he would have no more use for misguided zealots. After an attack of such magnitude on American soil, they would be eternally grateful and indebted to him for "finding" and turning in those responsible for the American tragedy that was about to take place.

A hint of perfume, the whisper of silk, and a light touch at his elbow drew him from his reverie. He turned to his wife.

"Some of the guests would like to speak to you," Fatima said. She inclined her head toward three tuxedo-clad men, the mayors of Memphis and Nashville, and the governor of Tennessee.

Donning his most engaging smile, he entwined his arm with Fatima's and strolled to join the waiting sycophants.

* * * * * *

Joseph scanned the faces of those under his protection. He felt he was betraying their trust, but his hands were tied. Sarah, Rachel, and Paul, seated around the table with him, stared back. Even little Abby gazed at him with solemnity. Despite Joseph's arguments and a request for a leave of absence so he could remain with Aaron's family, he had been ordered to leave for Memphis the following day. He was to head a security team at the Inter-Faith Conference. The president was due to arrive the day after.

At least they knew Aaron was all right. They finally received a phone call from him, although he hadn't been able to give any details as to where he was or when he would return.

"Special Agent Larry Martin is taking over for me. He's a good man, a good agent, and someone I trust." Joseph glanced at his watch. "He'll be here in a few minutes. After I brief him, I'm leaving to go home for the night." His gaze met Sarah's blue eyes. "Even after I leave, you can reach me anytime on my cell. It will be all right, I promise."

"Thank you, Joseph," Sarah said. "I trust your judgment. Do you know how long we're going to have to stay here?"

"I don't know. I hope not much longer."

Rachel reached over to Paul and they clasped hands. She seemed a little less confident in the situation than Sarah.

"Joseph," Paul said, "please be careful. I . . . well, I have a bad feeling."

Joseph gave him a smile meant to be reassuring. "I'll be careful, don't worry."

Paul looked in him in the eye. "I just have a feeling your role in all this isn't finished."

* * * * * *

A jolt of turbulence made Aaron groan. The bumpy ride battered his bruised body. The drone of the plane, fatigue, and injuries should have served as the perfect recipe for sleep, even on a lumpy cot in the rear of the C-17 Globemaster. But each bump of the plane was agonizing. Their wounds treated, and cleared for travel by a physician, Derek, Aaron, and the team boarded their plane for the flight home with all the data collected in Syria. Their prisoners, the weapons cache found there, and Chavez, were left behind. Aaron had no idea what the fate of Abdul-Qadir or the weapons would be, but Chavez had been taken to a local military hospital. He lost a great deal of blood, but it appeared as if he would pull through.

Aaron stood and stretched. A glimpse at his watch told him they had been in the air for over eight hours, so he must have slept. They must be near home, he thought. Well, Fort Bragg, anyway. For the moment that was good enough. The plane swayed beneath his feet and he sank back to the cot. He squirmed in an attempt to find a comfortable position. The cot squeaked and squawked with each move. He was sure he must have woken everyone else. A glance around the cabin told him no one noticed his fidgeting. The rest of the men either slept or read, and none looked in his direction.

Stretched out on the next cot, Derek opened his eyes. "You okay?"

"Fine," Aaron said. "Just sore and tired." He leaned up on an elbow. "Derek, I got involved in all this because of some phone calls and e-mails that were intercepted. Won't the bad guys know what we've been up to?"

"No. Not from our communications, anyway. We've only used se-cure transmissions."

"Are you going to tell me what's going on? Why didn't you want me to tell anyone about my last dream?"

Derek sat up and leaned close to Aaron, speaking in a whisper. "Somebody knew we were coming." He scanned the cabin, ensuring no one was eavesdropping. "To Nineveh, and to the base in Syria."

"How?"

"I don't know. Maybe Hal will have some answers."

Aaron nodded and settled back into the mattress. The overwhelming nature of the past few days' events made his head swim. Talk about bap-tism by fire. There was so much he didn't understand, so many ques-tions. He slipped the Bible out of his pocket and traced the gold letter-ing on its cover with a finger. Of one thing he could now be certain: this book contained the answers.

* * * * * *

The whine of engines, the screech of rubber on asphalt, and the bump of the wheels as they impacted the runway jerked Aaron from a dream-less slumber. He had been sleeping on his back, mouth wide open, a snore still ringing in his ears. Embarrassed, he glanced around, but no one seemed to notice or care. The team packed their gear, preparing to deplane. Aaron wiped a hand across his mouth, longing for a toothbrush and a shower. The plane taxied. Shadows passed over the windows and blocked the blazing morning sunlight. When they stopped, Derek threw a switch. Hydraulics whirred and the ramp at the rear of the plane began to drop, revealing the interior of a metal hanger.

Aaron followed Derek down the ramp. The giant roaring propellers bathed them in a weakening breeze as the engines shut down. Immense metal doors slid closed behind the plane. Aaron shielded his eyes against the glare beaming through them. The doors closed with a metallic clang, and he blinked to adjust his eyes. Neon lights in the high ceiling and dust-stained windows now provided the only light. The interior of the hanger was vast to accommodate the colossal C-17.

Hal Bouie extracted himself from a swarm of suited men scrambling to set up lab and computer equipment, and reached the ramp as it scraped the Tarmac. He exchanged a salute with Derek then grasped his hand in a two-handed shake. He turned to Aaron and did the same. "Good to see you two." He released his grip on Aaron's hand. "Mr. Henderson, you had me worried. If anything had happened to you, it would have cost me hours of paperwork." He narrowed his eyes. "And I *hate* unnecessary paperwork."

Aaron dropped his hand and stared. "Um . . . I'm glad I didn't inconvenience you."

Hal stepped between them and gave them gentle nudges on the back. "I've set up a room over there." He nodded toward a suite of offices on the north side of the hanger. He turned to Derek. "We need to discuss your cold." Hal patted Aaron on the back. "Why don't you get some rest? You've earned it."

"No," Derek said. "He needs to be in on this . . . consultation."

As they moved down the ramp, Hal's people swarmed the plane and began offloading.

"If you say so." Hal led them into a small office space with no windows and no furniture, closing the door behind them. "All right. Talk to me."

No sooner had the door clicked in place than Derek began speaking. "Someone is hemorrhaging information. We've been compromised."

"What makes you say that?" Hal said.

Derek moved to the wood paneled wall and leaned against it, crossing his arms. "They knew we were coming. The ambush at Nineveh. There's no way they set that up in the few minutes after they heard the chopper approaching. Then in Syria. It just seemed . . . off somehow. Rayhan's body was cold. It was supposed to look like he was killed in battle. I don't buy it. The wound was to the forehead. Fired at close range. The blood on the floor was already congealed." He shook his head. "No. He had been dead for at least a couple of hours. And the maps. A little too obvious. They shouted hey, look, this is what we're planning. It just seemed like a set-up."

Hal leaned against the opposite wall. "The only people privy to the op were me, you, and your team . . ." He touched the tip of a new finger with each name. "The deputy director of National Intelligence, the Director of National Intelligence, and"—He directed a glare at Aaron and jabbed an accusing finger—"you."

"What? No, I . . ." Aaron stammered.

"Easy, Hal," Derek said. "It's not him. He's been the only reliable source of intel we've had. He risked his life for us, for me." He shook his head again. "No. I'm sure of it. It's not anyone on the team, either." He locked eyes with Hal. "It's higher up the chain."

Hal snapped his fingers. "That *bastard*," He straightened from the wall. "I knew he was dirty." He was silent for a moment while he stroked his chin with his thumb and forefinger. "You guys get some rest and some chow. We've set up a temporary barracks for all of you. We need to take a look at what you brought back. We'll talk more later. I need to think this through." He opened the door and they filed from the room.

"Let's find the showers," Derek said.

The thought of hot water washing over his stiff and sore muscles sounded like bliss to Aaron. He whispered to Derek, "Thanks. I promise you, I didn't—"

"I know. Don't give it another thought." He reached over and patted Aaron on the back. "It was a little dicey there for a while, wasn't it?"

Aaron smiled and nodded. "Yeah. A little."

CHAPTER XXX

HAL clicked a button on the remote and the TV screen went blank. The tape they watched showed Abdul-Qadir Rayhan, leader of the Fist of Allah, screaming and ranting while shaking his fist. Hal paced, which seemed to be a habit, while Derek and Aaron perched on the edges of two very uncomfortable metal folding chairs. They occupied a small office in the hangar, and a large window allowed them a view of the analysts combing through the reams of papers, maps, and files brought back from Syria. A small window-mounted air conditioner strained valiantly to cool the room but failed. Aaron wiggled on the hard surface of the chair and tugged at his sweaty tee-shirt. After discussing Aaron's latest dream, Hal had played them the tape found at the base in Syria.

"Well, I'm sure the two of you recognized him," Hal said, pointing at the TV with the remote. "That was a taped confession claiming responsibility for attacks planned for tomorrow, Mr. Henderson. Attacks on the Saudi Royal Family and British Parliament with cooperation from other terrorist groups." He finally stopped pacing and leaned against the desk. "But there is no mention of an attack on U.S. or Israeli soil."

His words referred to Aaron's earlier dreams. Hal glanced over his shoulder and pulled a folder off the desk, then passed it to Aaron. "Open it."

Aaron did as instructed. The only item in the folder was an eight-by-ten photo. He resisted the urge to shiver at the sight of the black and white image staring at him.

"Is that the guy?" Hal asked. "The Hawk?"

"Yes."

"No doubt? One-hundred percent certain?"

Aaron nodded and Hal took the folder from his hands. "This man is Hussaam Uzeen Zaafir. He is the founder and president of a multinational pharmaceutical conglomerate." Hal raised his eyebrows. "We haven't found *anything* in what you guys brought back to implicate him or his company." Apparently unable to think while standing still, Hal began marching back and forth across the room again, hands clasped behind him. "The guys who attacked Aaron on the street won't talk." He stared at Aaron. "As much as I hate to say it, at this point all I've got to go on is what you've told us. But without concrete proof, moving against Zaafir will be a tough sell."

Derek stood and restrained Hal's pacing with a gentle hand on the shoulder. Hal mumbled, "Sorry." This was obviously a dance they had danced before. In spite of the tension Aaron couldn't help smiling.

"I think Qadir was a captive," Derek said. "The admission on the tape forced. More than likely to avert suspicion."

"I agree," Hal said. "Qadir didn't have the wherewithal or influence to build the facility in Nineveh. I've alerted the British and Saudi governments, anyway. Just in case."

"What about the attack here?" Aaron asked.

"Zaafir's U.S. headquarters are located in Memphis, Tennessee." Hal frowned. "Mr. Zaafir arrived there yesterday."

"He's there? Now?" The news made Aaron's stomach sink.

"Yes, he's there. He's scheduled to speak at the International Conference on Inter-Faith Relations tomorrow morning. Along with an international contingent of religious leaders, the prime minister of England, and the president—yes, the president—are also scheduled to speak at the conference tomorrow."

"You have to call the conference off!" Aaron said. "You can't let the president go. The city has to be evacuated!"

"I'm sorry, Aaron, it doesn't work that way. There are threats both real and imagined, some serious and some not, made on the president's life every day. There are threats made to this country every day. It's our job to stop them. To separate reality from fiction. We can't clear a city every time there's a threat unless we have *actionable* intelligence. It's the Secret Service's job to protect the president. They've been informed of our fears." Hal puffed his cheeks and blew out a blast of air. "As of right now his trip is still on. Not showing up would send the wrong message: we can't protect our president on our own soil. That we can't protect our guests. And don't worry. They were informed . . . indirectly."

"But—" Aaron's argument was silenced by a raised hand from Hal.

"It's up to us, to me, to get incontrovertible proof. Put a stop to it. Or both. I have a team in place in Memphis. Some men I trust. Agents are watching Mr. Zaafir, his property, and his people. They were instructed to be discreet. If he is up to something, we don't want him to know we're on to him and force him underground. Aaron, can you tell me anything else that might help?"

"No. I can't think of anything else. I've told you everything."

"Well, here is what we do know." Hal began pacing again.

Derek glanced at Aaron and shrugged his shoulders. "Once he gets going, its impossible to stop him."

Hal cleared his throat with a loud *harumph*. "There *is* a pyramid in Memphis. It's the Memphis Pyramid Arena, built in 1991. The Interfaith Conference is being held there."

Aaron swallowed a lump forming in his throat.

Hal flicked open his briefcase, pulled out a folder, and scattered its contents over the top of the desk. He pointed to another photo of the Hawk. "Hussaam Uzeen Zaafir was nicknamed 'the Hawk' in his teens. It is common belief that he's Jordanian. He's not. His parents were Palestinian. His father was killed in front of him when he was a small boy, by Israeli soldiers. His mother is dead of natural causes. There's a vague reference to a brother. But we can't verify it. If he ever existed he has to be dead, too."

"Who are those two?" Derek pointed at two burly men who appeared in almost every picture with Hussaam.

"Those are Mr. Zaafir's personal bodyguards. All we know about them are their names, Basil and Rashad, and that they are also Palestinian." Hal pointed to a women and young boy. "That's his wife, Fatima, and son, Haytham." Hal tapped his finger on a photo of Zaafir. "Mr. Hussaam Zaafir is clean. We can't find any evidence of wrongdoing. We can't find any connection or affiliation to any terrorist groups, Palestinian or otherwise. The man has a doctorate in pharmacology and a master's in microbiology from the University of Cairo. He went to work for a pharmaceutical company out of college and rose quickly through the ranks with inventions and breakthroughs that made the company a fortune. After his success there, he started his own company, which he named . . ." Hal paused for affect, ". . . Hawk Pharmaceuticals."

The lump in Aaron's throat and the sinking feeling in his stomach returned with a vengeance.

"His company has been, to say the least, very successful." Hal rubbed his hands together as if to say, *Now it gets really good.* He scanned the documents on the desk and plucked one from the stack. "His first breakthrough was a medicine that reduced the detrimental affects of chemotherapy on cancer patients. He administered this medicine to the former monarch of Jordan, King Hussein, who was dying of cancer. The treatment prolonged his life. This gained Hussaam favor, and he was granted the privilege of marrying into the royal family of Jordan. He's considered to be one of the wealthiest men in the world, with international holdings." Hal pointed to some newspaper and magazine clippings. "Mr. Zaafir's benevolence is well documented. We've all seen the news stories. Seen the pictures of his blue trucks with the white Hawk logo. He even received a Nobel Peace prize for his philanthropic efforts."

Head bowed, Aaron stroked his forehead in an attempt to stave of the headache creeping its way from up from his tight shoulders. *A Nobel Prize winner?*

"So," Hal said, placing his hands on his hips, "What could a man like Hussaam Uzeen Zaafir have to gain from orchestrating terror attacks? Why would he need to amass weapons?"

Aaron didn't know if Hal really expected an answer or if the question was strictly rhetorical.

"Power. Revenge. Who knows?" Derek said.

Hal inclined his head toward the swarm of analysts in the hanger. "I doubt we'll find anything answers in there, either, except what they wanted us to know."

Derek sat down and propped his elbows on his knees. "So, what's our next move?"

"We," Hal said, pointing a finger at Derek and himself, "are going to stop Zaafir. "*You* are going home."

Derek stood and put a hand on Aaron's shoulder. "No. I don't think that's a good idea. He's the only thing even keeping us in the game." Derek looked at Aaron. "I hate to ask you. And I'll understand if you don't want to. But are you willing to see this through?"

Aaron pushed up from the chair. His legs were so sore he nearly gasped from the pain. "Of course. I don't see how I can just quit now." He wished he felt as confident as his words.

Hal stared at them and seemed to be considering. Aaron gently gripped Hal's arm. "As much as I want to go home, I have to see this through." He dropped his hand. "I can help Derek. You need me there. There is, or soon will be, a bomb in that pyramid. How can I quit now, knowing that? I may be able to help you find it. Please."

Hal exhaled a long breath. "Okay. Against my better judgment, okay. You two are going to Memphis. Make contact with my team. Find *something*. Until further notice, not one word of this op's true nature is to be repeated. Give my team in Memphis only enough information to let them do their job. No more. For now, I don't even want your own team informed, Derek." He reached into the pocket of his blazer, pulled out an envelope, and passed it to Derek. "If anything happens to me, make sure the president gets this. Put it in his hands yourself."

"I will," Derek said. "What are you going to do?"

"See about this cold."

CHAPTER XXXI

THE Gulf Stream banked in a lazy circle as they approached a small airport on the outskirts of Memphis. The intercom buzzed. "We'll be on the ground in a minute, guys." The pilot's voice sounded tinny and muffled through the speakers.

According to the map on Aaron's lap, the airport's landing strip ran between the Mississippi River and Lake McKellar. He studied the map to familiarize himself with the city. He had driven through Memphis many times and was familiar with the interstate circling it, but he didn't know much about the interior of the city. That same interstate would have him home in less than three hours. All it would take is a stop at the rental-car counter. It was very tempting. Home.

The wings dipped as they lined up for the final approach, allowing Aaron a view of the river below. The sky was bright red and orange as the sun dipped below the horizon, and warm light cascaded over the immensity of the mighty Mississippi. Mammoth barges chugging along in the current appeared to be floating on a sea of red. He prayed it wasn't an ill omen. A great weight settled onto him, an awesome sense of responsibility. Thousands, perhaps hundreds of thousands of lives, might depend on him. His own included. The rental car seemed more appealing all the time.

With a rustle of paper he mashed the map closed and shoved it down on the seat next to him. He leaned his head back, drew in a long breath, and blew it out with a moan.

Derek sat in the opposite aisle, eyes closed, chest hardly moving, head against the backrest. For most of the two-hour flight from Fort Bragg, he had been quiet. His eyes popped open and he swiveled his head to face Aaron.

"Sorry. Did I wake you?" Aaron said.

"No. It's fine. I heard the pilot's announcement."

"Sleep much?"

"A little. I hate to admit, but I started off praying and . . . well . . . I drifted off."

"I'm sure He understands." Aaron glanced toward the sky. "You've had a rough couple of days."

Flaps whirred, the planed bumped, and rubber screeched on concrete. "Welcome to Isle-A-Port airstrip," the pilot said over the intercom.

Derek swung open the door and said, "You comin'?"

Aaron stood, reaching for the seat in front of him for support. He instantly regretted the movement and clutched the bandage on the outside of his left bicep. The wound wasn't serious, but it burned. He walked to the hatch and descended the steps to the Tarmac. A stiff breeze carrying the scent of water whipped his clothing. The tang of moisture swirled in the air.

"Here's our ride." Derek tilted his head toward an approaching car.

A large black sedan with tinted windows sped toward them. Derek's bags lay at his feet, his arms crossed, his right hand beneath his coat, inches from the gun strapped in a shoulder holster. The car skidded to a stop a few feet away. A woman with wavy shoulder-length hair wearing a dark and slightly rumpled suit stepped out of the driver's side. She held a wallet open as she approached. "Captain Galloway, I'm agent Jaime Pendleton."

Derek looked at the woman, then at her CIA credentials. He uncrossed his arms, and they exchanged a brief handshake.

The CIA agent stuck a hand out to Aaron. "Agent Pendleton. Glad to meet you."

Aaron opened his mouth to answer, but Derek interrupted. "My companion isn't here."

"Understood," Pendleton said. "I was told to bring this car to you and show you to the command center."

"Were you able to get the gear I requested?" Derek picked up his bags. "We left on short notice. I didn't have time to pack properly."

"Everything you asked for is in the trunk," Agent Pendleton said.

"Good. Thank you. Are we ready to go?"

"Yes, sir." Pendleton slid into the driver's seat.

Derek joined her in the front seat and Aaron climbed in the back. With a slight screech of tires they pulled toward the gated exit of the small airport. The gates swung open and they hung a left. Pendleton opened the throttle and they headed north.

The sedan sped over the street as dusk's long shadows turned to evening. Bouncing over bumps and potholes, they traveled due north, the river always to their left. Aaron clutched a handgrip mounted near his head and squeezed the edge of the seat with the other. The car hit a particularly large pothole and he thought his head would go through the roof. *Go back, I think you missed one.*

After a thorough tour of Memphis' bumpy streets, they slowed as they entered an industrial complex. Aaron released his stranglehold on the car. Large metal warehouses surrounded them. A convergence of train tracks was a focal point of activity. Men, cranes, and forklifts loaded and unloaded boxes and crates of all sizes and shapes. In the distance, the hulking silhouettes of massive barges dotted the horizon.

On a poorly lit out-of-the-way street they turned into a nondescript parking area. Pendleton parked in front of a large steel building. It appeared deserted. There were more windows missing and broken than intact. Those that remained were stained with dust and dirt, and the dingy exterior walls were blemished with fading graffiti. The car's headlights hit two large metal doors that slowly slid open. Pendleton guided the sedan between the doors into the dimly lit interior of the warehouse. Once they were clear, two men shut the doors behind them. In the ruby glow from the brake lights, Aaron could see that the agents manning the doors carried small automatic rifles slung over their shoulders.

Derek stepped out of the vehicle and Aaron followed. The slamming of the car doors echoed from the two-story-high ceiling and bare metal walls.

Agent Pendleton pointed to a thin rectangle of light beaming through an open door. "Through there."

Heels clicking on the concrete, they maneuvered between several other parked cars. Aaron passed through the door, blinking as his eyes adjusted to the glare, and stepped into a large open room encompassing the entire warehouse. Men with their shirtsleeves rolled up and ties hanging loosely from their necks surrounded a workspace consisting of folding tables and chairs. Communications equipment and computers were stacked haphazardly on the tabletops. The glow from free-standing flood lamps created a pool of light that did little to penetrate the gloom beyond the workstation. Bundles of power cords snaked into the darkness.

One of the men left the group hovering over the equipment and moved to greet them. He extended a hand to Derek. "Captain Galloway, I'm Randy Nicholas, the agent in charge."

"Good to meet you."

The agent shook hands with Aaron but didn't seem to notice, or care, that he wasn't introduced.

"I was instructed to brief you as soon as you arrived." Nicholas waved them toward a table with folders and pictures scattered over its top. "The Hawk Pharmaceuticals plant is just a few blocks from here." He pointed to a group of pictures. A broad angle revealed the entire plant. Close-ups showed guards clad in blue jump-suits. "I have a team watching the plant. As you can see, it's well guarded. A little too well, if you ask me. There's a small army there." He glanced at Derek, apparently waiting to see if he would comment.

He didn't.

"Right now his wife and son are at their home," Nicholas said. "Mr. Zaafir is in his office at the plant. Right here." He pointed to a picture of a three-story brick building tucked in a corner of the Hawk Pharmaceuticals complex. He passed a file folder to Derek. "The top page is Zaafir's itinerary for tomorrow." Nicholas reached in and flipped the page to expose a photo. It showed Hussaam from a distance, flanked by two large men. "This, of course, is Zaafir. The men beside him are his personal bodyguards. It seems as if the three are inseparable." He flipped through several more photos of Zaafir, his bodyguards, uniformed guards patrolling his property, his wife, his son, his house. "A twelve-man strike team is assembled and ready as instructed." The CIA man leaned over, hands propped on the table. "I don't suppose you can clue me in on what this is about."

"I can only tell you this. We have intel on a credible threat to Memphis and the inter-faith conference."

"And you think Zaafir is involved?"

Derek paused, seeming to consider what to say. "Yes." He tapped a finger on a photo of Zaafir. "This goes no further. Clear?"

The agent nodded.

"We also have information that suggests he, or someone in his organization, may be planning on detonating a nuclear device, at or near the conference."

Agent Nicholas gawked at Derek before gathering his composure. "You're serious."

"Very."

The agent pushed away from the table and smoothed his shirt front. "What do you need us to do?"

"We need proof. Hard evidence. But we can't let him know we're on to him. With his resources, he can disappear like that." Derek snapped his fingers. "Keep your teams on him and be ready to move when I tell you. I want to know every move he makes. And please, whatever you do, don't let him pick up your surveillance."

"Shouldn't we contact the FBI and Homeland Security?"

"Absolutely not. Not yet, anyway." Derek said. "Your people are not to breathe one word of this to *anyone* else until I say so. Don't worry. Our operational clearance comes from the top."

"Good enough." Agent Nicholas passed over a small cell phone. "Press and hold 'one' and it will dial me." He held up his own phone. "Your number is programmed in here."

Derek took the phone and tucked it in his pocket. "Thanks. I'll be in touch." He tapped Aaron's shoulder. "Come on. We have some things to do."

With a nod to Nicholas, Aaron followed Derek to the car. Derek climbed behind the wheel and Aaron jumped into the passenger's seat. As the engine roared to life, the agents manning the doors slid them open. Leaning against another sedan, the glow of a lit cigarette reflecting on her face, Agent Jaime Pendleton tapped two fingers to her forehead in a half wave, half salute.

A couple of blocks from the warehouse, Derek pulled the car to the side of the road and parked in an area of deep shadow between street-lights. "I'll be right back." He popped the trunk and retrieved a small black bag. He settled back in to the driver's seat, raised the center arm-rest, and placed the bag between them.

Aaron scanned the contents of the bag. Electronics and weapons. Derek pulled out a handheld PDA and a mounting device which he plugged into the cigarette lighter. The gadget powered up, bathing the car's interior with its glow. Using the stylus, Derek brought up a map-ping program. With a couple of more clicks, the small screen filled with a map of Memphis.

Curious what they were up to, Aaron remained quiet.

Derek must have noticed his interest. "GPS with a map overlay. The blinking dot is us." He clicked the screen a few times, shrinking and ex-panding the map. "You tired?"

"A little. But I'm okay." Aaron was actually very tired and very sore. Every move of his left arm brought a sharp twinge. "Nothing a couple of aspirin won't cure." He marveled at Derek's ability to absorb punishment. It seemed as if the beating in the desert hadn't fazed him.

"Are you very familiar with Memphis?"

"No. Just the main roads."

"Me either. Are you up to a little recon?"

"Sure. How 'bout Graceland?"

The trace of a smile appeared on Derek's face. "If you don't mind, we'll check out Hawk Pharmaceuticals and the pyramid first. I also want to drive the roads in case we need to get somewhere in a hurry." He made a couple more clicks with the stylus. "Before we go." Derek looked up from the PDA screen. "I know I asked you to come along. I didn't want to, but I felt I had to. As before, you are to stay out of the action and do as I say. Are we clear?"

"Clear." Aaron grinned. "I'll be careful. Promise." He stared at the profile of his enigmatic companion. They were still strangers in so many ways, yet they had formed a bond through their extraordinary circumstances. He knew Derek was virtuous and courageous. He also knew gushing sentiment was not the man's style. Derek's warnings were not bravado, or an attempt at bullying, but the words of a person concerned about Aaron's welfare. Friendship with a man like Captain Derek Galloway wasn't easily won, and no matter what happened, Aaron was glad to know him.

Derek pulled away from the curb. As they eased along the road, he periodically checked the glowing PDA screen. Windows down, the night air blew into the sedan carrying with it the distant sounds of barge whistles, the hiss of steam engines, and the beep-beeping of forklifts and cargo carriers. Scattered streetlights with ancient bulbs cast weak blue islands of light on the otherwise dark street. Warehouses were recessed from the road with windows black as pitch, like ghostly sentinels glowering at their passing.

Derek made a left, traveled a block south, and turned right. "That should be it ahead."

The street glowed from higher-quality lighting. Over the tops of the trees, Aaron saw it. A sign bearing the white hawk on the field of blue. Hawk Pharmaceuticals. He shivered as if from a blast of cold air. The immense compound was surrounded by a twelve-foot-high fence. Beyond it, a vast band of black shadow marked the location of the Mississippi River. A barge docked at the compound's edge swarmed with men and equipment as crates and boxes of all shapes and sizes were extracted from its hold. The cargo was being transferred to a warehouse dominating the interior of the compound. In front of a three story brick and glass office building tucked away in a rear corner of the property was parked a white stretch limo.

Zaafir. The Hawk.

Another shudder coursed through Aaron.

They approached the main gate, protected by a guardhouse. Men in blue uniforms with the hawk symbol emblazoned on their chests seemed to patrol every square inch of the property.

Aaron could swear he heard the cry of a hawk. He envisioned giant claws flying at him out of the night and resisted the urge to roll up his window.

They continued past the perimeter of the half-mile long property. At the next cross street, Derek turned right. He scanned the area and pulled into the parking lot of a small brick building. No lights showed through the buildings' windows and the front door was barred and chained. He parked on the opposite side of the only other vehicle on the lot, a white cargo van. "I'm going to look around," he said. "Stay put. If any cars come by, duck out of sight. If by chance the police see you and get suspicious, show them this, and tell them you're on a case." He reached into the bag and tossed Aaron a small leather wallet. Aaron flipped it open to reveal a CIA badge and an ID card with Derek's picture on it.

Derek stepped out of the car, slipped off his blazer, and removed his shoulder holster and button-down shirt. His muscles were mottled with purple and green bruises. He shrugged into a snug black tee-shirt, replaced his shoulder holster and SIG, added a second holster and gun, and tucked his sheathed CQ-7 in his belt at the small of his back. Ready, he donned his dark blazer. "I'll be back in thirty minutes. No more than an hour." He glanced at the black bag on the seat. "There's another SIG and the forty-five in there if you need it."

Window down, elbow propped on the car door, Aaron drummed his fingers. He squirmed in the seat in an attempt to get comfortable. Alone, his thoughts turned to the macabre. Every scenario he imagined became a rabbit trail which he followed to his death. Would he be killed by a bullet or a bomb? Who would die with him? Every shadow, every sound startled him as he envisioned everything from gang bangers to professional assassins stepping out of the gloom.

Under Derek's bag lay the dossier on Zaafir. Aaron grabbed it and rifled through Derek's bag until he found a pen-sized flashlight. Desperate to occupy his mind, Aaron studied the dossier. He scanned every photo and read every line.

The driver's side door clicked open and the interior light flashed on. Aaron's breath caught and his head snapped to the left. He dropped the file and the flashlight as he brought up his hands to protect himself.

Derek plopped into the driver's seat and pulled the door closed behind him. "Did I scare you?"

Aaron leaned back in his seat and put his hand to his heart. "What? Me? Of course not."

The look on Derek's face was skeptical.

"Okay. Maybe a little."

Derek shook his head and tried to hide a smile behind his hand. "Well, there's something going on at Zaafir's facility. I just know it." His hands gripped the steering wheel. "There's a *lot* of activity and way too many guards. Zaafir has a small army there." He fished in his pants pocket and pulled out his phone. He held down a key and placed the phone to his ear. "Hal, I want my team here by morning. Tell Lane to bring the gear we need for an assault on a fenced, well-guarded compound."

"I have a bad feeling," Derek continued into the phone. "That's all I can tell you at the moment. We're doing recon of our own now. I want my guys here to back us up. Something's going down. I'm sure the locals are fine. But fine may not be good enough." His free hand clamped down on the steering wheel. "Have you heard anything about Chavez?" As Derek listened, his face became tense, his jaw muscles clenched, his brow furrowed. "Okay. I'll call you back in a couple of hours."

"Well. What about Chavez?" Aaron asked.

"They say he's going to be fine." Derek glanced away, staring out of the window. Before he spoke he cleared his throat. "His leg has severe damage, though. They say he probably won't ever get full mobility back." He smacked both hands against the steering wheel and shook his head. "Whatever happens, it looks like his career is over. In the field, at least." He twisted the key in the ignition and the car roared to life. Jamming the car in reverse, they shot out of the parking space.

Aaron didn't know what to say. A feeble, "I'm sorry," was the best he could do.

"It's okay." Derek sighed. "He knew the risks. It's just . . . well, ending it this way. It's going to kill him."

CHAPTER XXXII

HAL tugged the solid light-blue tie against his throat and shoved the tail of a white dress shirt into his pants. He grabbed the blazer of his best gray suit from the bed and slid it over his arms. For some reason, he wanted to look his best for the meeting with the devil. He studied his reflection in the mirror. Satisfied that he looked as good as he possibly could, he moved to the door of his bedroom. He listened while he glanced left and right into the hall. Anne and the kids were downstairs.

He pushed the bedroom door closed and locked it. Retrieving the phone from his pocket he called Tim. "Where are you?"

"Home."

"I need you to meet me at Russell's house. I need a face-to-face."

"Why?"

"Can you get me in or not?"

"Sure." Tim paused. "But you've got to give me something."

"Someone's been leaking information on my operation. I'm pretty sure it's coming from Russell. The question is whether or not it's intentional. I need to sweat him. Find out if he sold us out. See if I can find out what's really going on. He's attempted to stall my investigation from the beginning. I'm going to find out why."

"I don't know, Hal. This doesn't sound like a good career move."

"To hell with that. Lives are on the line. A lot of them."

"What if you're wrong?"

"Then I'm screwed. Look, just do this for me. Don't let him know I'm coming. Make up some excuse why you needed to see him." Hal glanced at his watch. "If you leave now, you can be there in thirty minutes. I'll be there in forty." Hal hung up. Tim would do what he asked.

Hal opened the closet door. He flipped a switch, bathing the fastidiously neat rows of hanging clothes in white light. The large walk-in closet smelled detergent fresh with a hint of cypress. Anne had installed cypress planks on the walls to protect their clothing from moths. The wood also emanated a pleasant scent. He moved to the back of the closet and shoved aside a group of seldom worn clothes to reveal the door of a safe, which he opened twisting the knob in the correct sequence of numbers. Pushing aside a stack of emergency cash and an envelope containing a number of documents supporting an array of clandestine identities from his field days, he extracted a silver case.

He set the case on the bed, fingered in the combination, and pulled open the lid. The black padded interior of the case contained his Glock 18, with two extra magazines, a box of full jacket .9 mm ammo, and a clip-on holster. Next to it lay a Kel-Tec P-11 pocket pistol. Also a .9 mm. He thumbed cartridges into the magazines of both weapons. After engaging the safeties of both pistols, he placed the Glock in its holster and tucked it beneath the waistband of his pants at the small of his back. The small Kel-Tec he slipped into his front pocket.

He replaced the case in the safe and moved the clothes back into place. He flipped off the closet light and moved back to the mirror, turning from side to side. The guns weren't visible. He hoped he wouldn't need them. If he did, he hoped he still had what it took to use them.

Hal moved to the bedside table and picked up a family photo. Anne, William, Benjamin, and himself at the beach. He stroked a thumb across the glass. There was a lot to lose. A knot of fear made his breath quicken. Should he let it go? Just stay comfortable within the status quo? He could just go the president. Confess his fears. Hal shook his head. No. It was his duty. Any other way, and the element of surprise would be gone. Tracks could be covered. He placed the picture on the table. *I hope you can understand.*

He went downstairs, kissed his wife long and deeply, told his boys he loved them, and drove away.

* * * * * *

Hussaam's office seemed to have grown small. Its walls pressed on him. Even the window commanding a view of the plant and the river provided no relief from the feeling of confinement. Something was wrong.

He stalked to the wall and freed his favorite blade from its scabbard. Thirty-six inches of gleaming steel, and the hilt added another foot. He admired the flawless and beautiful weapon. It was fashioned similar to a light Chinese sword called a *jian*: straight blade, small hand guard, hilt adorned at the end with a small decorative knob. But unlike the Chinese blade his was fashioned to resemble, it was heavy, formidable. Its weight soothed him.

He walked back and forth in the space between his desk and the window, hands clenching and unclenching the hilt, slashing the blade through the air. His bodyguards stood to either side of the room. Had Basil and Rashad been men of eloquence they might have described Hussaam as a fox scenting danger, nose in the air, ears twitching. He sensed a hunter he couldn't see but somehow knew was there. The two men wisely remained silent.

A tap on the door stilled Hussaam's traipsing. He set the blade on the desk and took his chair, steepling his fingers on his chin. "Come."

Thomas Cable led a member of his local security team into the office, a man named Mark who resembled Basil enough to be his brother.

Hussaam asked, "Mark, are you clear on your assignment?"

The man nodded. "Yes, sir."

"Good. If you do well this time, I may require your services again in the future." A lie was hidden behind Hussaam's best disarming smile, the one he used when the cameras rolled. The one called "warm" and "genuine" by his admirers in the media. He stepped from behind the desk and passed Mark an envelope stuffed with large bills.

"Thank you, sir. Thank you. I really appreciate it. I won't let you down."

"I know." Hussaam patted the security man on the back and motioned toward the door. "We have things to discuss. Please wait for us outside." As the door closed, Hussaam stalked back to his desk and leaned over it, palms inches from the sword's hilt, his back to Thomas Cable. "Tell me you have something. Anything."

"I'm sorry, sir, but I don't know where they are. I'm still working on it."

Hussaam glanced for the thousandth time at the two files laid open on his desk: Dossiers on one Aaron Henderson and one Paul Jenkins. Every feature of their faces was etched into Hussaam's memory, thanks to the pictures in the files. A graphic designer? A preacher? How? Why?

"Maybe this is just some kind of fluke," Cable said. "They probably don't know anything. If you told me more, maybe I could help you more."

Hussaam grabbed the sword and spun around, leveling the blade inches from the man's face. No trace of the smile remained. "You know all you need to know." He allowed the sword's tip to drop. "Wait for me in the hall." The man spun without a word and walked brusquely through the door. Jalal was dead, unfortunately, but his purpose had been served. Assurances had been made that Hussaam's plans had not been compromised. But still . . . something. He could not shake a gnawing suspicion. No matter. He would proceed until he had reason not to.

Hussaam turned and replaced the sword in its sheath. "Basil, you know what to do. It is up to you now. Do not fail me."

* * * * * *

Derek turned off the raised interstate onto the exit ramp. The sedan glided down to ground level, and Aaron stared.

The pyramid. He didn't yet have a full view of it, for as they passed under bridges and buildings, it popped in and out of view. The mass of gleaming steel and glass dominated the skyline.

They emerged from the shadows beneath the overpass, allowing a full view of the structure, exactly as in his dream, down to the last detail. His eyes scanned from the broad foundation to the pointed tip. As they drew closer, the immense building filled the windshield and details of a statue came into focus. An imperious bare-chested figure clutched a scepter, glaring at all beneath it.

Rameses the Great.

Aaron didn't realize he groaned until the noise reached his ears. He wanted to scream and slam his fists into the dashboard. He settled for rubbing his temples.

Derek found a parking spot near an entrance to the pyramid. "What's wrong?"

"It's exactly like I dreamed. I just hoped it wouldn't be."

Derek laughed. "Yeah. Me, too."

They climbed out of the car, scanning the exterior of the unique building.

"Come on," Derek said. "Let's check it out."

Secret Service agents already swarmed the building and its surroundings in preparation for the arrival of the president, foreign dignitaries, and religious leaders. Security checkpoints and parking barriers were being erected and the grounds swept for threats. On the way inside, Derek was forced to flash his credentials three times.

They pushed through a set of glass doors into a spacious hallway. Uniformed guards and Secret Service agents were in abundance.

"How could anyone get a bomb in here?" Aaron asked.

"They couldn't."

Using signs for direction, they found the arena security office. A guard sat hunched over his desk reading a paper.

Derek tapped on the doorjamb. "Excuse me. I know this is a bad time, but do you have anyone who could show us around?"

The guard studied Derek as he folded his newspaper then glanced at his watch. "My shift's almost over. I can give you a tour."

* * * * * *

Aaron plopped into the passenger seat, stretched, and yawned. Nothing. They hadn't found anything. The security guard led them through the building from top to bottom. At Derek's prodding, they were shown the basement parking garage and the sub-basement. The lowest level of the building was a labyrinthine maze of concrete passages, pipes, electrical conduits, and environmental equipment.

He turned to Derek, "What do think? Wild goose chase?"

"No. There's something about that sub-basement. I just can't put my finger on it." Derek raised an eyebrow. "You up for a little more recon?"

"Sure." He was actually up for a shower and a bed.

CHAPTER XXXIII

HAL'S dark blue Grand Marquis rolled smoothly along the tree-lined boulevard, headlights flashing across ornate entrances. Though simply named, River Bluff Estates was anything but. The exclusive neighborhood was a collection of stately mansions, all gated, all on one acre plus lots. The ones on the right side of the road were situated on a bluff overlooking the Potomac River. Most were guarded by private security. The street was home to captains of industry, silver spooners, and high profile politicos. Old and new money. He drove slow, allowing him to read the addresses on the gates.

He passed an open gate and glanced back. Small numbers inscribed on one side of the opened entry read "1706." His destination. *Here I am.* He pulled abreast of the open gates and stared down the driveway. The house wasn't visible beyond the trees. He pulled on to the cobblestone drive, which probably cost more than he made in a year, and after a bend in the road, he encountered a second gate and a guardhouse.

A uniformed sentry stepped from the small building and held up a hand. Hal rolled to a stop and lowered his window.

"Mr. Bouie?"

"Yes."

"May I see some identification, sir?"

Hal flipped open his wallet and passed over his CIA credentials. The man looked from the ID to Hal's face and handed it back.

"Go right in. They're expecting you."

Hal nodded and pulled away. He rubbed his forehead to clear the moisture collecting there, swallowing to clear a lump in his throat. He continued along the driveway and a sprawling two-story Victorian manor constructed of stone and brick with arching windows and steeply angled roof lines became visible through the trees. In the rear of the property sat a smaller version of the house, either a guest house or servant's quarters. Servant's quarters? Hal had never liked Russell. This place gave him all the more reason. A public servant. Right.

Hal stepped out of the car, lit a cigarette, and listened, but there were no sounds aside from the river-scented breeze through the trees. The clichéd thought, *too quiet*, came to mind. A form moved in the distance near the perimeter fence. A guard and a dog. The guest house was ablaze with lights, but few lights burned in the main house. The front door was ajar.

Hal inhaled a long drag from his smoke, dropped it, and ground the butt beneath his shoe. He adjusted his suit and walked toward the front door. His heels clicked on the stone path, and he lightened his step, a sudden need for stealth overwhelming him. He shook it off. Nerves.

He mounted the steps to the front door, his hand hovered near the chime, debating whether or not to ring it. He stood in the doorway, staring into the dim interior, ears cocked. A wood floored hall, decorated with paintings, all no doubt expensive originals, led into the home's interior. The hall ended on the far side of the house and he could vaguely make out a room beyond. Most of the doors lining the hall were closed. But one, halfway down, stood ajar, a dim light shining from within. Not a solitary sound could be heard.

Hal called out in little more than a whisper. "Tim? Director Russell?" No answer.

He moved into the hall, aiming for the open door. Everything felt wrong, but he resisted the urge to draw a weapon, satisfying himself by placing a hand over the gun in his pocket. As he approached the door, the faint scent of cigar smoke wafted to his nostrils. "Hello." *Where the hell is everybody? Is the director on to me? Has he done something to Tim?*

He stepped into the small rectangle of light shining through the open door of a study sporting shelves lined with books, walls decked with outdoorsy paintings, thick burgundy carpet, and an unlit stone fireplace.

Centered near the wall sat a massive mahogany desk. The tip of the director's dark head was visible over the backrest, and his hands rested on the chair's arm, one held a smoking cigar, the other a tumbler filled with a light brown liquid; probably Scotch, Hal thought.

Hal cleared his throat. "Director Russell." The man didn't respond. Hal spoke again, louder. "Director Russell."

When he didn't respond the second time, Hal moved around the desk, trying to ignore the thump of his heart. "Hey." The man's face was cloaked in shadow. Hal stepped closer, gripped the back of the chair, and spun it toward him. The Director of National Intelligence, Robert Russell, stared back sightlessly. A wound in his forehead dripped blood, and the movement of the chair caused his head to loll to the side.

Hal jumped a step away from the body and reached to his back. Before he could grab his pistol, a voice spoke. "Don't."

He froze, blood seeming to gel in his veins, too thick for his heart to pump. The quiet command startled him, but what chilled him to the bone was who spoke the words. He swiveled his head toward the deep shadows in the opposite corner of the room.

Tim Greene stepped into view from the shadow of an antique wardrobe, preceded by the elongated barrel of a silenced weapon.

Hal's hand floated near his hip, inches from the holster at his waist. Could he reach it? Would Tim hesitate to gun him down?

"I mean it, Hal. Leave the Glock in its holster where it belongs. I don't want to shoot you. But I will." Tim's words, though believable and spoken in earnest, betrayed resignation and a tone of inevitability.

"What are playing at, Tim? Whatever it is, we can work through it."

"Stretch your arms over your head," Tim said. "Turn around." He emphasized his words with a wave of the gun.

Hal complied.

"Now take your right hand, reach to your shoulder, and pull the back of your jacket up. Slowly."

Hal grabbed the cloth of his coat and tugged on it, exposing the holster. Footsteps rushed toward, the gun was ripped from his waistband, and the steps retreated.

"Okay. You can relax."

Hal turned to find Tim's gun still aimed at his chest.

"Dammit, Hal. Why couldn't you just leave it alone?"

"It was you? The leak? *You?*" Hal tried to swallow back the acid roiling in his stomach, burning the back of his throat.

"I don't know how you found out information was being leaked, but when you wanted to confront the director, I knew I wouldn't be able to talk you out of it. I also knew that when you realized he wasn't the source of the leak, it wouldn't take long for you to figure out who was. You forced my hand. I didn't want it to come to this."

"All this time you've been playing me?" Hal licked his dry lips. "It's all been a lie?"

"No. I didn't want this. You weren't supposed to find out. No one was." Tim moved to the opposite side of the desk and grabbed an attaché case. The gun remained locked on Hal's chest. "I know it doesn't matter to you, but I didn't have a choice in this."

"There's always a choice." Hal used a sleeve to wipe the perspiration from his brow. "So, what now? Do you kill me, too? Leave Anne without a husband? William and Benjamin without a father?"

"Stop it." Tim's calm seemed to slip.

"You killed the director, bro. They'll be after you, no matter what you do next. Killing me won't help. I'm sure his personal alarm has already gone off." All top cabinet members carried personal alarms, small devices designed to be concealed within a pocket, equipped with GPS, bio monitors, and an emergency button.

"You know I'm not that stupid." Tim sat the briefcase down and patted his pocket. "Russell's vital signs are normal." The deputy director shook his gun, a Glock 18. "Besides. I didn't kill the director. You did."

With every word Hal's heart sank. His hopes of surviving were dashed. "You don't have to kill me. When they find me with the body, I'll be an instant suspect. By the time it's sorted out, you can be long gone."

Tim worked his jaw. "I wish it was that easy. I really do. But I can't. It's not just about getting away with it. I can't be involved. It's not just about me."

"Explain it to me. You at least owe me that." Hal had to keep him talking. He just needed a slip in the man's concentration.

"I have a brother. As a matter of fact, you've been looking for him: Hussaam Zaafir, The Hawk." Tim shook his head in obvious frustration. "He sent me here when I was seven. Set me up with a family." He nodded. "Yes. Mom and dad. They're not my real parents."

"But you look just like them."

"Yes. My brother is nothing if not thorough. He groomed me. Got me in to the best schools. A favor from him even got me in the agency."

"What's the game?"

"The destruction of Israel. Taking the throne of Jordan. Eventually, he'll topple all the little despot dictators in the Middle East. Create a nation. A superpower. A place where my people can live and be free from oppression."

"Your people? You mean the Palestinians?"

Tim nodded. "So you discovered my brother's—and my—heritage." He licked his lips. "Don't think Hussaam can't pull this all off, either. He will."

This conversation was causing Hal's head to swim. Everything he knew about his friend seemed to be a falsehood. "So, the setup in Syria was just to throw me off. What about Memphis?"

"A distraction." Tim's eyes narrowed.

Hal couldn't reconcile this callousness coming from his friend. Speaking of the death of tens of thousands of people as if it were nothing.

"Wait. How did you know about that? You can't know about that."

Hal knew his time was short. Too much had been revealed to him. If he could just keep him dialoging . . . "So, it's all been a lie."

"No. That's the problem. I love you. And your family. More than you know. You're the only real family I've ever known. I love this country. It's just . . . my brother . . . you can't understand." He stepped closer. "How do you know about Memphis?"

The betrayal. Hal couldn't wrap his mind around it. He vacillated between red-hot burning anger and overwhelming sorrow, with sorrow finally edging out the anger. This man had stood at his wedding, was his children's godfather, and was named in Hal's will as their guardian if anything should happen to him or his wife. They had shared laughter, comforted each other in grief, saved each other's lives too many times to count. Their exploits in the field were the stuff of legend. They shared an intimacy Hal couldn't even have with his wife, since she didn't and couldn't know most of what he had done and seen. They were brothers, sharing a bond of loyalty he thought could never be severed. By anything. Closer than blood. Hal trembled, feeling as if a vital organ had been removed, his body no longer able to function normally.

"I have to know who you've told about Memphis." Tim's eyes tightened. "Tell me, now."

Hal knew Tim was going to kill him, no matter what was said. The weight of the gun in Hal's pocket gave no reassurance. No way he could reach it. The door was the obvious choice. He stumbled, feigning weakness, placing his palms on the desk. "Please, Tim. For the love of God, don't do this. I'm begging you."

Tim's chest expanded as he drew in a long breath. When he blinked, Hal acted.

He shot out his hand and used his palm like a racquet, swatting the desk lamp toward Tim's face. Tim raised an arm to protect his head and fired, but Hal was already on the move, digging his right hand into his pocket. As he took his first step pain erupted, a bullet striking him high, just beneath his right shoulder, spinning him. He went with the force, stumbling backwards through the door. As he passed the threshold a bullet grazed his stomach, burning a furrow in his skin.

He smashed into the wall on the opposite side of the corridor, forcing a *whoof* of air from his lungs. His right arm useless, he ripped the pistol from his right pocket with his left hand, tearing the cloth to free it. As he thumbed the safety, Tim stepped into view, firing in Hal's general direction. Bullets ripped into the wall paneling before Hal could line up Tim in his sights.

Tim centered his gun on Hal's chest. Unable to force his legs to move, he allowed them to collapse beneath him as Tim squeezed off another round. Hal aimed while he fell, landing on his side. He ignored the pain bursting in his shoulder and squeezed the Kel-Tec's trigger. His first shot went wide, but the second didn't. Tim's gun burst fire though his aim was ruined when a bullet ripped through his stomach. He attempted to pull the pistol back on target, but Hal hammered him with shots to the torso, emptying his magazine.

Crimson stains bloomed in Tim's chest and stomach, forcing him back against the desk. He opened his mouth to speak then crumpled face-first to the floor.

Hal tried to force air into his lungs. He gathered his legs beneath him and crawled toward Tim, clutching his right arm against his chest. His vision clouded, and every move brought agonizing surges of pain. Footsteps sounded in the hall.

Hal knelt by the fallen man and gripped his shoulder, groaning as he flipped the man onto his stomach. Hal reached into Tim's blazer, removed the director's personal alarm, and activated the emergency button.

Two uniformed security guards burst through the door with large caliber revolvers leading the way. "Don't move!"

"No problem." Hal sank to the floor. "Do you think you can call me an ambulance?" He closed his eyes and laid his head back, pulling Tim's briefcase close, draping it with a protective arm.

CHAPTER XXXIV

HUSSAAM woke before dawn, his skin clammy and moist with perspiration. He glanced at Fatima. She breathed softly and deeply, cocooned in the silk sheets. Apparently his restlessness had not disturbed her. Phantoms and demons plagued his sleep, bizarre dreams pervaded with images of torment, and a vision of his brother's death had finally woken him. *Nonsense.* He eased his feet into the slippers next to the bed, moved to the window, and peeled the curtain back. Faint purple light at the edge of the horizon hinted at the coming dawn.

Tying on his robe as he strolled down the hall, he stuck his head into Haytham's bedroom. Fast asleep. The room was filled with things that brought an eight-year-old joy. Hussaam grimaced at the images of cartoon characters and the collection of dolls. Calling them "action figures" to make it palatable for boys to play with them did not change the fact they were dolls. He shook his head and pulled the door closed.

Satisfied everything was as it should be on the second floor, he explored the lower rooms of his house and scanned the grounds through windows, ensuring guards were in place. He checked the surveillance cameras, his e-mails, and phone messages. Nothing seemed amiss, but still something nagged at him, a sense of dread, of being hunted. He trusted his instincts and wouldn't ignore them.

He glanced at his watch. Five a.m. He retrieved a phone from his robe pocket and dialed Thomas Cable.

The man answered on the first ring. "You were right. There are surveillance teams watching your house and the warehouse. They're good. It took us awhile to pick them up."

"Who are they?" *And why had he not been informed? Was someone working off the grid?*

"I don't know yet."

"What do you mean you don't know?" Hussaam's teeth clenched. "That is not acceptable."

"Like I told you, they're good."

He blinked. Did he detect a hint of insolence? "I want to know who is having me watched and why. Do *whatever* it takes. Am I making myself clear?"

"Yes, s—"

Before the man could finish his reply, Hussaam thumbed the phone's end key and punched another number. "Have my plane fueled and ready. My wife and son will be leaving within the hour. Secure another plane for my disposal. Now. I don't care if you have to buy it. Make sure my helicopter is ready for take-off on a moment's notice. See that the boat is ready and I want another car waiting at the warehouse. Understood?"

"Understood."

He hung up the phone and began to pace, considering. Finally, he decided to break protocol and contact his brother.

* * * * * *

The phone rang three times before Aaron's eyes opened. Bone weary, his head throbbed with each shrill clang of the outdated telephone. A lamp left on overnight illuminated the too-bright and slightly garish hotel-room décor, stinging his eyes. Kicking and squirming his way out of the tangled sheets, he reached for the phone. As tired as he was, sleep hadn't come easily. A racing mind, pain, a hard mattress, and anxiety kept him tossing and turning until after midnight. He grabbed the receiver on the fifth ring.

"Time to get up." Derek's voice boomed. "I thought I would let you sleep in."

Aaron glanced at the glowing red numbers on bedside clock: 5:30 a.m. He tried to force a reply through his gravelly throat.

"Get dressed and meet me in the dining room in thirty minutes."

"Okay." He rubbed his gritty eyes which seemed to be full of sand. As he stood and stretched his hands toward the ceiling, he winced at the pain of stiff and sore muscles. Of course, this was to be expected when one flew around the world and ran for one's life through the desert battling lunatics and foreign soldiers. "I need coffee." He groaned to the hotel walls as he stumbled to the bathroom.

* * * * * *

Thanking the waitress after she refilled his coffee cup for the third time, Aaron wolfed down his breakfast. The caffeine kicked in and once the Aleve he'd popped worked its magic, he might feel almost human again.

Between bites of pancakes, Derek spoke. "Neither Hal's team nor the local CIA guys have been able to find anything on Zaafir. He and his two bodyguards left his facility on the river last night and went to his house. They've been there ever since." He took a sip of juice. "Hal called. He's been shot."

"Is he okay? What happened?"

"He'll be fine. He didn't give me all the details, but Zaafir apparently had a brother."

"Had?"

Derek stirred the scrambled eggs around on his plate with his fork. "Hal shot him. He's dead. Hal also got hold of their real plans. England and Saudi Arabia were misinformation. The real targets are Jordan and Israel." He leaned back and placed his napkin on the table. "The right authorities were informed." Derek looked Aaron in the eye. "Hal finally decided to listen to you. He gave the Israeli's the locations you pointed out to us on the maps. There is still a lot of area to cover, but they found several chemical weapons caches."

Mouth suddenly dry, Aaron washed down a bite of biscuit with a swig of water. "What are we going to do?"

"Right now, the Israelis are frantically searching for a portable nuclear device. They haven't found it. Hal's leaving it up to us to stop Zaafir. After we do a little more scouting and I get my team ready, we're heading to the conference. That's where it's going down." Derek placed a twenty on the table to cover their check. He swiped the edge of his mouth with a white linen napkin, pushed his chair back, and rose to his feet. "It wouldn't hurt to pray."

Aaron drained his coffee and pushed himself back from the table. If they failed, he could die. A lot of people could die. He could flee. Find a car and speed home. The thought was fleeting and he shook it away. If he ran now, he would always be running, looking over his shoulder. He also couldn't live with himself if he walked away. If his dream came to pass, the ghosts of the dead and the tears of their families left behind would haunt him all his days. He felt, no, he *knew* he had more to do. He had to see it through. He would just have to rely on faith.

A few minutes later, he sat in the passenger seat of the sedan gazing out of the window. They were crossing Beale Street; he wished he was there to eat the world-famous barbecue and listen to the blues. As early as it was, people scurried down the brick paved streets, most of them on the way to work. Too early for tourists, Aaron thought. Some walked with folded papers tucked under their arms, others with cell phones stuck to their ears, a few nibbled pastries. Steaming foam cups were in abundance. An ancient, grizzled old man and a beautiful little girl lounged on a park bench. The girl giggled as she fed pigeons beneath the shade of a tree. Near them, the statue of W.C. Handy, trumpet in hand, watched. Bustling humanity.

People so often angered Aaron with their selfishness, their complete lack of regard for others. They would run over you in traffic, he thought to himself, chatter incessantly and loudly on cell phones in restaurants and theaters, step in front of you in line. But am I any different? Well, maybe.

But in the end, when pushed to the edge, the same people who so angered him could perform acts of selfless love and sacrifice that were, well, Biblical in scope. The thought of those people dying today, that fair-haired little girl and thousands like her having their lives ripped away by a power hungry lunatic—no. He smacked his fist against the armrest.

As they passed, the old man noticed him staring and lifted a hand in greeting. Aaron returned the wave and tried to smile. He wouldn't let these people die. *I will swallow my fear, and I will save them.*

Derek drove with one hand, the other pressed a phone to his ear. Since breakfast, the device had been in constant use. Now he was talking to Hal. "The team will be landing in about thirty minutes. I'm sending them to hook up with the local CIA guys."

Before Derek hung up, Aaron tapped him on the shoulder. "Let me talk to him."

Derek told Hal to hold and passed over the phone.

"Any word on my family?" Aaron asked.

A slight pause and an intake of breath before Hal answered caused Aaron a moment of panic. "They're fine. But your friend Joseph Harris has been pulled off the guard detail."

"What?"

"Aaron, everything's fine. I promise." His voice sounded tired, his words a little slurred. "I spoke to Agent Harris myself. He was ordered to report to Memphis to aid with security at the conference. He hand-picked his replacement. Your family is well guarded. I promise."

Aaron went cold. Not because he was any more worried about his family, he knew Joseph wouldn't put them at risk. But now Joseph was here, in harm's way.

"Aaron." Hal groaned before he continued. "Sorry. I hurt like hell. The Israelis can't find a nuclear device, and we don't think they've located all of the chemical weapons. The Mossad—Israel's intelligence agency—is frantic. Can you give me something to pass along to them?"

"I'm sorry. I can't think of anything I haven't told you. I'm sure you know this already, but you can be sure the bomb will be placed for the most dramatic affect. If there are any big events planned . . . something important people might attend, that's where I'd look."

"I'll pass that along. Let me know if you can think of anything else."

* * * * * *

They pulled onto Auction Avenue at 8:15 a.m., forty-five minutes before the conference was due to begin. They wanted to arrive in plenty of time to scour the pyramid once more. Derek planned to be in place before Hussaam arrived so they could watched him first hand. The Secret Service reported that nothing had been found on the arena grounds.

Aaron stared as the statue of Rameses loomed over them as they drove. A knot of liquid ice seemed to form in his stomach. His breathing became hurried and shallow, and his pulse began to race.

Aaron knew he should have been used to it by now, but he felt on the verge of panic as terror overwhelmed him. He concentrated in an attempt to gain control of his emotions. Without warning, his vision clouded. The image of a small black case formed in his mind's eye. It lay open on the ground in a room he recognized. Inside, a metallic device with a key sticking out of a switch and a ten-digit keypad were illuminated in a soft green light. The light came from numbers flickering across an LCD screen.

4:00:29.

4:00:28.

4:00:27.

Aaron blinked, the bright sunlight burning his eyes. Had he actually seen that or was it his imagination?

Stopped at a barricaded entrance, Derek presented his credentials to a Secret Service agent. He glanced at Aaron with lowered eyebrows. "You okay?"

"Fine."

The agent held Derek's credentials and eyed them both carefully before folding the leather wallet and passing it back. He nodded to two other agents, and they pulled the barrier to the side.

Aaron leaned over and spoke through the open window. "Excuse me, sir. Can you tell me if Special Agent Joseph Harris is here?"

The man peered at them, suspicious.

"He's a friend of mine," Aaron said. "He's not answering his cell. Please. I need to reach him."

"He's here. But I'm sure he's very busy."

"Will you radio him and see if he'll meet me in the foyer?"

"Please," Derek added. "It's important."

"What's your name, sir?"

"Aaron. Aaron Henderson."

The agent nodded. "Okay. I'll tell him. But I can't promise he'll do it." He waved them through.

"What's going on?" Derek asked.

"I just had . . . well, a . . . vision. I guess. I don't know. Anyway, I think it's here. The bomb. It's in the basement."

"You're sure?" Derek didn't bother to argue the point of how or when. Or to remind him a search of the basement hadn't yielded anything. He didn't even blink upon hearing the news. "None of Hussaam's people have been close to this place."

"Pretty sure."

"Good enough."

* * * * * *

After parking, they were required to pass through two more checkpoints consisting of uniformed police officers, Secret Service agents, and metal detectors. At the final checkpoint before entering the building, an agent, apparently a supervisor, pulled them to the side. Aaron understood the necessity for the tight security—of course he did—but his blood pressure rose with each passing second. The Secret Service had been informed of a possible threat to the conference and no chances were being taken. The blood throbbed in Aaron's temples and he debated breaking protocol and screaming, *"There's a bomb in the building!"* The longer they stood there, the less time they had to search for the bomb.

"Stan, let 'em through." Joseph strolled up, flashing his badge.

Without thinking, Aaron grabbed his friend and squeezed him in a bear hug. "Oh, man. I'm glad to see you." Glancing over Joseph's shoulder Aaron glimpsed the stone-faced Secret Servicemen surrounding them. Aaron relinquished his hold and smoothed the fabric of Joseph's blazer. "Uh . . . sorry."

Joseph grimaced and rubbed his shoulder.

"Are you all right?" Aaron asked.

"Fine. I'll tell you about it later." He grinned and a patted Aaron on the back. "Good to see you too, old man." Joseph shook hands with Derek and led them past the checkpoint through a set of large glass doors. They bypassed a line of people waiting to walk through a metal detector and entered the foyer. At the rear of the room an immense banner announced: "Welcome to the International Conference on Interfaith Relations!"

A crowd milled about and conversations buzzed as early arrivals waited for the conference to begin. Joseph pulled them into a corner, out of the tide of moving bodies. "Aaron, I know what you're thinking. But I promise your family is fine. I left them in good hands."

"I know." Aaron said.

"Now." Joseph placed his fists on his hips and stared at Derek and Aaron in turn. "Would you care to explain just what in the heck you guys are doing here?"

Aaron glanced at Derek and received a nod, along with a look conveying that he'd better be careful what he said. Aaron explained to Joseph what brought them there, giving the Cliff's Notes version of their adventures, ending with the fact they feared a bomb was in the basement.

Although Derek hadn't interrupted the story, apparently Aaron's explanation broached sensitive information. "Agent Harris," Derek said, "please treat what you just heard as classified."

"Well," Joseph stroked his chin, "that explains a lot. I take it you guys are responsible for the intel on the potential threat to the conference?" Before they could answer, Joseph glanced at his watch. "This entire building was swept again thirty minutes ago."

"What about the sub-basement?" Derek asked.

"I don't know. But I feel sure it was checked."

For the first time since arriving, Aaron examined his surroundings. The foyer and the entrance to the coliseum were filled with men and women of myriad faiths and skin tones. People in suits, robes, frocks, smocks, and turbans carried Bibles, Qurans, and Torahs. Print and television reporters carried pen and paper or microphones and cameras. The conference was an event of momentous import. A disaster here could and probably would lead to more fear, terror attacks, and war. Panic would lead to more distrust and uncertainty. Jihadists would claim it as an excuse to slaughter more innocents. It would be a disaster of epic proportions.

Some in the crowd turned toward the entrance and reporters scrambled into position beyond the security checkpoint. Cameras flashed as a figure moved through the metal detector. Aaron swallowed a lump in his throat.

Hussaam Uzeen Zaafir. The Hawk.

His dark features handsome and confident, he strode into the foyer, smiling, waving, and nodding his head. His gray suit, with a blue shirt and matching tie, was impeccably tailored and appeared as if it had been crafted by an artisan. In his wake stalked the two ever-present bodyguards.

Aaron studied them. Something nagged in his mind. Something seemed . . . off. What?

"Aaron. Move back," Derek said.

Aaron felt a tug at his elbow, but he was rooted to the spot. When he didn't budge, Derek stepped away, melting into the crowd.

Hussaam approached, eyes scanning the crowd as he greeted wellwishers. His head swiveled in Aaron's direction. Aaron wanted to move but couldn't. He was the proverbial deer caught in the headlights. Hussaam's gaze swept past him and, like a laser, snapped back. Their eyes locked and held.

Aaron went cold while his brow dampened with sweat. The dark predatory eyes appeared to soak in the entirety of his being. Their eyes remained fixed only a split second, an eternity.

The Hawk broke the stare, his stride unbroken as if nothing was amiss.

Aaron knew better. Derek materialized beside him. "He saw me. He knew me," Aaron said.

They watched Hussaam as he marched into the arena. People cleared the way for him, some moved to shake his hand. Microphones were stuck in front of his face as reporters asked him questions, and cameras flashed and recorded his every move. The Hawk handled the situation with practiced ease, smiling and waving for the cameras. Grasping a hand here, giving a one-line answer there. From the crowd's reaction, it was as if Elvis himself had entered the building.

Aaron swiped the perspiration from his forehead. If he wasn't sure before, he was sure now. Something in Hussaam's eyes, a brief flicker, a flash, revealed his nature.

He hated. The man was evil incarnate. He smiled and posed while plotting mass murder.

Aaron studied the bodyguards' broad backs. Their heads swiveled, vigilant, watchful. The one on the left turned to speak to his partner, revealing his full profile. Something about him troubled Aaron. Like a pebble in his shoe or a grain of sand in his eye, he felt a minute chafing. Then it hit him. It wasn't the same man as in the photos. "Derek, hand me the file."

Derek retrieved a folded and bent manila folder from his back pocket.

"Would you guys care to clue me in?" Joseph asked.

Aaron thumbed through the file until he located a photograph of Hussaam's bodyguards. He tapped his finger on the form in the picture. "Look."

Joseph and Derek leaned in.

"The bodyguard on the left. It's a different man."

* * * * * *

Hussaam recognized Aaron Henderson instantly. Their eyes met for only a moment, and he doubted the man even noticed.

This was no coincidence.

He continued to smile and wave at the walking dead.

At the first chance he pulled Rashad close. "Something is wrong. Be ready."

He strode into the immense auditorium, eyes scanning every corner, searching. He couldn't escape the feeling he was trapped in a cage. No word from his brother, Jalal dead. That man here. It was time to go. The plan was in motion and would fail or succeed; there was no reason for him to take any risks. He would disappear until he knew for certain.

CHAPTER XXXV

A tug on Aaron's sleeve made him scramble for footing. He and Joseph were jerked from where they stood as Derek grabbed them by their sleeves and pulled them through the crowd. Once out of the throng, Derek released his grip and marched at a near run along the hallway.

Joseph caught Aaron's eye and spread his arms, palms up.

Aaron just shrugged his shoulders. He didn't know their destination, either.

Picking up the pace, Joseph came abreast of Derek. "Where are—"

"Here." Derek stopped in front of a service elevator and pressed the call button. A ding announced the arrival of the elevator. When the doors slid open he shooed his companions into the waiting car. He pushed the button for the basement parking garage.

"Um, guys," Joseph said, "would one of you please clue me in here? The president and the prime minister will be here." He waved his finger in a circle over his head. "Today."

Derek handed over the dossier. "Our information suggests that Zaafir doesn't go anywhere without his bodyguards."

Joseph's brow crinkled but he didn't interrupt. He flipped through the documents.

"Why would Zaafir bring a look-alike instead of . . ." Derek appeared unable to recall the name then snapped his fingers. ". . . Basil. So, where is Basil?"

"Sick?"

"Not likely. The tail we put on them reports Basil is still with Zaafir."

The elevator bumped to a stop and the doors slipped open. Two Secret Service agents blocked the exit. "This area is off limits."

Joseph stepped up and opened his badge. "They're with me." The trio exited the elevator and entered a concrete cavern. The slate gray uniformity of the parking garage was only broken by pillars and yellow lines. "No cars were allowed in here. Too easy to hide a bomb," Joseph said. He turned to the agents. "I don't guess you've seen anything."

Both shook their heads.

"Okay. We're going . . ." Joseph glanced at Derek.

"Over there." Derek pointed to a set of double doors on the opposite side of the garage.

"That way," Joseph said. "Keep your eyes peeled."

Derek pushed himself between the other agents and jogged toward the doors.

Aaron mumbled, "Excuse me," and followed.

Joseph caught up. "Okay. Now will you finish clueing me in?"

"Aaron believes there may be a bomb in the sub-basement. Zaafir's bodyguard is AWOL. I don't like the way that adds up."

"Don't you think we should report this?"

They reached the doors and Derek turned. "What will you tell them? Let's see what we can find first." He put his hand on the door. "Besides. If there's anyone down here, it will be a small group. More people will just get in my way." He reached beneath his blazer and extracted two semi-automatic pistols. "Agent Harris, I don't mean to step on your toes, here. But if you're coming, you have to follow my lead."

Joseph nodded and drew his own gun.

Tucking a gun under his left arm, Derek pulled open one of the doors. He held it open with his foot, allowing him to resume his two-fisted pistol wielding. He scanned the area beyond for a moment and stepped through. Aaron went in last. A steep set of dimly lit concrete steps ended at another door. Beyond it was the sub-basement.

As they approached the metal door, Derek turned. "Aaron, is there any point in my asking you to wait here?"

Yes. May I? Please? "No. I'm going."

"Aaron," Joseph said, "there's no reason for—"

"I'm going."

"All right," Derek said. "You two stay on my tail and do *exactly* what I tell you. Aaron, stay behind us. No more talking. If there's anyone down here, I don't want them to hear us." He peered through a rectangular piece of glass in the door before easing it open a crack. He listened before shouldering through the door. Stepping into the passageway, he spread his arms and panned his pistols to the left and right before motioning his companions to follow.

The last one through the door, Aaron eased it shut. The lock clicked into place and the sound seemed to reverberate off the walls. He grimaced, but his companions didn't seem to notice. Straight ahead and to the right and left, long concrete hallways faded into the distance. A faint hum gently throbbed in his ears. Overhead pipes and electrical conduits ran lengthwise down all the passages. Dim yellow bulbs in metal casings spaced intermittently along the walls provided feeble lighting.

Derek stood still, eyes swiveling as he scanned the area. Using the barrel of the pistol in his left hand, he pointed to the pipes on the ceiling. He took a step back, close enough to whisper to Joseph, "These pipes lead to a large equipment room in the center of the structure. That's where we're headed." He nodded to the passage straight ahead.

As far as they could see in the weak lighting, the hall was dissected every few feet by cross passages.

Derek pulled Aaron into whispering range. "If anyone starts shooting at us, don't hug against the walls. These concrete passages will act like a funnel if a bullet is fired into them. Stay low, make yourself as small a target as possible, and hustle into the next cross passage." Derek turned the butt of one of his large pistols toward Aaron. "Here. You may need this."

Aaron shook his head, but Derek pressed the heavy weapon into the palm of his hand. As he turned away, Aaron grabbed his arm. "This will do more good in your hands than mine. I don't want it."

They exchanged a look and Derek retrieved the weapon and snapped it into its holster. He either understood or simply didn't want to take the time to argue.

He placed a finger to his lips and led them into the corridor. They crept down its center. Joseph and Derek held their guns in two-handed grips. Aaron was afraid he wouldn't be able to hear anything over the blood pounding in his ears and the noise of his ragged breathing. At the first intersection, Derek held up a hand. He pointed at Aaron's feet. *Stay put.*

Derek tapped Joseph and pointed to the right. They nodded to each other and crouched with their backs against the wall at the edge of the intersection. Another nod and they spun in unison, pointing their guns into the cross corridor in opposite directions. When they lowered their weapons and turned back, Derek motioned Aaron forward. They continued into the bowels of the pyramid, repeating the process at every intersection.

As they approached the end of the long concrete corridor, the whir and hum of electrical equipment grew louder. The passage ended with a metal-railed catwalk. Aaron knew from the previous night's exploration that beyond was an expansive room filled with a myriad of large electrical boxes and equipment. A metallic clink pierced the throbbing of electric apparatus.

Derek held up his hand and they stopped, ears pricked. The sound didn't repeat. Gesturing for them to stay put, Derek crawled on his belly to the end of passage then rolled onto his back and tugged a small rolled-up case from his pocket. Small pockets were filled with gleaming metal tools of indeterminate uses. He extracted what appeared to be a dental mirror and replaced the case in his pocket. Stretching his arm, he pushed the mirror past the opening and panned it left and right. After replacing the mirror in his pocket, he edged toward the opening and peered through. Crawling backward until he was out of the threshold, he crouched and shuffled back to them. He motioned them a few yards back down the passage. They huddled close and Derek whispered, "There are two men down there. One of them is Hussaam's bodyguard. It looks like he's arming a nuclear device. There's another one standing watch." He paused just a moment and seemed to be formulating a plan.

Joseph attempted to reach his colleagues on the radio. He shook his head. "Too much interference. I can't raise them." He flipped open his cell phone. "No signal."

"Aaron, work your way back to the two agents stationed at the basement elevator," Derek said. "Have them bring backup. And we need a bomb squad." He put a hand on Aaron's shoulder. "Keep your eyes open. There may be more of them." Derek turned to Joseph. "I'm going to get as close to them as I can." He inclined his head toward the opening at the end of the passage. "You set up there and cover me. We've got to get to that bomb before it's armed." He aimed a glare at Aaron and pointed back down the corridor. "Go."

A knot in Aaron's stomach attempted to lodge itself in his throat. He swallowed and slipped down the passage. *When did it get so hot?* At the first intersecting hallway he looked over his shoulder. Derek stepped onto the metal catwalk at the end of the passage and disappeared. Joseph leaned against the wall facing the room beyond, his gun in a two-fisted grip.

Aaron glanced left and right and hurtled through the junction. He dashed along the passage on tiptoes, attempting to move quickly but quietly. Every sound—a change in pitch of the constant electrical hum, a drip of water, the whir of electric motors—startled him. He picked up speed, flying along the concrete passage. As fast as he moved through the intersections, he didn't believe anyone would have time to take a shot at him.

* * * * * *

Derek crept onto the catwalk to avoid any creaking of metal. He bent low in an attempt to remain hidden. He leaned forward and risked a glance into the room below.

The room was immense, a forest of electronic gizmos, pipes, and large electric boxes. Hussaam's burly bodyguard hunched over a suitcase bomb, brow wrinkled in deep concentration. Another man stared over his shoulder at the device. Both were dressed in black bodysuits, their feet bare. No, not bodysuits. Wetsuits. They still dripped water.

So that's how they did it. They found a way in from the river.

Staying low, gun trained on the men's backs, Derek moved toward a set of stairs on his left. He placed his foot on each step with care, transferring his weight slowly to avoid causing any squeaks.

He reached the bottom and stepped onto the concrete floor. Undetected, he darted behind one of the large electrical boxes. He placed his back against it and slid toward the edge. He glanced up and caught Joseph's eye. He nodded and received a nod in return. *Here we go.*

With one eye past the edge of his hiding place, Derek stole a glimpse at the two men to confirm they were in the same position. He whirled to the left, with his gun gripped in both hands, trained on the back of Hussaam's bodyguard. "Don't move!"

Out of the corner of Derek's eye, in the midst of several large electrical boxes, a metal grate had been slid to the side of an opening in the floor. Diving equipment was stacked around it, including four sets of full face-masked rigs, the type used for deep sea or lengthy dives.

Four sets.

A curse welled in his throat, but before it could reach his lips, a blur of movement in his periphery silenced it.

* * * * * *

Hussaam made his way through the vast auditorium toward the seats on the front row. Seats he would share with the president of the United

States and the prime minister of England. Well-wishers, many of them renowned religious leaders, spoke and grasped his hands. Bulbs flashed and cameras clicked with each brief encounter. Through it all he felt separated, almost as if he were watching from outside himself. Eyes scanning the arena, he identified the multitude of suited Secret Service agents stoically surveying their surroundings while trying to blend into the background. Uniformed security patrolled the arena and guarded each entrance.

Hussaam's nerves were taut. He was so close. The sight of Aaron Henderson had been startling, enough that Hussaam's mask of serenity had almost slipped. Henderson had been conversing with a man with the unmistakable bearing of a soldier, and a Secret Service agent. Hussaam squeezed his hands into fist and gritted his teeth. He tugged at his collar and reached into his jacket pocket for a handkerchief to swipe the perspiration from his brow. Perspiration? His eyes darted around the room, searching for . . . Were those guards staring at him?

They reached the aisle containing his seat and Hussaam paused. He allowed Rashad and Basil's double to come abreast of him. He reached for Rashad's elbow and whispered, "We are leaving. Now." He would trust his instincts.

Without hesitation, Rashad moved toward a set of doors to the right of the stage intended for use by speakers and musicians. Two uniformed men guarded the doors and eyed them warily until they recognized Hussaam behind his bodyguard.

"Mr. Zaafir has taken ill," Rashad said as they approached. The two guards nodded and held the doors open. After they passed into the antechamber, Rashad placed a call to their driver. "Bring the car to the rear entrance. Now."

CHAPTER XXXVI

AARON approached the last cross passage and finally saw the metal door leading to the stairs. Making sure the way was clear, he stepped into the intersection. The hair on the back of his neck stood on end and chill bumps covered the skin on his arms. He stopped. A sound. The scuff of a foot on concrete? Standing still, he strained his ears. He pivoted his head a hundred and eighty degrees but saw nothing. He glanced toward Joseph's back, small and blurred by dim light and distance. Nothing. He was jumping at shadows.

Just as Aaron flexed his legs to step forward he heard it again. Behind him. He stared toward the exit, still about thirty feet away. He had to move. Now. He ducked into the cross passage on his right and flattened his back against the wall. Breathing hard, he slid to the floor. Crawling on hands and knees, he moved to the edge of the intersection. Mashing his nose against the wall, he peeked around the corner. A dark form emerged from an intersection midway between Aaron and Joseph. Aaron pulled his head back attempting to calm his breathing and slow his pounding heart, certain the intruder would be able to hear him. He risked a second look. The man's back was to him. He wore a form-fitting black suit, his feet were bare, and he held the barrel of an automatic rifle in one hand, its trigger cradled in the other. As Aaron watched, the man crept on the balls of his feet toward Joseph.

* * * * * *

Joseph nodded to Captain Galloway. The man was ready to make his play and he would back it. He was grateful Aaron had been sent away. One less thing to fret over. Joseph checked his radio again and heard nothing but static.

Galloway slid out of sight behind the electrical box below. Joseph squatted with his shoulder against the concrete for support. He resisted the urge to squeeze the handle of his gun and readied it with a relaxed two-handed grip, his right finger caressing the trigger.

Galloway appeared on the opposite side of the electrical box, gun extended. He shouted, "Don't move." But a third man sprinted out of the shadows toward him, a metal crowbar raised over his head. The assailant struck at Galloway's gun, attempting to disarm him. The crowbar flashed down and struck nothing but air. Galloway moved impossibly fast, retracting his arms and stepping back. He grabbed the back of the attacker's head with his left hand and, using the man's own forward momentum, bashed his skull into the metal railing on the staircase.

The burly man hovering over the bomb never wavered; his attention remained fixed on his tinkering. The other spun toward the disturbance, raising his gun to fire at Galloway. Joseph expelled his breath and squeezed the trigger three times. The gun bucked in his hands and he automatically leveled it after each shot. The first shot caught the man high in the shoulder, spinning him away from Galloway. The man tracked his pistol toward the shots, attempting to draw a bead on Joseph. The second and third shots slammed into the man's torso, ruining his attempt to return fire as his feet were ripped from beneath him. He crashed to the floor.

Joseph glanced at Galloway. The crowbar-wielding assailant lay slumped at his feet. Shifting his aim to the bodyguard's back, Joseph's senses tingled. Someone was behind him.

* * * * * *

Vaulting away from the wall, Aaron spun into the corridor. He sprinted toward the intruder sneaking up behind Joseph. Gunfire erupted and his step faltered as he ducked his head. He regained his balance and raced down the passage as the walls blurred past. Joseph fired three times.

The wetsuit-clad man raised his rifle and targeted Joseph's back. Aaron leaned forward in an attempt to gain more speed. He was within fifteen feet of the man. The man nestled the gun against his cheek to fire.

Aaron yelled, "Hey!"

The man swiveled for a glance over his shoulder. Aaron jumped and the low ceiling brushed the top of his head. The would-be assassin pivoted and swung his gun around. Aaron pulled his right knee into his chest as he leaped and kicked at the center of the man's forehead. The flying kick snapped his head back. Unable to halt, Aaron crashed into the man's chest. As both of them fell, Aaron pulled his feet in and tucked into a roll. Tumbling over, he spun to face the assassin. The man lay unmoving.

"Catch," Joseph said. He tossed a set off handcuffs and returned his attention to the area below him.

Aaron snatched the cuffs, kicked the man's gun away, and flipped him onto his stomach. After securing his wrists, Aaron checked the neck for a pulse and felt a steady throb.

Go or stay?

Unsure of what to do, Aaron moved toward Joseph and peered over his friend's shoulder. Joseph's gun pointed toward Basil who busily worked over what must have been the nuclear device. A man lay in a pool of blood near him. Derek turned away from a limp form at his feet.

"Step away from the bomb or I will shoot!" Joseph shouted. "Now!"

The large man froze and began to spread his arms. With swiftness belying his bulk, a hand shot out and turned a key on the bomb. He grabbed for a gun lying beside the bomb, but shots boomed from Joseph's gun forced him to spring away. Derek's gun joined the cacophony. With bullets careening all about him, the man did a series of zigzagging leaps and dives. His evasive maneuvers seemed to Aaron to defy gravity as he moved toward Derek.

A bullet from Derek's gun struck Basil's left shoulder. A crimson bloom sprouted from the wound, soaking his shirt in a rapidly expanding stain. The injury did nothing to halt his momentum. The brawny man lowered his shoulders to barrel into Derek, but Derek stepped to the side, evading the tackle. The bodyguard whizzed past but shot his right hand out, ripping the gun from Derek's grasp.

Joseph tracked the combatants with his gun. "I can't risk a shot."

Derek's gun clattered to the floor; Basil pivoted and lunged at Derek. Two meaty hands clasped Derek's throat, encompassing it. He shoved Derek into an electrical box, pinning him to it and lifting his feet off the ground.

Derek reached over the top of the stranglehold and gripped the back of his attacker's right hand and twisted. He raised his opposite hand and smashed his elbow across the man's wrists. Regaining his feet as the hold was broken, Derek pulled the man's arm straight out, elbow up. He smacked a palm strike into the exposed joint, breaking the right arm with a pop loud enough to be heard over the electrical drone.

The bull-like man didn't even pause to wince. As he dropped to his knees from the force of the blow, he reached for a sheath on his left leg and whipped out a large knife. He attempted an upward stab, but Derek stepped away and delivered a vicious kick to the face that rocked his assailant's head back.

The man rose and wiped blood from his nose with the back of the knife-wielding hand, his right arm dangling loose at his side. Derek reached beneath his coat and whipped the CQ-7 combat knife from its sheath at the small of his back. He flicked the blade open and eased into a comfortable fighting stance.

Frustrated in his attempts for a clear shot, Joseph moved toward the stairs. Aaron followed, unable to rip his eyes from the brawl.

Basil sprang forward, delivering a vicious overhand stab. Derek moved and parried with his own blade. In a whirl of motion the combatants' blades flashed, and steel rang on steel. Knife edges gleamed as they slashed, cut, and stabbed. Even in the fury of the melee, it soon became obvious to Aaron which man was the more competent fighter. Derek met each furious assault with impenetrable defense. He circled, avoiding each attack with a dodge or block while inflicting damage with parries and attacks of his own.

Basil dripped blood. His massive chest heaved. Though he must have realized defeat was inevitable, he raised his knife over his head. With a bellow of rage, he rushed forward and executed a desperate overhand stab with all his weight. Derek stepped to the side as his left hand darted in a circular blocking motion, sweeping the man's knife hand down and away. Derek thrust his own blade into the man's abdomen, burying it to the hilt before pulling it free.

The man remained standing, staring blankly ahead. His blade clattered to the floor and he swayed on his feet. His hand reached down to cover the wound to his stomach, and he sank to his knees. His lips moved in an attempt to speak, but he pitched forward on his face.

Joseph and Aaron reached Derek at a sprint. "Are you all right?" Aaron asked.

Derek nodded. He checked for the bodyguard's pulse and shook his head. "He's dead."

Joseph cuffed the unconscious man lying on the floor then dragged the other down the stairs and secured both of them to the railing of the stairs.

Derek moved to the bomb. The glowing LCD numbers counted backward. Three hours and fifty-eight minutes remained on the display. "If I had the tools, I might be able to disarm it. But we'd better let the experts have it. At least there's time. Let's get topside."

CHAPTER XXXVII

THE Secret Service was informed of the situation and a bomb squad summoned. The arena was locked down and an attempt to arrest Hussaam Zaafir was made, but his seats were empty.

Derek reached Agent Pendleton and was informed that Zaafir had left fifteen minutes prior and appeared to be heading toward the Hawk Pharmaceuticals compound. "Okay," Derek said. "Get your people in place around his facility. My team is on the way. We'll assume that's where he's heading. If it looks like he's going anywhere else, I need to know immediately." He flipped the phone closed. "Aaron, I can take it from here. You've done more than anyone could ask. I understand if you—"

"I'm going."

"Me, too," Joseph said. "I'll come along and try to keep him out of trouble."

Derek studied the pair for a moment. "Okay. Come on." As they ran toward the car, Derek placed another call, this one to his team.

* * * * * *

From the center of the backseat Aaron stared past his companions' shoulders and gripped the edge of his seat. Cars, lane lines, and signs blurred in and out of his vision as they weaved through traffic. It wasn't Derek's driving that caused his nervousness; the man handled the black sedan with the skill of a concert cellist. His fear was based on what he felt—what he *knew*—was coming at the end of their headlong journey. A reckoning. A showdown. But what would be the outcome? Would Abby be fatherless? Sarah a widow? Memphis a graveyard?

He had felt a moment of vast relief when the bomb squad had been called. The pandemic threat of attack on the Inter-Faith conference had been neutralized. But Aaron knew his role was not done. The Hawk was still free to pursue his nefarious plans, to kill and destroy. Aaron knew he remained on a headlong path to an inexorable showdown with the Hawk. Everything he had been through was leading him to some moment of truth. Whatever role his companions were to play, Aaron felt—no he knew—the ultimate responsibility of ending the Hawk's schemes once and for all belonged to him alone. The only question was whether or not he would survive. No, Aaron was not out of the woods. Not by a long shot.

"We've got company," Derek said.

Glancing over his shoulder, Aaron noticed a car weaving in and out of traffic. It pulled alongside in the lane to their left. Derek accelerated and Aaron's head rocked back. As they pulled away, the glass in the rear window erupted. Shards of glass showered him and he threw his hands up to protect his face.

"Get down!" Derek shouted.

Joseph ripped his pistol from its holster and thumbed off the safety.

Aaron lunged to the seat and lay flat on a bed of broken glass. Wind whipped and swirled into the car along with the unfiltered noise of traffic. Brakes screeched and horns blared.

The sound of gunfire exploded on top of him. Automatic bullets riddled the sedan with a *whapping-tinging* sound accompanying each impact.

"Hold on," Derek said.

The car swerved and metal screeched against metal as he broadsided the gunmen's car. Pistol in hand, Joseph waited for a clear shot. Derek drew his own weapon and fired three quick shots into the passenger side of the other vehicle. In the confined space, the shots were deafening. Aaron stole a peek through the rear window. There were very few cars remaining in their vicinity. Behind them the road and the shoulder were jammed with a line of stopped traffic. A gunman wielding an automatic rifle slumped forward in the front seat of the next car. A man in the backseat aimed a weapon.

Derek stomped on the brakes. Tires and metal squealed. Their sedan slid along the body of the car beside them. As they came even with car's rear quarter panel, Derek stomped the gas and jerked the wheel to the left. The sedan's front bumper shoved the gunmen's rear wheel, forcing the car into a clockwise spin. Its left tires grabbed the pavement and the right side lifted off the road. Derek pulled the wheel to the right and created some distance. The assailant's car tumbled forward in a half flip onto its roof. Metal and glass flew as the car slid to a stop.

"Here comes another one," Derek said.

A jolt rocked the sedan forward and as another car smashed into their rear bumper. As Aaron regained his bearings, another bump shook the car. They accelerated as yet another bash rattled them. The fear painted on Aaron's face must have been obvious to Derek as he caught the civilian's eyes in the rearview mirror.

"Don't worry," Derek said. "They won't do any real damage as long as they keep hitting us straight on like that."

"If you say so," Aaron said.

Derek turned to Joseph. "Can you take care of that?"

"Lie down and cover your ears," Joseph said. The sedan slowed and their pursuers bumped them again. Gunfire accompanied the impact.

Joseph leaned over the back seat and aimed his pistol, the glassless rear window offering an unobstructed field of fire. He snapped off three quick shots, panned his pistol to the right, and fired two more. Tires screeched, and Joseph settled into his seat.

Aaron uncovered his ears and peered over the back seat. The car behind them careened out of control toward the side of the road, its windshield shattered, two men slumped over in the front seat. Aaron turned to the front and closed his eyes. How much more death would he be forced to witness?

* * * * * *

Aaron breathed in through his nose attempting to retain his composure.

With one hand on the wheel and the other pressing a cell phone to his ear, Derek spoke to Lane. "According to the CIA team, Hussaam just entered his complex. Are you in position?"

As he listened, he maneuvered their heavily damaged car onto Plant Road, a street bordering the Mississippi River and the location of the Hawk Pharmaceuticals compound. The sedan shook and rattled as it lumbered along the road. Curious onlookers gaped through their windows as they sped past. Police sirens faded in the distance, and Aaron thought their highway combat must have drawn hot pursuit from the local authorities. A flurry of calls from Joseph's cell dissuaded them from the chase.

"We can't let him get away," Derek informed Lane. "I'm coming in hot. When I crash the gates, I want you on my six." With a flick of the wrist he snapped the phone closed and tossed it on the seat. He caught Aaron's eye in the rearview mirror and seemed about to say something.

Joseph interrupted him, saying, "Captain Galloway, please pull the car over." He turned in his seat. "Aaron, you're getting out. I'll send someone back for you when it's over."

Aaron stared back at his friend. "I have to see this through."

"There's no point in arguing," Derek said to Joseph. "We could force him out of the car." A smile split his lips as he glanced in the mirror again. "And that might not be so easy."

Joseph drew in a chest full of air, intending to continue the dispute.

"I'm staying," Aaron said. "Period."

Joseph's chest deflated with a groan. "Whatever you say, old man. Just watch yourself."

"The back seat folds down," Derek said. "Can you get my bag out of the trunk?"

Aaron avoided the broken glass, found the latch, and folded the seat forward. He leaned into the opening and pulled the heavy black bag onto the seat next to him.

"Unzip it."

Aaron unfastened the zipper revealing the cornucopia of guns, explosives, electronic devices, and combat equipment. At Derek's request, he passed up a belt with ammunition and grenades attached and a second one to Joseph. He then handed both men small automatic machine guns and lightweight armored vests.

"Yours is in there, too," Derek said. "I suggest you grab it."

Retrieving the .45 from the bag, Aaron turned it in his hands. He studied the weapon with the same deadly fascination one studied a coiled serpent, wanting to run but afraid to look away. He knew it made sense to carry it, but that did little to assuage the images of all the carnage he had witnessed playing like a film-loop in his head. Steeling himself, he ratcheted the slide back, jacking a bullet into the chamber. He ejected the clip, thumbed another bullet in, and rammed it home. He shrugged out of his blazer, removed the Bible from the inside pocket and ran his thumb along its edges. *Lord, help us.* Aaron tucked the Bible into the back pocket of his pants and slipped into the armored vest.

"Okay," Derek said. "Hussaam has men stationed on the fence line. All armed. He's obviously aware we're on to him." He patted the dashboard of the battered car. "He's got a chopper waiting on the roof of his office building. I can't allow him to reach it. We could take the chopper down, but Hal wants him alive. We're gonna crash the gates. My team and the CIA guys will be right behind us."

The Hawk Pharmaceuticals compound appeared on their right. Behind a guardhouse at the front entrance, the gates were closed and a barrier arm blocked access. Two gun-carrying guards in light blue uniforms stood behind the barrier. Hussaam's army was ready for them.

"Keep your head down back there, Aaron." As they approached the front gates, Derek swung the car out in a wide arc before angling back toward them. He reached beneath his shirt and clutched the silver cross. "Here we go." The engine roared as they sped toward the closed gate. A barrage of bullets pelted their grille.

Aaron threw himself on the backseat.

Joseph ducked, leaving only his eyes above the dashboard. The front windshield exploded and he stuck the muzzle of his gun through the new breach, panning the barrel as he laid a blazing trail of return fire.

Aaron felt and heard the car crash through the gates. The heavy sedan barely slowed. The car was riddled with gunfire as Derek drove past the guardhouse, his head barely showing over the dashboard.

Another fusillade erupted behind them and the onslaught on their car ceased. Aaron popped his head up to risk a look. The guards were falling victim to Derek's team. Where had they been hiding? The team swarmed the gates, securing it in moments.

Derek sped through the compound with smoke pouring from beneath the hood,. They approached the three-story office building and saw the white limo parked in front, its rear doors flung open. Hussaam and his bodyguards disappeared through the front entrance.

They screeched to a halt. Derek and Joseph threw their doors open and squatted behind them for cover, guns extended through glassless windows. Aaron flicked off the safety of his .45 and hurled his own door open.

* * * * * *

Hussaam pushed open the double glass doors into the lobby and reception area. His stunned-looking receptionist was seated behind a desk angled in the corner. "Mr. Zaafir, what's happening?" she yelled. "Should I call the police?"

Hussaam ground his teeth and refused to acknowledge the hysterical woman. Basil's double attempted to calm her and instructed her to hide behind the desk and remain quiet. Two guards stepped through a door on the opposite side of the room, and a bank of closed-circuit monitors behind them showed the attack on his compound. They stared, waiting for instructions.

"Where's Thomas Cable?" Hussaam asked the frantic receptionist.

"He's gone. I don't know where. He was carrying a duffle bag when he left."

Hussaam glanced over his shoulder as a bullet-riddled black sedan slid to a halt near his limousine. He grabbed Rashad's arm. "I don't know what happened to Basil, but he knows where to find us. Stay here and keep our company occupied. I have to grab some things from my office. I'll wait for you in the helicopter."

Ever faithful, Rashad nodded and drew his weapon.

Fool, thought Hussaam.

The doors of the black car flew open, and Hussaam could not believe his eyes. Aaron Henderson rolled out of the back seat! Incredible. He longed to wrap his hands around the man's neck and look into his eyes as he crushed the life out of him.

Hussaam refused to allow his anger to control him. He spun from the door, and dashed into the hallway beyond the lobby. He couldn't resist the feeling that something had happened to his brother, that his role in Hussaam's plot had been discovered. Soon he would find out for certain. A lump formed in his throat and he cursed his weakness. Other than his parents, his brother was one of the few human beings on this planet whom Hussaam had ever loved. The only person he would be willing to sacrifice his life for. Hussaam shook off the dread; he had to focus on the moment.

He always believed his plan would work but had been pragmatic enough to plan for failure. With his wealth and some reconstructive surgery, he would rise from the ashes. One of his safe-houses was outfitted with a full laboratory, and enough material had been transported there to begin again. The Russians would be only too happy to sell him more nuclear devices.

This was not the end. Simply a minor set-back.

He pushed the call button on the elevator. Rashad barked orders, and the guards fanned out in the lobby.

Hussaam entered the elevator and turned. As he pressed the button for the third floor Rashad glanced in his direction.

I will miss you, my old friend.

CHAPTER XXXVIII

THE gunfire grew louder and Aaron glanced over his shoulder. Derek's team sprinted across the compound with Lane in the lead and the CIA team in tow, dealing death as they moved. More of Hussaam's guards poured out of a warehouse adjacent to the brick office building. As they burst forth, they began firing. Aaron wondered how Zaafir garnered such support. They couldn't win. Even if his men beat back the forces here, there was only the one helicopter. They couldn't all escape.

"There may be innocent people inside, but we can't wait." Derek stared at Hussaam's helicopter on the roof, its blades rotating faster. "I'm going to use a flash-bang."

Aaron knew from his crash course in combat that a flash-bang grenade emitted a short, intense burst of light accompanied by a deafening concussion wave. It was non-lethal, but anyone within range would be blinded and unable to hear.

Derek raised his gun and blasted the windows out of the lobby doors, aiming high to reduce the risk of hitting noncombatants who might be inside. He pulled a grenade from his belt, flicked out the pin, and hurled it into building. "Close your eyes and cover your ears!"

Aaron counted to eight, and a flash of light penetrated his closed eyes, visible even behind his squeezed eyelids. The shockwave thrummed against his covered ears. A hand tugged at his shoulder.

"Come on," Derek said. "Stay with me." He donned a headset from the bag in the backseat and radioed Lane. "Fire some gas canisters into the second and third floor windows."

As the trio stormed into the building, glass broke over their heads and gas canisters were fired into the building., They sprinted into the lobby and their footsteps crackled on shards of glass. Three men lay prostrate on the floor groaning, one of them the double of Hussaam's bodyguard.

"Nobody move!" Derek yelled.

Shielded behind his two companions, Aaron stared between them to the end of the hall. Beyond the limited range of the flash-bang, the doors of an elevator slid closed. Behind them were the glaring eyes of the Hawk. His stare was defiant and challenging.

Aaron shoved past his comrades and raced toward the elevator. As he passed the receptionist's desk, a form emerged from behind it, gun in hand: Hussaam's other bodyguard, Rashad.

Aaron felt the shot before he heard it. It hammered his side, spinning him, stealing his breath. Gasping for air, he tumbled into the shelter of the hall and leaned against the wall.

Joseph and Derek opened fire. A deluge of bullets sprayed the corner sheltering Aaron's assailant. No way the man could have survived the onslaught, Aaron thought.

Aaron dashed down the hallway. He sprinted to a door leading to the stairwell. He placed his hand on the metal handle.

"Aaron, wait!" Joseph shouted. More of Hussaam's guards rushed toward the front doors, weapons blazing.

Aaron and Joseph exchanged a look. Joseph's eyes implored caution before he turned to help Derek fight off the attack.

Aaron shoved the door open and ducked into the stairwell. A set of concrete steps bordered by a metal railing led down to the left and straight up in front of him.

Wheezing for breath, he ripped off the Velcro straps of his vest, slipped his arms out, and examined it. An indentation in the side was the only indication of the bullet's impact. He untucked his shirt and analyzed his ribcage. A large red welt bloomed on his skin. His fingers traced it gingerly and found it tender. He didn't think a rib was broken; it was painful but not incapacitating.

He scanned the stairwell. Up or down? Up. He vaulted the stairs two at a time. Arriving at the second-level door, he peered through a rectangle of glass. An empty corridor billowed with smoke from the gas canisters. Holding his breath, he stuck his head into the hallway: to the left, a broken window with a smoking gas canister beneath it. To the right, elevator doors. He squinted with stinging eyes at the numbers over the doors. The number three glowed.

Aaron turned and hurdled up the next flight of steps. He grabbed the handle on the exit door and pressed his face against the window to see another smoke-filled, yet otherwise empty hallway. He opened the door a crack, just enough to allow for a peek toward the elevator. Its doors were closed but a figure disappeared through an office door at the end of the hall. Hussaam.

Aaron shoved the door open and leaned into the hall, the barrel of the .45 panning left, then right. Satisfied he was alone in the hall, he raced after Hussaam. As he reached the open office door, he flattened himself against the wall, wiped the tears from his eyes with his palm, and gripped the gun.

He pivoted left. Chest to the wall, one eye peeping past the doorframe, he pointed his pistol into the room. Where did he Hussaam go?

A blur of motion.

Too late, Aaron attempted to draw back. A wooden staff crashed into his hand and knocked the gun from his grip. A foot shot out and kicked the weapon away. Aaron jerked his stinging hand back and flexed his fingers.

"Come in, Mr. Henderson."

He stepped into the office, large, luxurious, and dominated by a window overlooking the Mississippi River. His eyes were drawn to the multitude of weapons mounted on the right wall.

Twirling a staff, Hussaam stepped into view and kicked the gun farther into a corner of the room. He strolled to his desk and stood behind it. The staff ceased whirling, and he leaned on it, staring.

As Aaron took a tentative step into the room, Hussaam's hand shot out and pressed a button on his desk. A concealed metal door slammed closed behind Aaron, clanging shut with a whoosh of displaced air, missing his foot by centimeters.

The Hawk's lips parted in a smile that didn't reach his narrowed eyes. Gas clouded the air in the room, not as thick as in the hall but enough to tear the eyes and cause difficulty breathing. He tossed the staff to the side and turned to open a window, allowing in fresh air and the sound of gunfire.

Aaron attempted to appear calm. He drew himself up to his full height. "Give up," he said. "You can't get away. They'll just bring the helicopter down."

With a chuckle, Hussaam turned. The raspy sound held no humor. It sounded more like brittle paper as it was crushed in a fist. "I think the term you southerners use is 'bait and switch.' The helicopter will take off, but I will not be on it." He tilted his head to a corner of the room and pushed another button. A section of paneling on the wall slid open, revealing another door. "I'll be leaving by either car or boat. That passage leads to my freedom. How could someone like you ever expect to best someone like me?" He smiled, seeming to relish in his opportunity to gloat. "You see. I have thought of everything." The smile faded. "Of course, that information will die with you."

Aaron's eyes darted to the pistol on the floor, gauging his chances. The weapons on the wall and the way the man handled the staff told him all he needed to know.

"So, Mr. Henderson, before you die, who are you? I am truly curious. How did an insignificant flea like yourself find out about my plans?" Hussaam shuffled sideways and plucked a sword from the wall, a straight Chinese blade in a decorative sheath. He took up a position between Aaron and the .45.

Aaron stood half a head taller than Hussaam and outweighed him by twenty or so pounds, but that provided no comfort. The two men held each other's eyes, and Aaron sidled to the wall. So this was how it was to be? Keeping his opponent in his field of vision, Aaron chose a Japanese *katana* and snatched the sword from its resting place. Its heft told him it was a fine weapon, about three feet in length.

"Well?" The man's calm veneer slipped for a moment as anger flashed in his dark eyes.

Aaron's forehead was damp and his mouth dry, yet he managed to summon his voice. "Who am I?" He considered the question another moment before an answer came. Along with it came a feeling of . . . calm. "I'm the man God has chosen to stop you."

"*God?*" Hussaam laughed. "There is no god but power. I *am* god." He grabbed the hilt of his sword. "What makes you think you have stopped anyone? It is not over, simply postponed. My empire will be built and the loss of your pitiful life will have been for nothing." He slid his blade from its scabbard. It gleamed with reflected light, sharp and deadly. He dropped the sheath to the floor and stepped forward, gripping the sword in both hands like an extension of his arms. He eased his feet into a fighting position. "You may have saved some people today, but your *God*, your *Bible*, say that grace requires a sacrifice of blood." He slashed the air in front of him with a practice cut. "Your blood will be the price of their lives."

The sounds of gunfire became more sporadic. The battle below must have been almost over. All Aaron had to do was delay the man until help arrived. No matter the outcome, thousands, if not hundreds of thousands, of innocent people had been saved. His fear subsided and as it ebbed, a wave of anger replaced it. The man's narcissistic arrogance, his willingness to mass murder to fulfill his twisted desires . . . and to Aaron's surprise, the way the man spoke the name of the Lord, made his blood boil.

God, please help me. Forgive me. Grant me strength.

He flung the katana's scabbard away and slid into a left-foot-forward fighting stance, gripping the sword with both hands.

Hussaam sprang forward and delivered an overhead blow toward Aaron's head. Aaron stepped left and made a desperate parry. Steel rang as the blades met. Hussaam's strike was blocked and as they disengaged, his blade nicked Aaron's right forearm, drawing blood before Aaron had a chance to counter.

The brief exchange was telling: Aaron was outclassed with a sword.

Hussaam launched another attack, a straight stab at Aaron's abdomen. Aaron struck down, deflecting the blade. As it was swept aside, Hussaam flicked his wrist and inflicted another wound, this one on the calf. Aaron reversed his blade and counterattacked with a sweeping diagonal slash at Hussaam's neck. The attempted cut was ruined by a deft block as Hussaam spun out of the way.

Their blades moved in a blur as each man struck, blocked, and retreated. Steel rang on steel, pealing like silver chimes.

Aaron sweated profusely, his breathing ragged. The ordeals of the last few days exacted their toll. Hussaam appeared fresh and unperturbed. Each time their blades met, Aaron was able to protect his center of mass, even as Hussaam inflicted a minor cut. None were too serious, but they covered Aaron's arms and legs. He was capable enough to force some caution from his opponent, but the more experienced swordsman was slowly bleeding him. Eventually, Aaron would weaken. Then he would fall.

He pressed the attack, reigning blows at Hussaam's head, body, and legs. None connected. They separated, circling, each searching for an opening. Aaron couldn't continue much longer. He retreated and placed all his weight on his rear leg, attempting to draw his adversary toward him. Hussaam moved to close the gap. Aaron raised his sword over his head and vaulted forward. With all his strength, he executed a furious diagonal slash at Hussaam's neck.

Sweeping his blade in an arc, Hussaam sidestepped and parried the attack. Aaron's sword was brushed aside and his balance upset. He was forced to continue forward, as all his weight was on his front foot. As he stepped by, Hussaam's blade raked his ribcage.

He winced in pain as he turned and raised his sword. The cut was severe. Blood flowed warm and sticky down his side. He weakened. His legs trembled, the sword grew heavy in his hands and his breathing labored. He glanced toward the pistol in the corner.

Reading Aaron's intent, Hussaam stepped in front of the gun, a smile on his thin lips. Aaron stumbled, his ebbing strength causing the tip of his blade to dip toward the floor.

* * * * * *

Derek ejected a spent clip and snapped in a new one, his ears ringing in the relative quiet after the fierce firefight. Sirens approached in the distance and his men surrounded the surviving guards. Joseph bled from a wound in his shoulder and a bullet was buried in his vest. "Are you all right?" Derek asked.

"I'm fine. We need to find Aaron."

Derek nodded his agreement.

"Captain!" Lane hollered. "You okay in there?"

"Fine. Get half the guys in here to help us secure the building. Leave the rest outside to form a perimeter." Derek ripped the sleeve from his ruined blazer and bound Joseph's shoulder.

"Save him."

His head swiveled, his eyes searched. *What?* "Did you hear that?"

"Hear what?" Joseph rubbed his shoulder.

Movement caught Derek's eye. He stared down the hall. The door to the stairwell swung closed. No one had gone in there. Had they? "Let's find Aaron," he said. "Follow me."

They rushed down the hall to the stairwell entry and Derek peered through the glass. Gun gripped in front of him, he booted the door open and burst through. He scanned the stairs.

Which way? Up or down? Probably up, but . . .

From up the stairs something flickered in his peripheral vision, a flash he couldn't identify. He whipped his gun toward the movement. Nothing. But he knew.

"This way," he said.

* * * * * *

Hussaam roared and sprang forward, sword overhead, intending to end the battle with a fatal blow.

When the man reached the apex of his swing, Aaron moved. In a do-or-die gambit, he tossed his sword toward Hussaam's face. The man flinched, and Aaron shot forward and caught Hussaam's wrists in both of his hands as the blade flashed down. Using Hussaam's forward momentum, Aaron pivoted and tugged on the man's arms, pulling him forward and off balance. As his opponent was drawn abreast of him, Aaron yanked down in the opposite direction and knelt on one knee. Hussaam's waist was bent double until his hands swept past his legs, forcing his feet off the floor. Hussaam was flipped onto his back. As the Hawk's back smacked the floor, Aaron gave his wrist a sharp twist and jerked the sword from his hands.

Hussaam flipped over, spun on a knee, and delivered a kick to Aaron's face that rattled his teeth followed by a punch to his nose.

On his knees and unable to get the sword in play, Aaron allowed it to slip from his hands. He swept the blow aside and delivered a head-snapping palm strike to Hussaam's chin. He jumped to his feet followed closely by Hussaam. Shouts and banging on the door joined the ringing in Aaron's ears. He didn't have the breath required to yell a reply. They circled, searching for openings, probing with punches and kicks. Aaron longed to end it, but forced himself to remain patient.

Hussaam rushed in, feinting with a left jab while unleashing a vicious roundhouse kick toward Aaron's temple. Aaron stepped in and interrupted the kick with his right palm against Hussaam's knee. With his left hand Aaron grabbed the leg, pinning it between his forearm and bicep. He kicked backward in a sweeping motion, lifting Hussaam's other leg from the floor while striking his throat with a claw hand. Aaron clutched Hussaam's leg as the man fell, eyes wide, as his head and shoulders crashed to the floor. Aaron stepped over and pinned Hussaam's leg between his own in a scissor hold. He twisted sharply and snapped his

knee. The man didn't even flinch. He had already been knocked unconscious from the impact with the floor.

Hammering on the steel door grew louder, more urgent. Aaron
glanced down at his blood-stained clothes, grimacing as pain and weakness washed over him, robbing his strength. Light-headed, he sank to
his knees. His vision clouded as consciousness slipped away. He fumbled in his pocket and wriggled the Bible free, then squeezed the book
in his hands as he slumped to the floor.

Lord, please watch over my family.

* * * * * *

Joseph pounded on the door. "Are you sure they're in there?"

"Positive." Derek paced the hall, searching for something to pry the
door open. Shots boomed and ricocheted in the hall. He dove and rolled
up in a crouch, pistol tracking toward the gunfire.

Joseph held his gun, aimed at the metal door, curses pouring from
his lips.

"That's a reinforced metal door," Derek said. "That won't do it." He
snapped his fingers. With a kick, he smashed open the door of the next
office and ran to the window. He slid the glass open and leaned out.
The next window was too far; he couldn't make it.

He had to get to Aaron, he was responsible for him. If anything happened . . . Derek stared at the plasterboard lining the office wall. He
grabbed a wooden chair, smashed it over a desk, and tore the legs free.
Using one of the chair's legs, he gouged a hole in the wall, repeatedly
ramming it until a fist sized hole exposed the framing beneath.

Joseph appeared at the door. Derek's intent was obvious, and Joseph
joined him. Together they tore a section of the wall away.

When the opening was wide enough, Derek drove the chair leg into
the wall of the next office. It took three strikes but it finally punctured a
small hole. "It's not reinforced." Derek peeked through the hole. Two
slumped forms lay on the floor. Aaron's body was covered in blood, and
he didn't appear to be breathing.

Derek ripped a grenade from his belt, jerked the pin free, and
mashed it into the hole, placing the fuse assembly in first so the blast
would be directed away from Aaron. "Go!" He pushed Joseph into the
shelter of the hall and counted to eight. The grenade blew and smoke
poured from the office. Derek ran into the room holding his breath and

waving his arms to clear the smoke. The grenade created a hole large enough for him to squeeze through. "I'll get the door open," Derek said. "Get a medic up here, quick."

"Is he . . .?" Joseph's anguish was written on his face, and he couldn't complete the question, as if saying the word would make it true.

"I don't know. Go. Bring help."

CHAPTER XXXIX

The smell of fresh air fills his nostrils. He lies on his back but feels weightless. He opens his eyes to find himself in the midst a vast meadow. A breeze waves the grass he lies upon and tousles trees with canopies stretching high enough to dwarf a redwood. Gurgling streams, singing birds, buzzing insects, the lowing and calling of beasts create a concerto unrivaled by the masters. Herds of gazelle, antelope, impalas, a vast array of deer-like animals, prance over the fields. Elephants and emus share water from the same stream. Every creature imaginable grazes, plays, or sleeps. He glances toward a group of bleating lambs. Their fur is cottony white, without blemishes. Near them a lion lies in the grass. It glances at him and yawns, its gaping mouth revealing teeth the size of daggers, before it returns to licking its paws.

Glancing down, he notices his feet are bare and his tattered clothes have been replaced by a white linen robe. His attention is drawn to a range of mountains beyond the meadow. Soaring peaks are shrouded in roiling mist. The mist parts to reveal a gleaming white city on a plateau. The city's spires stretch like fingers probing the heavens. His eyes follow them to their tips.

The wonder steals his breath: it is as if the universe somehow fits into the sky above him. Planets of every conceivable color and hue, some with rings, some filled with gaseous clouds, some with small glowing moons, swirl around suns. Meteors zoom and comets flash. Star clusters glow, their light painting the celestial expanse.

"He comes."

The voice startles him. He leans toward it.

A man sits beside him. His hair is so golden it shines with its own radiance. His eyes are a deep cerulean blue. Though Aaron has seen the face but once, and it was no longer covered by grime and whiskers, he recognizes it instantly as belonging to the homeless man. Even more familiar than the face is the voice. The voice from his dreams. The man's lips part revealing even, white teeth.

"Who?" he asks.

"Our Lord. He comes. There." A finger points toward the white city in the hills.

A gate opens and a figure emerges. Though the distance obscures details, it appears to be a man, bathed in a nimbus of white-hot light, bursts of blue radiance swirl and flicker within the glow. The city is miles away, but with each step the form covers an impossible distance and the ground shudders from peals of distant thunder. As he approaches, the stars and planets seem to be drawn towards Him, as if the power of His presence exerts a force they can't resist.

Aaron is forced to cover his burning eyes with a hand, though the light is still visible through the skin. His body thrums with vibration. His mind whirls with emotion. Calm and anger, joy and sorrow, swirl together, overwhelming him. Tears flow from his eyes and laughter bubbles in his throat.

The quivering in his body and the churning of emotions cease as suddenly as they began. The air goes still and an overwhelming sense of love overwhelms him. The light behind his hand fades.

A voice speaks, deep and resonant. "Now, that's better isn't it?"

Aaron opens his eyes. A man stands a few feet away. He is tall and strong with sun-darkened skin, clad in a gleaming white robe, feet wrapped by leather sandals. The handsome face is crowned by short, wavy brown hair. Deep brown eyes beam kindness from their depths. Gentle lines form in the corners of his eyes as he smiles and reaches out a hand. "Just like you imagined?"

Aaron stumbles for words. "Sir?"

"All this." He waves his hand around them. "Just like you imagined it would be. It makes it easier. I'm afraid you're not quite ready to see it as it really is."

He stretches his hand to Aaron and pulls him to his feet. He looks into the gentle eyes and drops his gaze in shame.

A hand gently raises his chin. "Why do you look away?"

"I'm ashamed. I doubted You. I still don't understand why I was chosen."

"Ah. But I never doubted you. In your heart, you always believed in Me. What you doubted were those who claimed to be my messengers. Don't be ashamed of that."

"There's just so much I don't understand. All the pain. The suffering . . . I . . ." He stops, embarrassed by the outburst.

"Man has been seeking the answer to those questions since Adam and Eve were cast from the garden. The answer isn't simple. But I will give you something to consider. Do you love your Abby?"

The thought of his baby girl made his heart ache. He missed her terribly. "Yes. Of course. With all my heart."

"In an effort to save her pain, would you lock her away and never let her experience life? Just as laughter, fun, play, and love teach us about life, so do pain and trial. Adversity builds and reveals character." He reaches out taps Aaron's forehead. "You were also given this beautiful mind, and free will to go with it. Our Father would have you love Him—love Us—because you choose to. Would you rather have been created with no freedom of choice?" Their eyes lock and Aaron can't pull his gaze away. "Your life on earth is not even a fingernail's breadth of your full existence. The physical life readies you, tries you, so that you may enter into the Kingdom of our Father. If the world was perfect, why would you need faith?" Turning away, He spreads His hands, gesturing around them. "What if the world were perfect for you? Your perfection would inevitably cause another pain. You pray for sun, another prays for rain . . . you are both righteous men. Whose prayer should be answered? This is a simple explanation, I know, but you will see for yourself. Never forget. We care for all humanity. More than you can grasp." He turns to walk away and glances over his shoulder. "You've done well."

"Am I dead?"

Another smile beams from His face. "Not yet." A chuckle shakes his shoulders. "You still have much to do." He points a finger and looks stern. "Not the least of which is to raise your daughter to know Me."

"What do I do now?"

"You'll know. There are always those who will need your help." He turns away and begins walking toward the city.

"Please. Wait."

He calls over his shoulder. "If you have doubts, look to the words of Isaiah. Chapter forty-three, verse one." He reaches the city gates and disappears again into the mist.

His companion, silent throughout the exchange, smiles. "It's time to go," he says.

* * * * * *

Aaron's eyes opened and just as quickly snapped shut. He gulped in air as waves of pain racked his body. Hands pressed on him and something jabbed his arm. He eased his eyelids apart and risked a peek. A medic swathed him in bandages. His eyes followed an IV tube from his arm to the hand holding it.

Derek.

A smile split the soldier's face. "You sure gave us a scare."

A gentle squeeze on Aaron's other hand drew his attention. He lolled his head to the side.

"Hey, old man." Joseph's eyes were red-rimmed, his face pale.

"Hey, yourself." Aaron almost coughed out the words, his parched throat protesting speech. He gave his friend's hand a squeeze. "I'm fine. Don't worry." He began to feel light, as if he was drifting, weightless. His pain drifted away as well. Drugs in the IV. "Is it over?" he mumbled.

"Yes," Derek said. "Now, be quiet. Save your strength."

Two paramedics rushed in carrying a stretcher. Aaron's eyes closed and he attempted to grin. "Yes, sir."

CHAPTER XL

AARON woke to the sound of people talking in hushed tones. Occasional laughter broke the conversation. He opened his eyes and blinked against the harsh sunlight. He lay in a bed in a large hospital room. A picture window allowed the sun's beams to bring cheerful light to the dreary space. Tubes ran from his arms, and a sensor on the tip of his finger led to a heart-rate monitor.

His left hand was held in a soft grip by his wife. He couldn't remember ever being so glad to see anyone. As his eyes adjusted and he gathered his wits, the heart monitor beeped. Sarah stopped talking and turned toward the sound.

Aaron cleared his throat. "Hey."

Sarah's head snapped to meet his gaze. Her eyes lit up and a smile brightened her features. She leaned down and showered his face with kisses. Placing both hands on his face, she stroked it and kissed him again and again, as if she was afraid he would disappear if she quit touching him. She stood but refused to let go, grasping his hand in a firm two-handed clasp. Tears pooled at the corners her eyes and spilled down her cheeks.

The other occupants of the room surrounded the bed: Derek, Hal, Joseph, Rachel, and Paul. All of them talked at once, each asking how he felt. Rachel and Paul stood together, shoulder to shoulder, hands and fingers entwined.

That explained much.

Paul held his right arm against his side and his shirt was untucked. He seemed stiff and grimaced when he moved to pat Aaron on the arm.

Aaron squeezed his wife's hand and smiled at the group circling his bed. "How long have I been out?"

"Almost a whole day," Joseph said. "How do you feel?"

Aaron took a deep breathe and worked his muscles. Mistake. The pain wasn't sharp but a dull ache, all over. It felt as if he had been beaten. Oh, yes: he had. He lifted the sheets and examined the bandages covering his arms and legs. "Not too bad. I'm pretty sore."

"Do you feel like talking?" The question came from Hal. His face was pale and his right arm was in a sling. He looked as if he should be the one in bed. "Someone would like to say something to you."

"Sure." Aaron's voice was thick. "I could use a swallow of water, though."

Sarah helped him lean up and fluffed the pillows. She poured a glass of water from a sweating pitcher and placed it to his lips. Aaron gulped the cool liquid until Sarah pulled it away. "Not too much," she said. "It might make you sick to your stomach."

Hal placed a call with his cell phone. "Sir, he's awake."

Aaron wrinkled his eyebrows. He expected Hal to call Chavez, but he doubted the man would address the corporal as "sir."

Hal handed the phone over, and Aaron pressed it to his ear. "Hello?"

"Mr. Henderson, this is the president." The familiar voice was deep and resonant with a distinct southern drawl.

Aaron raised his eyebrows and glanced at Hal.

"It's really him," Hal said.

"Hello, Mr. President. Please, sir, just call me Aaron."

"Well, Aaron, I wanted to take the time to thank you for your service to our country, and to the world, for that matter. You saved a lot of lives. It's not fair, but we can't publicize most of what you've done. I'm afraid your involvement will have to remain between us."

Aaron grinned. "Mr. President, I'd prefer it that way. I really don't want that kind of attention. I don't want to have to look over my shoulder for the rest of my life. I've got a family to think about."

"Good enough, son. We'll see to it. Thank you again. The nation and the world owe you a debt of gratitude. You take care now."

"I will. Thank you, sir." Aaron handed the phone back to Hal. "So, what's happened? While I was out, I mean."

"I'm sure you figured out that the bomb in the pyramid was diffused." Hal glanced out of the window toward the Memphis skyline. "I found another tape. Another confession from Rayhan, leader of the Fist of Allah, claiming responsibility for attacks in Israel and Jordan . . . which were thwarted, thanks to you."

"Where did you get it?" Aaron said.

"Let's just say a friend gave it to me, along with a briefcase full of other useful information." His eyes misted and he shook his head. "And that's all I can say." He rubbed a hand over his eyes and continued. "The Jordanians found chemical agents planted in the palace that, had they not been found, would've killed the entire royal family in the midst of their annual celebration, making Zaafir the de facto king of Jordan. The Israelis found a nuclear device much the same as the one you found here and were also able to disarm it. Some of their settlements weren't so lucky. Some chemical weapons were used, but the loss of life was minimized by our warnings. The majority of the weapons were found before they were used. Some arrests have been made, and based on the information the suspects in custody have passed along, more will be coming soon. We're still working out a lot of the details. Hussaam's wife and son have been detained, but they apparently didn't know about his plans. That's really all I can tell you. I thought you deserved to know at least that much." Hal gripped Aaron's hand and gave it a firm shake. "I've got to go." He placed a card on the bedside table. "Thank you, Aaron. If you ever need *anything*, all you have to do is call me." He released his grip on Aaron's hand and strode to the door, groaning as he moved. "Derek, you coming?"

"I'll be right there." Derek reached around his neck and removed the cross hanging there. He pressed it into Aaron's hand and held on for a moment. "I want you to have this. No arguments." He leaned down. "I need to go, too. But I'll be in touch." He patted Aaron on the shoulder and followed Hal into the hall. As he stepped through the door, he turned and looked at Sarah. "Take care of him."

"I will," she said.

Derek disappeared into the hall, and Aaron pushed away a sudden pang of sorrow. He opened his fist and dangled the silver cross in front of his eyes. *Thank you, Derek.*

Paul picked up the Bible laying next to Hal's card on the table. It seemed to Aaron as if he had given it to him a lifetime ago. "Looks like this got some use," Paul said.

Aaron chuckled. "You have no idea." His mind wandered. The sight of the Bible brought questions with it. What did he do now? What was expected of him? He wasn't sure what was in store for him, but he knew his life would never be quite the same.

As Paul flipped through the pages of the Bible, Aaron's last dream came to him. The dream had seemed so real. He could still hear the animals, smell the grass. "Paul, can you find the book of Isaiah? Chapter forty-three, verse one."

"Sure." Paul flicked the pages with his thumb. "Got it."

"Would you read it to us, please?"

He smiled. "It would be my pleasure." He raised the Bible and began to read. "But now, this is what the LORD says—he who created you, O Jacob, he who formed you, O Israel . . ." Paul stopped reading and raised his eyes to Aaron's. Another smile flashed across his face. He straightened his back and took a deep breath. In a resonant voice, fit for the pulpit, he finished reading the scripture. ". . . Fear not, for I have redeemed you; I have summoned you by name; you are Mine!

ABOUT THE AUTHOR

Photo by Melinda Courtney

CRAIG ALEXANDER has always dreamed of being a novelist. He spent countless hours reading as a youth, many times by flashlight after being instructed to turn off his light. The writers that influenced him the most as an adolescent were J.RR. Tolkien, C.S. Lewis, and Louis L'amour. He remains an avid reader with varied interests. In 2003 with the help of an intriguing dream, he began plotting a story which turned into his first novel, The Nineveh Project.

Craig is a martial artist of eighteen years experience. He is a third-degree black belt in Tae Kwon Do and Hapkido, and a first degree black belt in Han Mu Do, and has studied many other styles. He is an instructor at Sun Bi Martial Arts in Madison, MS and has competed and trained internationally.

He is a member of Pinelake Church in Brandon, MS and leads a men's small group Bible study. Craig's hobbies include: Tennis, basketball, reading, movies, and video games. He lives in Flowood, MS with his wife and daughter and can be reached at craigalexander@bellsouth.net.

Visit him on the web at: www.craigalexanderonline.com.

ALSO AVAILABLE FROM
BREAKNECK BOOKS

By Jeremy Robinson
"...a rollicking Arctic adventure that explores the origins of the human species." -- James Rollins, bestselling author of Black Order and The Judas Strain

www.breakneckbooks.com/rtp.html

By James Somers
"...a nice read of battle, honor, and spirituality... that left me wanting more." -- Fantasybook spot.com

www.breakneckbooks.com/soone.html

By Sean Young
"...captures the imagination and transports you to another time, another way of life and makes it real." -- Jeremy Robinson, author of Raising the Past and The Didymus Contingency

www.breakneckbooks.com/sands.html

BREAKNECK BOOKS
PUBLISHING COMPANY

ALSO AVAILABLE FROM
BREAKNECK BOOKS

By Jeremy Robinson
"[A] unique and bold thriller. It is a fast-paced page-turner like no other. Not to be missed!" – James Rollins, bestselling author of Black Order and The Judas Strain

http://www.breakneckbooks.com/didymus.html

By Jules Verne
This Special Edition of the original high speed thriller features discussion questions, a design challenge and the complete and unabrideged text.

www.breakneckbooks.com/mow.html

By Edgar Rice Burroughs
This Special Edition features all three Caspak novels (*The People that Time Forgot* and *Out of Time's Abyss*) in one book, the way it was originally intended to be read.

www.breakneckbooks.com/land.html

Printed in the United States
105760LV00001B/319/A

9 780978 655174